FATHERS & SONS

FATHERS & SONS
AN anthology

ALBERTO MANGUEL

RAINCOAST BOOKS

See page 292 for a continuation of the copyright page.

First published in Canada in 1998 by
Raincoast Books
8680 Cambie Street
Vancouver, B.C.
V6P 6 M9
(604) 323-7100

First published in the U.S. by Chronicle Books.
Canadian Cataloguing in Publication Data
Main entry under title:
Fathers and Sons

   ISBN 1-55192-129-4

   1. Fathers and sons—Fiction. I. Manguel, Alberto, 1948–
PN6120.95.F3F3 1998   808.83'935204   C97-910873-X

Book designed by Carole Goodman
Book composition by Suzanne Scott

Printed in the United States of America.

10 9 8 7 6 5 4 3 2 1

To Jean-Daniel and Fabian Reynaud

TABLE OF contents

INTRODUCTION

One of the moments of greatest joy in my life—of sheer, untouched, astounded joy—was the birth of my son. His appearance in the world, the only *true* act of creation I can say I've witnessed, moved me more than anything I have ever experienced. From that moment, his existence demanded a relationship, the building of bridges and walls and the marking of common land between us.

One day in Paris, thirteen years later, I was confiding to Richard Ford small parental worries and asked him, in a conversational way, what he thought was the best thing a father could do for his son. "The best thing a father can do for his son," he answered in a low Midwestern drawl, "is die."

It is a bewildering paradox that Father Time (who in the ancient Greek myth, in order not to die, castrates his old man and devours his own children) builds and demolishes us all at an equal and hurried pace. We know, of course, that in the end the labors of his left hand will outwit the labors of his right one, and of his carefully constructed edifices nothing will remain but tottering frames inhabited by a few fleeting memories. In that gloomy light, fatherhood aspires to a species of immortality it seldom attains.

Like everything in the world (which, according to Spinoza, wants to persist in its own being—the stone wants to be a stone throughout eternity, the dog a dog), we apparently aspire to persist in ourselves through the perseverent links of fathers and sons: links like those woven in blood by the prophets all the way to the bosom of Abraham. For Virgil, the links of Rome crept back to Venus and the defenders of Troy. His Aeneas, rescuing his father from the captured city, illustrates both the reward and the price of such perseverance: the son carrying on his back the feeble father as well as the father's unfulfilled ambitions, becoming for posterity the leader-warrior his father never was. Immortality of this sort not only grants old men beyond the grave a name and a face, but also condemns young men to a face and a name beyond the grave. "I'm looking for the face I had before the world was made," wrote William Butler Yeats, who carried to the end of his life the legacy of his father's signature and features.

In spite of Ford's glum advice, even death might not grant us freedom, as Hamlet found out when his father's ghost returned to instruct him on unfinished business. From his grave in Prague's Jewish cemetery, Kafka's father continued to frighten the boy he had put out onto the cold balcony of the family flat to cure him of his nightmares. And Henry James, at an older age than his father was when he died, still remembered the warning issued by the patriarch to his adolescent son: "Every man who has reached even his intellectual teens begins to suspect that life is no farce; that it is not genteel comedy even; that it flowers and fructifies on the contrary out of the profoundest tragic depths of the essential dearth in which its subject's roots are plunged. The natural inheritance of everyone who is capable of spiritual life is an unsubdued forest where the wolf howls and the obscene bird of night chatters."

I argued with Ford: isn't a father's legacy ever beneficent? Ford changed the subject.

It may be that few experiences are, in themselves, purely good or evil. It may be that our use, our experience of the experience, as it were, turns the complexity of being a father (or being a son) to our advantage or disadvantage, allows us to rebuild on it or to crumble away the little that is left. In this sense, stories can help us by putting into words shreds of memory, intuitions of causes, old wounds, or ancient joys, setting our son next to the son we were and our father next to the father we have become.

We consider such comparisons with some trepidation: it is an unsettling experience to imagine ourselves, in the unthinkable future, as our son's contemporary or, in the ineffable past, the contemporary of our father.

> *What man has bent o'er his son's sleep, to brood*
> *How that face shall watch his when cold it lies?—*
> *Or thought, as his own mother kissed his eyes,*
> *Of what her kiss was when his father wooed?*

wrote Dante Gabriel Rossetti. Very few, I should imagine. Our baggage of assumptions and ideals, of our social and intimate vocabularies, of our lessons in history and geography, doesn't travel at all well. We are of this time and place and cannot follow our reflection backward or forward. Nadine Gordimer, in a brilliant short story, gave voice to Kafka's father and helped him write a letter to answer his son's accusations, to no avail. The image of the evil Hermann Kafka persists. In the seventh century, the Venerable Bede described our short lives as one long hall crossed by a bird flying from darkness into darkness. We are, at least in part, the memory of ourselves in our son as he goes into the darkness ahead, as we are, at least in part, the shadow of our father reaching us from the darkness behind. Wherever we stand, we stand between open doors.

And yet, sometimes (as Ford ultimately acknowledged) fatherhood elicits successful partnerships, delicate balances of respect and dependency—though literature has recorded few of this kind. Perhaps our victory (over the demonic playfulness of Time and his invidious family relationships) is best reflected in the open-minded, honest, and yet generous account of Edmund Gosse, writing in 1907 about his loving and tyrannical father. Under the ferule of Gosse Senior, the boy grew up in a household fearful of a willful God, warned against the snares of fiction and the flesh. These strictures excited in the boy not servility, but curiosity. When told by his father, for instance, of the terrors of idolatry, Gosse secretly placed a chair on top of a table and

10

proceeded to adore it with the invocation "Oh Chair!" expecting now something terrible to take place. "But nothing happened; there was not a cloud in the sky, not an unusual sound in the street," Gosse recalled. "I had committed idolatry, flagrantly and deliberately, and God did not care." The result of this experiment did not lead him to question the existence of God, but "to lessen still further my confidence in my Father's knowledge of the Divine mind" and eventually to repudiate the idea "that my father was responsible to God for my secret thoughts and my most intimate convictions."

This, then, is Gosse's conclusion, the "bond of allegiance" between a son that wishes to live and a father who need not, as Ford suggested, die: "The young man's conscience threw off once and for all the yoke of his 'dedication,' and, as respectfully as he could, without parade or remonstrance, he took on a human being's privilege to fashion his inner life for himself." In that expectation we can, perhaps, rejoice.

Alberto Manguel
London
June 1997

Sean O'Faolain

Born in the first year of the twentieth century in Cork, Sean O'Faolian's career followed the political fortunes of Ireland in our time. The avatars of the Irish Rebellion, the constraints of Irish Catholicism, the tug-of-war relationship with England, and the internal strife and eternal factions of Irish life are the subject matter of his novels and stories. Fatherhood, which (according to George Bernard Shaw) the Irish see "as an almost exclusive Irish institution" is at the core of much of O'Faolian's writing.

Fathers learn from their son's interaction with the world: in him, they see themselves play, desire, love, attack, lie, conform, rebel. Gerard Manley Hopkins, taking up Wordsworth's celebrated line about the father's debt to the son, opened the question up again:

> "The child is father to the man."
> How can he be? The words are wild.
> Suck any sense from them who can:
> "The child is father to the man."
> No; what the poet did write ran
> "The man is father to the child."
> "The child is father to the man"!
> How can he be? The words are wild.

INNOCENCE

sean o'faolain

all this month the nuns have been preparing my
little boy for his first Confession. In a few days he will go in a
crocodile from the school to the parish church; enter the strange-
looking cabinet in the corner of the aisle and see in the dusk of
this secretive box an old priest's face behind a grille. He will
acknowledge his wickedness to this pale, criss-crossed face. He
will be a little frightened but he will enjoy it too, because he does
not really believe any of it—for him it is a kind of game that the
nuns and priest are playing between them.

How could he believe it? The nuns tell him that the
Infant Jesus is sad when he is wicked. But he is never wicked, so
what can it matter? If they told him instead of the sorrow he
causes the Weasel, or Two Toes, or the Robin in the Cow's Ear, all
of which live in the fields below our house, he would believe it in
just the same way. To be sure he tells lies, he is a terrible liar, and
when he plays Rummy with me he cheats as often as he can, and
when he is slow and I flurry him he flies into furious rages and his
eyes swim with tears and he dashes the cards down and calls me
A Pig. For this I love him so much that I hug him, because it is so
transparent and innocent; and at night if I remember his tears I
want to go into his room and hold his fat, sweaty hand that lies on

the coverlet clutching some such treasure as an empty reel. How, then, can he believe that God could be angry with him because he tells lies or calls his daddy A Pig?

Yet, I hate to see him being prepared for his first Confession because one day he will really do something wicked, and I know the fear that will come over him on that day—and I cannot prevent it.

I have never forgotten the first time I knew that I had committed sin. I had been going to Confession for years, ever since I was seven, as he is now, telling the same things time after time, just as he will do. 'Father, I told a lie . . . Father, I forgot to say my morning prayers . . . Father, I was disobedient to my parents . . . And that is all, Father.' It was always quite true: I had done these things; but, as with him, it was only true as a fable or a mock-battle is true since none of these things were any more sinful that his childish lies and rages. Until, one dim, wintry afternoon, not long after Christmas, when I went as usual to Confession in an old, dark, windy church called Saint Augustine's, down a side-lane, away from the city's traffic, a place as cold and damp and smelly as a tomb. It has since been pulled down and if they had not pulled it down it must soon have fallen down. It was the sort of church where there was always a beggar or two sheltering from the weather in the porch or in the dusky part under the back gallery; and always some poor shawled woman sighing her prayers in a corner like the wind fluttering in the slates. The paint was always clean and fresh, but the floor and the benches and the woodwork were battered and worn by the generations. The priests dressed in the usual black Augustinian garment with a cowl and a leather cincture. Altogether, a stranger would have found it a gloomy place. But I was familiar with it ever since my mother brought me there to dedicate me to Saint Monica, the mother of Augustine, and I loved the bright candles before her picture, and the dark nooks under the galleries, and the painted tondos on the ceiling, and the stuffy confessional boxes with their heavy purple curtains underneath which the heels of the penitents stuck out when they knelt to the grille.

14

There I was, glad to be out of the January cold, kneeling before Saint Monica, brilliant with the candles of her mendicants. I was reading down through the lists of sins in my penny prayer-book, heeding the ones I knew, passing over the ones I didn't know, when I suddenly stopped at the name of a sin that I had hitherto passed by as having nothing to do with me.

As I write down these words I again feel the terror that crept into me like a snake as I realized that I knew that sin. I knew it well. No criminal who feels the sudden grip of a police-man on his arm can have felt more fear than I did as I stared at the horrible words. . . .

I joined the long silent queue of penitents seated against the wall. I went, at last, into the dark confessional. I told my usual innocent litany. I whispered the sin.

Now, the old priest inside the confessional was a very aged man. He was so old and feeble that the community rarely allowed him to do anything but say Mass and hear Confessions. Whenever they let him preach he would ramble on and on for an hour; people would get up and go away; the sacristan would peep out in despair through the sacristy door; and in the end an altar-boy would be sent out to ring the great gong on the altar-steps to make him stop. I have seen the boy come out three times to the gong before the old man could be lured down from the pulpit.

When this old priest heard what I said to him he gave a groan that must have been heard in the farthest corner of the church. He leaned his face against the wire and called me his 'child', as all priests in the confessional call every penitent. Then he began to question me about the details. I had not counted on this. I had thought that I would say my sin and be forgiven: for up to this every priest had merely told me that I was a very good little boy and asked me to pray for him as if I were a little angel whose prayers had a special efficacy, and then I would be dismissed jumping with joy.

To his questions I replied tremulously that it had hap-pened 'more than once'—How soon we begin to evade the truth!—

15

and, I said, 'Yes, Father, it was with another.' At this he let out another groan so that I wanted to beg him to be quiet or the people outside would hear him. Then he asked me a question that made my clasped hands sweat and shake on the ledge of the grille. He asked me if any harm had been done to me. At first I didn't know what he meant. Then horrible shapes of understanding came creeping towards me along the dark road of my ignorance, as, in some indistinct manner, I recognized that he was mistaking me for a girl! I cried out that nothing at all had happened, Father. Nothing! Nothing! Nothing! But he only sighed like the south wind and said:

'Ah, my poor child, you won't know for several months.'

I now had no desire but to escape. I was ready to tell him any story, any lie, if he would only stop his questions. What I did say I don't know but in some fashion I must have made the old man understand that I was a male sinner. For his next question, which utterly broke me, was:

'I see, I see. Well, tell me, my poor child. Was she married or unmarried?'

I need hardly say that as I remember this now I laugh at it for an absurd misadventure, and I have sometimes made my friends laugh at his questions and his groans, and at me with my two skinny heels sticking out under the curtains and knocking like castanets, and the next penitents wondering what on earth was going on inside the box. But, then, I was like a pup caught in a bramble bush, recanting and retracting and trying to get to the point where he would say the blessed words 'Absolve te . . .' and tell me what my penance would be.

What I said I cannot recall. All I remember distinctly is how I emerged under the eyes of the queue, walked up the aisle, as far away as I could get from the brightness of Saint Monica into the darkest corner under the gallery where the poorest of the poor crowd on Sundays. I saw everything through smoke. The scarlet eye of the sanctuary lamp—the only illumination apart from the candles before the shrine—stared at me. The shawled woman sighed at me. The wind under my bare knees crept away from me. A beggar in a corner, picking his nose and scratching himself, was Purity itself compared to me.

In the streets the building stood dark and wet against the after-Christmas pallor of the sky. High up over the city there was one tiny star. It was as bright and remote as lost innocence. The blank windows that held the winter sky were sullen. The wet cement walls were black. I walked around for hours. When I crept home my mother demanded angrily where I had been all these hours and I told her lies that *were* lies, because I wanted to deceive her, and I knew that from this point on I would always be deceiving everybody because I had something inside me that nobody must ever know. I was afraid of the dark night before me. And I still had to face another Confession when I would have to confess all these fresh lies that I had just told the old priest and my mother.

17

It's forty years ago, now: something long since put in its unimportant place. Yet, somehow, when I look across at this small kid clutching his penny prayer-book in his sweaty hands and wrinkling up his nose at the hard words—I cannot laugh. It does not even comfort me when I think of that second Confession, after I had carefully examined those lists of sins for the proper name of my sin. For, what I said to the next priest was: 'Father, I committed adultery.' With infinite tenderness he assured me that I was mistaken, and that I would not know anything about that sin for many years to come, indeed, that I would have to be married before I could commit it—and then asked me to pray for him, and said I was a very good little boy and sent me away jumping with joy. When I think of that and look at this small Adam he becomes like that indescribably remote and tender star, and I sigh like that old, dead priest, and it does not help. I know that he is playing a fable of—'Father, I told lies . . . Father, I forgot to say my morning prayers. . . . Father, I called my daddy A Pig.'

Franz Kafka

Of all literary father-son relationships, that of Kafka with his loutish father is one of the most infamous, revealed in a letter Kafka wrote to his father and never sent. In that sense, Kafka's father is one of Kafka's most enduring literary creations. Since the posthumous publication of the letter by Kafka's friend and literary executor, Max Brod, the reader senses the shadow of paternal fear hanging over Kafka's work, either in the stories that concern, at least in part, a father and a son (such as "Metamorphosis") or in its many incarnations: fear of the law, fear of official authority, fear of the all-seeing eye of God. As a peace offering, Kafka dedicated the short story collection, *A Country Doctor*, to his father. "Not as if I could appease Father," he wrote to Brod, "the roots of this hostility are irradicable."

On September 23, 1912, Kafka noted in his diary, "This story, 'The Judgement,' I wrote at one sitting during the night of the 22nd–23rd, from ten o'clock at night to six o'clock in the morning. I was hardly able to pull my legs from under the desk, they had got so stiff from sitting. The fearful strain and joy, how the story developed before me, as if I were advancing over water. Several times during this night I heaved my own weight on my back. How everything can be said, how for everything, for the strangest fancies, there waits a great fire in which they perish and rise up again." And he concluded, "Only in this way can writing be done, only with such coherence, with such a complete opening out of the body and the soul."

THE JUDGEMENT

franz kafka

it was a Sunday morning at the height of spring.
George Bendemann, a young businessman, was sitting in his room
on the first floor of one of the low, flimsily built houses that
stretched in a long row along the river bank, distinguished in little
more than height and colour. He had just completed a letter to a
boyhood friend now living abroad; he sealed it with frivolous
deliberation and then, propping his elbows on the desk, looked
out of the window at the river, the bridge, and the hills on the
other side with their hint of green.

He was thinking about how the friend, not content with
his progress at home, had years before quite literally escaped to
Russia. He now ran a business in Petersburg that had started
extremely well but had apparently been falling off for some time, as
the friend complained on his less and less frequent visits. There he
was, far from home, wearing himself out to no purpose, the foreign-
looking full beard imperfectly concealing the face George had
known so well since childhood, with the yellow skin that seemed to
suggest some developing illness. By his own account he had no
proper contact with his compatriots, who formed a colony in the city,
and virtually no social intercourse with Russian families either, so
that he was settling down to a life of permanent bachelordom.

What was one to write to such a man, who had obviously got stuck in a rut and whom one could pity but not help? Ought one perhaps to advise him to come home, to move back again, resuming all the old friendships—nothing stood in the way of that—and for the rest relying on his friends' assistance? But that would be tantamount to telling him at the same time—and the more solicitously one did it, the more offensive would be the effect—that his efforts up to now had been abortive, that he should desist from them once and for all, that he should come back and have everyone stare open-mouthed at the man who had come back for good, that only his friends knew what was what, and that he was an overgrown baby who must simply do as his successful friends, who had stayed at home, instructed him. And was it even certain that all the bother one would have to put him to was going to serve some purpose? Perhaps there would be no getting him to come home at all—he said himself that he no longer felt he had the hang of things in his native land—and he would stay there in spite of everything, still abroad and now, embittered by all the advice he had received, alienated even further from his friends. If on the other hand he took the advice and, having come back, succumbed to depression—not of course through any fault except that of circumstances—if he failed to get along with his friends and failed to get along without them, suffered humiliation, and in the end had no real home any more and no friends, would it not have been much better for him to have stayed abroad where he was? Was it in fact thinkable in such circumstances that he would ever get anywhere back at home?

For these reasons it was not possible, supposing one wanted to keep up a correspondence with him in the first place, actually to tell him things in the way that one would have no hesitation in telling them to the most casual acquaintance. The friend had not been back for over three years now on the thoroughly makeshift pretext of the unstable political situation in Russia, as if this would not permit even the briefest absence on the part of a small businessman when hundreds of thousands of Russians happily travelled all over the globe. As it happened, in the course of those three years many things had changed as far as George was concerned. News of the death of George's mother some two years previously, since when George had been living with his aged father, had in fact reached his friend's ears and the friend had expressed his condolences in a letter of such dryness as could be accounted for only by assuming that grief at that sort of event is quite inconceivable to one living abroad. Since that time, however, George had thrown himself into everything, including his business, with greater determination. Possibly while his mother was alive his father had blocked any genuinely autonomous activity on George's part by allowing only his own views to prevail in business matters; possibly since his mother's death his father, while continuing to work for the firm, had made his presence less felt; possibly—as was in fact very likely—a series of happy accidents had played a more important role; at any rate, the business had expanded quite unexpectedly in those two years, they had had to take on twice as many staff, turnover was five times what it had been, and further progress was undoubtedly just around the corner.

21

The friend, however, had no idea of this change. He had previously—the last occasion had perhaps been that letter of condolence—tried to persuade George to emigrate to Russia, outlining in detail the prospects that existed for George's particular line of business in Petersburg. The figures had been infinitesimal in relation to the size George's firm had since assumed. But George had not felt inclined to write to his friend about his business successes, and to have made good the omission now would have created a curious impression to say the least.

George therefore confined himself to writing to his friend about such insignificant events as come to mind in no particular order when one sits down to think on a quiet Sunday. His sole aim was to leave undisturbed the conception that his friend had presumably formed of his native city in the long time he had been away and to which he had presumably become reconciled. It had happened, for example, that George notified his friend of the engagement of a person of no consequence to a girl of equally little consequence three times in letters written at quite long intervals apart—so that eventually the friend, very much contrary to George's intention, had begun to show interest in this curious fact.

George, however, much preferred to write to him about things like that than admit that he had himself become engaged a month before to a Miss Frieda Brandenfeld, the daughter of a wealthy family. He often talked to his fiancée about this friend and the peculiar relationship in which he stood to him through his letters. 'Then he certainly won't come to our wedding,' she said, 'and I have the right to meet all your friends.' 'I don't want to bother him,' George replied. 'You see, he probably would come, at least I think he would, but he'd feel that I was getting at him, that I was putting him on the spot; he might envy me, and he'd certainly feel discontented and incapable of ever shaking off that discontentment and travelling back alone. Do you know what that means—alone?' 'Yes, but might he not hear about our getting married through some other channel?' 'I can't prevent that, of course, but it's unlikely in view of the kind of life he leads.' 'George, if you have friends like that you shouldn't have got engaged at all.' 'I know, we're both to blame there; but I wouldn't have it any different even now.' And when, panting between his kisses, she went on to say, 'No, I'm hurt, I really am,' there did indeed seem no harm at all in writing to tell his friend everything. 'That's the way I am, and that's the way he must accept me,' he said to himself. 'I can't carve another person out of myself who might be better suited for friendship with him than I am.'

So it was that in the long letter he wrote on that Sunday morning he informed his friend of his engagement in the following words: 'I've kept the best news till last. I've become engaged to a Miss Frieda Brandenfeld, the daughter of a wealthy family that came to live here long after you left, so you're hardly likely to know them. There will be other opportunities to tell you more about my fiancée; let me just say for now that I am very happy and that the only change this has made to our relationship is that, instead of having a perfectly ordinary friend in me, you will now have a happy friend. You will also have, in the person of my fiancée, who sends you her best wishes and who will be writing to you herself very shortly, a sincere friend of the opposite sex, which for a bachelor is not without importance. I know how many things stand in the way of your paying us a visit, but wouldn't my wedding provide just the occasion to sweep all obstacles aside for once? Well, be that as it may, make no allowances but do only as you think fit.'

With this letter is his hand and with his face turned to the window, George continued to sit at his desk for a long time. An acquaintance passing in the street who wished him good morning received no more acknowledgement than a vacant smile.

Eventually, putting the letter in his pocket, he went out of his room and straight across a small landing into his father's room, where he had not set foot for months. Not that there was any need for him to do so in the ordinary course of events since he was in constant contact with his father at the office, they lunched at the same time in a restaurant, and in the evenings, though each looked after himself, they usually—when George was not out with friends or visiting his fiancée, as most often happened—sat up for a while, each with his newspaper, in the sitting-room that they shared between them.

George was amazed at how dark his father's room was, even on that sunny morning. What a shadow it cast, that high wall beyond the narrow courtyard! His father was sitting by the window, in a corner of the room that was adorned with various mementoes of George's late mother; he was reading the newspaper, holding it up to his eyes at an angle in an attempt to compensate for some deficiency in his eyesight. On the table stood the remains of his breakfast, not much of which appeared to have been consumed.

'Ah, George!' his father said, coming across the room towards him. His heavy dressing-gown fell open as he walked, the flaps swirling about him—'He's still a giant, my father,' George said to himself.

Then he said, 'It's intolerably dark in here.'

'It's dark, all right,' his father replied.

'And you have the window shut?'

'I prefer it that way.'

'It's really warm outside,' said George, as if following up his earlier remark. He took a seat.

His father cleared the breakfast things away and put them on top of a cupboard.

'I just wanted to tell you,' George went on, following the old man's movements with a forlorn look, 'that I've sent word of my engagement to Petersburg after all.' He pulled the letter out of his pocket a little way; then let it drop back.

'Why to Petersburg?' his father asked.

'To my friend, *you* know,' said George, looking his father in the eye. 'He's not at all like this in the office,' he was thinking, 'sitting there so four-square with his arms across his chest!'

'Quite. Your friend,' his father said with emphasis.

'But I told you, father, how I didn't want to tell him of my engagement at first. Purely out of consideration, for no other reason. You know yourself how difficult he is. What I said to myself was, he may hear about my engagement from someone else, though it's hardly likely in view of the solitary life he leads—I can't help that—but he's not going to hear about it from me.'

'And now you've changed your mind, is that it?' his father inquired, putting his huge newspaper down on the window-sill, placing his spectacles on top of it, and covering the spectacles with his hand.

'Yes, now I've changed my mind. If he's a good friend of mine, I said to myself, then my being happily engaged will make him happy too. That's why I no longer had any hesitation in notifying him of the fact. But before I posted the letter I wanted to tell you what I'd done.'

'George,' his father said, pulling his toothless mouth into a broad slit, 'listen to me! You've come to me with this thing because you want to talk it over with me. That does you credit, no

24

doubt about it. But it's no good, in fact it's less than no good, if you're not going to tell me the whole truth. I don't want to stir up things that have no place here. Since the death of your beloved mother certain not very nice things have been happening. Maybe there's a time for them too, and maybe that time comes sooner than we expect. A great deal escapes me in the office, though perhaps not because it's kept from me—the last thing I'm trying to suggest is that things are being kept from me—but I haven't the strength any more, my memory is beginning to go, and I no longer have an eye for all the little details. This is simply nature taking its course for one thing, and for another, Mummy's death hit me much harder than it did you. But as long as we're on the subject of this letter, promise me one thing, George: don't try to hoodwink me. It's a trifle, it's not worth bothering about, so don't try to hoodwink me. Do you really have this friend in Petersburg?'

George stood up in embarrassment. 'Never mind about my friends. A thousand friends could never take the place of my father. Do you know what I think? You don't look after yourself enough. Old age is demanding its due. I can't do without you in the office, you know that as well as I do, but if the business should ever start undermining your health I'd shut up shop for good tomorrow. I'm not having that. No, we're going to have to start a new regimen for you. Radically new, I mean. Here you are, sitting in the dark, when in the living-room it would be lovely and light for you. You peck at your breakfast instead of building yourself up properly. You sit around with the window shut when fresh air would do you so much good. No, Father, no! I'll get the doctor round and we'll do exactly what he says. We'll swap rooms: you move into the front room and I'll come in here. There'll be no difference as far as you're concerned because we'll move all your things over too. But there's time enough for all that. You go back to bed for a bit now; you've got to take things easy. Here, I'll help you get undressed. I can, you know. Or would you like to go in the front room now? You can have my bed for the time being. In fact that would be a very sensible arrangement.'

George was standing right beside his father, whose head of shaggy white hair had sunk to his breast.

'George,' his father said softly, not moving.

George immediately knelt down beside his father; he looked into his father's weary face and into the huge pupils staring out at him from the corners of his father's eyes.

'You have no friend in Petersburg. You've always liked to have your little joke, even with me. How should you have a friend there, of all places! I find that too much to believe.'

'Think back for a moment, father,' George said, heaving the old man out of his chair and, as he stood there in a really extremely weak condition, pulling off his dressing-gown. 'Nearly three years ago now my friend came here to see us. You didn't particularly like him, I remember. On at least two occasions I disowned him in conversation with you, although he was sitting in my room at the time. I could understand your dislike of him perfectly well; my friend has his peculiarities. But then there was that other time when you got on with him very well. I was really proud of the fact that you listened to him, nodded at what he said, and asked questions. Think back—you must remember. He was telling us those incredible stories about the Russian Revolution. About how for example on a business trip to Kiev he had become involved in a disturbance and seen a priest up on a balcony cut a large, bleeding cross in the flat of his hand, hold the hand in the air, and shout to the crowd. You've even recounted the story yourself on occasion.'

In the meantime George had managed to lower his father into his chair again, carefully remove the woollen trousers he wore over his linen pants, and pull off his socks. Seeing the not particularly clean state of his father's underwear, he reproached himself for having neglected to ensure that his father changed his clothes whenever necessary. He and his fiancée had not yet discussed in so many words how they were going to arrange his father's future; they had tacitly assumed that he would stay on in the old flat by himself. Now, however, George resolved on the spur of the moment to take his father with him when he set up house. In fact, on second thought, it looked as if the care and attention he planned to give his father there might almost come too late.

He picked his father up and carried him into bed. An awful feeling came over him as he became aware during the few steps to the bed that his father, curled up in his arms, was playing with the watch chain at his lapel. So firmly did his father grasp the watch chain that for a moment George was unable to put him to bed.

Once he was in bed, however, everything seemed to be fine. He arranged the bedclothes himself, pulling the quilt unusually high over his shoulders. He looked up at George in a not unfriendly fashion.

'You do remember him, don't you?' George asked, nodding encouragingly.

'Am I covered up now?' asked his father, as if he could not tell whether his feet were adequately covered.

'See, you like it in bed,' said George, tucking the quilt in around him.

'Am I covered up?' his father asked again. He seemed to be particularly interested in what the answer would be.

'Don't worry, you're well covered up.'

'No, I'm not!' his father shouted, slamming the answer down on the question, and he threw the quilt back with such force that for a moment it opened out completely in flight. He stood up in bed, one hand pressed lightly to the ceiling. 'You wanted to cover me up, you scoundrel, I know you did, but I'm not covered up yet. If it's my last ounce of strength it's enough for you—more than enough for you. I know your friend, all right. A son after my own heart, he'd have been. That's why you've been deceiving him all these years, isn't it? Why else? Do you think I haven't wept for him? That's why you shut yourself in your office—the boss is busy, no one's to disturb him—purely in order to write your lying notes to Russia. But luckily for your father he doesn't need anyone to teach him to see through his son. And now that you thought you'd got the better of him, so much so that you could plant your bottom down on him and he wouldn't move, what does my high and mighty son do but decide to get married!'

George looked up at this terrifying vision of his father. The friend in Petersburg, whom his father suddenly knew so well, affected him as never before. He thought of him, lost in the depths of Russia. He saw him at the door of his empty, looted shop against a background of smashed-up shelving, ransacked stock, and bent gas brackets, barely able to stand. Why had he had to go so far away?

'Look at me, will you!' his father shouted, and George almost distractedly ran over to the bed to take everything in but came to a halt halfway there.

'Because she hauled up her skirts,' his father began in a slimy falsetto, 'because she hauled up her skirts like this, the filthy bitch,' and by way of illustration he lifted the hem of his nightshirt so high that the war wound on his thigh was exposed, 'because she hauled up her skirts like this and like this and like this you had to have a go at her, and to make sure you can have your way with her undisturbed you defile your mother's memory, betray your friend, and stick your father in bed where he can't budge. Well, can he budge or can't he?'

And he stood without holding on at all and kicked his legs in the air. His eyes blazed with insight.

George was now standing in a corner, as far away from his father as possible. A long time ago he had made up his mind to keep a really close watch on everything lest he should ever, by some devious means, either from behind or from above, be caught by surprise. He recalled his long-forgotten resolution and promptly forgot it, like drawing a short thread through the eye of a needle.

'But the friend isn't betrayed after all!' his father shouted, and a wagging forefinger corroborated this. 'I was his locum tenens here.'

'Playactor!' George could not refrain from shouting; realizing his mistake he immediately, though too late—there was a

28

glazed look in his eyes—bit his tongue so hard that he doubled up in pain.

'Of course I've been playacting! Hah, that's just the word for it! What other consolation was left to your old widowed father? Tell me—and for the space of your answer be my living son still— what else was left to me in my little back room, persecuted by disloyal staff, an old man to the marrow of my bones? And my son went about rejoicing, clinching deals that I had set up, giddying himself with pleasure, and departing from his father's presence with the opaque face of a man of honour! Do you think I didn't love you—having fathered you?'

'Now he's going to lean forward,' George thought. 'If only he'd fall and smash to pieces!' The words went hissing through his head.

His father leant forward but did not fall. Since George did not approach as he had expected, he straightened up again.

'Stay where you are, I don't need you! You think you still have the strength to come over here and are just holding back because you want to. Well, don't delude yourself! I'm still the stronger by far. On my own I might have had to stand down, but mother has left me her strength. I'm in business with your friend in a big way; I've got your customer right here in my pocket!'

'He's even got pockets in his nightshirt!' George said to himself, thinking that he could make him look ridiculous in the eyes of the whole world by this remark. He only thought it for a moment, because he always forgot everything.

'Just you take your fancy woman on your arm and come up and see me! I'll swat her away from your side for you, you'll see if I don't!'

George made a face as if he did not believe it. His father simply nodded, driving home the truth of his words, in the direction of George's corner.

'You made me laugh today, coming to ask whether you should write to your friend about your engagement! He knows everything, stupid, he knows everything! I wrote to him myself,

29

because you forgot to take my writing things away. That's why he
hasn't been here for years. He knows everything a hundred times
better than you do yourself. He screws your letter up unread in
his left hand while holding up my letters to read in his right!'

He waved an arm about enthusiastically above his head.
'He knows everything a thousand times better!' he yelled.

'Ten thousand times!' George said to poke fun at his
father, but even before the words had left his lips they had a
deadly serious sound.

'For years I've been waiting for you to come along with
that question! Do you think I care about anything else? Do you
think I read the papers? Here!' And he threw George a sheet of
newspaper that had somehow got carried into bed with him. An
old newspaper with a name George did not begin to recognize.

'The time it's taken you to grow up! Your mother had to
die, she was not to see the joyful day, your friend's going to rack
and ruin in Russia, he looked as if he was on his last legs three
years ago, and you can see for yourself the state I'm in! You've got
eyes, haven't you?'

'So you've been trying to catch me out!' cried George.

Sympathetically his father observed, 'You wanted to say
that before, probably. Now it's completely out of place.'

And in a louder voice: 'So now you know what else
there was apart from you; up to now you only knew about yourself!
You were an innocent child, to tell the truth—though to tell the
whole truth you were the devil incarnate! Therefore know: I hereby
sentence you to death by drowning!'

George felt himself thrust from the room, the thud
with which his father fell on the bed behind him still echoing in
his ears. On the stairs, which he took at a rush as if descending
an inclined plane, he surprised his cleaning lady, who was going
up to tidy the flat after the night. 'Jesus!' she cried, hiding her
face in her apron, but he had already gone. Out of the door he
shot, his momentum carrying him across the road to the water's
edge. He clutched the railing as a hungry man will clutch at food.

He vaulted over it, expert gymnast that he had been in his boyhood days, much to his parents' pride. Still holding on with weakening grip, he glimpsed a bus through the bars, knew it would easily cover the noise of his fall, called softly, 'Dear parents, I did love you, always,' and let himself drop.

Crossing the bridge at that moment was a simply endless stream of traffic.

Kenzaburō Ōe

"Sooner murder an infant in his cradle than nurse unacted desires," wrote William Blake in his *Proverbs of Hell*. The line became Kenzaburō Ōe's motto. He was hailed a genius while still in high school upon the publication of a novella, "Prize Stock," but it was not until 1964, when Ōe was twenty-nine, that he found both his theme and his voice. That year Ōe's son was born with brain damage, and in that personal nightmare Ōe saw a reflection of his country's tragedy, the bombing of Hiroshima. For Ōe, both events cancelled out the past and its expectations. A few months after his son's birth, he wrote two books—*A Personal Matter*, the first of a series of novels dealing with brain-damaged children, and *Hiroshima Notes,* a collection of essays—and asked his publisher to release both the same day as proof of their interrelation.

His son—whom he calls his "obstacled boy"—became his guide through the hell of private anguish and public despair. "There's a boat," Ōe said during an interview in Toronto, "and a small pilot who shows the way to a big ship. If I may use the gorgeous example in Dante's *Inferno*, Dante finds a pilot, a teacher. My son is a kind of small, funny pilot for me. My son is my pilot ship."

AGHWEE THE SKY MONSTER

kenzaburō ōe

Translated from the Japanese by John Nathan

alone in my room, I wear a piratical black patch over my right eye. The eye may look all right, but the truth is I have scarcely any sight in it. I say scarcely, it isn't totally blind. Consequently, when I look at this world with both eyes I see two worlds perfectly superimposed. A vague and shadowy world on top of one that's bright and vivid. I can be walking down a paved street when a sense of peril and unbalance will stop me like a rat just scurried out of a sewer, dead in my tracks. Or I'll discover a film of unhappiness and fatigue on the face of a cheerful friend and clog the flow of an easy chat with my stutter. I suppose I'll get used to this eventually. If I don't, I intend to wear my patch not only in my room when I'm alone but on the street and with my friends. Strangers may pass with condescending smiles—what an old-fashioned joke!—but I'm old enough not to be annoyed by every little thing.

The story I intend to tell is about my first experience earning money; I began with my right eye because the memory of that experience ten years ago revived in me abruptly and quite out of context when violence was done to my eye last spring. Remembering, I should add, I was freed from the hatred uncoiling in my heart and beginning to fetter me. At the very end I'll talk about the accident itself.

Ten years ago I had twenty-twenty vision. Now one of my eyes is ruined. *Time* shifted, launched itself from the spring-board of an eyeball squashed by a stone. When I first met that sentimental madman I had only a child's understanding of *time*. I was yet to have the cruel awareness of *time* drilling its eyes into my back and *time* lying in wait ahead.

Ten years ago I was eighteen, five feet six, one hundred and ten pounds, had just entered college, and was looking for a part-time job. Although I still had trouble reading French, I wanted a cloth-bound edition in two volumes of *L'Ame Enchanté*. It was a Moscow edition, with not only a foreword but footnotes and even the colophon in Russian and wispy lines like bits of thread connecting the letters of the French text. A curious edition to be sure, but sturdier and more elegant than the French, and much cheaper. At the time I discovered it in a bookstore specializing in East European publications. I had no interest in Romain Rolland, yet I went immediately into action to make the volumes mine. In those days I often succumbed to some weird passion and it never bothered me, I had the feeling there was nothing to worry about so long as I was sufficiently obsessed.

As I had just entered college and wasn't registered at the employment centre, I looked for work by making the rounds of people I knew. Finally my uncle introduced me to a banker who came up with an offer. 'Did you happen to see a movie called *Harvey*?' he asked. I said yes, and tried for a smile of moderate but unmistakable dedication, appropriate for someone about to be employed for the first time. *Harvey* was that Jimmy Stewart film about a man living with an imaginary rabbit as big as a bear; it had made me laugh so hard I thought I would die. 'Recently, my son has been having the same sort of delusions about living with a monster.' The banker didn't return my smile. 'He's stopped work-ing and stays in his room. I'd like him to get out from time to time but of course he'd need a—companion. Would you be interested?'

I knew quite a bit about the banker's son. He was a young composer whose avant-garde music had won prizes in France and Italy and who was generally included in the photo roundups in the weekly magazines, the kind of article they always called 'Japan's Artists of Tomorrow'. I had never heard his major works, but I had seen several films he had written the music for. There was one about the adventures of a juvenile delinquent that had a short, lyrical theme played on the harmonica. It was beautiful. Watching the picture, I remember feeling vaguely troubled by the idea of an adult nearly thirty years old (in fact, the composer was twenty-eight when he hired me, my present age), working out a theme for the harmonica, I suppose because my own harmonica had become my little brother's property when I had entered elementary school. And possibly because I knew more about the composer, whose name was D, than just public facts; I knew he had created a scandal. Generally I have nothing but contempt for scandals, but I knew that the composer's infant child had died, that he had gotten divorced as a result, and that he was rumoured to be involved with a certain movie actress. I hadn't known that he was in the grips of something like the rabbit in Jimmy Stewart's movie, or that he had stopped working and secluded himself in his room. How serious was his condition, I wondered, was it a case of nervous breakdown, or was he clearly schizophrenic?

'I'm not certain I know just what you mean by companion,' I said, reeling in my smile. 'Naturally, I'd like to be of service if I can.' This time, concealing my curiosity and apprehension I tried to lend my voice and expression as much sympathy as possible without seeming forward. It was only a part-time job, but it was the first chance of employment I had had and I was determined to do my accommodating best.

'When my son decides he wants to go somewhere in Tokyo, you go along—just that. There's a nurse at the house and she has no trouble handling him, so you don't have to worry about violence.' The banker made me feel like a soldier whose cowardice had been discovered. I blushed and said, trying to recover lost ground, 'I'm fond of music, and I respect composers more than anyone, so I look forward to accompanying D and talking with him.'

'All he thinks about these days is this thing in his head, and apparently that's all he talks about!' The banker's brusqueness made my face even redder. 'You can go out to see him tomorrow,' he said.

'At—your house?'

'That's right, did you think he was in an asylum?' From the banker's tone of voice I could only suppose that he was at bottom a nasty man.

'If I should get the job,' I said with my eyes on the floor, 'I'll drop by again to thank you.' I could easily have cried.

'No, he'll be hiring you' (All right then, I resolved defiantly, I'll call D my employer), 'so that won't be necessary. All I care about is that he doesn't get into any trouble outside that might develop into a scandal . . . There's his career to think about. Naturally, what he does reflects on me—'

So that was it! I thought, so I was to be a moral sentinel guarding the banker's family against a second contamination by the poisons of scandal. Of course I didn't say a thing, I only nodded dependably, anxious to warm the banker's chilly heart with the heat of reliance on me. I didn't even ask the most pressing question, something truly difficult to ask: This monster haunting your son, sir, is it a rabbit like Harvey, nearly six feet tall? A creature covered in bristly hair like an Abominable Snowman? What kind of monster is it? In the end I remained silent and consoled myself with the thought that I might be able to pry the secret out of the nurse if I made friends with her.

Then I left the executive's office, and as I walked along the corridor grinding my teeth in humiliation as if I were Julien Sorel after a meeting with someone important, I became self-conscious to the tips of my fingers and tried assessing my attitude and its effectiveness. When I got out of college I chose not to seek nine-to-five employment, and I do believe the memory of my dialogue with that disagreeable banker played a large part in my decision.

Even so, when classes were over the next day I took a train out to the residential suburb where the composer lived. As

I passed through the gate of that castle of a house, I remember a roaring of terrific beasts, as at a zoo in the middle of the night. I was dismayed, I cowered—what if those were the screams of my employer? A good thing it didn't occur to me then that those savage screams might have been coming from the monster haunting D like Jimmy Stewart's rabbit. Whatever they were, it was so clear that the screaming had rattled me that the maid showing me the way was indiscreet enough to break into a laugh. Then I discovered someone else laughing, voicelessly, in the dimness beyond a window in an annex in the garden. It was the man who was supposed to employ me; he was laughing like a face in a movie without a soundtrack. And boiling all around him was that howling of wild beasts. I listened closely and realized that several of the same animals were shrieking in concert. And in voices too shrill to be of this world. Abandoned by the maid at the entrance to the annex, I decided the screaming must be part of the composer's tape collection, regained my courage, straightened up, and opened the door.

Inside, the annex reminded me of a kindergarten. There were no partitions in the large room, only two pianos, an electric organ, several tape recorders, a record player, something we had called a 'mixer' when I was in the high-school radio club—there was hardly room to step. A dog asleep on the floor, for example, turned out to be a tuba of reddish brass. It was just as I had imagined a composer's studio; I even had the illusion I had seen the place before. His father had said D had stopped working and secluded himself in his room; could he have been mistaken?

The composer was just bending to switch off the tape recorder. Enveloped in a chaos that was not without its own order, he moved his hands swiftly and in an instant those beastly screams were sucked into a dark hole of silence. Then he straightened and turned to me with a truly tranquil smile.

Having glanced around the room and seen that the nurse was not present I was a little wary, but the composer gave me no reason in the world to expect that he was about to get violent.

'My father told me about you. Come in, there's room

over there,' he said in a low, resonant voice.

I took off my shoes and stepped up onto the rug without putting on slippers. Then I looked around for a place to sit, but except for a round stool in front of the piano and the organ, there wasn't a bit of furniture in the room, not even a cushion. So I brought my feet together between a pair of bongo drums and some empty tape boxes and there I stood uncomfortably. The composer stood there too, arms hanging at his sides. I wondered if he ever sat down. He didn't ask me to be seated either, just stood there silent and smiling.

'Could those have been monkey voices?' I said, trying to crack a silence that threatened to set more quickly than any cement.

'Rhinoceros—they sounded that way because I speeded the machine up. And I had the volume way up, too. At least I think they're rhinoceros—rhino is what I asked for when I had this tape made—of course I can't really be sure. But now that you're here, I'll be able to go to the zoo myself.'

'I may take that to mean that I'm employed?'

'Of course! I didn't have you come out here to test you. How can a lunatic test a normal person?' The man who was to be my employer said this objectively and almost as if he were embarrassed. Which made me feel disgusted with the obsequiousness of what I had said—I may take that to mean that I'm employed? I had sounded like a shopkeeper! The composer was different from his businessman father and I should have been more direct with him.

'I wish you wouldn't call yourself a lunatic. It's awkward for me.' Trying to be frank was one thing, but what a brainless remark! But the composer met me half-way. 'All right, if that's how you feel. I suppose that would make work easier.'

Work is a vague word, but, at least during those few months when I was visiting him once a week, the composer didn't get even as close to work as going to the zoo to record a genuine rhino for himself. All he did was wander around Tokyo in various conveyances or on foot and visit a variety of places. When he mentioned work, he must therefore have had me in mind. And I worked quite a lot; I even went on a mission for him all the way to Kyoto.

'Then when should I begin?' I said.

'Right away if it suits you. Now.'

'That suits me fine.'

'I'll have to get ready—would you wait outside?'

Head lowered cautiously, as though he were walking in a swamp, my employer picked his way to the back of the room past musical instruments and sound equipment and piles of manuscript to a black wooden door which he opened and then closed behind him. I got a quick look at a woman in a nurse's uniform, a woman in her early forties with a longish face and heavy shadows on her cheeks that might have been wrinkles or maybe scars. She seemed to encircle the composer with her right arm as she ushered him inside, while with her left hand she closed the door. If this was part of the routine, I would never have a chance to talk with the nurse before I went out with my employer. Standing in front of the closed door, in the darkest part of that dim room, I shuffled into my shoes and felt my anxiety about this job of mine increase. The composer had smiled the whole time and when I had prompted him he had replied. But he hadn't volunteered much. Should I have been more reserved? Since outside might have meant two things and since I was determined that everything should be perfect on my first job, I decided to wait just inside the main gate, from where I could see the annex in the garden.

D was a small, thin man, but with a head that seemed larger than most. To make the bony cliff of his forehead look a little less forbidding he had combed his pale, well-washed, and fluffy hair down over his brow. His mouth and jaw were small, and his teeth were horribly irregular. And yet, probably due to the colour of his deeply recessed eyes, there was a static correctness about his face that went well with a tranquil smile. As for the overall impression, there was something canine about the man. He wore flannel trousers and a sweater with stripes like fleas. His shoulders were a little stooped, his arms outlandishly long.

When he came out of the back door of the annex, my

employer was wearing a blue wool cardigan over his other sweater and a pair of white tennis shoes. He reminded me of a grade-school music teacher. In one hand he held a black scarf, and as if he were puzzling whether to wrap it around his neck, there was perplexity in his grin to me as I waited at the gate. For as long as I knew D, except at the very end when he was lying in a hospital bed, he was always dressed this way. I remember his outfit so well because I was always struck by something comical about an adult man wearing a cardigan around his shoulders, as if he were a woman in disguise. Its shapelessness and nondescript colour made that sweater perfect for him. As the composer pigeon-toed toward me past the shrubbery, he absently lifted the hand that held the scarf and signalled me with it. Then he wrapped the scarf resolutely around his neck. It was already four in the afternoon and fairly cold out-of-doors.

40

D went through the gate, and as I was following him (our relationship was already that of employer and employee) I had the feeling I was being watched and turned around: behind the same window through which I had discovered my employer, that forty-year-old nurse with the scarred—or were they wrinkled?—cheeks was watching us the way a soldier remaining behind might see a deserter off, her lips clamped shut like a turtle's. I resolved to get her alone as soon as I could to question her about D's condition. What was wrong with the woman, anyway? Here she was taking care of a young man with a nervous condition, maybe a madman, yet when her charge went out she had nothing to say to his companion! Wasn't that professional negligence? Wasn't she at least obliged to fill in the new man on the job? Or was my employer a patient so gentle and harmless that nothing had to be said?

When he got to the sidewalk D shuttered open his tired-looking eyes in their deep sockets and glanced swiftly up and down the deserted, residential street. I didn't know whether it was an indication of madness or what—sudden action without any continuity seemed to be a habit of his. The composer looked up at the clear, end-of-autumn sky, blinking rapidly. Though they were sunken, there was something remarkably expressive about his deep brown eyes. Then he stopped blinking and his eyes seemed to focus, as though he were searching the sky. I stood obliquely behind him, watching, and what impressed me most vividly was the movement of his Adam's apple, which was large as any fist. I wondered if he had been destined to become a large man; perhaps something had impeded his growth in infancy and now only his head from the neck up bespoke the giant he was meant to be.

Lowering his gaze from the sky, my employer found and held my puzzled eyes with his own and said casually, but with a gravity that made objection impossible, 'On a clear day you can see things floating up there very well. He's up there with them, and frequently he comes down to me when I go outdoors.'

Instantly I felt threatened. Looking away from my employer, I wondered how to survive this first ordeal that had confronted me so quickly. Should I pretend to believe in 'him', or would that be a mistake? Was I dealing with a raving madman, or was the composer just a poker-faced humorist trying to have some fun with me? As I stood there in distress, he extended me a helping hand: 'I know you can't see the figures floating in the sky, and I know you wouldn't be aware of him even if he were right here at my side. All I ask is that you don't act amazed when he comes down to earth, even if I talk to him. Because you'd upset him if you were to break out laughing all of a sudden or tried to shut me up. And if you happen to notice when we're talking that I want some support from you, I'd appreciate it if you'd chime right in and say something, you know, affirmative. You see, I'm explaining Tokyo to him as if it were a paradise. It might seem a lunatic paradise to you, but maybe you could think of it as a satire and be affirmative anyway, at least when he's down here with me.'

I listened carefully and thought I could make out at least the contours of what my employer expected of me. Then was he a rabbit as big as a man after all, nesting in the sky? But that wasn't what I asked; I permitted myself to ask only: 'How will I know when he's down here with you?'

'Just by watching me; he only comes down when I'm outside.'

'How about when you're in a car?'

'In a car or a train, as long as I'm next to an open window he's likely to show up. There have been times when he's appeared when I was in the house, just standing next to an open window.'

'And . . . right now?' I asked uncomfortably. I must have sounded like the class dunce who simply cannot grasp the multiplication principle.

'Right now it's just you and me,' my employer said graciously. 'Why don't we ride in to Shinjuku today; I haven't been on a train in a long time.'

We walked to the station, and all the way I kept an eye peeled for a sign that something had appeared at my employer's side. But before I knew it we were on the train and, so far as I could tell, nothing had materialized. One thing I did notice: the composer ignored the people who passed us on the street even when they greeted him. As if he himself did not exist, as if the people who approached with hellos and how-are-yous were registering an illusion which they mistook for him, my employer utterly ignored all overtures to contact.

The same thing happened at the ticket window; D declined to relate to other people. Handing me one thousand yen he told me to buy tickets, and then refused to take his own even when I held it out to him. I had to stop at the gate and have both our tickets punched while D swept through the turnstile onto the platform with the freedom of the invisible man. Even on the train, he behaved as if the other passengers were no more aware of him than of the atmosphere; huddling in a seat in the furthest corner of the car, he rode in silence with his eyes closed. I stood in front of him and watched in growing apprehension for whatever it was to float in through the open window and settle at his side. Naturally, I didn't believe in the monster's existence. It was just that I was determined not to miss the instant when D's delusions took hold of him; I felt I owed him that much in return for the money he was paying me. But, as it happened, he sat like some small animal playing dead all the way to Shinjuku Station, so I could only surmise that he hadn't had a visit from the sky. Of course, supposition was all it was: as long as other people were around us, my employer remained a sullen oyster of silence. But I learned soon enough that my guess had been correct. Because when the moment came it was more than apparent (from D's reaction, I mean) that something was visiting him.

We had left the station and were walking down the street. It was that time of day a little before evening when not many people are out, yet we ran across a small crowd gathered on a corner. We stopped to look; surrounded by the crowd, an old man was turning around and around in the street without a glance at anyone. A dignified-looking old man, he was spinning in a frenzy, clutching a briefcase and an umbrella to his breast, mussing his grey, pomaded hair a little as he stamped his feet and barked like a seal. The faces in the watching crowd were lustreless and dry in the evening chill that was stealing into the air; the old man's face alone was flushed, and sweating, and seemed about to steam.

Suddenly I noticed that D, who should have been standing at my side, had taken a few steps back and had thrown one arm around the shoulders of an invisible something roughly his own height. Now he was peering affectionately into the space slightly above the empty circle of his arm. The crowd was too intent on the old man to be concerned with D's performance, but I was terrified. Slowly the composer turned to me, as if he wanted to introduce me to a friend. I didn't know how to respond; all I could do was panic and blush. It was like forgetting your silly lines in the junior high-school play. The composer continued to stare at me, and now there was annoyance in his eyes. He was seeking an explanation for that intent old man turning singlemindedly in the street for the benefit of his visitor from the sky. A paradisical explanation! But all I could do was wonder stupidly whether the old man might have been afflicted with Saint Vitus' dance.

When I sadly shook my head in silence, the light of

43

inquiry went out of my employer's eyes. As if he were taking leave of a friend, he dropped his arm. Then he slowly shifted his gaze skyward until his head was all the way back and his large Adam's apple stood out in bold relief. The phantom had soared back into the sky and I was ashamed; I hadn't been equal to my job. As I stood there with my head hanging, the composer stepped up to me and indicated that my first day of work was at an end: 'We can go home, now. He's come down today already, and you must be pretty tired.' I did feel exhausted after all that tension.

We rode back in a taxi with the windows rolled up, and as soon as I'd been paid for the day, I left. But I didn't go straight to the station; I waited behind a telephone pole diagonally across from the house. Dusk deepened, the sky turned the colour of a rose, and just as the promise of night was becoming fact, the nurse, in a short-skirted, one-piece dress of a colour indistinct in the dimness, appeared through the main gate pushing a brand-new bicycle in front of her. Before she could get on the bicycle, I ran over to her. Without her nurse's uniform, she was just an ordinary little woman in her early forties; vanished from her face was the mystery I had discovered through the annex window. And my appearance had unsettled her. She couldn't climb on the bike and pedal away, but neither would she stand still; she had begun to walk the bike along when I demanded that she explain our mutual employer's condition. She resisted, peevishly, but I had a good grip on the bicycle seat and so in the end she gave in. When she began to talk, her formidable lower jaw snapped shut at each break in the sentence; she was absolutely a talking turtle.

'He says it's a fat baby in a white cotton night-gown. Big as a kangaroo, he says. It's supposed to be afraid of dogs and policemen and it comes down out of the sky. He says its name is Aghwee! Let me tell you something, if you happen to be around when that spook gets hold of him, you'd better just play dumb, you can't afford to get involved. Don't forget, you're dealing with a loony! And another thing, don't you take him anyplace funny, even if he wants to go. On top of everything else, a little gonorrhea is all we need around here!'

I blushed and let go of the bicycle seat. The nurse, jangling her bell, pedalled away into the darkness as fast as she could go with legs as round and thin as handlebars. Ah, a fat baby in a white cotton night-gown, big as a kangaroo!

When I showed up at the house the following week, the composer fixed me with those clear brown eyes of his and rattled me by saying, though not especially in reproof, 'I hear you waited for the nurse and asked her about my visitor from the sky. You really take your work seriously.'

That afternoon we took the same train in the opposite direction, into the country for half an hour to an amusement park on the banks of the Tama river. We tried all kinds of rides and, luckily for me, the baby as big as a kangaroo dropped out of the sky to visit D when he was up by himself in the Sky Sloop, wooden boxes shaped like boats that were hoisted slowly into the air on the blades of a kind of windmill. From a bench on the ground, I watched the composer talking with an imaginary passenger at his side. And until his visitor had climbed back into the sky, D refused to come down; again and again a signal from him sent me running to buy him another ticket.

Another incident that made an impression on me that day occurred as we were crossing the amusement park toward the exit, when D accidentally stepped in some wet cement. When he saw that his foot had left an imprint he became abnormally irritated, and until I had negotiated with the workmen, paid them something for their pains and had the footprint trowelled away, he stubbornly refused to move from the spot. This was the only time the composer ever revealed to me the least violence in his nature. On the way home on the train, I suppose because he regretted having barked at me, he excused himself in this way: 'I'm not living in present time anymore, at least not consciously. Do you know the rule that governs trips into the past in a time machine? For example, a man who travels back ten thousand years in time doesn't dare do anything in that world that might remain behind him. Because he doesn't exist in time ten thousand years ago, and if he left anything behind him there the result would be a warp, infinitely slight maybe but still a warp, in all of history from then until now, ten thousand years of it. That's the way the rule goes, and since I'm not living in present time, I mustn't do anything here in this world that might remain or leave an imprint.'

'But why have you stopped living in present time?' I asked, and my employer sealed himself up like a golf ball and ignored me. I regretted my loose tongue; I had finally exceeded the limits permitted me, because I was too concerned with D's problem. Maybe the nurse was right; playing dumb was the only way, and I couldn't afford to get involved. I resolved not to.

We walked around Tokyo a number of times after that, and my new policy was a success. But the day came when the composer's problems began to involve me whether I liked it or not. One afternoon we got into a cab together and, for the first time since I had taken the job, D mentioned a specific destination, a swank apartment house designed like a hotel in Daikan Yama. When we arrived, D waited in the coffee shop in the basement while I went up the elevator alone to pick up a package that was waiting for me. I was to be given the package by D's former wife, who was living alone in the apartment now.

I knocked on a door that made me think of the cell blocks at Sing Sing (I was always going to the movies in those days; I have the feeling about ninety-five percent of what I knew came directly from the movies) and it was opened by a short woman with a pudgy red face on top of a neck that was just as pudgy and as round as a cylinder. She ordered me to take my shoes off and step inside, and pointed to a sofa near the window where I was to sit. This must be the way high society receives a stranger, I remember thinking at the time. For me, the son of a poor farmer, refusing her invitation and asking for the package at the door would have taken the courage to defy Japanese high society, the courage of that butcher who threatened Louis XIV. I did as I was told, and stepped for the first time in my life into a studio apartment in the American style.

The composer's former wife poured me some beer. She seemed somewhat older than D, and although she gestured grandly and intoned when she spoke, she was too round and over-weight to achieve dignity. She was wearing a dress of some heavy cloth with the hem of the skirt unravelled in the manner of a squaw costume, and her necklace of diamonds set in gold looked like the work of an Inca craftsman (now that I think about it, these observations, too, smell distinctly of the movies). Her window overlooked the street of Shibuya, but the light pouring through it into the room seemed to bother her terrifically; she was continually shifting in her chair, showing me legs as round and bloodshot as her neck, while she questioned me in the voice of a prosecutor. I suppose I was her only source of information about her former husband. Sipping my black, bitter beer as if it were hot coffee, I answered her as best I could, but my knowledge of D was scant and inaccurate and I couldn't satisfy her. Then she started asking about D's actress girl-friend, whether she came to see him and things like that, and there was nothing I could say. Annoyed, I thought to myself, what business was it of hers, didn't she have any woman's pride?

47

'Does D still see that Phantom?'

'Yes, it's a baby the size of a kangaroo in a white cotton night-gown and he says its name is Aghwee, the nurse was telling me about it,' I said enthusiastically, glad to encounter a question I could do justice to. 'It's usually floating in the sky, but sometimes it flies down to D's side.'

'Aghwee, you say. Then it must be the ghost of our dead baby. You know why he calls it Aghwee? Because our baby spoke only once while it was alive and that was what it said—Aghwee. That's a pretty mushy way to name the ghost that's haunting you, don't you think?' The woman spoke derisively; an ugly, corrosive odour reached me from her mouth. 'Our baby was born with a lump on the back of its head that made it look as if it had two heads. The doctor diagnosed it as a brain hernia. When D heard the news he decided to protect himself and me from a catastrophe, so he got together with the doctor and they killed the baby—I think they only gave it sugar water instead of milk no matter how loud it screamed. My husband killed the baby because he didn't want us to be saddled with a child who could only function as a vegetable, which is what the doctor had predicted! So he was acting out of fantastic egotism more than anything else. But then there was an autopsy and the lump turned out to be a benign tumour. That's when D began seeing ghosts; you see he'd lost the courage he needed to sustain his egotism, so he declined to live his own life, just as he had declined to let the baby go on living. Not that he committed suicide, he just fled from reality into a world of phantoms. But once your hands are all bloody with a baby's murder, you can't get them clean again just by running from reality, anybody knows that. So here he is, hands as filthy as ever and carrying on about Aghwee.'

The cruelness of her criticism was hard to bear, for my employer's sake. So I turned to her, redder in the face than ever with the excitement of her own loquacity, and struck a blow for D. 'Where were you while all this was going on? You were the mother, weren't you?'

'I had a Caesarean, and for a week afterwards I was in a coma with a high fever. It was all over when I woke up,' said D's former wife, leaving my gauntlet on the floor. Then she stood up and moved toward the kitchen. 'I guess you'll have some more beer?'

'No, thank you, I've had enough. Would you please give me the package I'm supposed to take to D?'

'Of course, just let me gargle. I have to gargle every ten minutes, for pyorrhoea—you must have noticed the smell?'

D's former wife put a brass key into a business envelope and handed it to me. Standing behind me while I tied my shoes, she asked what school I went to and then said proudly: 'I hear there's not even one subscriber to the T—— *Times* in the dormatories there. You may be interested to know that my father will own that paper soon.'

I let silence speak for my contempt.

I was about to get into the elevator when doubt knifed through me as though my chest were made of butter. I had to think. I let the elevator go and decided to use the stairs. If his former wife had described D's state of mind correctly, how could I be sure he wouldn't commit suicide with a pinch of cyanide or something taken from a box this key unlocked? All the way down the stairs I wondered what to do, and then I was standing in front of D's table and still hadn't arrived at a conclusion. The composer sat there with his eyes tightly shut, his tea untouched on the table. I suppose it wouldn't do for him to be seen drinking materials from this time now that he had stopped living in it and had become a traveller from another.

'I saw her,' I began, resolved all of a sudden to lie, 'and we were talking all this time but she wouldn't give me anything.'

My employer looked up at me placidly and said nothing, though doubt clouded his puppy eyes in their deep sockets. All the way back in the cab I sat in silence at his side, secretly perturbed. I wasn't sure whether he had seen through my lie. In my shirt pocket the key was heavy.

But I only kept it for a week. For one thing, the idea of D's suicide began to seem silly; for another, I was worried he might ask his wife about the key. So I put it in a different envelope and mailed it to him special delivery. The next day I went out to the house a little worried and found my employer in the open space in front of the annex, burning a pile of scores in manuscript. They must have been his own compositions: that key had unlocked the composer's music.

We didn't go out that day. Instead I helped D incinerate his whole opus. We had burned everything and had dug a hole and I was burying the ashes when suddenly D began to whisper. The phantom had dropped out of the sky. And until it left I continued working, slowly burying those ashes. That afternoon Aghwee (and there was no denying it was a mushy name) the monster from the sky remained at my employer's side for fully twenty minutes.

From that day on, since I either stepped to one side or

dropped behind whenever the baby phantom appeared, the composer must have realized that I was complying with only the first of his original instructions, not to act amazed, while his request that I back him up with something affirmative was consistently ignored. Yet he seemed satisfied, and so my job was made easier. I couldn't believe D was the kind of person to create a disturbance in the street; in fact his father's warning began to seem ridiculous, our tours of Tokyo together continued so uneventfully. I had already purchased the Moscow edition of *L'Ame Enchanté* I wanted, but no longer had any intention of giving up such a wonderful job. My employer and I went everywhere together. D wanted to visit all the concert halls where works of his had been performed and all the schools he had ever been to. We would make special trips to places he had once enjoyed himself—bars, movie theaters, indoor swimming pools—and then we would turn back without going inside. And the composer had a passion for all of Tokyo's many forms of public transportation: I'm sure we rode the entire metropolitan subway system. Since the monster baby couldn't descend from the sky while we were underground, I could enjoy the subway in peace of mind. Naturally, I tensed whenever we encountered dogs or officers of the law, remembering what the nurse had told me, but those encounters never coincided with an appearance by Aghwee. I discovered that I was loving my job. Not loving my employer or his phantom baby the size of a kangaroo. Simply loving my job.

One day the composer approached me about making a trip for him. He would pay travelling expenses, and my daily wage would be doubled; since I would have to stay overnight in a hotel and wouldn't be back until the second day, I would actually be earning four times what I usually made. Not only that, the purpose of the trip was to meet D's former girl-friend the movie actress in D's place. I accepted eagerly; I was delighted. And so began that comic and pathetic journey.

D gave me the name of the hotel the actress had mentioned in a recent letter and the date she was expecting him to arrive.

Then he had me learn a message to the girl: my employer was no longer living in present time; he was like a traveller who had arrived here in a time machine from a world ten thousand years in the future. Accordingly, he couldn't permit himself to create a new existence with his own signature on it through such acts as writing letters.

I memorized the message, and then it was late at night and I was sitting opposite a movie actress in the basement bar of a hotel in Kyoto, with a chance first to explain why D hadn't come himself, next to persuade his mistress of his conception of time, and finally to deliver his message. I concluded: 'D would like you to be careful not to confuse his recent divorce with another divorce he once promised you he would get; and since he isn't living in present time anymore, he says it's only natural that he won't be seeing you again.' I felt my face colour; for the first time I had the sensation that I had a truly difficult job.

51

'Is that what D-boy says? And what do you say? How do you feel about all this that you'd run an errand all the way to Kyoto?'

'Frankly, I think D is being mushy.'

'That's the way he is—I'd say he's being pretty mushy with you, too, asking this kind of favour!'

'I'm employed; I get paid by the day for what I do.'

'What are you drinking there? Have some brandy.'

I did. Until then I'd been drinking the same dark beer D's former wife had given me, with an egg in it to thin it down. By some queer carom of a psychological billiard, I'd been influenced by a memory from D's former wife's apartment while waiting to meet his mistress. The actress had been drinking brandy all along. It was the first imported brandy I'd ever had.

'And what's all this about D-boy seeing a ghost, a baby as big as a kangaroo? What did you call it, Raghbee?'

'Aghwee! The baby only spoke once before it died and that was what it said.'

'And D thought it was telling him its name? Isn't that darling! If that baby had been normal, it was all decided that D was going to get a divorce and marry me. The day the baby was born we were in bed together in a hotel room and there was a phone call and then we knew something awful had happened. D jumped out of bed and went straight to the hospital. Not a word from him since—' The actress gulped her brandy down, filled her glass to the brim from the bottle of Hennessy on the table as if she were pouring fruit juice, and drained her glass again.

Our table was hidden from the bar by a display-case full of cigarettes. Hanging on the wall above my shoulder was a large colour poster with the actress's picture on it, a beer advertisement. The face in the poster glittered like gold, no less than the beer. The girl sitting opposite me was not quite so dazzling, there was even a depression in her forehead, just below the hairline, that looked deep enough to contain an adult thumb. But it was precisely the fault that made her more appealing than her picture.

She couldn't get the baby off her mind.

'Look, wouldn't it be terrifying to die without memories or experiences because you'd never done anything human while you were alive? That's how it would be if you died as an infant— wouldn't that be terrifying?'

'Not to the baby, I don't imagine,' I said deferentially.

'But think about the world after death!' The actress's logic was full of leaps.

'The world after death?'

'If there is such a thing, the souls of the dead must live there with their memories for all eternity. But what about the soul of a baby who never knew anything and never had any experiences? I mean what memories can it have?'

At a loss, I drank my brandy in silence.

'I'm terribly afraid of death so I'm always thinking about it—you don't have to be disgusted with yourself because you don't have a quick answer for me. But you know what I think? The minute that baby died, I think D-boy decided not to create any new memories for himself, as if he had died, too, and that's why he stopped living, you know, positively, in the present time. And I bet he calls that baby ghost down to earth all over Tokyo so he can create new memories for it!'

At the time I thought she must be right. This tipsy movie actress with a dent in her forehead big enough for a thumb is quite an original psychologist, I thought to myself. And much more D's type, I thought, than the pudgy, tomato-faced daughter of a newspaper baron. All of a sudden I realized that, even here in Kyoto with hundreds of miles between us, I, the model of a faithful employee, was thinking exclusively about D. No, there was something else, too, there was D's phantom. I realized that the baby whose appearance I waited for nervously every time my employer and I went out together hadn't been off my mind for a minute.

It was time for the bar to close and I didn't have a room. I'd managed to get as old as I was without ever staying in a hotel and I knew nothing about reservations. Luckily, the actress was known at the hotel, and a word from her got me a room. We went up in the elevator together, and I started to get off at my floor when she suggested we have one last drink and invited me to her room. It was from that point that memories of the evening get comic and pathetic. When she had seated me in a chair, the actress returned to the door and looked up and down the hall, then went through a whole series of nervous motions, flounced on the bed as if to test the springs, turned lights on and switched them off, ran a little water in the tub. Then she poured me the brandy she had promised and, sipping a Coca-Cola, she told me about another man who had courted her during her affair with D, and finally going to bed with him, and D slapping her so hard the teeth rattled in her mouth. Then she asked if I thought today's college students went in for 'heavy petting'? It depended on the student, I said—suddenly the actress had become a mother scolding a child for staying up too late and was telling me to find my own room and go to sleep. I said good-night, went downstairs, and fell asleep immediately. I woke up at dawn with a fire in my throat.

The most comic and pathetic part was still to come. I understood the minute I opened my eyes that the actress had invited me to her room intending to seduce a college student who was wild for heavy petting. And with that understanding came rage and abject desire. I hadn't slept with a woman yet, but this humiliation demanded that I retaliate. I was drunk on what must have been my first Hennessy VSOP, and I was out of my head with the kind of poisonous desire that goes with being eighteen. It was only five o'clock in the morning and there was no sign of life in the halls. Like a panther wild with rage I sped to her door on padded feet. It was ajar. I stepped inside and found her seated at the dresser mirror with her back to me. Creeping up directly behind her (to this day I wonder what I was trying to do), I lunged at her neck with both hands. The actress whirled around with a broad smile on her face, rising as she turned, and then she had my hands in her own and was pumping them happily up and down as if she were welcoming a guest and sing-songing, 'Good morning! Good morning! Good morning!' Before I knew it I had been seated in a chair and we were sharing her toast and morning coffee and reading the newspaper together. After a while the movie actress said in a tone of voice she might have used to discuss the weather: 'You were trying to rape me just now, weren't you!' She went back to her makeup and I got out of there, fled downstairs to my own room and burrowed back into bed, trembling as though I had malaria. I was afraid that a report of this incident might reach D, but the subject of the movie actress never came up again. I continued to enjoy my job.

54

Winter had come. Our plan that afternoon was to bicycle through D's residential neighborhood and the surrounding fields. I was on a rusty old bike and my employer had borrowed the nurse's shiny new one. Gradually we expanded the radius of a circle around D's house, riding into a new housing development and coasting down hills in the direction of the fields. We were sweating, relishing the sensation of liberation, more and more exhilarated. I say 'we' and include D because that afternoon it was evident that he was in high spirits, too. He was even whistling a theme from a Bach sonata for flute and harpsichord called Siciliana. I happened to know that because when I was in high school I had played flute. I never learned to play well but I did develop a habit of thrusting out my upper lip the way a tapir does. Naturally, I had friends who insisted my buck teeth were to blame. But the fact is, flautists frequently look like tapirs.

As we pedalled down the street, I picked up the tune and began to whistle along with D. Siciliana is a sustained and elegant theme, but I was out of breath from pedalling and my whistle kept lapsing into airy sibilance. Yet D's phrasing was perfect, absolutely legato. I stopped whistling then, ashamed to go on, and the composer glanced over at me with his lips still pursed in a whistle like a carp puckering up to breathe and smiled his tranquil smile. Granted there was a difference in the bikes, it was still unnatural and pathetic that an eighteen-year-old student, skinny maybe, but tall, should begin to tire and run short of breath before a twenty-eight-year-old composer who was a little man and sick besides. Unjust is what it was, and infuriating. My mood clouded instantly and I felt disgusted with the whole job. So I stood up on the pedals all of a sudden and sped away as furiously as a bicycle racer. I even turned down a narrow gravel path between two vegetable fields purposely. When I looked back a minute later, my employer was hunched over the handlebars, his large, round head nodding above his narrow shoulders, churning the gravel beneath his wheels in hot pursuit of me. I coasted to a stop, propped a foot on the barbed wire fence that bordered the field and waited for D to catch up. I was already ashamed of my childishness.

His head still bobbing, my employer was approaching fast. And then I knew the phantom was with him. D was racing his bike down the extreme left of the gravel path, his face twisted to the right so that he was almost looking over his right shoulder, and the reason his head appeared to bob was that he was whispering encouragement to something running, or maybe flying, alongside the bicycle. Like a marathon coach pacing one of his runners. Ah, I thought, he's doing that on the premise that Aghwee is neck and neck with his speeding bike. The monster as large as a kangaroo, the fat, funny baby in a white cotton night-gown was bounding—

like a kangeroo!—down that gravel path. I shuddered, then I kicked the barbed-wire fence and slowly pedalled away, waiting for my employer and the monster in his imagination to catch up.

Don't think I had let myself begin to believe in Aghwee's existence. I had taken the nurse's advice, sworn not to lose sight of the anchor on my common sense as in those slightly solemn slapstick comedies where, for example, the keeper of the mad-house goes mad; consciously derisive, I was thinking to myself that the neurotic composer was putting on a show with his bicycle just to follow up a lie he had told me once, and what a lot of trouble to go to! In other words, I was keeping a clinical distance between myself and D's phantom monster. Even so, there occurred a strange alteration in my state of mind.

It began this way: D had finally caught up and was biking along a few feet behind me when, as unexpectedly as a cloudburst, and as inescapably, we were enveloped by the belling of a pack of hounds. I looked up and saw them racing towards me down the gravel path, young adult Dobermans that stood two feet high, more than ten of them. Running breathlessly behind the pack, the thin black leather leashes grasped in one hand, was a man in over-alls, chasing the dogs perhaps, or maybe they were dragging him along. Jet-black Dobermans, sleek as wet seals, with just a dusting of dry chocolate on their chests and jowls and pumping haunches. And down on us they howled, filling the gravel path, keening for the attack at such a forward tilt they looked about to topple on their foaming snouts. There was a meadow on the other side of the field; the man in overalls must have been training the beasts there and now he was on his way home with them.

Trembling with fear, I got off my bike and helplessly surveyed the field on the other side of the fence. The barbed wire came up to my chest. I might have had a chance myself but I would never have been able to boost the little composer to safety on the other side. The poisons of terror were beginning to numb my head, but for one lucid instant I could see the catastrophe that was bound to occur in a few seconds. As the Dobermans neared,

D would sense that Aghwee was being attacked by a pack of the animals it most feared. He would probably hear the baby's frightened crying. And certainly he would meet the dogs head-on, in defense of his baby. Then the Dobermans would rip him to pieces. Or he would try to escape with the baby and make a reckless leap to clear the fence and be just as cruelly torn. I was rocked by the pity of what I knew must happen. And while I stood there dumbly without a plan, those giant black-and-chocolate devils were closing in on us, snapping in the air with awful jaws, so close by now that I could hear their alabaster claws clicking on the gravel. Suddenly I knew I could do nothing for D and his baby, and with that knowledge I went limp, unresisting as a pervert when he is seized in the subway, and was swallowed whole in the darkness of my fear. I backed off the gravel path until the barbed wire was a fire in my back, pulled my bike in front of me as if it were a wall, and shut my eyes tight. An animal stench battered me, together with the howling of the dogs and the pounding of their feet, and I could feel tears seeping past my eyelids. I abandoned myself to a wave of fear and it swept me away . . .

57

On my shoulder was a hand gentle as the essence of all gentleness; it felt like Aghwee touching me. But I knew it was my employer; he had let those fiendish dogs pass and no catastrophe of fear had befallen him. I continued crying anyway, with my eyes closed and my shoulders heaving. I was too old to cry in front of other people; I suppose the shock of fright had induced some kind of infantile regression in me. When I stopped crying, we walked our bikes past that barbed-wire fence like prisoners in a concentration camp, in silence, our heads hanging, to the meadow beyond the field where strangers were playing ball and exercising dogs (D wasn't occupied with Aghwee anymore, the baby must have left while I was crying). We laid our bikes down and then sprawled on the grass ourselves. My tears had flooded away my pretensions and my rebelliousness and the perverse suspicion in my heart. And D was no longer wary of me. I lay back on the grass and clasped my hands beneath my head, curiously light and dry after all that crying. Then I closed my eyes and listened quietly while D peered down at me with his chin in his hand and spoke to me of Aghwee's world.

'Do you know a poem called "Shame" by Chuya Nakahara? Listen to the second verse:

The mournful sky
High where branches tangle
Teems with dead baby souls;
I blinked and saw
above the distant fields
fleece knit into a dream
of mastodons.

58   'That's one aspect of the world of the dead baby I see. There are some Blake engravings, too, especially one called "Christ Refusing the Banquet Offered by Satan"—have you ever seen it? And there's another, "The Morning Stars Singing Together". In both there are figures in the sky who have the same reality about them as the people on the ground, and whenever I look at them I'm sure Blake was hinting at an aspect of this other world. I once saw a Dali painting that was close, too, full of opaque beings floating in the sky about a hundred yards above the ground and glowing with an ivory white light. Now that's exactly the world I see. And you know what those glowing things are that fill the sky? Beings we've lost from our lives down here on earth, and now they float up there in the sky about a hundred yards above the ground, quietly glowing like amoebas under a microscope. And sometimes they descend the way our Aghwee does (my employer said it and I didn't protest, which doesn't mean I acquiesced). But it takes a sacrifice worthy of them to acquire the eyes to see them floating there and the ears to detect them when they descend to earth, and yet there are moments when suddenly we're endowed with that ability without any sacrifice or even effort on our part. I think that's what happened to you a few minutes ago.'

Without any sacrifice or even effort on my part, just a few tears of expiation, my employer seemed to have wanted to say. The truth was I had shed tears out of fear and helplessness and a kind of vague terror about my future (my first job, an experiment in a kind of microcosm of life, was guarding this mad composer, and since I had failed to do that adequately, it was predictable that situations I couldn't cope with would recur as one of the patterns of my life), but instead of interrupting with a protest, I continued to listen docilely.

'You're still young, probably you haven't lost sight of anything in this world that you can never forget, that's so dear to you you're aware of its absence all the time. Probably the sky a hundred yards or so above your head is still nothing more than sky to you. But all that means is that the storehouse happens to be empty at the moment. Or have you lost anything that was really important to you?'

The composer paused for my answer, and I found myself remembering his former mistress, that movie actress, with a dent in her forehead as big as an adult thumb. Naturally, no crucial loss of mine could have had anything to do with her, all that crying had eroded my head and a sentimental honey was seeping into the crevices.

'Well, have you?' For the first time since we had met, my employer was insistent. 'Have you lost anything that was important to you?'

Suddenly I had to say something silly to cover my embarrassment.

'I lost a cat,' I tried.

'A Siamese or what?'

'Just an ordinary cat with orange stripes; he disappeared about a week ago.'

'If it's only been a week he might come back. Isn't it the season for them to wander?'

'That's what I thought, too, but now I know he won't

be back.'

'Why?'

'He was a tough tom with his own territory staked out. This morning I saw a weak-looking cat walking up and down his block and it wasn't even on its guard—my cat won't be coming back.' When I'd stopped talking I realized I'd told a story intended for laughs in a voice that was hoarse with sadness.

'Then there's a cat floating in your sky,' my employer said solemnly.

Through closed eyes I pictured an opaque cat as large as an ad balloon, glowing with an ivory-white light as it floated through the sky. It was a comical flight all right, but it also made me wistful.

'The figures floating in your sky begin to increase at an accelerating rate. That's why I haven't been living in present time ever since that incident with the baby, so I could stop that spreading. Since I'm not living in our time, I can't discover anything new, but I don't lose sight of anything, either—the state of my sky never changes.' There was profound relief in the composer's voice.

But was my own sky really empty except for one bloated cat with orange stripes? I opened my eyes and started to look up at the clear, now almost evening sky, when dread made me close my eyes again. Dread of myself, for what if I had seen a glowing herd of numberless beings I had lost from time down here on earth!

We lay on the grass in that meadow for quite a while, ringed by the passive affinity two people have for one another when the same gloom is gripping them. And gradually I began to get my perspective back. I reproached myself: how unlike the eighteen-year-old pragmatist I really was to have let myself be influenced by a mad composer! I'm not suggesting my equilibrium was perfectly restored. The day I succumbed to that strange panic, I drew closer than ever to the sentiments of my employer and to that glowing herd in the sky one hundred yards above the ground. To an extent, what you might call the after-effects remained with me.

And then the final day came. It was Christmas Eve. I'm

60

certain about the date because D gave me a wristwatch with a little apology about being a day early. And I remember that a powdery snow fell for about an hour just after lunch. We went down to the Ginza together but it was already getting crowded, so we decided to walk out to Tokyo harbour. D wanted to see a Chilean freighter that was supposed to have docked that day. I was eager to go, too; I pictured a ship with snow blanketing her decks. We had left the Ginza crowds and were just passing the Kabuki Theatre when D looked up at the dark and still snowy sky. And Aghwee descended to his side. As usual, I walked a few steps behind the composer and his phantom. We came to a wide intersection. D and the baby had just stepped off the curb when the light changed. D stopped, and a fleet of trucks as bulky as elephants heaved into motion with their Christmas freight. That was when it happened. Suddenly D cried out and thrust both arms in front of him as if he were trying to rescue something; then he leaped in among those trucks and was struck to the ground. I watched stupidly from the curb.

'That was suicide; he just killed himself!' said a shaky voice at my side.

But I had no time to wonder whether it might have been suicide. In a minute that intersection had become backstage at a circus, jammed with milling trucks like elephants, and I was kneeling at D's side, holding his bloody body in my arms and trembling like a dog. I didn't know what to do, a policeman had dashed up and then disappeared on the run again.

D wasn't dead; it was more awful than that. He was dying, lying there in the filthy wet that had been a light snow, oozing blood and something like tree-sap. The dark and snowy pattern of the sky ripped open and the stately light of a Spanish pieta made my employer's blood glisten like silly fat. By that time a crowd had gathered, snatches of 'Jingle Bells' wheeled above our heads like panic-stricken pigeons, and I knelt at D's side listening hard for nothing in particular and hearing screaming in the distance. But the crowd just stood there silently in the cold, as if indifferent to the screams. I have never listened so hard on a street corner again,

61

nor again heard screams like that.

An ambulance finally arrived and my employer was lifted inside unconscious. He was caked with blood and mud, and shock seemed to have withered his body. In his white tennis shoes, he looked like an injured blind man. I climbed into the ambulance with a doctor and an orderly and a young man about my age who seemed haughty and aloof. He turned out to be the driver's helper on the long-distance truck that had hit D. The congestion was getting worse all the time as the ambulance cut across the Ginza (according to some statistics I saw recently, there were record crowds that Christmas Eve). Those who heard the siren and stopped to watch us pass, nearly all of them, shared a look of circumspectly solemn concern. In one corner of my dazed head I reflected that the so-called inscrutable Japanese smile, while it seemed likely to exist, did not. Meanwhile D lay unconscious on that wobbly stretcher, bleeding his life away.

When we arrived at the hospital, two orderlies who didn't even pause to change out of shoes into slippers rushed D away to some recess of the building. The same policeman as before appeared out of nowhere again and calmly asked me a lot of questions. Then I was permitted to go to D. The young worker from the truck had already found the room and was sitting on a bench in the corridor next to the door. I sat down next to him and we waited for a long time. At first he would only mutter about all the deliveries he still had to make, but when two hours had passed he began to complain that he was hungry in a surprisingly young voice, and my hostility toward him dwindled. We waited some more, then the banker arrived with his wife and three daughters, who were all dressed up to go to a party. Ignoring us, they went inside. All four of the women had fat, squat bodies and red faces; they reminded me of D's former wife. I continued to wait. It had been hours by then, and the whole time I had been tormented by suspicion—hadn't my employer intended to kill himself from the beginning? Before taking his life he had settled things with his ex-wife and former mistress, burned his manuscripts, toured the city saying goodbye to places he would miss—hadn't he hired me because he needed some good-natured help with those chores? Kept me from seeing his plan by inventing a monster baby floating in the sky? In other words, wasn't it the case that my only real function had been to help D commit suicide? The young labourer had fallen asleep with his head on my shoulder and every minute or two he would convulse as though in pain. He must have been dreaming about running over a man with a truck.

It was pitch black outside when the banker appeared in the door and called me. I eased my shoulder from under the worker's head and stood up. The banker paid me my salary for the day and then let me into the room. D lay on his back with rubber tubes in his nostrils as in a joke. His face gave me pause: it was black as smoked meat. But I couldn't help voicing the doubt that had me so afraid. I called out to my dying employer: 'Did you hire me just so you could commit suicide? Was all that about Aghwee just a cover-up?' Then my throat was clogged with tears and I was surprised to hear myself shouting, 'I was about to believe in Aghwee!'

At that moment, as my eyes filled with tears and things began to dim, I saw a smile appear on D's darkened, shrivelled face. It might have been a mocking smile and it might have been a smile of friendly mischief. The banker led me out of the room. The young man from the truck was stretched out on the bench asleep. On my way out, I slipped the thousand yen I had earned into his jacket pocket. I read in the evening paper the next day that the composer was dead.

And then it was this spring and I was walking down the street when a group of frightened children suddenly started throwing stones. It was so sudden and unprovoked, I don't know what I had done to threaten them. Whatever it was, fear had turned those children into killers, and one of them hit me in the right eye with a rock as big as a fist. I went down on one knee, pressed my hand to my eye and felt a lump of broken flesh. With my good eye I watched my dripping blood draw in the dirt in the street as though magnetically. It was then that I sensed a being I knew and missed leave the ground behind me like a kangaroo and soar into the teary blue of a sky that retained its winter brittleness. Goodbye, Aghwee, I heard myself whispering in my heart. And then I knew that my hatred of those frightened children had melted away and that time had filled my sky during those ten years with figures that glowed with an ivory-white light, I suppose not all of them purely innocent. When I was wounded by those children and sacrificed my sight in one eye, so clearly a gratuitous sacrifice, I had been endowed, if for only an instant, with the power to perceive a creature that had descended from the heights of my sky.

Sergio Ramírez

In Nicaragua, baseball has acquired the status of the top-ranking national sport, whether among the Sandinistas or the Contras, and Nicaraguan players carry abroad the pride of beating the gringos at their own game. Like the Spanish religion that the Indians and black slaves adapted to their own beliefs in the seventeenth and eighteenth centuries, the North American culture of our time has also undergone translation, so that in Nicaragua, the game has become not merely a communal entertainment but a ritual, a learning game for fathers and sons in which the pupil must end by outplaying the teacher.

Before the Sandinista Revolution of 1979 that toppled the dictatorship of Anastasio Somoza, Sergio Ramírez had begun writing novels in the "indigenist" tradition—novels that lend the Latin American Indian a new kind of heroic stature. After the Revolution, when he became Nicaragua's vice-president, his subject matter broadened, and since 1985, he has published fiction that sets out to rescue heroic dimensions in every man's and woman's life.

THE PERFECT GAME

sergio ramírez

Translated by Nick Caistor

usually as he rushed out of the tunnel into the stands, his eyes went straight to the bullpen to see if the kid was warming up. Had the manager finally decided to use him as starter? Tonight, though, his bus had broken down on the South Highway, and he had arrived so late that the Boer-San Fernando game was already well under way. Back in the urine-smelling tunnel he'd heard the umpire's screech of "Strike!"; so now, with dinner pail under one arm and bottle under the other, he hurried out into the dazzling whiteness, which seemed to float down like a milky haze from the depths of the starry sky.

He always tried to get to the stadium before the San Fernando manager had handed his team's lineup to the head umpire, while the pitchers were still warming up in the bullpen. Sometimes his son would be one of them, so he would press up against the wire fence, his fingers gripping the wire, to show him he was there, that he had arrived. The boy was too shy to acknowledge his presence and invariably kept on practising in that silent, ungainly way of his. But by the beginning of the game he had always been back on the bench: never once since San Fernando had signed him for the big league at the opening of the season had he started as pitcher. Some nights he hadn't even warmed up, and he would shake his head at his father from the shadows of the dugout: No, it wasn't going to be tonight either.

And now, just when he had got there so late, he scanned the green of the floodlit field and spotted him at once on the pitcher's mound. There he was, a thin, slightly hunched figure, following the catcher's signals intently. Before his father could put the dinner pail down to adjust his glasses, he saw him wind up and pitch.

"Strike!" he heard the umpire shout a second time in the sweltering night. He peered down again, shielding his eyes with his hand: it was him, his boy was pitching, they'd put him on to start. He saw him casually field the ball the catcher returned to him, then wipe the sweat from his brow with the glove. He still needs a bit of polish, he's still raw, his father thought proudly.

He picked up the dinner pail and, as if frightened of making any noise, walked carefully, almost on tiptoe, to the limit of the cheap seats behind home plate, as close as he could get to the San Fernando dugout. He had no idea of how the game stood. He was aware only that at last his boy was up there on the mound under the floodlights, while out beyond the scoreboard and the stands stretched the vast black night.

He paused as a harmless infield fly floated up. The shortstop took a few steps back and spread his arms wide to show it was his catch. He caught it safely, threw the ball back to the mound, then the whole team trotted off to the dugout. End of inning. His boy strolled off, staring at his feet.

The stadium was almost empty. There was no applause or shouting, the atmosphere was more like a practice match when a few curious onlookers drift into the stadium and huddle together in tiny groups, as if to keep warm.

Still standing, he looked over at the scoreboard above the brightly colored billboards, high in the stadium beyond the direct light of the floodlights and already half in shadow. The scoreboard itself was like a housefront with windows. The men who hung the figures in the two windows that showed the score for each inning were silhouetted against it. One of these shadows was busy closing the window for the bottom of the fourth inning with a nought.

	1	2	3	4	5	6	7	8	9	H	E
SAN FERNANDO	0	0	0	0						0	0
BOER	0	0	0	0						0	0

Boer hadn't managed to hit against his boy, and his team had made no errors, so he was pitching a perfect game. A perfect game—as he cleaned his glasses, breathing on them then wiping them on his shirt, with the bottle still tucked under one arm and the dinner pail on the floor beside him.

He walked up a few steps to be with the nearest group of spectators. He sat next to a fat man with a blotchy white face who sold lottery tickets. He was surrounded by a halo of peanut shells. He split the shells with his teeth, spat them out, then chewed on the nuts. The father carefully set the dinner pail and the bottle down. He had brought the dinner his wife always prepared for the boy to eat after the game. The bottle was full of milky coffee.

"No runs at all?" he looked back awkwardly to ask the others, to make sure the scoreboard was correct. A stiff neck he'd had for years made it hard for him to turn his head. The fat man looked at him with the easy familiarity of baseball fans. Everybody in the stands knows one another, even if they've never met before.

"Runs?" he exclaimed, as though taken aback by a blasphemy, but still chewing steadily. "They haven't even got to first base with that skinny kid pitching for San Fernando."

"He's only a boy," a woman in the row behind said, pursing her lips in pity as if he really were still a small child. She had gold teeth and wore pebble glasses. Between her feet was a large handbag, at which she kept glancing down anxiously.

Another of the spectators sitting higher up chuckled a toothless grin, "Where the hell did they dig up such a beanpole?" The father struggled to turn his head properly so he could see who was insulting his boy. He fiddled with his glasses to get a clearer view of him and to glare his reproach. One of the sidepieces of his glasses was missing, so he had them tied around one ear with a shoelace.

"He's my son," he announced to the whole group, staring at them defiantly despite the crick in his neck. The gap-toothed heckler still had a sarcastic smile on his face, but didn't say a word. Still spitting out shells, the fat man patted his leg. No runs, no hits, no errors? His son was out there, pitching for the first time, and he had a clean sheet. He felt at home in the stands.

And now he heard on the rumbling loudspeakers that it was his boy who was going to open the inning for San Fernando. He didn't last long. One of the assistants threw a jacket around his shoulders to keep his arm warm.

"He's no great shakes as a batter," his father explained, to no one in particular.

69

"There's no such thing as a pitcher who can bat," the woman answered. It was strange to see her without her husband, alone in this group of men. She ought to be at home in bed at that time of night, he thought; but she knows a thing or two about the game. His own wife had never wanted to go with him to the stadium at night. She prepared the boy's food, then sat in the room that served as shoe repair shop, kitchen and dining room, glued to the radio, though she couldn't really follow the action.

The San Fernando team was taking to the field again after getting nothing from their half-inning. His boy was strolling back to the mound. Bottom of the fifth inning.

"Let's see how he does," the fat man grunted affectionately. "I've been a Boer fan all my life, but I take my hat off to a good pitcher." With that, he swept off his yellow cap with its Allis-Chalmer badge in salute.

Boer's fourth batter was the first at the plate. He was a Yankee import and was chewing gum or tobacco. To judge by the bulging cheek and the way he spat constantly, it must have been tobacco. All his boy needed were three pitches. Three marvellous strikes—the last of them a curve that broke beautifully over the outer edge of the plate. The Yank never even touched it. He looked stunned.

"He didn't see them," the woman laughed. "That kid's growing up fast."

Then there was an easy grounder to the shortstop. The last batter popped out to the third baseman. All three were out in no time.

"Will you look at that," gap-tooth shouted. "That bean-pole's no pushover." Too bad there were so few people to hear him. The stands all around them were empty, and he could see only a few cigarette butts glowing down in the reserved seats section under the lights from the radio commentators' boxes. This time he didn't even bother to turn around to the smart-ass. Fifteen outs in a row. Would his wife be beside the radio back home? She must have understood some of it, if only the name of her boy.

The San Fernando team was batting again. The top of the sixth inning. One of them got to first with a quick bunt, then the catcher, number five in their line-up, hit a double, and the man on first made a desperate run of the bases and just scraped home. That was all: the top of the sixth was over—with one run on the scoreboard.

"Well," the fat Boer supporter said sadly, "now your boy is one up."

That was the first time he'd called him "your boy." And there he was, strolling out hunched and frail, back to the mound, his features lengthened under the shadow of his cap. Just a kid, as the woman had said.

"He'll be eighteen in June," he confided to his neighbor, but the fat man was suddenly on his feet cheering, because the ball was flying off the bat out to centerfield. His own heart leapt as he saw the ball soaring into the outfield, but over by the billboards, where the lettering glistened as though it had just rained, the centerfielder was running back to make the catch. He collided noisily with the fence, but held the ball. Disappointed, the fat man sat down again. "Good hit," was all he said.

Next there was a grounder behind third base. The third baseman scooped it up behind the bag and threw it as hard as he could. Out at first.

"The team's doing all it can for your boy," the woman said.

"Whose side are you on now, Doña Teresa?" the fat man asked, annoyed.

"I never take sides. I only come to bet, but today there's nothing going," she replied, unruffled. Her bag was full of money to bet on anything: ball or strike, base hit or error, run or not. And the fat man came to sell his lottery tickets in those little packets.

The third man hit a chopper right in front of the plate. The catcher grabbed it and threw to first. The batter didn't even bother to run. This incensed the fat man.

"What are they paying that chicken for? . . . Up yours!" he bawled through cupped hands.

Someone strolled down from the deserted stands, a small blue plastic transistor pressed to his ear. The fat man called to him by name, "What does Sucre make of this?"

"He says there's the chance of a perfect game," the man replied, imitating the voice of the famous commentator, Sucre Frech.

"Is that what he says?" the father gasped, his voice thick with emotion. He fiddled with the loop of the shoelace behind his ear, as though that would help him hear better.

"Turn your radio up," the fat man demanded. The other put it down on the ground and turned it louder. The fat man lifted his hand in an automatic gesture of throwing a peanut into his mouth, then began to chew . . . "All of you who couldn't be bothered to turn up tonight are missing out on something really fantastic: the first chance in the history of the country to see a perfect game. You've no idea what you're missing."

It was the top of the seventh: the fateful inning. San Fernando was batting. The first man walked, but then was picked off trying to steal. The second hit the ball straight back at the pitcher. The third was struck out. The game was fast and furious.

Now it was Boer's turn to bat in the lucky seventh. His

boy would have to take on the big guns, who were bound to make him squirm. The seventh inning: the one for the stretch, for surprises and scares. Everyone sweating with anticipation.

He was trembling, in the grip of a fever despite the heat. He looked back painfully to see the gap-tooth's expression, but the man was sitting silently and seemed miles away, all his attention turned to the radio. Sucre Frech's voice was lost in a crackle of static on the warm breeze.

The umpire's shout was real, tangible. "Strike three!" His boy had struck out the first batter.

"That beanpole is hurling rocks out there," the man behind muttered, his chin cupped in his hands as though he were praying.

He caught sight of the ball floating gently up into the white light. The left fielder raced down the line to get under it . . . got into position . . . waited . . . caught the ball! The second out. The woman slapped her knees excitedly. "That's the way, that's the way!" The stands appeared back-to-front in the thick pebbles of her glasses. The fat man kept on chewing air without a word.

The first ball was too high. The gap-tooth stood up as though to stretch his legs, but nobody was fooled. A foul off to the back. Strike one.

That made it one and one. Another foul. One and two. The field stretched out, calm and peaceful. The outfielders stood motionless halfway back to the fence. A truck rumbled in the distance along the South Highway.

Another foul to the back—three in a row. The batter wouldn't give up. "Strike!" The ball sped right down the middle. The batter didn't even have time to react and stood there with his bat still aloft. End of the seventh inning!

A ripple of applause, like the rustle of dry leaves. The clapping drifted slowly up to him in the deserted stand. He laughed out loud, knowing that all of them in the group around him, even gap-tooth and the fat man, were as pleased as he was.

"This is a great moment," the fat man declared. "I wouldn't have missed this for anything, even though it hurts."

72

Sucre Frech was talking about Don Larsen, who in a World Series only two years previously had pitched the *only* perfect game in the *history* of the major leagues . . . "and now it looks as if this unknown Nicaraguan pitcher is about to achieve the same feat, step by step, pitch by pitch."

They were talking in the same breath of Don Larsen and his boy, who at that moment was walking back to the dugout, where he sat calmly at the far end, like it was nothing. His team-mates were chatting, again like it was nothing. Their manager looked unconcerned. Managua was slumbering in the dark, like it was nothing. And he too was sitting there as if nothing had happened—he hadn't even gone down to the fence, as he usually did, to let the kid know he was there.

"An obscure rookie who I'm told is from Masatepe, signed only this season by San Fernando. This is his first time to start as a pro, his first chance, and here he is pitching a perfect game. Who could believe it?"

"A perfect game means glory," the fat man concurred, listening devotedly to the radio.

"It's straight to the major leagues, first thing tomorrow. And you can scoop the jackpot," the woman cackled, rubbing her fingers together. The father felt keyed up, floating on air. He gave a mocking sideways glance at his tormentor, as though to say: "What d'you make of your beanpole now?" but the gap-toothed man simply nodded his head without demur.

The loudspeakers repeated the name of San Fernando's first batter. He reached first base with an infield hit. The second man hit into a double play to the shortstop. The last batter was struck out, and the inning was over.

"Get a move on, I want to see the beanpole pitch!" gap-tooth shouted as Boer trooped off the field, but nobody found it funny. "Sshh!" the fat man silenced him.

Once again all the lights for strikes and outs disappeared from the distant scoreboard. Now for the bottom of the eighth. Everybody hold on to your hats!

His boy was back on the mound. Sweat was coursing down his face as he again studied the catcher's signals. What he'd done that night was real enough, he was making history with his arm. Did they know in Masatepe? Would the people on his block have stayed up to listen? Surely they must have heard the news. They'd have flung open their doors, switched on all the lights, gathered on street corners, to hear how a local boy was pitching a perfect game.

Strike one! Straight past the batter.

It was the Yank's turn again. He punched the air with the bat, the wad of tobacco bulging in his cheek. Before he even realized, the kid had sent a second strike past him. He never pitched a bad one, every single pitch was on target. Another lightning throw: Strike three, and out! The Yank flung down the bat so furiously it nearly bounced into the Boer dugout. The gap-toothed fan jeered him.

"Know something?" the fat man with the lottery tickets nudged the old man. "Another five outs and you'll join the ranks of the immortals too, because you're his father."

Sucre Frech was talking about immortality at that very moment on the little blue radio rattling on the cement steps. About the immortals of this sport of kings. The whole of Managua ought to be there to witness the entry of a humble, obscure young man into immortality. He nodded, chill with fear, yes, the whole of Managua should have been there, hurrying out of the tunnels, filling all the seats, dressed in pyjamas, slippers, nightshirts. They should be leaping out of bed, hailing taxis or scurrying on foot to see this great feat, this unrepeatable marvel . . . a line drive cutting between center and left field . . . the fielder appeared out of nowhere, running forward with his arm outstretched to stop the ball as if by magic; then he coolly threw it back. The second out of the inning!

He wanted to get to his feet, but his courage failed him. The woman had covered her face in her hands, and was peering through spread fingers. The toothless wonder tapped him on the shoulder.

"They want to interview you on Radio Mundial when this inning is over. Sucre Frech in person," he said, whistling tunelessly through the gap in his teeth.

"How do they know he's the boy's father?" the fat man enquired.

"I told them," grinned the other man smugly . . . a low ball near first base, the first baseman stopped it, the pitcher assisted, another easy out! End of inning!

"We'll all go," the fat man said imperiously.

They stood up. The fat man led the way up to the Radio Mundial commentary box. When they got there, high up beyond the empty rows of seats, Sucre Frech passed the microphone out his window. The father grasped it fearfully. Gap-tooth pushed in next to him. The woman, her handbag full of money clamped firmly on her arm, stood there grinning, showing off all her gold teeth as if she were having her portrait taken by a photographer. The fat man cocked his head to listen.

"You tell 'em, old fella," he encouraged the father.

He can't remember what he said, apart from sending greetings to all the fans everywhere in Nicaragua, and especially those in Masatepe, to his wife, the pitcher's mother, and to everyone in *barrio* Veracruz.

He would have liked to add: It was me who made a pitcher of him, I've been training that arm since he was thirteen; at fifteen he started for the General Moncada team for the first time; I used to take him on the back of my bike every day to practice; I sewed his first glove in my shoe shop; it was me who made those spikes he's wearing.

But he had no time for any of that. Sucre Frech snatched the microphone back to begin his commentary on San Fernando's ninth and final inning. They were still in the lead, one to nothing. Just think what all of you who stayed at home are missing.

Again San Fernando failed to add to their score. By the time the group was back in its place in the stand, one of the batters had been struck out and the others followed in rapid succession. Now came the moment of truth everyone had been waiting for.

Boer's last chance, the final challenge for the boy whose stature
had grown so immensely as the evening wore on:

	1	2	3	4	5	6	7	8	9
SAN FERNANDO	0	0	0	0	1	0	0	0	0
BOER	0	0	0	0	0	0	0	0	

All that was needed was one last circle on the board, to
close the last window where in the distance the score keeper's
head was visible. They wouldn't even trouble to put up the final
score; they never did at the end of the game.

There was a respectful silence as his boy sauntered out
to the center of the diamond, as though he were leaving for a long
journey. From high in the stands, his father saw him shoot a
glance in his direction, to reassure himself that he was there, that
he hadn't failed to come on this of all nights. Should I have gone
down there? he reproached himself.

"I'm right not to have gone down there, aren't I?" he
asked his neighbor in a low voice.

"Sure," the fat man gave his judgment, "when his perfect game is over, we'll all go down and congratulate him."

Ball—too high, the first pitch. The catcher had to go on
tiptoe to take it. Bottom of the ninth inning: one ball, no strikes.

"I can't bear to look," the woman said, ducking behind
her handbag.

Up at bat was a black Cuban from the Sugar Kings. The
kid had already struck him out once. He stood there, wiry and
muscular in his freshly laundered uniform, impatiently tapping his
heels with the bat.

"That black's out to bust the stitching off the ball," gap-
toothed pronounced.

The second pitch was too high as well. With no sign of
emotion, the umpire turned aside to note down another ball. Two
balls, no strikes.

"This is a fine time to crack up, kid," the gap-tooth man
muttered, speaking for all the group.

76

The third pitch is also a ball, Sucre Frech screamed into the microphone.

"What's going on?" the woman asked from behind her bag.

"What a crying shame," the fat man commiserated, looking at him with genuine pity. But all he was aware of was the sweat soaking his hatband.

The catcher called time-out and trotted over to the mound to talk to the boy. He listened hard, slapping the ball into his glove the whole while.

The discussion on the mound was over. The catcher slipped his mask back on, and the batter returned to the plate. If the next throw was a ball, the black man in the starched white uniform could throw down the bat mockingly and stroll to first base, jubilant at someone else's misfortune.

"Strike!" shouted the umpire in the hushed silence, flailing his arm in the air. As his cry died away, it was so quiet they could almost hear the lights hissing on top of their towers.

"Bound to happen," said the gap-toothed Boer fan.

Now the score stood at three balls, one strike. No outs. Sucre Frech was silent too. A buzz of static was the only sound from the radio.

The father sat bent over, hugging his knees, but still feeling exposed, unprotected. In his mind though he was sailing off into the same milky vapor that drifted down from the flood-lights, from the sky full of stars. He floated painfully away.

"Strike!" the umpire's voice rang out again.

"The whole of Managua heard that one," the fat man chortled.

The Cuban had flung himself at the ball with all his might. He spun around, and stood teetering, trying to regain his balance.

"If he does connect, we'll never see the ball again," the toothless tormentor said, still preaching in the wilderness.

Three balls, two strikes. Anyone with heart problems had better switch off their radio now and read what happened in tomorrow's papers.

His boy caught a new ball. He studied it quizzically. Still cowering behind her handbag, the woman wanted to know what was happening now. "Shut up!" the fat man snapped.

The black man blasted a high fly, which the wind carried over to the San Fernando dugout, close by where they were sitting. The catcher chased it desperately, but in the end the ball bounced harmlessly on the roof of the covered seats.

"That leaves the count at three and two," gap-tooth mimicked the radio.

"Are you trying to be funny?" the fat man had his blood up . . . a grounder between shortstop and third, the shortstop chased it, picked it up, threw to first base. Out!

All his hope flooded to his throat, then burst out in a triumphant shout that washed all over them. Would his boy come straight back with him to Masatepe? Fireworks, everybody in the streets: he'd have to lock up, he didn't want everything stolen.

The red eye on the scoreboard showed the first out.

"Nearly there, nearly there," crooned the woman.

The fat man put an arm around his shoulder, and the gap-toothed man was cheekily patting him on the back. The owner of the radio had turned it up full volume to celebrate.

"Don't congratulate me yet," he begged them, shrugging them off. But what he really felt like saying was yes, congratulate me, hug me all of you, let's laugh and enjoy ourselves.

The sudden crack of the bat made them all swivel their gaze back to the field. The white shape of the ball stood out sharply as it bounced near second base. The fielder was waiting for it behind the bag. He ran to one side, stopped, picked it up, pulled it from his glove to throw to first. He fumbled it, juggled with the ball for what seemed an eternity, finally held it, threw . . . threw wide!

The batter sped past first base. The father turned to the others. He still had a smile on his face, but now he was imploring them to confirm that this was crazy, that it hadn't happened. Yet there was the first base umpire in black, bent almost double, his arms sweeping the ground, while the batter stood his ground defiantly and tossed his protective helmet away.

The radio owner turned the sound down, so they could no longer make out what Sucre Frech was saying up in the box.

"After the error comes the hit," the gap-toothed man prophesied pitilessly.

The few photographers at the game gathered around home plate.

Another clear thud from the bat pulled him out of himself as out of a lonely, miserable well.

The ball bounced far out into centerfield and hit the fence. The runner on first easily reached third; the throw was aimed at the catcher to stop him there, but it sailed yards wide, and almost hit the dugout. The flashbulbs told them the tying run had been scored.

The second batter was rounding third base, the ball was still loose; the second man slid home in a cloud of dust, the cameras flashed again.

"Boer has done it, you jerks!" the fat man chortled. Crestfallen, the father blinked at his companions. "What now?" he asked in a feeble voice.

"That's the way it goes," the gap-toothed man behind him said, already standing up to leave.

The small crowd was hurrying out the gates, all the excitement forgotten. The fat man smoothed his trousers down, feeling for change in his pocket. San Fernando had already left the field. The fat man and the woman trundled off, deep in conversation.

The father picked up the dinner pail and the bottle of by-now-cold coffee. He pushed open the wire gate and walked out onto the field. Swallowed up in the darkness of the dugout, the players were busy changing to go home. He sat on the bench next to his boy and untied the cloth around the dinner pail. His uniform soaked in sweat, his spikes caked with dirt, the boy began silently to eat. With every mouthful, he looked over at his father. He chewed, took a drink from the bottle, looked at him.

The boy took off his cap for the sweat in his hair to dry. A sudden gust of wind swept a cloud of dust from the diamond and plucked the cap from the bench. His father jumped up and ran after it, finally catching up with it beyond home plate.

From right field they began to put out the lights. Only the two of them were left in the stadium, surrounded by the silent stands that the night was reclaiming.

He walked back with the cap and replaced it gently on his son's head. The boy kept on eating.

Ben Okri

Ben Okri was born in Nigeria, but his home is in England. His first novel, *Flowers and Shadows,* was published when he was barely twenty-six, in 1980. Since then, he has been recognized as the leading Nigerian writer of his generation. In both his father-lands, however, Okri is a rebel son, like the son in "In the Shadow of War" who acknowledges a different reality than his father. His subtle stories belong neither to Africa nor to Europe; they have a cosmopolitan view of tragedy and are rooted in language, rather than in place.

"Africa," Okri said in a lay sermon delivered in Cambridge, "is a land bristling with too many stories and moods. This overabundance of stories, this pollution, is a sort of chaos. A land of too many stories is a land that doesn't necessarily learn from its stories. It should trade some of its stories for clarity. Stories hint both at failure and celebration. Dying lands breed stories in the air like corpses breed worms. A land beginning to define itself, to create beauty and order from its own chaos, moves from having too many moods and stories in the air to having clear structures, silences, clear music, muted and measured celebrations, lucid breezes, freed breathing, tentative joys, the limpid freshness of new dawns over places sighted across the sea for the first time. If suffering breeds stories, then the transformation of suffering into a higher order and beauty and functionality breathes tranquility."

IN THE SHADOW OF WAR

ben okri

that afternoon three soldiers came to the village. They scattered the goats and chickens. They went to the palm-frond bar and ordered a calabash of palm-wine. They drank amidst the flies.

Omovo watched them from the window as he waited for his father to go out. They both listened to the radio. His father had bought the old Grundig cheaply from a family that had to escape the city when the war broke out. He had covered the radio with a white cloth and made it look like a household fetish. They listened to the news of bombings and air raids in the interior of the country. His father combed his hair, parted it carefully, and slapped some aftershave on his unshaven face. Then he struggled into the shabby coat that he had long outgrown.

Omovo stared out of the window, irritated with his father. At that hour, for the past seven days, a strange woman with a black veil over her head had been going past the house. She went up the village paths, crossed the Express road, and disappeared into the forest. Omovo waited for her to appear.

The main news was over. The radio announcer said an eclipse of the moon was expected that night. Omovo's father wiped the sweat off his face with his palm and said, with some bitterness:

'As if an eclipse will stop this war.'

'What is an eclipse?' Omovo asked.

'That's when the world goes dark and strange things happen.'

'Like what?'

His father lit a cigarette.

'The dead start to walk about and sing. So don't stay out late, eh.'

Omovo nodded.

'Eclipses hate children. They eat them.'

Omovo didn't believe him. His father smiled, gave Omovo his ten kobo allowance, and said:

'Turn off the radio. It's bad for a child to listen to news of war.'

Omovo turned it off. His father poured a libation at the doorway and then prayed to his ancestors. When he had finished he picked up his briefcase and strutted out briskly. Omovo watched him as he threaded his way up the path to the bus-stop at the main road. When a danfo bus came, and his father went with it, Omovo turned the radio back on. He sat on the window-sill and waited for the woman. The last time he saw her she had glided past with agitated flutters of her yellow smock. The children stopped what they were doing and stared at her. They had said that she had no shadow. They had said that her feet never touched the ground. As she went past, the children began to throw things at her. She didn't flinch, didn't quicken her pace, and didn't look back.

The heat was stupefying. Noises dimmed and lost their edges. The villagers stumbled about their various tasks as if they were sleep-walking. The three soldiers drank palm-wine and played draughts beneath the sun's oppressive glare. Omovo noticed that whenever children went past the bar the soldiers called them, talked to them, and gave them some money. Omovo ran down the stairs and slowly walked past the bar. The soldiers stared at him. On his way back one of them called him.

'What's your name?' he asked.

Omovo hesitated, smiled mischievously, and said:
'Eclipse.'
The soldier laughed, spraying Omovo's face with spit.
He had a face crowded with veins. His companions seemed unin-
terested. They swiped flies and concentrated on their game. Their
guns were on the table. Omovo noticed that they had numbers on
them. The man said:
'Did your father give you that name because you have
big lips?'
His companions looked at Omovo and laughed. Omovo
nodded.
'You are a good boy,' the man said. He paused. Then he
asked, in a different voice:
'Have you seen that woman who covers her face with a
black cloth?'
'No.'
The man gave Omovo ten kobo and said:
'She is a spy. She helps our enemies. If you see her
come and tell us at once, you hear?'
Omovo refused the money and went back upstairs.
He re-positioned himself on the window-sill. The soldiers occasionally looked at him. The heat got to him and soon he fell asleep
in a sitting position. The cocks, crowing dispiritedly, woke him
up. He could feel the afternoon softening into evening. The soldiers dozed in the bar. The hourly news came on. Omovo listened
without comprehension to the day's casualties. The announcer
succumbed to the stupor, yawned, apologized, and gave further
details of the fighting.
Omovo looked up and saw that the woman had already
gone past. The men had left the bar. He saw them weaving between
the eaves of the thatch houses, stumbling through the heat-mists.
The woman was further up the path. Omovo ran downstairs and
followed the men. One of them had taken off his uniform top.
The soldier behind had buttocks so big they had begun to split his
pants. Omovo followed them across the Express road. When they

got into the forest the men stopped following the woman, and took a different route. They seemed to know what they were doing. Omovo hurried to keep the woman in view.

He followed her through the dense vegetation. She wore faded wrappers and a grey shawl, with the black veil covering her face. She had a red basket on her head. He completely forgot to determine if she had a shadow, or whether her feet touched the ground.

He passed unfinished estates, with their flaking ostentatious signboards and their collapsing fences. He passed an empty cement factory: blocks lay crumbled in heaps and the workers' sheds were deserted. He passed a baobab tree, under which was the intact skeleton of a large animal. A snake dropped from a branch and slithered through the undergrowth. In the distance, over the cliff edge, he heard loud music and people singing war slogans above the noise.

He followed the woman till they came to a rough camp on the plain below. Shadowy figures moved about in the half-light of the cave. The woman went to them. The figures surrounded her and touched her and led her into the cave. He heard their weary voices thanking her. When the woman reappeared she was without the basket. Children with kwashiorkor stomachs and women wearing rags led her half-way up the hill. Then, reluctantly, touching her as if they might not see her again, they went back.

He followed her till they came to a muddied river. She moved as if an invisible force were trying to blow her away. Omovo saw capsized canoes and trailing water-logged clothes on the dark water. He saw floating items of sacrifice: loaves of bread in polythene wrappings, gourds of food, Coca-Cola cans. When he looked at the canoes again they had changed into the shapes of swollen dead animals. He saw outdated currencies on the riverbank. He noticed the terrible smell in the air. Then he heard the sound of heavy breathing from behind him, then someone coughing and spitting. He recognized the voice of one of the soldiers urging the others to move faster. Omovo crouched in the shadow of a tree.

The soldiers strode past. Not long afterwards he heard a scream. The men had caught up with the woman. They crowded round her.

'Where are the others?' shouted one of them.

The woman was silent.

'You dis witch! You want to die, eh? Where are they?'

She stayed silent. Her head was bowed. One of the soldiers coughed and spat towards the river.

'Talk! Talk!' he said, slapping her.

The fat soldier tore off her veil and threw it to the ground. She bent down to pick it up and stopped in the attitude of kneeling, her head still bowed. Her head was bald, and disfigured with a deep corrugation. There was a livid gash along the side of her face. The bare-chested soldier pushed her. She fell on her face and lay still. The lights changed over the forest and for the first time Omovo saw that the dead animals on the river were in fact the corpses of grown men. Their bodies were tangled with river-weed and their eyes were bloated. Before he could react, he heard another scream. The woman was getting up, with the veil in her hand. She turned to the fat soldier, drew herself to her fullest height, and spat in his face. Waving the veil in the air, she began to howl dementedly. The two other soldiers backed away. The fat soldier wiped his face and lifted the gun to the level of her stomach. A moment before Omovo heard the shot a violent beating of wings just above him scared him from his hiding place. He ran through the forest screaming. The soldiers tramped after him. He ran through a mist which seemed to have risen from the rocks. As he ran he saw an owl staring at him from a canopy of leaves. He tripped over the roots of a tree and blacked out when his head hit the ground.

When he woke up it was very dark. He waved his fingers in front of his face and saw nothing. Mistaking the darkness for blindness he screamed, thrashed around, and ran into a door. When he recovered from his shock he heard voices outside and the radio crackling on about the war. He found his way to the balcony, full of wonder that his sight had returned. But when he got there he was surprised to find his father sitting on the sunken cane chair, drinking palm-wine with the three soldiers. Omovo rushed to his father and pointed frantically at the three men.

'You must thank them,' his father said. 'They brought you back from the forest.'

Omovo, overcome with delirium, began to tell his father what he had seen. But his father, smiling apologetically at the soldiers, picked up his son and carried him off to bed.

José García Villa

José García Villa's upbringing was strict. His father was a doctor of nationalistic leanings who had been chief of staff to General Emilio Aguinaldo, leader of the Filipino rebels against both Spain and the United States. García Villa senior had wanted the boy to follow in his footsteps and study medicine; the boy embraced his father's nationalist politics but not his interest in science. At the age of fifteen, he was expelled from the University of Quezón in the Philippines for publishing a poem regarded as obscene. The boy accepted the expulsion as a challenge and escaped to the United States, settling first in New Mexico and then in New York. He wrote a series of short stories (all in English) and published his first collection before his twentieth birthday. Later he brought out several volumes of experimental poetry, praised by the likes of Marianne Moore.

From his earliest childhood, García Villa was a voracious reader. He read the Spanish and American classics as well as the Filipino writers, especially José Rizal, the man who inspired the Philippine Nationalist Movement in the late nineteenth century and who himself combined the ambitions of father and son, being both a doctor and a novelist. Rizal's first novel, *Noli me tangere,* a fierce denunciation of his country's unjust Spanish rule, was written in Tagalog and awakened the public's consciousness in a way comparable to *Uncle Tom's Cabin* in the United States. Accused of rebellion, he was tried for sedition by the military and executed by firing squad in Manila in 1896.

THE SON OF RIZAL

josé garcía villa

last December thirtieth I boarded the last afternoon train for Lucena, Tayabas. I had waited until the afternoon to
leave, for in the morning my wife, my children, and I had gone to
the Luneta to view the annual Rizal Day parade. On the morning
of the thirty-first I had to close an important land deal in Lucena.

From my compartment in the train I could see that the
third-class cars were filling with returning provincials who had
come to the city—Manila—to celebrate the day. They formed a
motley, obstreperous group and crowded both the station platform
and the steps of the cars. They bustled and palavered loudly like
little children. Some were students going home for a day or two,
and they were easily distinguishable from the rest by their modern, flashy clothes. There was a short, ducklike fellow among
them who hummed "Ramona," but nobody listened to him, for
another was cracking a joke about women.

There was much pushing and jostling on the steps to
the cars, and a woman whose feet had been stepped on issued a
string of shrill invectives: "Goats! Pigs! Brutes!" she cried to those
about her: did they have no regard for women, did they have no
conscience, and oh! of what advantage being a woman if you had
to be trampled upon like a mat!

But there was one person especially of all this crowd who caught my attention—or was it a feeling of pity? I felt guilty that I should think myself so superior as to bestow compassion on a fellow creature. Yet there I was, feeling it, and unable to help myself. He was a small, bark-colored man, lugging a long, narrow buri bag, which in the native tongue is called *bayong*. He found difficulty in pushing through the group on the steps to the car, and finally retreated quietly to the platform. On his thin face was written a fear that the train might start before he had got on. Then the locomotive bell began to ring its slow, annunciative notes, and the man got more and more nervous.

In my pocket I had two tickets, for not quite fifteen minutes ago my eldest son had insisted on going along with me, but had later on decided not to. The tickets had been bought, and I could not find the nerve to return the other. In such little things I am most sensitive, and would feel myself brazen and shameless if I returned with indifference the things already paid for. Compassionately again (and I hated myself for it) I thought of offering the other ticket to the man.

Half guiltily I whistled to him, and he glanced confusedly in my direction. I beckoned him to approach, which I saw he was reluctant to do—so afraid was he that he would lose more time and not get on the train at all. But I raised my two tickets for him to see, and I surmised that he understood my intention, for he hobbled hurriedly to my window. In brief words I explained to him that I had an extra ticket, and would he be kind enough to share my company in my compartment? I was alone, I said. Timidly yet eagerly he accepted my invitation.

The steps to the first-class cars are often, if not always, clear, and soon he was at the door of my compartment. He mumbled a deferential greeting, removing his black-green hat. I told him to step in, and he did so, silently lifting the buri bag and depositing it on the iron net above our heads; beside it he placed the hat. Then he settled himself awkwardly on the seat opposite mine, and regarded me with soft, pathetic eyes. The train started.

He was sparely built and poorly dressed. He wore the poor man's *camisa-chino,* but it was clean and freshly starched. He had on white drill trousers and red velvet slippers.

He smiled shyly at me and I smiled in return.

"You see, I've got my ticket," he tried to explain, pulling it out of his *camisa-chino*'s pocket, "but it was hard to get in. I cannot afford to ride in *here,* you know," he confessed, half embarrassed. His thick lips moved slowly, docilely, and his voice was thin, slow, and sad. His melancholy eyes lowered in humility.

I told him I was glad to help him. I said I was bound for Lucena, and he where?

"Calamba. That is where I live. I have three children—two little girls and a boy. Their mother—she died at childbirth."

I expressed my sympathy and told him I hoped the children were well.

"They are good children," he said contentedly.

We fell into a warm, friendly chat. He was well-mannered in speech, and although he did not talk fluently—sometimes he was tongue-tied—he managed to convey his thoughts.

We became confidential, and I spoke to him of my business. I said I was married and had more children that he had, and was a commercial agent. I said I was tired of the work but was not sure I should be more successful in other lines.

In return he spoke to me about himself and his trade. His name was Juan Rizal and he was a shoemaker. He had a little shop in the front of his house. "It is not a big house," he said.

I said, "You have a good name—Juan Rizal."

"My father is Rizal," he answered.

"Then maybe you are a relative of the hero," I said inferentially. "Near relation, I suppose."

"No. Rizal is my *father,*" he said. "Rizal. Doctor Rizal," he emphasized, and I saw a brilliant light of pride in his small button-like eyes. "Yes," he affirmed himself with not a little bombast.

I said I had not heard and did not know that Rizal had a son.

"Yes, he *has*," he said matter-of-factly. "I am *he*." And he looked at me superiorly.

"The books do not speak of Rizal having a son," I said.

"They don't know," he negated with perfect self-confidence. "They don't know, at all. I *am* the son of Rizal."

As he said this, he set himself erect, lifted his chest out, and plaited together his fingers on his lap. He was little and thin, and when he stretched himself to look great and dignified, he became pathetically distorted. Now he looked elongated, disconcertingly elongated, like an extending, crawling leech.

And I was moved, and I lied:

"I am glad to know you, I am glad to know the son of Rizal."

"Rizal had only *one* son," he explained. "*I* am he, that son—yes, *I* am he. But people won't believe me. They are envious of me."

There was a slight whispering, protesting note in his voice. His thick lips quivered and a film covered his eyes. I thought he was going to cry and I began to feel uncomfortable.

"They are *envious* of me," he repeated, and could not say more. A choking emotion had seized him. He swayed slightly as though he would fall.

I realized the intensity of his feeling and I kept quiet. When he returned to himself, he asked me in a half fearful, half apologetic tone:

"Do you believe me?"

"Yes," I said, but faltering a little.

A happy light beamed in his doglike eyes.

He said, "Thank you. Thank you. Thank you."

There were minutes of silence, and we looked through the window at the passing scenes. The greenery in the soft sunlight was beautiful and healthy, imparting to the eyes a sense of coolness, of vastness. The air, though rather warm, we felt cool and soothing. The train moved smoothly, like a vessel on a very peaceful sea.

It was I who broke the silence. I said I had gone to the Luneta that morning to see the parade. The sun had been hot, and my wife, the children, and I had perspired a lot. "It is a trial, waiting for and watching a parade," I said.

He said I was right and that he too had seen the parade. He had come to Manila for that purpose only. "I go once a year. It is a sort of—pilgrimage. But—I love my father, you see."

It was a naïve, full-souled statement. His eyes ceased for the moment being dull and inexpressive. The soft warmth of gentleness, of a supreme devotional love, filled them. They became the eyes of a dove.

"I love my father," he repeated wistfully, softly, as though he were chanting a most sacred song.

But I (and may God punish me for my cruelty!) remarked inadvertently that he didn't look like his father.

A look of immeasurable hurt stole into his eyes, and he looked at me imploringly, questioned me with those small, melancholy eyes that but a moment ago had been so happy, so inspired, so tender. Struggling out of impending defeat, clamoring to be saved, to be believed in, those eyes looked at me so that a lump rose unwillingly in my throat.

But as though he bore me no grudge at all for my cruel remark, he said softly, lowly, as though in solemn prayer: "I take— after my mother."

Yet he was disturbed, completely broken by my remark, I realized. It had cut him deeply, although he wanted to appear composed. But his efforts were futile. His unrest was visible everywhere in his person: his eyes grew painfully feverish, his nostrils quivered, his lips trembled. And he gave it up with a twitch of his lips, let himself be as he felt, and talked, to dispel my doubts, about his mother and his birth:

"My father and my mother—they lived together before they were married. They lived in Talisay, during my father's deportation, but I was born in Dapitan. People don't know that. When I was born they thought I was dead. Dead. But that is not true.

93

I was *alive*. People thought I was born so, because when my mother was in a delicate condition before my birth, my father played a prank on her and she sprang forward and struck against an iron stand. She became sick. I was born prematurely. But I was alive. Do you understand? I was born, and alive—and I lived." There was galvanic energy in his excited voice. "My mother, she was Irish—Josefina Bracken." He gazed deeper into my eyes. "I don't remember her well," he said. "I don't remember her. She had brown eyes and a little nose." He blew his nose with a cheap, colored handkerchief.

"My father liked her but maybe he did not love her. He loved Leonora. Leonora was his cousin. They were separated when my father went to Europe. Leonora's mother intercepted his letters. She withheld them from Leonora. When my father came back she was married." He stopped and brooded.

"I ran away from my mother when I was old enough to do so. I ran away to Calamba. My father was born there. I wanted to go there, to live there. I have lived there ever since. Have you ever been to Calamba?"

"No," I said.

"My father married my mother on the morning of his execution," he pursued. "My father was brave," he said. "He was not afraid of the Spaniards. He fell forward when they shot him. They wanted to shoot him in the back, but he turned around and fell forward."

He was greatly excited. His face was flushed. "They shot him—my father—the white scoundrels! They shot my father—as they would a dog!" He was indignant. His thin, sticklike fingers closed and opened frantically. He was so vituperative I was afraid he did not realize what he was saying.

I stretched a comforting hand to his to calm him down. He looked at me with quivering lips and I realized his helplessness. He told me that he had not meant to upset me. He begged tearfully for my forgiveness, clutching my hands tightly in his. "Please forgive me," he said. "Please forgive me."

I was afraid he would kneel down; so I moved over to his side and said I understood.

"Do you?" he said. "Do you?" His voice was pleading, full of pain.

"I do," I said.

He quieted down. He turned his face away from mine, ashamed that he had let his feelings run loose.

We were silent again. Only the chug-chug-chug of the train could be heard, and the wind-tossed laughter of those in the neighboring compartments. The air had grown cooler, dusk was fast approaching, and only a lone bird fluttered in the sky. There was a sweet, flowing sound as we crossed a rivulet.

My companion turned to me and made me understand that he was desirous of asking a question. I encouraged him.

"His books—you have read my father's books, the *Noli* and the *Filibusterismo*?" There was still a tremor in his voice, and he mispronounced the last title, calling it "Plisterismo."

"Only the *Noli*," I said. "I have not had the time to read the other."

We were approaching the station of Calamba, Laguna.

"We are nearing your place," I said.

"Yes," he said, and a sadness was now in his voice. "I wish," he murmured, "I could invite you home."

"I will drop in some day."

The train slackened speed and finally stopped.

I helped the son of Rizal lift the buri bag from the net.

"For my children," he explained, smiling. "I brought them fruits."

He asked me before he alighted:

"Do you really believe me?"

"I do."

He was very happy and shook my hands effusively.

"Good-bye," he said.

"Good-bye."

The train moved again.

95

The following month I went to Calamba on the invitation of a friend. It had been a long time, about six years, since we had last met in the city, and now I was to be godfather to his first-born. The choosing of a name depended on me, he had written. Aside from the customary baptismal gift, I brought with me a plaster bust of Rizal which I intended to present to Juan Rizal.

After the ceremony I asked my host if he knew anything about Juan Rizal.

"Yes," he said. "You mean Juan Kola."

I told him to explain.

"He is a shoemaker—owns a little shop near the edge of the town. The children call him Juan Sirá. You know what that means: nutty."

"Tell me more."

"Well, he calls himself Juan Rizal—tells that to people whom he meets. There is a sad story behind it. I will tell it to you:

"When Juan Kola was a small boy, his father was very cruel to him. He used to beat him for any or no reason at all. Naturally the boy grew to dislike his father—learned to hate him as much as he feared him. But when the boy was twelve or thereabouts, the father died. The boy knew no happiness so great; so he cried. Otherwise the boy would not have wept. He was so used to his father's meanness and cruelty that any sorrow, any pain, could not make him cry. He had forgotten how to cry, had learned to stifle that surging in the breast that brings tears to the eyes, and he would merely whine, dry-eyed, like a puppy that is kicked. But this time he wept, and for a long time afterwards you could see him in the streets crying. And when people asked him why he cried, he replied, 'I don't know. I just want to cry.' He was not evading the truth; the boy simply had no words for it. But the people knew.

"Then the boy began thinking of Rizal. Rizal was born here, you know, and that makes him closer to us than to you who live elsewhere. Rizal to us is a reality, a magnificent, potent reality, but to you he is only a myth, a golden legend. He is to you a star, faraway, bright, unreachable. To us he is not unreachable, for he is among us. We feel him, breathe with him, live with him. *Juan Kola lived with him—lives with him.* In his young untutored mind he knew that if Rizal were his father he would be a good father, a supremely beautiful father, and he, Juan Kola, would always be happy. And so Juan Kola, the little unhappy boy, made José Rizal his father.

"He was a poor boy, Juan Kola, and he could not go to school. He had to work and earn his living. He does not read or write, but he knows much about Rizal's life from the schoolteacher who boarded with the shoemaker to whom he was apprenticed. Of nights, when work was over, he would go to her, to this teacher, and ask her questions, and she, filled with sympathy for the boy, gave him of her time.

"When Juan's father died, he destroyed all his father's things. There was a picture left of his father, but he burned it, not wishing to remember anything of his true parent. He wanted to be fully the son of his adopted father. From then on he was the son of Rizal.

"And that," concluded my friend, "is the story of Juan Sirá. The children have misnamed him. It is cruel, unjust. He who can dream of beautiful things, and live in them, surely he is great—and wise."

"Take me to Juan Rizal," I said.

I presented my gift to Juan Rizal in his shabby little nipa home. Juan Rizal was exultant when he opened the package containing Rizal's bust. "I have always wanted one, but I could not afford it," he said with tremulous lips and adoring eyes.

Bruno Schulz

When the Germans occupied the Polish town of Orogo-
bych in 1941, Bruno Schulz was earning his living as a painter; his
writings didn't sell, in spite of a prize awarded to his book *The
Street of Crocodiles* by the Polish Academy of Letters, and as a
Jewish teacher his salary was meager. A year later, in November,
while bringing home a loaf of bread, he was shot dead in the street
by a Nazi officer who bore a grudge against another Nazi, Schulz's
temporary "protector," a man obviously interested in *Kultur* who
had become fond of Schulz's paintings.

A translator of Kafka, Schulz shared Kafka's own sense
of being "a parasite of metaphors." A year before Kafka's death in
1924, Gustav Janouch, Kafka's friend, visited Kafka in hospital.
Among their several conversations was one about the literary
device of turning people into animals, which Kafka had used so
effectively in "Metamorphosis." "But no," he said to Janouch. "The
theme is not mine. It belongs to our time—that is where I got it
from. Animals are now closer to us than man. Because of the bars
of the cage, you see."

"Father's Last Escape" is a metaphor of Schulz's vision
of his father, but it is also an account of his search for truth "to fill
in the gaps that official history leaves," as John Updike has said.
Updike quotes Schulz: "Where is truth to shelter, where is it to
find asylum if not in a place where nobody is looking for it?"

FATHER'S LAST ESCAPE

bruno schulz

Translated from the Polish by Celina Wieniewska

it happened in the late and forlorn period of complete disruption, at the time of the liquidation of our business.
The signboard had been removed from over our shop, the shutters
were halfway down, and inside the shop my mother was conducting an unauthorized trade in remnants. Adela had gone to America
and it was said that the boat on which she had sailed had sunk
and that all the passengers had lost their lives. We were unable to
verify this rumour, but all trace of the girl was lost and we never
heard of her again.

A new age began—empty, sober, and joyless, like a sheet
of white paper. A new servant girl, Genya, anaemic, pale, and bone-
less, mooned about the rooms. When one patted her on the back,
she wriggled, stretched like a snake, or purred like a cat. She had
a dull white complexion, and even the insides of her eyelids were
white. She was so absent-minded that she sometimes made a
white sauce from old letters and invoices: it was sickly and inedible.

At that time, my father was definitely dead. He had been
dying a number of times, always with some reservations that forced
us to revise our attitude towards the fact of his death. This had its
advantages. By dividing his death into instalments, Father had
familiarized us with his demise. We became gradually indifferent

to his returns—each one shorter, each one more pitiful. His features were already dispersed throughout the room in which he had lived, and were sprouting in it, creating at some points strange knots of likeness that were most expressive. The wallpaper began in certain places to imitate his habitual nervous tic; the flower designs arranged themselves into the doleful elements of his smile, symmetrical as the fossilized imprint of a trilobite. For a time, we gave a wide berth to his fur coat lined with polecat skins. The fur coat breathed. The panic of small animals sewn together and biting into one another passed through it in helpless currents and lost itself in the folds of the fur. Putting one's ear against it, one could hear the melodious purring unison of the animals' sleep. In this well-tanned form, amid the faint smell of polecat, murder, and nighttime matings, my father might have lasted for many years. But he did not last.

One day, Mother returned home from town with a preoccupied face.

'Look, Joseph,' she said, 'what a lucky coincidence. I caught him on the stairs, jumping from step to step'—and she lifted a handkerchief that covered something on a plate. I recognized him at once. The resemblance was striking, although now he was a crab or a large scorpion. Mother and I exchanged looks: in spite of the metamorphosis, the resemblance was incredible.

'Is he alive?' I asked.

'Of course. I can hardly hold him,' Mother said. 'Shall I place him on the floor?'

She put the plate down, and leaning over him, we observed him closely. There was a hollow place between his numerous curved legs, which he was moving slightly. His uplifted pincers and feelers seemed to be listening. I tipped the plate, and Father moved cautiously and with a certain hesitation on to the floor. Upon touching the flat surface under him, he gave a sudden start with all of his legs, while his hard arthropod joints made a clacking sound. I barred his way. He hesitated, investigated the obstacle with his feelers, then lifted his pincers and turned aside. We let him run in his chosen direction, where there was no furniture to give him shelter. Running in wavy jerks on his many legs, he reached the wall and, before we could stop him, ran lightly up it, no pausing anywhere. I shuddered with instinctive revulsion as I watched his progress up the wallpaper. Meanwhile, Father reached a small built-in kitchen cupboard, hung for a moment on its edge, testing the terrain with his pincers, and then crawled into it.

He was discovering the apartment afresh from the new point of view of a crab; evidently, he perceived all objects by his sense of smell, for, in spite of careful checking, I could not find on him any organ of sight. He seemed to consider carefully the objects he encountered on his path, stopping and feeling them with his antennae, then embracing them with his pincers, as if to test them and make their acquaintance; after a time, he left them and continued on his run, pulling his abdomen behind him, lifted slightly from the floor. He acted the same way with the pieces of bread and meat that we threw on the floor for him, hoping he would eat them. He gave them a perfunctory examination and ran on, not recognizing that they were edible.

Watching these patient surveys of the room, one could assume that he was obstinately and indefatigably looking for something. From time to time, he ran to a corner of the kitchen, crept under a barrel of water that was leaking, and, upon reaching the puddle, seemed to drink.

Sometimes he disappeared for days on end. He seemed to manage perfectly well without food, but this did not seem to affect his vitality. With mixed feelings of shame and repugnance, we concealed by day our secret fear that he might visit us in bed during the night. But this never occurred, although in the daytime he would wander all over the furniture. He particularly liked to stay in the spaces between the wardrobes and the wall.

We could not discount certain manifestations of reason and even a sense of humour. For instance, Father never failed to appear in the dining-room during mealtimes, although his participation in them was purely symbolic. If the dining-room door was by chance closed during dinner and he had been left in the next room, he scratched at the bottom of the door, running up and down along the crack, until we opened it for him. In time, he learned how to insert his pincers and legs under the door, and after some elaborate manoeuvres he finally succeeded in insinuating his body through it sideways into the dining-room. This seemed to give him pleasure. He would then stop under the table, lying quite still, his abdomen slightly pulsating. What the meaning of these rhythmic pulsations was, we could not imagine. They seemed obscene and malicious, but at the same time expressed a rather gross and lustful satisfaction. Our dog, Nimrod, would approach him slowly and, without conviction, sniff at him cautiously, sneeze, and turn away indifferently, not having reached any conclusions.

102   Meanwhile, the demoralization in our household was increasing. Genya slept all day long, her slim body bonelessly undulating with her deep breaths. We often found in the soup reels of cotton, which she had thrown in unthinkingly with the vegetables. Our shop was open non-stop, day and night. A continuous sale took place amid complicated bargainings and discussions. To crown it all, Uncle Charles came to stay.

He was strangely depressed and silent. He declared with a sigh that after his recent unfortunate experiences he had decided to change his way of life and devote himself to the study of languages. He never went out but remained locked in the most remote room—from which Genya had removed all the carpets and curtains, as she did not approve of our visitor. There he spent his time, reading old price lists. Several times he tried viciously to step on Father. Screaming with horror, we told him to stop it. Afterwards he only smiled wryly to himself, while Father, not realizing the danger he had been in, hung around and studied some spots on the floor.

My father, quick and mobile as long as he was on his feet, shared with all crustaceans the characteristic that when turned on his back he became largely immobile. It was sad and pitiful to see him desperately moving all his limbs and rotating helplessly around his own axis. We could hardly force ourselves to look at the conspicuous, almost shameless mechanism of his anatomy, completely exposed under the bare articulated belly. At such moments, Uncle Charles could hardly restrain himself from stamping on Father. We ran to his rescue with some object at hand, which he caught tightly with his pincers, quickly regaining his normal position; then at once he started a lightning, zigzag run at double speed, as if wanting to obliterate the memory of his unsightly fall.

I must force myself to report truthfully the unbelievable deed, from which my memory recoils even now. To this day I cannot understand how we became the conscious perpetrators of it. A strange fatality must have been driving us to it; for fate does not evade consciousness or will but engulfs them in its mechanism, so that we are able to admit and accept, as in a hypnotic trance, things that under normal circumstances would fill us with horror.

Shaken badly, I asked my mother in despair, again and again, 'How could you have done it? If it were Genya who had done it—but you yourself?' Mother cried, wrung her hands, and could find no answer. Had she thought that Father would be better off? Had she seen in that act the only solution to a hopeless situation, or did she do it out of inconceivable thoughtlessness and frivolity? Fate has a thousand wiles when it chooses to impose on us its incomprehensible whims. A temporary blackout, a moment of inattention or blindness, is enough to insinuate an act between the Scylla and Charybdis of decision. Afterwards, with hindsight, we may endlessly ponder the act, explain our motives, try to discover our true intentions; but the act remains irrevocable.

When Father was brought in on a dish, we came to our senses and understood fully what had happened. He lay large and swollen from the boiling, pale grey and jellified. We sat in silence, dumbfounded. Only Uncle Charles lifted his fork towards the dish, but at once he put it down uncertainly, looking at us askance. Mother ordered it to be taken to the sitting-room. It stood there afterwards on a table covered with a velvet cloth, next to the album of family photographs and a musical cigarette box. Avoided by us all, it just stood there.

But my father's earthly wanderings were not yet at an end, and the next instalment—the extension of the story beyond permissible limits—is the most painful of all. Why didn't he give up, why didn't he admit that he was beaten when there was every reason to do so and when even Fate could go no farther in utterly confounding him? After several weeks of immobility in the sitting room, he somehow rallied and seemed to be slowly recovering. One morning, we found the plate empty. One leg lay on the edge of the dish, in some congealed tomato sauce and aspic that bore the traces of his escape. Although boiled and shedding his legs on the way, with his remaining strength he had dragged himself some-where to begin a homeless wandering, and we never saw him again.

John Edgar Wideman

"Think of our country as a vast orphanage. The official policy of the institution is to keep its inmates confused by concealing from them their biological origins. Divide and conquer. Spread a lot of ugly rumors about some people's tainted births, glorify other people's impeccable bloodlines. Float some preposterous lies, dress up myth and legend as fact to explain and prove how different some kinds of people are from other kinds. Keep everybody guessing, confused, under suspicion." In 1994, John Edgar Wideman, after writing a moving memoir of his relationship with his imprisoned brother, published a short meditation on the nature of fathers and sons, *Fatheralong,* in which he tried to disentangle the identity of sons and fathers from the paradigm of race.

"Whose child are you? What's your name?" Wideman asks his own son. And as he looks back to the little he knows—the name of the town his grandfather lived in, the name of his own father—he reflects: "The men they were fade into a set of facts, sparse, ambiguous, impersonal, their intimate lives unretrievable, where what is known about a county, a region, a country and its practice of human bondage, its tradition of obscuring, stealing, or distorting black people's lives, begins to crowd out the possibility of seeing my ancestors as human beings. The powers and principalities that originally restricted our access to the life free people naturally enjoy still rise like a shadow, a wall between my grandfathers and myself, my father and me, between the two of us, father and son, son and father." Wideman concludes, "So we must speak these stories to one another."

CASA GRANDE

john edgar wideman

about a month ago I discovered a long-lost story written by my son:

A Trip to Jupiter

One morning I woke up floating in space because the gravity pull decreased. I was sailing nice and smoothly right towards Jupiter. I sailed for 0:100 hours and then landed. The atmosphere was very cool and I heard a sound: "Mee, Meep. Earthling intruder."

"Where are you earthling name caller." I asked.

"Right before your eyes. I am green with black spots but no thing can see me. I cannot see you. Where are you?"

"Who, me? Oh. Well I guess I might be near the end of the universe because it is very cool here. I also think I might be on Saturn because of the rings."

"Well, earthling you are dumb because you are on the biggest planet in the Universe, Jupiter. The rings you see are our moons. They make a circle around our planet. Earthling, are you well educated?"

"I am. I am. Mr. Unknown."

"Well you don't sound that way. Our schools are green and our only force is a cannon that shoots out Juperballs. Juperballs are balls from the sky and they kill whatever they touch. We have great leaders named: Nansi, Rasher, Lack, Spiritual and Malcomba. Spiritual is our only man from another planet, Earth. You live in Earth too, right?"

"I do. But how do you know?"

"We Jupers have 3 different powers. Each Juper has different powers. Mine happen to be: disappearing power, able to speak English, and E.S.P. My E.S.P. allows me to look into your body and know everything about you. For instance: You're 10 years old, you go to Washington school, and you're from a family of 5. Well I have to now go back to tending the Juperlies. Goodbye." And he went away. When I got back I told everyone what I had learned and where I had been and the writers named me student of the year. But when I told my parents they didn't believe one bit of it. They just laughed. "Ha, ha, ha," they said.

My son wrote his story, as he says, when he was ten years old. Eleven years later, just after he'd turned twenty-one and I had celebrated his birthday with him in the Arizona prison where he's serving a life sentence, I was attempting to write in my journal about the way it feels when the terrible reality of his situation comes down on me, when I exchange for a fraction of a second my life for his. Longer than that I can't bear. Even that fraction of a second, brief and illusory as it is, has the effect of a pebble dropped at dawn in a still, clear lake. Everything changes and keeps on changing, but not with the simple elegance of ripple within ripple expanding rhythmically outward. What I feel when I cannot help myself and our shadows collide, are superimposed for a millisecond, is the instability of the earth's core, the tremor of aging that's already started in my left thumb, convulsing my entire body, the planes and frames of being rattling and shattering, a voice too familiar to name crying out in pain and I can't do a damn thing about any of it. I couldn't write either so I straightened up my study instead. That's when I found "Trip to Jupiter" in a manila folder in a box of our kids' things and read it again for the first time in eleven years, thinking as I read, My god, here's something I've totally forgotten, totally lost.

That's what I thought anyway until later that same day, browsing my journal, I came across an entry from the previous year, written after another visit with my son:

He sits on a planet ten million light years away, waiting for time to change the place he is to another. Darkness shrouds him. He would be invisible from ten feet if there were someone else on the planet looking at the space where he sits. He peoples the darkness with many such *someones,* teaches them the language of this planet to which he is exiled, instructs them how not to be blind to his presence. They help him pass this time till it becomes another. To himself he is far too visible, a presence screaming light, insistent, tedious as neon. Dim warmth beneath his skin defines him, fills the void he must occupy until time drifts as far as it must drift to open again for him.

He dreams a forest of green creatures, some tall as trees, many man-size, others a foot or two high. They repeat themselves, could be the same prickly, stumped-armed form over and over until you dream differently, stare at the cacti clustered around you, scattered on rolling hills, in stark ranks on the desert floor.

They say the Hohokam dwelt here. Those who are gone, who are used up is what the word *hohokam,* borrowed from the Pima Indian language, means. Hohokam cremated their dead in shallow pits. Only ash and bits and pieces of ornament and bone remain. Named Hohokam by archeologists because the ones who dwelt here are gone, gone, gone and cannot speak their own names, sing their songs, claim this land they peopled nine centuries ago

when the Gila River was young and filled with fish and waterfowl
nested on its green banks and game roamed the marshes, when
this dry land supported fruits and vegetables and flowers no one
has seen growing here in a thousand years. Because they left so
little behind, not even skulls for anthropologists to measure, the
Hohokam culture remains mysterious. No one knows where they
originated nor why they disappeared completely after flourishing
here for hundreds of years, building towns, canals, their Casa
Grande I decide to visit since I've come this far anyway, this close,
and my heart is bursting so I'll come up for air here, near Coolidge,
Arizona, off Route 289, just fifteen miles from the prison at
Florence, blend in with the old white people hoping to find in these
ruins something they didn't bring with them, hoping to leave something burdensome behind in the dust they do not need or will not
miss when the vacation's over and its home again, home again.

On his distant planet he invents the word *hohokam*. It
slips into his unconscious as a way of understanding where he
once was. The sound of it almost like laughter, a joke on himself
he can tell over and over without becoming bitter. Where he stays
it doesn't snow but something is always falling from the sky, gritty,
grainy, like shredded husks of insects—wings, legs, antennae,
dried blood sucked from long-dead hosts, the desert floor lifted
and reserved so it is a ceiling, then shaken ever so gently, sifted
through the finest sieve down on his head *hohokam hohokam*. It
could be a word of welcome, a whispered promise, That which is,
soon goes away.

I can't help thinking the cacti are deformed. Truncated
men missing limbs, heads, fingers, feet. Clearly each cactus is
incomplete. Not what it should, could be. Or once was. Asymmetry
reigns. Ladders with rungs missing. Functionless protuberances.
Each cripple a warped facsimile of the perfect form yet to be
achieved by a builder who keeps trying in spite of countless disas-
ters jammed upright, headfirst into the desert sand.

Among these legions of failures some believe they are
better than others. They laugh at the lost ones, the outcast, the

hohokam. Their laughter rises and becomes dry rain on the planet where he sits in darkness, where time runs backwards, *Zamani* to *Sasa,* Great-time to Little-time, and oceans disappear down a drain no bigger than the pinhead upon which he dances his angels, counts them as they exhaust themselves and one by one plummet back to earth.

F. Scott Fitzgerald

All his life, Scott Fitzgerald wished to be what he was not. As a child, he decided he was not the son of his father, but told his neighbors that he had been found one night, wrapped in a blanket onto which was pinned a paper with the arms of the House of Stuart. He was young among the old, down-and-out among the high-lifers ("he couldn't distinguish between innocence and social climbing," said Saul Bellow), talented among the frivolous, poor among the rich ("I'm too poor to economize," he said, "economy is a luxury, our only salvation is in extravagance"). He was, at least in the popular imagination, the last romantic. After his death, his daughter called him "the key-note and prophet of his generation."

Fitzgerald's world is, in this wishful sense, an imaginary world: everyone in it lives just outside real life, dreaming of better (or worse) things. His raw material came, of course, from the men and women he knew; among his family, friends, and acquaintances, he plundered for good plots and dazzling, moonstruck characters. When his wife, Zelda, reviewed his early novel, *The Beautiful and the Damned,* she found so many traits of their own life in it that she observed, "Mr. Fitzgerald seems to believe that plagiarism begins at home." Pat Hobby, hero of seventeen stories written shortly before his death in 1940, is a luckless Hollywood writer with many of Fitzgerald's own traits; a late instance of one of those homebred imaginary lives.

PAT HOBBY,

PUTATIVE FATHER

f. scott fitzgerald

I

most writers look like writers whether they want to or not. It is hard to say why—for they model their exteriors whimsically on Wall Street brokers, cattle kings or English explorers—but they all turn out looking like writers, as definitely typed as 'The Public' or 'The Profiteers' in the cartoons.

Pat Hobby was the exception. He did not look like a writer. And only in one corner of the Republic could he have been identified as a member of the entertainment world. Even there the first guess would have been that he was an extra down on his luck, or a bit player who specialized in the sort of father who should *never* come home. But a writer he was: he had collaborated in over two dozen moving picture scripts, most of them, it must be admitted, prior to 1929.

A writer? He had a desk in the Writers' Building at the studio; he had pencils, paper, a secretary, paper clips, a pad for office memoranda. And he sat in an overstuffed chair, his eyes not so very bloodshot, taking in the morning's *Reporter.*

'I got to get to work,' he told Miss Raudenbush at eleven. And again at twelve:

'I got to get to work.'

At quarter to one, he began to feel hungry—up to this

point every move, or rather every moment, was in the writer's tradition. Even to the faint irritation that no one had annoyed him, no one had bothered him, no one had interfered with the long empty dream which constituted his average day.

He was about to accuse his secretary of staring at him when the welcome interruption came. A studio guide tapped at his door and brought him a note from his boss, Jack Berners:

> Dear Pat:
> Please take some time off and show these people
> around the lot.
> Jack

'My God!' Pat exclaimed. 'How can I be expected to get anything done and show people around the lot at the same time. Who are they?' he demanded of the guide.

'I don't know. One of them seems to be kind of coloured. He looks like the extras they had at Paramount for *Bengal Lancer*. He can't speak English. The other—'

Pat was putting on his coat to see for himself.

'Will you be wanting me this afternoon?' asked Miss Raudenbush.

He looked at her with infinite reproach and went out in front of the Writers' Building.

The visitors were there. The sultry person was tall and of a fine carriage, dressed in excellent English clothes except for a turban. The other was a youth of fifteen, quite light of hue. He also wore a turban with beautifully cut jodhpurs and riding coat.

They bowed formally.

'Hear you want to go on some sets,' said Pat. 'You friends of Jack Berners?'

'Acquaintances,' said the youth. 'May I present you to my uncle: Sir Singrim Dak Raj.'

Probably, thought Pat, the company was cooking up a Bengal Lancers, and this man would play the heavy who owned the Khyber Pass. Maybe they'd put Pat on it—at three-fifty a week. Why not? He knew how to write that stuff:

Beautiful Long Shot. The Gorge. Show Tribesman firing from behind rocks.

Medium shot. Tribesman hit by bullet making nose dive over high rock. (use stunt man)

Medium Long Shot. The Valley. British troops wheeling out cannon.

'You going to be long in Hollywood?' he asked shrewdly.

'My uncle doesn't speak English,' said the youth in a measured voice. 'We are here only a few days. You see—I am your putative son.'

II

'— And I would very much like to see Bonita Granville,' continued the youth. 'I find she has been borrowed by your studio.'

They had been walking toward the production office and it took Pat a minute to grasp what the young man had said.

'You're my what?' he asked.

'Your putative son,' said the young man, in a sort of sing-song. 'Legally I am the son and heir of the Rajah Dak Raj Indore. But I was born John Brown Hobby.'

'Yes?' said Pat. 'Go on! What's this?'

'My mother was Delia Brown. You married her in 1926. And she divorced you in 1927 when I was a few months old. Later she took me to India, where she married my present legal father.'

'Oh,' said Pat. They had reached the production office. 'You want to see Bonita Granville.'

'Yes,' said John Hobby Indore. 'If it is convenient.'

Pat looked at the shooting schedule on the wall.

'It may be,' he said heavily. 'We can go and see.'

As they started toward Stage 4, he exploded.

'What do you mean, "my potato son"? I'm glad to see you and all that, but say, are you really the kid Delia had in 1926?'

'Putatively,' John Indore said. 'At that time you and she were legally married.'

He turned to his uncle and spoke rapidly in Hindustani, whereupon the latter bent forward, looked with cold examination upon Pat and threw up his shoulders without comment. The whole business was making Pat vaguely uncomfortable.

When he pointed out the commissary, John wanted to stop there 'to buy his uncle a hot dog'. It seemed that Sir Singrim had conceived a passion for them at the World's Fair in New York, whence they had just come. They were taking ship for Madras tomorrow.

'—whether or not,' said John sombrely, 'I get to see Bonita Granville. I do not care if I *meet* her. I am too young for her. She is already an old woman by our standards. But I'd like to *see* her.'

It was one of those bad days for showing people around. Only one of the directors shooting today was an old timer, on whom Pat could count for a welcome—and at the door of that stage he received word that the star kept blowing up in his lines and had demanded that the set be cleared.

In desperation he took his charges out to the back lot and walked them past the false fronts of ships and cities and village streets, and medieval gates—a sight in which the boy showed a certain interest but which Sir Singrim found disappointing. Each time that Pat led them around behind to demonstrate that it was all phony Sir Singrim's expression would change to disappointment and faint contempt.

'What's he say?' Pat asked his offspring, after Sir Singrim had walked eagerly into a Fifth Avenue jewellery store, to find nothing but carpenter's rubble inside.

'He is the third richest man in India,' said John. 'He is disgusted. He says he will never enjoy an American picture again. He says he will buy one of our picture companies in India and make every set as solid as the Taj Mahal. He thinks perhaps the actresses just have a false front too, and that's why you won't let us see them.'

The first sentence had rung a sort of carillon in Pat's head. If there was anything he liked it was a good piece of money—not this miserable, uncertain two-fifty a week which purchased his freedom.

'I'll tell you,' he said with sudden decision. 'We'll try Stage 4, and peek at Bonita Granville.'

Stage 4 was double locked and barred, for the day—the director hated visitors, and it was a process stage besides. 'Process' was a generic name for trick photography in which every studio competed with other studios, and lived in terror of spies. More specifically it meant that a projecting machine threw a moving background upon a transparent screen. On the other side of the screen, a scene was played and recorded against this moving background. The projector on one side of the screen and the camera on the other were so synchronized that the result could show a star standing on his head before an indifferent crowd on 42nd Street—a *real* crowd and a *real* star—and the poor eye could only conclude that it was being deluded and never quite guess how.

Pat tried to explain this to John, but John was peering for Bonita Granville from behind the great mass of coiled ropes and pails where they hid. They had not got there by the front entrance, but by a little side door for technicians that Pat knew.

Wearied by the long jaunt over the back lot, Pat took a pint flask from his hip and offered it to Sir Singrim who declined. He did not offer it to John.

'Stunt your growth,' he said solemnly, taking a long pull.

'I do not want any,' said John with dignity.

He was suddenly alert. He had spotted an idol more glamourous than Siva not twenty feet away—her back, her profile, her voice. Then she moved off.

Watching his face, Pat was rather touched.

'We can go nearer,' he said. 'We might get to that ballroom set. They're not using it—they got covers on the furniture.'

On tip toe they started, Pat in the lead, then Sir Singrim, then John. As they moved softly forward Pat heard the words 'Lights' and stopped in his tracks. Then, as a blinding white glow struck at their eyes and the voice shouted 'Quiet! We're rolling!' Pat began to run, followed quickly through the white silence by the others.

The silence did not endure.

'Cut!' screamed a voice, 'What the living, blazing hell!'

From the director's angle something had happened on the screen which, for the moment, was inexplicable. Three gigantic silhouettes, two with huge Indian turbans, had danced across what was intended to be a New England harbour—they had blundered into the line of the process shot. Prince John Indore had not only seen Bonita Granville—he had acted in the same picture. His silhouetted foot seemed to pass miraculously through her blonde young head.

117

III

They sat for some time in the guard-room before word could be gotten to Jack Berners, who was off the lot. So there was leisure for talk. This consisted of a longish harangue from Sir Singrim to John, which the latter—modifying its tone if not its words—translated to Pat.

'My uncle says his brother wanted to do something for you. He thought perhaps if you were a great writer he might invite you to come to his kingdom and write his life.'

'I never claimed to be—'

'My uncle says you are an ignominious writer—in your own land you permitted him to be touched by those dogs of the policemen.'

'Aw—bananas,' muttered Pat uncomfortably.

'He says my mother always wished you well. But now she is a high and sacred Lady and should never see you again. He says we will go to our chambers in the Ambassador Hotel and meditate and pray and let you know what we decide.'

When they were released, and the two moguls were escorted apologetically to their car by a studio yes-man, it seemed to Pat that it had been pretty well decided already. He was angry. For the sake of getting his son a peek at Miss Granville, he had quite possibly lost his job—though he didn't really think so. Or rather he was pretty sure that when his week was up he would have lost it anyhow. But though it was a pretty bad break he remembered most clearly from the afternoon that Sir Singrim was 'the third richest man in India', and after dinner at a bar on La Cienega he decided to go down to the Ambassador Hotel and find out the result of the prayer and meditation.

It was early dark of a September evening. The Ambassador was full of memories to Pat—the Coconut Grove in the great days, when directors found pretty girls in the afternoon and made stars of them by night. There was some activity in front of the door and Pat watched it idly. Such a quantity of baggage he had seldom seen, even in the train of Gloria Swanson or Joan Crawford. Then he started as he saw two or three men in turbans moving around among the baggage. So—they were running out on him.

Sir Singrim Dak Raj and his nephew Prince John, both pulling on gloves as if at a command, appeared at the door, as Pat stepped forward out of the darkness.

'Taking a powder, eh?' he said. 'Say, when you get back there, tell them that one American could lick—'

'I have left a note for you,' said Prince John, turning from his Uncle's side. 'I say, you *were* nice this afternoon and it really was too bad.'

'Yes, it was,' agreed Pat.

'But we are providing for you,' John said. 'After our prayers we decided that you will receive fifty sovereigns a month—two hundred and fifty dollars—for the rest of your natural life.'

'What will I have to do for it?' questioned Pat suspiciously.

'It will only be withdrawn in case—'

John leaned and whispered in Pat's ear, and relief crept into Pat's eyes. The condition had nothing to do with drink and blondes, really nothing to do with him at all.

John began to get in the limousine.

'Goodbye, putative father,' he said, almost with affection.
Pat stood looking after him.

'Goodbye son,' he said. He stood watching the limousine go out of sight. Then he turned away—feeling like—like Stella Dallas. There were tears in his eyes.

Potato Father—whatever that meant. After some consideration he added to himself: it's better than not being a father at all.

IV

He awoke late next afternoon with a happy hangover—the cause of which he could not determine until young John's voice seemed to spring into his ears, repeating: 'Fifty sovereigns a month, with just one condition—that it be withdrawn in case of war, when all revenues of our state will revert to the British Empire.'

With a cry Pat sprang to the door. No *Los Angeles Times* lay against it, no *Examiner*—only *Toddy's Daily Form Sheet*. He searched the orange pages frantically. Below the form sheets, the past performances, the endless oracles for endless racetracks, his eye was caught by a one-inch item:

LONDON, SEPTEMBER 3RD. ON THIS MORNING'S DECLARATION BY CHAMBERLAIN, DOUGIE CABLES 'ENGLAND TO WIN. FRANCE TO PLACE. RUSSIA TO SHOW.'

Ambrose Bierce

"*Childhood:* The period of human life intermediate between the idiocy of infancy and the folly of youth—two removes from the sin of manhood and three from the remorse of old age," wrote Ambrose Bierce in his merciless *Devil's Dictionary,* a volume intended for "enlightened souls who prefer dry wines to sweet, sense to sentiment, wit to humour, and clean English to slang." Of his own childhood relationship with his father, Bierce left no clue.

A veteran of the Civil War, Ambrose Bierce became a journalist, first in San Francisco and then in England, where he began writing his bitter, poignant short stories at the age of thirty as well as collecting the definitions for his *Dictionary.* The memory of the war became for Bierce the source of many of his best stories, and the antagonism of its two American factions emblematic of the childlike antagonism bred within a family; "A Horseman in the Sky" makes this association movingly obvious. In 1913, after becoming disillusioned with American society, Bierce disappeared into Mexico's own conflict, in search of what he called "the good, kind darkness."

A HORSEMAN IN THE SKY

ambrose bierce

I

One sunny afternoon in the autumn of the year 1861 a soldier lay in a clump of laurel by the side of a road in western Virginia. He lay at full length upon his stomach, his feet resting upon the toes, his head upon the left forearm. His extended right hand loosely grasped his rifle. But for the some-what methodical disposition of his limbs and a slight rhythmic movement of the cartridge-box at the back of his belt he might have been thought to be dead. He was asleep at his post of duty. But if detected he would be dead shortly afterward, death being the just and legal penalty of his crime.

The clump of laurel in which the criminal lay was in the angle of a road which after ascending southward a steep acclivity to that point turned sharply to the west, running along the summit for perhaps one hundred yards. There it turned southward again and went zigzagging downward through the forest. At the salient of that second angle was a large flat rock, jutting out northward, overlook-ing the deep valley from which the road ascended. The rock capped a high cliff; a stone dropped from its outer edge would have fallen sheer downward one thousand feet to the tops of the pines. The angle where the soldier lay was on another spur of the same cliff. Had he been awake he would have commanded a view, not only of the short arm of the road and the jutting rock, but of the entire profile of the cliff below it. It might well have made him giddy to look.

The country was wooded everywhere except at the bottom of the valley to the northward, where there was a small natural meadow, through which flowed a stream scarcely visible from the valley's rim. This open ground looked hardly larger than an ordinary door-yard, but was really several acres in extent. Its green was more vivid than that of the inclosing forest. Away beyond it rose a line of giant cliffs similar to those upon which we are supposed to stand in our survey of the savage scene, and through which the road had somehow made its climb to the summit. The configuration of the valley, indeed, was such that from this point of observation it seemed entirely shut in, and one could but have wondered how the road which found a way out of it had found a way into it, and whence came and whither went the waters of the stream that parted the meadow more than a thousand feet below.

122

No country is so wild and difficult but men will make it a theatre of war; concealed in the forest at the bottom of that military rattrap, in which half a hundred men in possession of the exits might have starved an army to submission, lay five regiments of Federal infantry. They had marched all the previous day and night and were resting. At nightfall they would take to the road again, climb to the place where their unfaithful sentinel now slept, and descending the other slope of the ridge fall upon a camp of the enemy at about midnight. Their hope was to surprise it, for the road led to the rear of it. In case of failure, their position would be perilous in the extreme; and fail they surely would should accident or vigilance apprise the enemy of the movement.

II

The sleeping sentinel in the clump of laurel was a young Virginian named Carter Druse. He was the son of wealthy parents, an only child, and had known such ease and cultivation and high living as wealth and taste were able to command in the mountain country of western Virginia. His home was but a few miles from where he now lay. One morning he had risen from the breakfast-table and said, quietly but gravely: "Father, a Union regiment has arrived at Grafton. I am going to join it."

The father lifted his leonine head, looked at the son a moment in silence, and replied: "Well, go, sir, and whatever may occur do what you conceive to be your duty. Virginia, to which you are a traitor, must get on without you. Should we both live to the end of the war, we will speak further of the matter. Your mother, as the physician has informed you, is in a most critical condition; at the best she cannot be with us longer than a few weeks, but that time is precious. It would be better not to disturb her."

So Carter Druse, bowing reverently to his father, who returned the salute with a stately courtesy that masked a breaking heart, left the home of his childhood to go soldiering. By conscience and courage, by deeds of devotion and daring, he soon commended himself to his fellows and his officers; and it was to these qualities and to some knowledge of the country that he owed his selection for his present perilous duty at the extreme outpost. Nevertheless, fatigue had been stronger than resolution and he had fallen asleep. What good or bad angel came in a dream to rouse him from his state of crime, who shall say? Without a movement, without a sound, in the profound silence and the languor of the late afternoon, some invisible messenger of fate touched with unsealing finger the eyes of his consciousness— whispered into the ear of his spirit the mysterious awakening word which no human lips ever have spoken, no human memory ever has recalled. He quietly raised his forehead from his arm and looked between the masking stems of the laurels, instinctively closing his right hand about the stock of his rifle.

His first feeling was a keen artistic delight. On a colossal pedestal, the cliff,—motionless at the extreme edge of the capping rock and sharply outlined against the sky,—was an equestrian statue of impressive dignity. The figure of the man sat on the figure of the horse, straight and soldierly, but with the repose of a Grecian god carved in the marble which limits the suggestion of

123

activity. The gray costume harmonized with its aërial background; the metal of accoutrement and caparison was softened and subdued by the shadow; the animal's skin had no points of high light. A carbine strikingly foreshortened lay across the pommel of the saddle, kept in place by the right hand grasping it at the "grip"; the left hand, holding the bridle rein, was invisible. In silhouette against the sky the profile of the horse was cut with the sharpness of a cameo; it looked across the heights of air to the confronting cliffs beyond. The face of the rider, turned slightly away, showed only an outline of temple and beard; he was looking downward to the bottom of the valley. Magnified by its lift against the sky and by the soldier's testifying sense of formidableness of a near enemy the group appeared of heroic, almost colossal, size.

For an instant Druse had a strange, half-defined feeling that he had slept to the end of the war and was looking upon a noble work of art reared upon that eminence to commemorate the deeds of an heroic past of which he had been an inglorious part. The feeling was dispelled by a slight movement of the group; the horse, without moving its feet, had drawn its body slightly backward from the verge; the man remained immobile as before. Broad awake and keenly alive to the significance of the situation, Druse now brought the butt of his rifle against his cheek by cautiously pushing the barrel forward through the bushes, cocked the piece, and glancing through the sights covered a vital spot of the horseman's breast. A touch upon the trigger and all would have been well with Carter Druse. At that instant the horseman turned his head and looked in the direction of his concealed foeman— seemed to look into his very face, into his eyes, into his brave, compassionate heart.

Is it then so terrible to kill an enemy in war—an enemy who has surprised a secret vital to the safety of one's self and comrades—an enemy more formidable for his knowledge than all his army for its numbers? Carter Druse grew pale; he shook in every limb, turned faint, and saw the statuesque group before him as black figures, rising, falling, moving unsteadily in arcs of circles in a fiery sky. His hand fell away from his weapon, his head slowly dropped until his face rested on the leaves in which he lay. This courageous gentleman and hardy soldier was near swooning from intensity of emotion.

It was not for long; in another moment his face was raised from earth, his hands resumed their places on the rifle, his forefinger sought the trigger; mind, heart, and eyes were clear, conscience and reason sound. He could not hope to capture that enemy; to alarm him would but send him dashing to his camp with his fatal news. The duty of the soldier was plain: the man must be shot dead from ambush—without warning, without a moment's spiritual preparation, with never so much as an unspoken prayer, he must be sent to his account. But no—there is a hope; he may have discovered nothing—perhaps he is but admiring the sublimity of the landscape. If permitted, he may turn and ride carelessly away in the direction whence he came. Surely it will be possible to judge at the instant of his withdrawing whether he knows. It may well be that his fixity of attention—Druse turned his head and looked through the deeps of air downward, as from the surface to the bottom of a translucent sea. He saw creeping across the green meadow a sinuous line of figures of men and horses—some foolish commander was permitting the soldiers of his escort to water their beasts in the open, in plain view from a dozen summits!

125

Druse withdrew his eyes from the valley and fixed them again upon the man and horse in the sky, and again it was through the sights of his rifle. But this time his aim was at the horse. In his memory, as if they were a divine mandate, rang the words of his father at their parting: "Whatever may occur, do what you conceive to be your duty." He was calm now. His teeth were firmly but not rigidly closed; his nerves were as tranquil as a sleeping babe's—not a tremor affected any muscle of his body; his breathing, until suspended in the act of taking aim, was regular and slow. Duty had conquered; the spirit had said to the body: "Peace, be still." He fired.

III

An officer of the Federal force, who in a spirit of adventure or in quest of knowledge had left the hidden *bivouac* in the valley, and with aimless feet had made his way to the lower edge of a small open space near the foot of the cliff, was considering what he had to gain by pushing his exploration further. At a distance of a quarter-mile before him, but apparently at a stone's throw, rose from its fringe of pines the gigantic face of rock, towering to so great a height above him that it made him giddy to look up to where its edge cut a sharp, rugged line against the sky. It presented a clean, vertical profile against a background of blue sky to a point half the way down, and of distant hills, hardly less blue, thence to the tops of the trees at its base. Lifting his eyes to the dizzy altitude of its summit the officer saw an astonishing sight—a man on horseback riding down into the valley through the air!

Straight upright sat the rider, in military fashion, with a firm seat in the saddle, a strong clutch upon the rein to hold his charger from too impetuous a plunge. From his bare head his long hair streamed upward, waving like a plume. His hands were concealed in the cloud of the horse's lifted mane. The animal's body was as level as if every hoof-stroke encountered the resistant earth. Its motions were those of a wild gallop, but even as the officer looked they ceased, with all the legs thrown sharply forward as in the act of alighting from a leap. But this was a flight!

Filled with amazement and terror by this apparition of a horseman in the sky—half believing himself the chosen scribe of some new Apocalypse, the officer was overcome by the intensity of his emotions; his legs failed him and he fell. Almost at the same instant he heard a crashing sound in the trees—a sound that died without an echo—and all was still.

The officer rose to his feet, trembling. The familiar sensation of an abraded shin recalled his dazed faculties. Pulling himself together he ran rapidly obliquely away from the cliff to a point distant from its foot; there-about he expected to find his man; and there-about he naturally failed. In the fleeting instant of his vision his imagination had been so wrought upon by the apparent grace and ease and intention of the marvelous performance that it did not occur to him that the line of march of aërial cavalry is directly downward, and that he could find the objects of his search at the very foot of the cliff. A half-hour later he returned to camp.

This officer was a wise man; he knew better than to tell an incredible truth. He said nothing of what he had seen. But when the commander asked him if in his scout he had learned anything of advantage to the expedition he answered:

"Yes, sir; there is no road leading down into this valley from the southward."

The commander, knowing better, smiled.

IV

After firing his shot, Private Carter Druse reloaded his rifle and resumed his watch. Ten minutes had hardly passed when a Federal sergeant crept cautiously to him on hands and knees. Druse neither turned his head nor looked at him, but lay without motion or sign of recognition.

"Did you fire?" the sergeant whispered.

"Yes."

"At what?"

"A horse. It was standing on yonder rock—pretty far out. You see it is no longer there. It went over the cliff."

The man's face was white, but he showed no other sign of emotion. Having answered, he turned away his eyes and said no more. The sergeant did not understand.

"See here, Druse," he said, after a moment's silence, "it's no use making a mystery. I order you to report. Was there anybody on the horse?"

"Yes."

"Well?"

"My father."

The sergeant rose to his feet and walked away. "Good God!" he said.

Stephen Crane

Throughout his short life, Stephen Crane, the author of *The Red Badge of Courage,* tried to prove his own bravery in the eyes of his father. Once, during a camping trip with friends, he reached through the cracks of the floor of their cabin and suddenly pulled his hand out with a loud scream: "A snake bit me on the hand!" His companions laid him on a cot, cauterized his wound with a red-hot poker, and soused him in whiskey. These remedies didn't help, however, and Crane was visibly getting worse. As he bravely said a few farewells to family and friends, one of his companions suggested that, as an act of revenge, they should all seek out and kill the murderous reptile. Clutching sticks and stones, they approached the opening, when one of them shouted out, "By gosh, it's just a hen!" Everyone started to laugh hysterically; and Crane, pale on his cot, having given a fine demonstration of how a courageous man should die, then got splendidly drunk. Crane's father was not amused.

Willa Cather described Stephen Crane as a man who "drank life to the lees, but at the banquet table where other men took their ease and jested over their wine, he stood a dark and silent figure, somber as Poe himself, not wishing to be understood; and he took his portion in haste, with his loins girded, and his shoes on his feet, and his staff in his hand, like one who must depart quickly." Depart quickly he did, shortly after his twenty-ninth birthday. The poet Wallace Stevens covered his funeral for the *New York Tribune.*

THE SECOND GENERATION

stephen crane

I

Caspar Cadogan resolved to go to the tropic wars and do something. The air was blue and gold with the pomp of soldiering, and in every ear rang the music of military glory. Caspar's father was a United States Senator from the great State of Skowmulligan, where the war fever ran very high. Chill is the blood of many of the sons of millionaires, but Caspar took the fever and posted to Washington. His father had never denied him anything, and this time all that Caspar wanted was a little captaincy in the Army—just a simple little captaincy.

The old man had been entertaining a delegation of respectable bunco-steerers from Skowmulligan who had come to him on a matter which is none of the public's business.

Bottles of whiskey and boxes of cigars were still on the table in the sumptuous private parlor. The Senator had said, "Well, gentlemen, I'll do what I can for you." By this sentence he meant whatever he meant.

Then he turned to his eager son. "Well, Caspar?" The youth poured out his modest desires. It was not altogether his fault. Life had taught him a generous faith in his own abilities. If any one had told him that he was simply an ordinary damned fool he would have opened his eyes wide at the person's lack of judgment. All his life people had admired him.

The Skowmulligan war horse looked with quick disapproval into the eyes of his son. "Well, Caspar," he said slowly, "I am of the opinion that they've got all the golf experts and tennis champions and cotillion leaders and piano tuners and billiard markers that they really need as officers. Now, if you were a soldier—"

"I know," said the young man with a gesture, "but I'm not exactly a fool, I hope, and I think if I get a chance I can do something. I'd like to try. I would indeed."

The Senator lit a cigar. He assumed an attitude of ponderous reflection. "Y-yes, but this country is full of young men who are not fools. Full of 'em."

Caspar fidgeted in the desire to answer that, while he admitted the profusion of young men who were not fools, he felt that he himself possessed interesting and peculiar qualifications which would allow him to make his mark in any field of effort which he seriously challenged. But he did not make this graceful statement, for he sometimes detected something ironic in his father's temperament. The Skowmulligan war horse had not thought of expressing an opinion of his own ability since the year 1865, when he was young, like Caspar.

"Well, well," said the Senator finally. "I'll see about it. I'll see about it." The young man was obliged to await the end of his father's characteristic method of thought. The war horse never gave a quick answer, and if people tried to hurry him they seemed able to arouse only a feeling of irritation against making a decision at all. His mind moved like the wind, but practice had placed a Mexican bit in the mouth of his judgment. This old man of light, quick thought had taught himself to move like an ox cart. Caspar said, "Yes, sir." He withdrew to his club, where, to the affectionate inquiries of some envious friends, he replied, "The old man is letting the idea soak."

The mind of the war horse was decided far sooner than Caspar expected. In Washington a large number of well-bred, handsome young men were receiving appointments as lieutenants, as captains, and occasionally as majors. They were a strong, healthy, clean-eyed, educated collection. They were a prime lot. A German field marshal would have beamed with joy if he could have had them—to send to school. Anywhere in the world they would have made a grand show as material, but intrinsically they were not lieutenants, captains, and majors. They were fine men, though manhood is only an essential part of a lieutenant, a captain, or a major. But, at any rate, this arrangement had all the logic of going to sea in a bathing-machine.

The Senator found himself reasoning that Caspar was as good as any of them, and better than many. Presently he was bleating here and there that his boy should have a chance. "The boy's all right, I tell you, Henry. He's wild to go, and I don't see why they shouldn't give him a show. He's got plenty of nerve, and he's keen as a whiplash. I'm going to get him an appointment, and if you can do anything to help it along I wish you would."

Then he betook himself to the White House and the War Department and made a stir. People think that Administrations are always slavishly, abominably anxious to please the Machine. They are not; they wish the Machine sunk in red fire, for, by the power of ten thousand past words, looks, gestures, writings, the Machine comes along and takes the Administration by the nose and twists it, and the Administration dare not even yell. The huge force which carries an election to success looks reproachfully at the Administration and says, "Give me a bun." That is a very small thing with which to reward a Colossus.

The Skowmulligan war horse got his bun and took it to his hotel, where Caspar was moodily reading war rumors. "Well, my boy, here you are." Caspar was a captain and commissary on the staff of Brigadier General Reilly, commander of the Second Brigade of the First Division of the Thirtieth Army Corps.

"I had to work for it," said the Senator grimly. "They talked to me as if they thought you were some sort of empty-headed idiot. None of 'em seemed to know you personally. They

just sort of took it for granted. Finally I got pretty hot in the collar."
He paused a moment; his heavy, grooved face set hard; his blue
eyes shone. He clapped a hand down upon the handle of his chair.

"Caspar, I've got you into this thing, and I believe you'll
do all right, and I'm not saying this because I distrust either your
sense or your grit. But I want you to understand you've *got to make
a go of it*. I'm not going to talk any twaddle about your country and
your country's flag. You understand all about that. But now you're
a soldier, and there'll be this to do and that to do, and fighting to
do, and you've got to do *every damned one of 'em* right up to the
handle. I don't know how much of a shindy this thing is going to
be, but any shindy is enough to show how much there is in a man.
You've got your appointment, and that's all I can do for you; but
I'll thrash you with my own hands if, when the Army gets back,
the other fellows say my son is 'nothing but a good-looking dude.'"

He ceased, breathing heavily. Caspar looked bravely
and frankly at his father, and answered in a voice which was not
very tremulous. "I'll do my best. This is my chance. I'll do my best
with it."

The Senator had a marvelous ability of transition from
one manner to another. Suddenly he seemed very kind. "Well,
that's all right, then. I guess you'll get along all right with Reilly. I
know him well, and he'll see you through. I helped him along
once. And now about this commissary business. As I understand
it, a commissary is a sort of caterer in a big way—that is, he looks
out for a good many more things than a caterer has to bother his
head about. Reilly's brigade has probably from two to three thousand men in it, and in regard to certain things you've got to look out
for every man of 'em every day. I know perfectly well you couldn't
successfully run a boarding house in Ocean Grove. How are you
going to manage for all these soldiers, hey? Thought about it?"

"No," said Caspar, injured. "I didn't want to be a commissary. I wanted to be a captain in the line."

"They wouldn't hear of it. They said you would have to
take a staff appointment, where people could look after you."

"Well, let them look after me," cried Caspar resentfully; "but when there's any fighting to be done I guess I won't necessarily be the last man."

"That's it," responded the Senator. "That's the spirit." They both thought that the problem of war would eliminate to an equation of actual battle.

Ultimately Caspar departed into the South to an encampment in salty grass under pine trees. Here lay an Army corps twenty thousand strong. Caspar passed into the dusty sunshine of it, and for many weeks he was lost to view.

II

"Of course I don't know a blamed thing about it," said Caspar frankly and modestly to a circle of his fellow staff officers. He was referring to the duties of his office.

Their faces became expressionless; they looked at him with eyes in which he could fathom nothing. After a pause one politely said, "Don't you?" It was the inevitable two words of convention.

"Why," cried Caspar, "I didn't know what a commissary officer was until I *was* one. My old Guv'nor told me. He'd looked it up in a book somewhere, I suppose; but *I* didn't know."

"Didn't you?"

The young man's face closed with sudden humor. "Do you know, the word was intimately associated in my mind with camels. Funny, eh? I think it came from reading that rhyme of Kipling's about the commissariat camel."

"Did it?"

"Yes. Funny, isn't it? Camels!"

The brigade was ultimately landed at Siboney as part of an army to attack Santiago. The scene at the landing sometimes resembled the inspiriting daily drama at the approach to the Brooklyn Bridge. There was a great bustle, during which the wise man kept his property gripped in his hands lest it might march off into the wilderness in the pocket of one of the striding regiments. Truthfully, Caspar should have had frantic occupation, but men saw him wandering bootlessly here and there, crying, "Has anyone seen my saddlebags? Why, if I lose them I'm ruined. I've got everything packed away in 'em. Everything!"

They looked at him gloomily and without attention. "No," they said. It was to intimate that they would not give a rip if he had lost his nose, his teeth, and his self-respect. Reilly's brigade collected itself from the boats and went off, each regiment's soul burning with anger because some other regiment was in advance of it. Moving along through the scrub and under the palms, men talked mostly of things that did not pertain to the business at hand.

General Reilly finally planted his headquarters in some tall grass under a mango tree. "Where's Cadogan?" he said suddenly as he took off his hat and smoothed the wet gray hair from his brow. Nobody knew. "I saw him looking for his saddlebags down at the landing," said an officer dubiously. "Bother him," said the General contemptuously. "Let him stay there."

Three venerable regimental commanders came, saluted stiffly, and sat in the grass. There was a powwow, during which Reilly explained much that the division commander had told him. The venerable colonels nodded; they understood. Everything was smooth and clear to their minds. But still, the colonel of the Forty-fourth Regular Infantry murmured about the commissariat. His men—and then he launched forth in a sentiment concerning the privations of his men in which you were confronted with his feeling that his men—his men were the only creatures of importance in the universe, which feeling was entirely correct for him. Reilly grunted. He did what most commanders did. He set the competent line to doing the work of the incompetent part of the staff.

In time Caspar came trudging along the road merrily swinging his saddlebags. "Well, General," he cried as he saluted, "I found 'em."

"Did you?" said Reilly. Later an officer rushed to him tragically: "General, Cadogan is off there in the bushes eatin' potted ham and crackers all by himself." The officer was sent back into the bushes for Caspar, and the General sent Caspar with an order. Then Reilly and the three venerable colonels, grinning, partook of potted ham and crackers. "Tashe a' right," said Reilly, with his mouth full. "Dorsey, see if 'e got some'n else."

"Mush be selfish young pig," said one of the colonels, with his mouth full. "Who's he, General?"

"Son—Sen'tor Cad'gan—ol' frien' mine—dash 'im."

Caspar wrote a letter:

"*Dear Father:* I am sitting under a tree using the flattest part of my canteen for a desk. Even as I write the division ahead of us is moving forward and we don't know what moment the storm of battle may break out. I don't know what the plans are. General Reilly knows, but he is so good as to give me very little of his confidence. In fact, I might be part of a forlorn hope from all to the contrary I've heard from him. I understood you to say in Washington that you at one time had been of some service to him, but if that is true I can assure you he has completely forgotten it. At times his manner to me is little short of being offensive, but of course I understand that it is only the way of a crusty old soldier who has been made boorish and bearish by a long life among the Indians. I dare say I shall manage it all right without a row.

"When you hear that we have captured Santiago, please send me by first steamer a box of provisions and clothing, particularly sardines, pickles, and lightweight underwear. The other men on the staff are nice quiet chaps, but they seem a bit crude. There has been no fighting yet save the skirmish by Young's brigade. Reilly was furious because we couldn't get in it. I met General Peel yesterday. He was very nice. He said he knew you well when he was in Congress. Young Jack May is on Peel's staff. I knew him well in college. We spent an hour talking over old times. Give my love to all at home."

The march was leisurely. Reilly and his staff strolled out to the head of the long, sinuous column and entered the sultry gloom of the forest. Some less fortunate regiments had to wait among the trees at the side of the trail, and as Reilly's brigade passed them, officer called to officer, classmate to classmate, and in these greetings rang a note of everything from West Point to Alaska. They were going into an action in which they, the officers, would lose over a hundred in killed and wounded—officers alone—and these greetings, in which many nicknames occurred, were in many cases farewells such as one pictures being given with ostentation, solemnity, fervor. "There goes Gory Widgeon! Hello, Gory! Where you starting for? Hey, Gory!"

Caspar communed with himself and decided that he was not frightened. He was eager and alert; he thought that now his obligation to his country, or himself, was to be faced, and he was mad to prove to old Reilly and the others that after all he was a very capable soldier.

III

Old Reilly was stumping along the line of his brigade and mumbling like a man with a mouthful of grass. The fire from the enemy's position was incredible in its swift fury, and Reilly's brigade was getting its share of a very bad ordeal. The old man's face was the color of the tomato, and in his rage he mouthed and sputtered strangely. As he pranced along his thin line, scornfully erect, voices arose from the grass beseeching him to take care of himself. At his heels scrambled a bugler with pallid skin and clenched teeth, a chalky, trembling youth, who kept his eye on old Reilly's back and followed it.

The old gentleman was quite mad. Apparently he thought the whole thing a dreadful mess, but now that his brigade was irrevocably in it he was full-tilting here and everywhere to establish some irreproachable, immaculate kind of behavior on the part of every man-jack in his brigade. The intentions of the three venerable colonels were the same. They stood behind their lines, quiet, stern, courteous old fellows, admonishing their regiments to be very pretty in the face of such a hail of magazine-rifle and

machine-gun fire as had never in this world been confronted save
by beardless savages when the white man had found occasion to
take his burden to some new place.

And the regiments were pretty. The men lay on their
little stomachs, and got peppered according to the law, and said
nothing as the good blood pumped out into the grass; and even
if a solitary rookie tried to get a decent reason to move to some
haven of rational men, the cold voice of an officer made him look
criminal with a shame that was a credit to his regimental education. Behind Reilly's command was a bullet-torn jungle through
which it could not move as a brigade; ahead of it were Spanish
trenches on hills. Reilly considered that he was in a fix, no doubt;
but he said this only to himself. Suddenly he saw on the right
a little point of blue-shirted men already halfway up the hill. It
was some pathetic fragment of the Sixth United States Infantry.
Chagrined, shocked, horrified, Reilly bellowed to his bugler, and
the chalk-faced youth unlocked his teeth and sounded the charge
by rushes.

The men formed hastily and grimly, and rushed. Apparently there awaited them only the fate of respectable soldiers. But
they went because—of the opinions of others, perhaps. They went
because—no loud-mouthed lot of jailbirds such as the Twenty-
seventh Infantry could do anything that they could not do better.
They went because Reilly ordered it. They went because they went.

And yet not a man of them to this day has made a public speech explaining precisely how he did the whole thing and
detailing with what initiative and ability he comprehended and
defeated a situation which he did not comprehend at all.

Reilly never saw the top of the hill. He was heroically
striving to keep up with his men when a bullet ripped quietly
through his left lung, and he fell back into the arms of the bugler,
who received him as he would have received a Christmas present.
The three venerable colonels inherited the brigade in swift succession. The senior commanded for about fifty seconds, at the end of
which he was mortally shot. The junior colonel ultimately arrived

with a lean and puffing little brigade at the top of the hill. The men lay down and fired volleys at whatever was practicable.

In and out of the ditch-like trenches lay the Spanish dead, lemon-faced corpses dressed in shabby blue-and-white ticking. Some were huddled down comfortably like sleeping children; one had died in the attitude of a man flung back in a dentist's chair; one sat in the trench with his chin sunk despondently to his breast; few preserved a record of the agitation of battle. With the greater number it was as if death had touched them so gently, so lightly, that they had not known of it. Death had come to them rather in the form of an opiate than of a bloody blow.

But the arrived men in the blue shirts had no thought of the sallow corpses. They were eagerly exchanging a hail of shots with the Spanish second line, whose ash-colored entrenchments barred the way to a city white amid trees. In the pauses the men talked.

"We done the best. Old E Company got there. Why, one time the hull of B Company was *behind* us."

"Jones, he was the first man up. I saw 'im."

"Which Jones?"

"Did you see ol' Two-bars runnin' like a land crab? Made good time, too. He hit only in the high places. He's all right."

"The lootenant is all right, too. He was a good ten yards ahead of the best of us. I hated him at the post, but for this here active service there's none of 'em can touch him."

"This is mighty different from being at the post."

"Well, we done it, an' it wasn't b'cause *I* thought it could be done. When we started, I ses to m'self: 'Well, here goes a lot o' damned fools.'"

"'Tain't over yet."

"Oh, they'll never git us back from here. If they start to chase us back from here we'll pile 'em up so high the last ones can't climb over. We've come this far, an' we'll stay here. I ain't done pantin'."

"Anything is better than packin' through that jungle an' gettin' blistered from front, rear, an' both flanks. I'd rather tackle another hill than go trailin' in them woods, so thick you can't tell whether you are one man or a division of cav'lry."

"Where's that young kitchen-soldier, Cadogan, or whatever his name is? Ain't seen him today."

"Well *I* seen him. He was right in with it. He got shot, too, about half up the hill, in the leg. I seen it. He's all right. Don't worry about him. He's all right."

"I seen 'im, too. He done his stunt. As soon as I can git this piece of barbed wire entanglement out o' me throat I'll give 'm a cheer."

"He ain't shot at all, b'cause there he stands, there. See 'im?"

Rearward, the grassy slope was populous with little groups of men searching for the wounded. Reilly's brigade began to dig with its bayonets and shovel with its meat-ration cans.

IV

Senator Cadogan paced to and fro in his private parlor and smoked small brown, weak cigars. These little wisps seemed utterly inadequate to console such a ponderous satrap.

It was the evening of the Ist of July, 1898, and the Senator was immensely excited, as could be seen from the superlatively calm way in which he called out to his private secretary, who was in an adjoining room. The voice was serene, gentle, affectionate, low.

"Baker, I wish you'd go over again to the War Department and see if they've heard anything about Caspar."

A very bright-eyed, hatchet-faced young man appeared in a doorway, pen still in hand. He was hiding a nettle-like irritation behind all the finished audacity of a smirking, sharp, lying, untrustworthy young politician. "I've just got back from there, sir," he suggested.

The Skowmulligan war horse lifted his eyes and looked for a short second into the eyes of his private secretary. It was not a glare or an eagle glance; it was something beyond the practice of an actor; it was simply meaning. The clever private secretary grabbed his hat and was at once enthusiastically away. "All right, sir," he cried. "I'll find out."

The War Department was ablaze with light, and messengers were running. With the assurance of a retainer of an old house Baker made his way through much small-caliber vociferation. There was rumor of a big victory; there was rumor of a big defeat. In the corridors various watchdogs arose from their armchairs and asked him of his business in tones of uncertainty which in no wise compared with their previous habitual deference to the private secretary of the war horse of Skowmulligan.

Ultimately Baker arrived in a room where some kind of head clerk sat writing feverishly at a roll-top desk. Baker asked a question, and the head clerk mumbled profanely without lifting his head. Apparently he said: "How in the blankety-blank blazes do I know?"

The private secretary let his jaw fall. Surely some new spirit had come suddenly upon the heart of Washington—a spirit which Baker understood to be almost defiantly indifferent to the wishes of Senator Cadogan, a spirit which was not courteously oily. What could it mean? Baker's foxlike mind sprang wildly to a conception of overturned factions, changed friends, new combinations. The assurance which had come from experience of a broad political situation suddenly left him, and he would not have been amazed if someone had told him that Senator Cadogan now controlled only six votes in the State of Skowmulligan. "Well," he stammered in his bewilderment, "well—there isn't any news of the old man's son, hey?" Again the head clerk replied blasphemously.

Eventually Baker retreated in disorder from the presence of this head clerk, having learned that the latter did not give a damn if Caspar Cadogan were sailing through Hades on an ice yacht.

Baker stormed other and more formidable officials. In fact, he struck as high as he dared. They one and all flung him short, hard words, even as men pelt an annoying cur with pebbles. He emerged from the brilliant light, from the groups of men with anxious, puzzled faces, and as he walked back to the hotel he did not know if his name were Baker or Cholmondeley.

However, as he walked up the stairs to the Senator's rooms he contrived to concentrate his intellect upon a manner of speaking.

The war horse was still pacing his parlor and smoking. He paused at Baker's entrance. "Well?"

"Mr. Cadogan," said the private secretary coolly, "they told me at the Department that they did not give a cuss whether your son was alive or dead."

The Senator looked at Baker and smiled gently. "What's that, my boy?" he asked in a soft and considerate voice.

"They said—" gulped Baker, with a certain tenacity. "They said that they didn't give a cuss whether your son was alive or dead."

There was a silence for the space of three seconds. Baker stood like an image; he had no machinery for balancing the issues of this kind of situation, and he seemed to feel that if he stood as still as a stone frog he would escape the ravages of a terrible Senatorial wrath which was about to break forth in a hurricane speech which would snap off trees and sweep away barns. "Well," drawled the Senator lazily, "who did you see, Baker?"

The private secretary resumed a certain usual manner of breathing. He told the names of the men whom he had seen.

"Ye-e-es," remarked the Senator. He took another little brown cigar and held it with a thumb and first finger, staring at it with the calm and steady scrutiny of a scientist investigating a new thing. "So they don't care whether Caspar is alive or dead, eh? Well . . . maybe they don't. . . . That's all right. . . . However . . . I think I'll just look in on 'em and state my views."

When the Senator had gone, the private secretary ran to the window and leaned afar out. Pennsylvania Avenue was gleaming silver blue in the light of many arc-lamps; the cable trains groaned along to the clangor of gongs; from the window, the walks presented a hardly diversified aspect of shirtwaists and straw hats.

Sometimes a newsboy screeched.

Baker watched the tall, heavy figure of the Senator moving out to intercept a cable train. "Great Scott!" cried the private secretary to himself, "there'll be three distinct kinds of grand, plain practical fireworks. The old man is going for 'em. I wouldn't be in Lascum's boots. Ye gods, what a row there'll be."

In due time the Senator was closeted with some kind of deputy third assistant battery-horse in the offices of the War Department. The official obviously had been told off to make a supreme effort to pacify Cadogan, and he certainly was acting according to his instructions. He was almost in tears; he spread out his hands in supplication, and his voice whined and wheedled.

"Why, really, you know, Senator, we can only beg you to look at the circumstances. Two scant divisions at the top of that hill; over a thousand men killed and wounded; the line so thin that any strong attack would smash our Army to flinders. The Spaniards have probably received reinforcements under Pando; Shafter seems to be too ill to be actively in command of our troops; Lawton can't get up with his division before tomorrow. We are actually expecting . . . no, I won't say expecting . . . but we would not be surprised . . . nobody in the department would be surprised if before daybreak we were compelled to give to the country the news of a disaster which would be the worst blow the National pride has ever suffered. Don't you see? Can't you see our position, Senator?"

The Senator, with a pale but composed face, contemplated the official with eyes that gleamed in a way not usual with the big, self-controlled politician.

"I'll tell you frankly, sir," continued the other, "I'll tell you frankly that at this moment we don't know whether we are afoot or a-horseback. Everything is in the air. We don't know whether we have won a glorious victory or simply got ourselves in a deuce of a fix."

The Senator coughed. "I suppose my boy is with the two divisions at the top of that hill? He's with Reilly."

"Yes; Reilly's brigade is up there."

"And when do you suppose the War Department can tell me if he is all right? I want to know."

"My dear Senator, frankly, I don't know. Again I beg you to think of our position. The Army is in a muddle; it's a general thinking that he must fall back, and yet not sure that he *can* fall back without losing the Army. Why, we're worrying about the lives of sixteen thousand men and the self-respect of the nation, Senator."

"I see," observed the Senator, nodding his head slowly. "And naturally the welfare of one man's son doesn't—how do they say it?—doesn't cut any ice."

V

And in Cuba it rained. In a few days Reilly's brigade discovered that by their successful charge they had gained the inestimable privilege of sitting in a wet trench and slowly but surely starving to death. Men's tempers crumbled like dry bread. The soldiers who so cheerfully, quietly, and decently had captured positions which the foreign experts had said were impregnable, now in turn underwent an attack which was furious as well as insidious. The heat of the sun alternated with rains which boomed and roared in their falling like mountain cataracts. It seemed as if men took the fever through sheer lack of other occupation. During the days of battle none had had time to get even a tropic headache, but no sooner was that brisk period over than men began to shiver and shudder by squads and platoons. Rations were scarce enough to make a little fat strip of bacon seem of the size of a corner lot, and coffee grains were pearls. There would have been godless quarreling over fragments if it were not that with these fevers came a great listlessness, so that men were almost content to die if death required no exertion.

It was an occasion which distinctly separated the sheep from the goats. The goats were few enough, but their qualities glared out like crimson spots.

One morning Jameson and Ripley, two captains in the

Forty-fourth Foot, lay under a flimsy shelter of sticks and palm branches. Their dreamy, dull eyes contemplated the men in the trench which went to left and right. To them came Caspar Cadogan, moaning. "By Jove," he said, as he flung himself wearily on the ground, "I can't stand much more of this, you know. It's killing me." A bristly beard sprouted through the grime on his face; his eyelids were crimson; an indescribably dirty shirt fell away from his roughened neck; and at the same time various lines of evil and greed were deepened on his face, until he practically stood forth as a revelation, a confession. "I can't stand it. By Jove, I can't."

Stanford, a lieutenant under Jameson, came stumbling along toward them. He was a lad of the class of '98 at West Point. It could be seen that he was flaming with fever. He rolled a calm eye at them. "Have you any water, sir?" he said to his captain. Jameson got upon his feet and helped Stanford to lay his shaking length under the shelter. "No, boy," he answered gloomily. "Not a drop. You got any, Rip?"

"No," answered Ripley, looking with anxiety upon the young officer. "Not a drop."

"You, Cadogan?"

Here Caspar hesitated oddly for a second, and then in a tone of deep regret made answer, "No, Captain; not a mouthful."

Jameson moved off weakly. "You lay quietly, Stanford, and I'll see what I can rustle."

Presently Caspar felt that Ripley was steadily regarding him. He returned the look with one of half-guilty questioning.

"God forgive you, Cadogan," said Ripley, "but you are a damned beast. Your canteen is full of water."

Even then the apathy in their veins prevented the scene from becoming as sharp as the words sounded. Caspar sputtered like a child, and at length merely said: "No, it isn't." Stanford lifted his head to shoot a keen, proud glance at Caspar and then turned away his face.

"You lie," said Ripley. "I can tell the sound of a full canteen as far as I can hear it."

"Well, if it is, I—I must have forgotten it."

"You lie; no man in this Army just now forgets whether his canteen is full or empty. Hand it over."

Fever is the physical counterpart of shame, and when a man has the one he accepts the other with an ease which would revolt his healthy self. However, Caspar made a desperate struggle to preserve the forms. He arose and, taking the string from his shoulder, passed the canteen to Ripley. But after all there was a whine in his voice, and the assumption of dignity was really a farce. "I think I had better go, Captain. You can have the water if you want it, I'm sure. But—but I fail to see—I fail to see what reason you have for insulting me."

"Do you?" said Ripley stolidly. "That's all right."

Caspar stood for a terrible moment. He simply did not have the strength to turn his back on this—this affair. It seemed to him that he must stand for ever and face it. But when he found the audacity to look again at Ripley he saw the latter was not at all concerned with the situation. Ripley, too, had the fever. The fever changes all laws of proportion. Caspar went away.

"Here, youngster; here is your drink."

Stanford made a weak gesture. "I wouldn't touch a drop from his blamed canteen if it was the last water in the world," he murmured in his high, boyish voice.

"Don't you be a young jackass," quoth Ripley tenderly.

The boy stole a glance at the canteen. He felt the propriety of arising and hurling it after Caspar, but—he, too, had the fever.

"Don't you be a young jackass," said Ripley again.

VI

Senator Cadogan was happy. His son had returned from Cuba, and the 8:30 train that evening would bring him to the station nearest to the stone and red shingle villa which the Senator and his family occupied on the shores of Long Island Sound. The Senator's steam yacht lay some hundred yards from the beach. She had just returned from a trip to Montauk Point,

145

where the Senator had made a gallant attempt to gain his son from the transport on which he was coming from Cuba. He had fought a brave sea fight with sundry petty little doctors and ship's officers, who had raked him with broadsides, describing the laws of quarantine, and had used inelegant speech to a United States Senator as he stood on the bridge of his own steam yacht. These men had grimly asked him to tell exactly how much better was Caspar than any other returning soldier.

But the Senator had not given them a long fight. In fact, the truth came to him quickly, and with almost a blush he had ordered the yacht back to her anchorage off the villa. As a matter of fact, the trip to Montauk Point had been undertaken largely from impulse. Long ago the Senator had decided that when his boy returned the greeting should have something Spartan in it. He would make a welcome such as most soldiers get. There should be no flowers and carriages when the other poor fellows got none. He should consider Caspar as a soldier. That was the way to treat a man. But in the end a sharp acid of anxiety had worked upon the iron old man, until he had ordered the yacht to take him out and make a fool of him. The result filled him with a chagrin which caused him to delegate to the mother and sisters the entire business of succoring Caspar at Montauk Point Camp. He had remained at home conducting the huge correspondence of an active national politician and waiting for this son whom he so loved and whom he so wished to be a man of a certain strong, taciturn, shrewd ideal. The recent yacht voyage he now looked upon as a kind of confession of his weakness, and he was resolved that no more signs should escape him.

But yet his boy had been down there against the enemy and among the fevers. There had been grave perils, and his boy must have faced them. And he could not prevent himself from dreaming through the poetry of fine actions, in which visions his son's face shone out manly and generous. During these periods the people about him, accustomed as they were to his silence and calm in time of stress, considered that affairs in Skowmulligan might be most critical. In no other way could they account for this

146

exaggerated phlegm.

On the night of Caspar's return he did not go to dinner, but had a tray sent to his library, where he remained writing. At last he heard the spin of the dogcart's wheels on the gravel of the drive, and a moment later there penetrated to him the sound of joyful feminine cries. He lit another cigar; he knew that it was now his part to bide with dignity the moment when his son should shake off that other welcome and come to him. He could still hear them; in their exuberance they seemed to be capering like school-children. He was impatient, but this impatience took the form of a polar stolidity.

Presently there were quick steps and a jubilant knock at his door. "Come in," he said.

In came Caspar, thin, yellow, and in soiled khaki. "They almost tore me to pieces," he cried, laughing. "They danced around like wild things." Then as they shook hands he dutifully said: "How are you, sir?"

"How are you, my boy?" answered the Senator, casually but kindly.

"Better than I might expect, sir," cried Caspar cheerfully. "We had a pretty hard time, you know."

"You look as if they'd given you a hard run," observed the father in a tone of slight interest.

Caspar was eager to tell. "Yes, sir," he said rapidly. "We did, indeed. Why, it was awful. We—any of us—were lucky to get out of it alive. It wasn't so much the Spaniards, you know. The Army took care of them all right. It was the fever and the—you know, we couldn't get anything to eat. And the mismanagement. Why, it was frightful."

"Yes, I've heard," said the Senator. A certain wistful look came into his eyes but he did not allow it to become prominent. Indeed, he suppressed it. "And you, Caspar? I suppose you did your duty?"

Caspar answered with becoming modesty. "Well, I didn't do more than anybody else, I don't suppose, but—well, I got along all right, I guess."

"And this great charge up San Juan Hill?" asked the father slowly. "Were you in that?"

"Well—yes; I was in it," replied the son.

The Senator brightened a trifle. "You were, eh? In the front of it? or just sort of going along?"

"Well—I don't know. I couldn't tell exactly. Sometimes I was in front of a lot of them, and sometimes I was—just sort of going along."

This time the Senator emphatically brightened. "That's all right, then. And of course—of course you performed your commissary duties correctly?"

The question seemed to make Caspar uncommunicative and sulky. "I did when there was anything to do," he answered. "But the whole thing was on the most unbusinesslike basis you can imagine. And they wouldn't tell you anything. Nobody would take time to instruct you in your duties, and of course if you didn't know a thing your superior officer would swoop down on you and ask you why in the deuce such and such a thing wasn't done in such and such a way. Of course I did the best I could."

The Senator's countenance had again become somberly indifferent. "I see. But you weren't directly rebuked for incapacity, were you? No; of course you weren't. But—I mean—did any of your superior officers suggest that you were 'no good,' or anything of that sort? I mean—did you come off with a clean slate?"

Caspar took a small time to digest his father's meaning. "Oh, yes, sir," he cried at the end of his reflection. "The commissary was in such a hopeless mess anyhow that nobody thought of doing anything but curse Washington."

"Of course," rejoined the Senator harshly. "But supposing that you had been a competent and well-trained commissary officer. What then?"

Again the son took time for consideration, and in the end deliberately replied: "Well, if I had been a competent and well-trained commissary I would have sat there and eaten up my heart and cursed Washington."

"Well, then, that's all right. And now, about this charge up San Juan. Did any of the generals speak to you afterward and say that you had done well? Didn't any of them see you?"

"Why, n-n-no, I don't suppose they did . . . any more than I did them. You see, this charge was a big thing and covered lots of ground, and I hardly saw anybody excepting a lot of men."

"Well, but didn't any of the men see you? Weren't you ahead some of the time leading them on and waving your sword?"

Caspar burst into laughter. "Why, no. I had all I could do to scramble along and try to keep up. And I didn't want to go up at all."

"Why?" demanded the Senator.

"Because—because the Spaniards were shooting so much. And you could see men falling, and the bullets rushed around you in—by the bushel. And then at last it seemed that if we once drove them away from the top of the hill there would be less danger. So we all went up."

The Senator chuckled over this description. "And you didn't flinch at all?"

"Well," rejoined Caspar humorously, "I won't say I wasn't frightened."

"No, of course not. But then, you did not let anybody know it?"

"Of course not."

"You understand, naturally, that I am bothering you with all these questions because I desire to hear how my only son behaved in the crisis. I don't want to worry you with it. But if you went through the San Juan charge with credit I'll have you made a major."

"Well," said Caspar. "I wouldn't say I went through that charge with credit. I went through it all good enough, but the enlisted men around went through in the same way."

"But weren't you encouraging them and leading them

149

on by your example?"

Caspar smirked. He began to see a point. "Well, sir," he said with a charming hesitation, "aw—er—I—well, I dare say I was doing my share of it."

The perfect form of the reply delighted the father. He could not endure blatancy; his admiration was to be won only by a bashful hero. Now he beat his hand impulsively down upon the table. "That's what I wanted to know. That's it exactly. I'll have you made a major next week. You've found your proper field at last. You stick to the Army, Caspar, and I'll back you up. That's the thing. In a few years it will be a great career. The United States is pretty sure to have an Army of about a hundred and fifty thousand men. And, starting in when you did and with me to back you up—why, we'll make you a General in seven or eight years. That's the ticket. You stay in the Army." The Senator's cheek was flushed with enthusiasm, and he looked eagerly and confidently at his son.

But Caspar had pulled a long face. "The Army?" he said. "Stay in the Army?"

The Senator continued to outline quite rapturously his idea of the future. "The Army, evidently, is just the place for you. You know as well as I do that you have not been a howling success, exactly, in anything else which you have tried. But now the Army just suits you. It is the kind of career which especially suits you. Well, then, go in, and go at it hard. Go in to win. Go at it."

"But—" began Caspar.

The Senator interrupted swiftly. "Oh, don't worry about that part of it. I'll take care of all that. You won't get jailed in some Arizona adobe for the rest of your natural life. There won't be much more of that, anyhow; and besides, as I say, I'll look after all that end of it. The chance is splendid. A young, healthy, and intelligent man, with the start you've already got, and with my backing, can do anything—anything! There will be a lot of active service—oh, yes, I'm sure of it—and everybody who—"

"But," said Caspar, wan, desperate, heroic, "father, I

don't care to stay in the Army."

The Senator lifted his eyes and darkened. "What?" he said. "What's that?" He looked at Caspar.

The son became tightened and wizened like an old miser trying to withhold gold. He replied with a sort of idiot obstinacy, "I don't care to stay in the Army."

The Senator's jaw clenched down, and he was dangerous. But, after all, there was something mournful somewhere. "Why, what do you mean?" he asked gruffly.

"Why, I couldn't get along, you know. The—the—"

"The what?" demanded the father, suddenly uplifted with thunderous anger. "The what?"

Caspar's pain found a sort of outlet in mere irresponsible talk. "Well, you know—the other men, you know. I couldn't get along with them, you know. They're peculiar, somehow; odd; I didn't understand them, and they didn't understand me. We—we didn't hitch, somehow. They're a queer lot. They've got funny ideas. I don't know how to explain it exactly, but—somehow—I don't like 'em. That's all there is to it. They're good fellows enough, I know, but—"

"Oh, well, Caspar," interrupted the Senator. Then he seemed to weigh a great fact in his mind. "I guess—" He paused again in profound consideration. "I guess—" He lit a small brown cigar. "I guess you are no damn good."

December 2, 1899

Rose Tremain

A German folktale, collected by the brothers Grimm in the early nineteenth century but probably much older, tells of a carpenter who feeds his old father from a wooden bowl rather than a china plate deemed too fragile for the old man's trembling hands. Seeing this, the carpenter's son goes out into the yard and with his little axe begins to hack away at a large log. "What are you doing, my son?" asks the carpenter, bemused at the boy's earnest activity. The boy answered, "I'm building a trough for you to eat out of when you are old and feeble as grandfather."

We don't know how our lessons will be learned by our children. Our actions bear many translations, and we are seldom prepared to step into our own parents' place. In Rose Tremain's "Over," love and callousness, reflection and retribution, share the same actions and events, and it is almost impossible to make out where one begins and the other ends. Throughout her novels and short stories, Rose Tremain has explored these dubious areas, whether in contemporary settings or in the past, carefully avoiding taking sides with any one interpretation of the facts. In Colossians 3:21, Saint Paul warned, "Fathers, provoke not your children to anger, lest they be discouraged." This warning could stand as the epigraph of the following story.

OVER

rose tremain

waking is the hardest thing they ask of him.
The nurse always wakes him with the word 'morning,'
and the word 'morning' brings a hurting into his head which he
cannot control or ameliorate or do anything about. Very often, the
word 'morning' interrupts his dreams. In these dreams there was a
stoat somewhere. This is all he can say about them.

The nurse opens his mouth, which tastes of seed and
fills it with teeth. 'These teeth have got too big for me,' he sometimes remarks, but neither the nurse nor his wife replies to this
just as neither the nurse nor his wife laughs when from some part
of his ancient self he brings out a joke he did not know he could
still remember. He isn't even certain they smile at his jokes
because he can't see faces any longer unless they are no more and
no less than two feet from his eyes. 'Aren't you even smiling?' he
sometimes shouts.

'I'm smiling, Sir,' says the nurse.

'Naturally, I'm smiling,' says his wife.

His curtains are drawn back and light floods into the
room. To him, light is time. Until nightfall, it lies on his skin,
seeping just a little into the pores yet never penetrating inside
him, neither into his brain nor into his heart nor into any crevice

or crease of him. Light and time, time and light lie on him as weightless as the sheet. He is somewhere else. He is in the place where the jokes come from, where the dreams of stoats lie. He refuses ever to leave it except upon one condition.

That condition is so seldom satisfied, yet every morning, after his teeth are in, he asks the nurse: 'Is my son coming today?'

'Not that I know of, Sir,' she replies.

So then he takes no notice of the things he does. He eats his boiled egg. He pisses into a jar. He puts a kiss as thin as air on his wife's cheek. He tells the nurse the joke about the talking dog. He folds his arms across his chest. He dreams of being asleep.

But once in a while—once a fortnight perhaps, or once a month?—the nurse will say as she lifts him up on to his pillows: 'Your son's arrived, Sir.'

154

Then he'll reach up and try to neaten the silk scarf he wears at his throat. He will ask for his window to be opened wider. He will sniff the room and wonder if it doesn't smell peculiarly of water-weed.

The son is a big man, balding, with kind eyes. Always and without fail he arrives in the room with a bottle of champagne and two glasses held upside down, between his first and second fingers.

'How are you?' he asks.

'That's a stupid question,' says the father.

The son sits by the bed and the father looks and looks for him with his faded eyes and they sip the drink. Neither the nurse nor the wife disturbs them.

'Stay a bit,' says the father, 'won't you?'

'I can't stay long,' says the son.

Sometimes the father weeps without knowing it. All he knows is that with his son here, time is no longer a thing that covers him, but an element in which he floats and which fills his head and his heart until he is both brimming with it and buoyant on the current of it.

When the champagne has all been drunk, the son and the nurse carry the father downstairs and put him into the son's

Jaguar and cover his knees with a rug. The father and the son drive off down the Hampshire lanes. Light falls in dapples on the old man's temples and on his folded hands.

There was a period of years that arrived as the father was beginning to get old when the son went to work in the Middle East and came home only once or twice a year, bringing presents made in Japan which the father did not trust.

It was then that the old man began his hatred of time. He couldn't bear to see anything endure. What he longed for was for things to be over. He did the *Times* crossword only to fill up the waiting spaces. He read the newspaper only to finish it and fold it and place it in the waste-paper basket. He snipped off from the rose bushes not only the dead heads but the blooms that were still living. At mealtimes, he cleared the cutlery from the table before the meal was finished. He drove out with his wife to visit friends to find that he longed, upon arrival, for the moment of departure. When he made his bed in the morning, he would put on the bedcover then turn it down again, ready for the night.

His wife watched and suffered. She felt he was robbing her of life. She was his second wife, less beautiful and less loved than the first (the mother of his son) who had been a dancer and who had liked to spring into his arms from a sequence of three cartwheels. He sometimes dismayed the second wife by telling her about the day when the first wife did a cartwheel in the revolving doors of the Ritz. 'I've heard that story, darling,' she'd say politely, ashamed for him that he could tell it so proudly. And to her bridge friends she'd confide: 'It is as if he believes that by rushing through the *now* he'll get back to the *then*.'

He began a practice of adding things up. He would try to put a finite number on the oysters he had eaten since the war. He counted the cigarettes his wife smoked in a day and the number of times she mislaid her lighter. He tried to make a sum of the remembered cartwheels. Then when he had done these additions, he would draw a neat line through them, like the line a captive

155

draws through each recorded clutch of days, and fold the paper in half and then in quarters and so on until it could not be folded any smaller and then place it carefully in the waste-paper basket next to the finished *Times*.

'Now we know,' the wife once heard him mutter. 'Now we know all about it.'

When the war ended he was still married to the dancer. His son was five years old. They lived in a manor house with an ancient tennis court and an east-facing croquet lawn. Though his head was still full of the war, he had a touching faith in the future and he usually knew, as each night descended, that he was looking forward to the day.

Very often, in the summer of 1946, he would wake when the sun came up and, leaving the dancer sleeping, would go out on to the croquet lawn wearing his dressing gown and his slippers from Simpson's of Piccadilly and stare at the dew on the grass, at the shine on the croquet hoops and at the sky, turning. He had the feeling that he and the world made a handsome pair.

One morning he saw a stoat on the lawn. The stoat was running round the croquet hoops and then in and out of them in a strange repeated pattern, as if it were taking part in a stoat gymkhana. The man did not move, but stood and watched. Then he backed off into the house and ran up the stairs to the room where his son was sleeping.

'Wake up!' he said to the little boy. 'I've got something to show you.'

He took his son's hand and led him barefoot down the stairs and into the garden. The stoat was still running round and through the croquet hoops, jumping twice its height into the air and rolling over in a somersault as it landed, then flicking its tail as it turned and ran in for another leap.

The boy, still dizzy with sleep, opened his mouth and opened wide his blue eyes. He knew he must not move so he did not even look round when his father left his side and went back into the house. He shivered a little in the dewy air. He wanted to creep forward so that he could be in the sun. He tiptoed out across the gravel that hurt his feet on to the soft wet lawn. The stoat saw him and whipped its body to a halt, head up, tail flat, regarding the boy. The boy could see its eyes. He thought how sleek and slippery it looked and how he would like to stroke its head with his finger.

The father returned. 'Don't move,' he whispered to his son, so the boy did not turn.

The father took aim with his shotgun and fired. He hit the stoat right in the head and its body flew up into the air before it fell without a sound. The man laughed with joy at the cleanness and beauty of the shot. He laughed a loud, happy laugh and then looked down at his son to get his approval. But the boy was not there. The boy had walked back inside the house, leaving his father alone in the bright morning.

Anita Desai

Through his craft, a writer can help the sons he has created in fiction help their fictional father. In 300 B.C., the Sanskrit poet Valmiki, author of the *Ramayana,* tells of the sons of the god Rama searching for their father. In the woods they meet Valmiki himself, who teaches them using his own *Ramayana.* Valmiki and his disciples arrive at a feast given by Rama, where Rama's sons sing the poem. Rama hears them and, revealed by the poet's words, recognizes his sons.

Brought up in a German-Indian family in Delhi, Anita Desai lived in a world that combined European backdrops (the windblown moors of the Brontës, the lakes and pine forests of Heine, the steppes and dachas of Chekhov) with the homescape of her India: "verandas and plastered walls and ceiling fans, its garden of papaya and guava trees full of shrieking parakeets, the gritty dust that settled on the pages of a book before one could turn them." In such a brindled landscape, her characters partake of the best and worst of both worlds as they try valiantly to survive. As Salman Rushdie observed writing about Desai's work, "what seems to be a story of inevitable tragedies [as in "A Devoted Son"] turns out to be a tale of triumph over these tragedies."

A DEVOTED SON

anita desai

when the results appeared in the morning
papers, Rakesh scanned them, barefoot and in his pyjamas, at
the garden gate, then went up the steps to the veranda where
his father sat sipping his morning tea and bowed down to touch
his feet.

'A first division, son?' his father asked, beaming, reaching for the papers.

'At the top of the list, Papa,' Rakesh murmured, as if
awed. 'First in the country.'

Bedlam broke loose then. The family whooped and
danced. The whole day long visitors streamed into the small yellow house at the end of the road, to congratulate the parents of
this *Wunderkind,* to slap Rakesh on the back and fill the house
and garden with the sounds and colours of a festival. There were
garlands and *halwa,* party clothes and gifts (enough fountain pens
to last years, even a watch or two), nerves and temper and joy, all
in a multicoloured whirl of pride and great shining vistas newly
opened: Rakesh was the first son in the family to receive an education, so much had been sacrificed in order to send him to school
and then medical college, and at last the fruits of their sacrifice
had arrived, golden and glorious.

To everyone who came to him to say, '*Mubarak, Varma-ji,* your son has brought you glory,' the father said, 'Yes, and do you know what is the first thing he did when he saw the results this morning? He came and touched my feet. He bowed down and touched my feet.' This moved many of the women in the crowd so much that they were seen to raise the ends of their saris and dab at their tears while the men reached out for the betel leaves and sweetmeats that were offered around on trays and shook their heads in wonder and approval of such exemplary filial behaviour. 'One does not often see such behaviour in sons any more,' they all agreed, a little enviously perhaps. Leaving the house, some of the women said, sniffing, 'At least on such an occasion they might have served pure *ghee* sweets,' and some of the men said, 'Don't you think old Varma was giving himself airs? He needn't think we don't remember that he comes from the vegetable market himself, his father used to sell vegetables, and he has never seen the inside of a school.' But there was more envy than rancour in their voices and it was, of course, inevitable—not every son in that shabby little colony at the edge of the city was destined to shine as Rakesh shone, and who knew that better than the parents themselves?

And that was only the beginning, the first step in a great, sweeping ascent to the radiant heights of fame and fortune. The thesis he wrote for his M.D. brought Rakesh still greater glory, if only in select medical circles. He won a scholarship. He went to the U.S.A. (that was what his father learnt to call it and taught the whole family to say—not America, which was what the ignorant neighbours called it, but, with a grand familiarity, 'the U.S.A.') where he pursued his career in the most prestigious of all hospitals and won encomiums from his American colleagues which were relayed to his admiring and glowing family. What was more, he came *back*, he actually returned to that small yellow house in the once-new but increasingly shabby colony, right at the end of the road where the rubbish vans tipped out their stinking contents for pigs to nose in and rag-pickers to build their shacks on, all steaming and smoking just outside the neat wire fences and well-tended gardens. To this Rakesh returned and the first thing he did on entering the house was to slip out of the embraces of his sisters and brothers and bow down and touch his father's feet.

As for his mother, she gloated chiefly over the strange fact that he had not married in America, had not brought home a foreign wife as all her neighbours had warned her he would, for wasn't that what all Indian boys went abroad for? Instead, he agreed, almost without argument, to marry a girl she had picked out for him in her own village, the daughter of a childhood friend, a plump and uneducated girl, it was true, but so old-fashioned, so placid, so complaisant that she slipped into the household and settled in like a charm, seemingly too lazy and too good-natured to even try and make Rakesh leave home and set up independently, as any other girl might have done. What was more, she was pretty—really pretty, in a plump, pudding way that only gave way to fat—soft, spreading fat, like warm wax—after the birth of their first baby, a son, and then what did it matter?

For some years Rakesh worked in the city hospital, quickly rising to the top of the administrative organization, and was made a director before he left to set up his own clinic. He took his parents in his car—a new, sky-blue Ambassador with a rear window full of stickers and charms revolving on strings—to see the clinic when it was built, and the large sign-board over the door on which his name was printed in letters of red, with a row of degrees and qualifications to follow it like so many little black slaves of the regent. Thereafter his fame seemed to grow just a little dimmer—or maybe it was only that everyone in town had grown accustomed to it at last—but it was also the beginning of his fortune for he now became known not only as the best but also the richest doctor in town.

However, all this was not accomplished in the wink of an eye. Naturally not. It was the achievement of a lifetime and it took up Rakesh's whole life. At the time he set up his clinic his father had grow into an old man and retired from his post at the kerosene dealer's depot at which he had worked for forty years, and his mother died soon after, giving up the ghost with a sigh that sounded positively happy, for it was her own son who ministered to her in her last illness and who sat pressing her feet at the last moment—such a son as few women had borne.

For it had to be admitted—and the most unsuccessful and most rancorous of neighbours eventually did so—that Rakesh was not only a devoted son and a miraculously good-natured man who contrived somehow to obey his parents and humour his wife and show concern equally for his children and his patients, but there was actually a brain inside this beautifully polished and formed body of good manners and kind nature and, in between ministering to his family and playing host to many friends and coaxing them all into feeling happy and grateful and content, he had actually trained his hands as well and emerged an excellent doctor, a really fine surgeon. How one man—and a man born to illiterate parents, his father having worked for a kerosene dealer and his mother having spent her life in a kitchen—had achieved, combined and conducted such a medley of virtues, no one could fathom, but all acknowledged his talent and skill.

It was a strange fact, however, that talent and skill, if displayed for too long, cease to dazzle. It came to pass that the most admiring of all eyes eventually faded and no longer blinked at his glory. Having retired from work and having lost his wife, the old father very quickly went to pieces, as they say. He developed so many complaints and fell ill so frequently and with such mysterious diseases that even his son could no longer make out when it was something of significance and when it was merely a peevish whim. He sat huddled on his string bed most of the day and developed an exasperating habit of stretching out suddenly and lying absolutely still, allowing the whole family to fly around him in a flap, wailing and weeping, and then suddenly sitting up, stiff and gaunt, and spitting out a big gob of betel juice as if to mock their behaviour.

He did this once too often: there had been a big party in the house, a birthday party for the youngest son, and the celebrations had to be suddenly hushed, covered up and hustled out of the way when the daughter-in-law discovered, or thought she discovered, that the old man stretched out from end to end of his string bed, had lost his pulse; the party broke up, dissolved, even turned into a band of mourners, when the old man sat up and the distraught daughter-in-law received a gob of red spittle right on the hem of her new organza sari. After that no one much cared if he sat up cross-legged on his bed, hawking and spitting, or lay down flat and turned grey as a corpse. Except, of course, for that pearl amongst pearls, his son Rakesh.

It was Rakesh who brought him his morning tea, not in one of the china cups from which the rest of the family drank, but in the old man's favourite brass tumbler, and sat at the edge of his bed, comfortable and relaxed with the string of his pyjamas dangling out from under his fine lawn night-shirt, and discussed or, rather, read out the morning news to his father. It made no difference to him that his father made no response apart from spitting. It was Rakesh, too, who, on returning from the clinic in the evening, persuaded the old man to come out of his room, as bare and desolate as a cell, and take the evening air out in the garden, beautifully arranging the pillows and bolsters on the divan in the corner of the open veranda. On summer nights he saw to it that the servants carried out the old man's bed onto the lawn and himself helped his father down the steps and onto the bed, soothing him and settling him down for a night under the stars.

All this was very gratifying for the old man. What was not so gratifying was that he even undertook to supervise his father's diet. One day when the father was really sick, having ordered his daughter-in-law to make him a dish of *soojie halwa* and eaten it with a saucerful of cream, Rakesh marched into the room, not with his usual respectful step but with the confident and rather contemptuous stride of the famous doctor, and declared, 'No more *halwa* for you, Papa. We must be sensible, at your age. If you must have something sweet, Veena will cook you a little *kheer,* that's light, just a little rice and milk. But nothing fried, nothing rich. We can't have this happening again.'

163

The old man who had been lying stretched out on his bed, weak and feeble after a day's illness, gave a start at the very sound, the tone of these words. He opened his eyes—rather, they fell open with shock—and he stared at his son with disbelief that darkened quickly to reproach. A son who actually refused his father the food he craved? No, it was unheard of, it was incredible. But Rakesh had turned his back to him and was cleaning up the litter of bottles and packets on the medicine shelf and did not notice while Veena slipped silently out of the room with a little smirk that only the old man saw, and hated.

Halwa was only the first item to be crossed off the old man's diet. One delicacy after the other went—everything fried to begin with, then everything sweet, and eventually everything, everything that the old man enjoyed. The meals that arrived for him on the shining stainless steel tray twice a day were frugal to say the least—dry bread, boiled lentils, boiled vegetables and, if there were a bit of chicken or fish, that was boiled too. If he called for another helping—in a cracked voice that quavered theatrically—Rakesh himself would come to the door, gaze at him sadly and shake his head, saying, 'Now, Papa, we must be careful, we can't risk another illness, you know,' and although the daughter-in-law kept tactfully out of the way, the old man could just see her smirk sliding merrily through the air. He tried to bribe his grandchildren into buying him sweets (and how he missed his wife now, that generous, indulgent and illiterate cook), whispering, 'Here's fifty *paise'* as he stuffed the coins into a tight, hot fist. 'Run down to the shop at the crossroads and buy me thirty *paise* worth of *jalebis,* and you can spend the remaining twenty *paise* on yourself. Eh? Understand? Will you do that?' He got away with it once or twice but then was found out, the conspirator was scolded by his father and smacked by his mother and Rakesh came storming into the room, almost tearing his hair as he shouted through compressed lips, 'Now, Papa, are you trying to turn my little son into a liar? Quite apart from spoiling your own stomach, you are spoiling him as well—you are encouraging him to lie to his own parents.

You should have heard the lies he told his mother when she saw him bringing back those *jalebis* wrapped up in filthy newspaper. I don't allow anyone in my house to buy sweets in the bazaar, Papa, surely you know that. There's cholera in the city, typhoid, gastro-enteritis—I see these cases daily in the hospital, how can I allow my own family to run such risks?' The old man sighed and lay down in the corpse position. But that worried no one any longer.

There was only one pleasure left the old man now (his son's early morning visits and readings from the newspaper could no longer be called that) and those were visits from elderly neighbours. These were not frequent as his contemporaries were mostly as decrepit and helpless as he and few could walk the length of the road to visit him any more. Old Bhatia, next door, however, who was still spry enough to refuse, adamantly, to bathe in the tiled bathroom indoors and to insist on carrying out his brass mug and towel, in all seasons and usually at impossible hours, into the yard and bathe noisily under the garden tap, would look over the hedge to see if Varma were out on his veranda and would call to him and talk while he wrapped his *dhoti* about him and dried the sparse hair on his head, shivering with enjoyable exaggeration. Of course these conversations, bawled across the hedge by two rather deaf old men conscious of having their entire households over-hearing them, were not very satisfactory but Bhatia occasionally came out of his yard, walked down the bit of road and came in at Varma's gate to collapse onto the stone plinth built under the temple tree. If Rakesh were at home he would help his father down the steps into the garden and arrange him on his night bed under the tree and leave the two old men to chew betel leaves and discuss the ills of their individual bodies with combined passion.

'At least you have a doctor in the house to look after you,' sighed Bhatia, having vividly described his martyrdom to piles.

'Look after me?' cried Varma, his voice cracking like an ancient clay jar. 'He—he does not even give me enough to eat.'

'What?' said Bhatia, the white hairs in his ears twitching. 'Doesn't give you enough to eat? Your own son?'

'My own son. If I ask him for one more piece of bread, he says no, Papa, I weighed out the *ata* myself and I can't allow you to have more than two hundred grammes of cereal a day. He *weighs* the food he gives me, Bhatia—he has scales to weigh it on. That is what it has come to.'

'Never,' murmured Bhatia in disbelief. 'Is it possible, even in this evil age, for a son to refuse his father food?'

'Let me tell you,' Varma whispered eagerly. 'Today the family was having fried fish—I could smell it. I called to my daughter-in-law to bring me a piece. She came to the door and said No . . .'

'Said No?' It was Bhatia's voice that cracked. A *drongo* shot out of the tree and sped away. '*No?*'

'No, she said no, Rakesh has ordered her to give me nothing fried. No butter, he says, no oil—'

'No butter? No oil? How does he expect his father to *live?*'

Old Varma nodded with melancholy triumph. 'That is how he treats me—after I have brought him up, given him an education, made him a great doctor. Great doctor! This is the way great doctors treat their fathers, Bhatia,' for the son's sterling personality and character now underwent a curious sea change. Outwardly all might be the same but the interpretation had altered: his masterly efficiency was nothing but cold heartlessness, his authority was only tyranny in disguise.

There was cold comfort in complaining to neighbours and, on such a miserable diet, Varma found himself slipping, weakening and soon becoming a genuinely sick man. Powders and pills and mixtures were not only brought in when dealing with a crisis like an upset stomach but became a regular part of his diet—became his diet, complained Varma, supplanting the natural foods he craved. There were pills to regulate his bowel movements, pills to bring down his blood pressure, pills to deal with his arthritis and, eventually, pills to keep his heart beating. In between there were panicky rushes to the hospital, some humiliating experiences with the stomach pump and enema, which left him frightened and helpless. He cried easily, shrivelling up on his bed, but if he complained of a pain or even a vague, grey fear in the night, Rakesh would simply open another bottle of pills and force him to take one. 'I have my duty to you, Papa,' he said when his father begged to be let off.

'Let me be,' Varma begged, turning his face away from the pills on the outstretched hand. 'Let me die. It would be better. I do not want to live only to eat your medicines.'

'Papa, be reasonable.'

'I leave that to you,' the father cried with sudden spirit. 'Let me alone, let me die now, I cannot live like this.'

'Lying all day on his pillows, fed every few hours by his daughter-in-law's own hands, visited by every member of his family daily—and then he says he does not want to live "like this,"' Rakesh was heard to say, laughing, to someone outside the door.

'Deprived of food,' screamed the old man on the bed, 'his wishes ignored, taunted by his daughter-in-law, laughed at by his grandchildren—*that* is how I live.' But he was very old and weak and all anyone heard was an incoherent croak, some expressive grunts and cries of genuine pain. Only once, when old Bhatia had come to see him and they sat together under the temple tree, they heard him cry, 'God is calling me—and they won't let me go.'

The quantities of vitamins and tonics he was made to take were not altogether useless. They kept him alive and even gave him a kind of strength that made him hang on long after he ceased to wish to hang on. It was as though he were straining at a rope, trying to break it, and it would not break, it was still strong. He only hurt himself, trying.

In the evening, that summer, the servants would come into his cell, grip his bed, one at each end, and carry it out to the veranda, there setting it down with a thump that jarred every tooth in his head. In answer to his agonized complaints they said the Doctor Sahib had told them he must take the evening air and the evening air they would make him take—thump. Then Veena, that smiling, hypocritical pudding in a rustling sari, would appear and pile up the pillows under his head till he was propped up stiffly into a sitting position that made his head swim and his back ache. 'Let me lie down,' he begged. 'I can't sit up any more.'

'Try, Papa, Rakesh said you can if you try,' she said, and drifted away to the other end of the veranda where her transistor radio vibrated to the lovesick tunes from the cinema that she listened to all day.

So there he sat, like some stiff corpse, terrified, gazing out on the lawn where his grandsons played cricket, in danger of getting one of their hard-spun balls in his eye, and at the gate that opened onto the dusty and rubbish-heaped lane but still bore, proudly, a newly touched-up signboard that bore his son's name and qualifications, his own name having vanished from the gate long ago.

At last the sky-blue Ambassador arrived, the cricket game broke up in haste, the car drove in smartly and the doctor, the great doctor, all in white, stepped out. Someone ran up to take his bag from him, others to escort him up the steps. 'Will you have tea?' his wife called, turning down the transistor set, 'or a Coca-Cola? Shall I fry you some *samosas*?' But he did not reply or even glance in her direction. Ever a devoted son, he went first to the corner where his father sat gazing, stricken, at some undefined spot in the dusty yellow air that swam before him. He did not turn his head to look at his son. But he stopped gobbling air with his uncontrolled lips and set his jaw as hard as a sick and very old man could set it.

'Papa,' his son said, tenderly, sitting down on the edge of the bed and reaching out to press his feet.

Old Varma tucked his feet under him, out of the way, and continued to gaze stubbornly into the yellow air of the summer evening.

'Papa, I'm home.'

Varma's hand jerked suddenly, in a sharp, derisive movement, but he did not speak.

'How are you feeling, Papa?'

Then Varma turned and looked at his son. His face was so out of control and all in pieces, that the multitude of expressions that crossed it could not make up a whole and convey to the famous man exactly what his father thought of him, his skill, his art.

'I'm dying,' he croaked. 'Let me die, I tell you.'

'Papa, you're joking,' his son smiled at him, lovingly. 'I've brought you a new tonic to make you feel better. You must take it, it will make you feel stronger again. Here it is. Promise me you will take it regularly, Papa.'

Varma's mouth worked as hard as though he still had a gob of betel in it (his supply of betel had been cut off years ago). Then he spat out some words, as sharp and bitter as poison, into his son's face. 'Keep your tonic—I want none—I want none— I won't take any more of—of your medicines. None. Never,' and he swept the bottle out of his son's hand with a wave of his own, suddenly grand, suddenly effective.

His son jumped, for the bottle was smashed and thick brown syrup had splashed up, staining his white trousers. His wife let out a cry and came running. All around the old man was hubbub once again, noise, attention.

He gave one push to the pillows at his back and dislodged them so he could sink down on his back, quite flat again. He closed his eyes and pointed his chin at the ceiling, like some dire prophet, groaning, 'God is calling me—now let me go.'

Virginia Moriconi

I was given Virginia Moriconi's "Simple Arithmetic" to read by a wise and caustic teacher in my third year of high school. I never forgot the three-person dialogue in which one of the participants is silent, another deaf to the pain, the third pitilessly sinking into the learning of despair. To an adolescent, this was a true portrayal of adolescence, a ritual passage through time unseen by the adult world, what the Spanish poet Vicente Gaos described as "powerful night, air-tight darkness, gigantic stone weighing down on the principles of beauty."

For many years, this story was all I could find by Moriconi. At last, I traced a collection of her short fiction, *The Mark of St. Crispin,* and a novel, *Black Annis,* both published in England but neither carrying any useful biographical information. I included "Simple Arithmetic" in an anthology I was compiling, and then, out of the blue, I received a kind letter from the author who was, at the time, living in Italy. I wrote back, delighted. The letter was returned shortly afterward with a note explaining that Virginia Moriconi had died. "Simple Arithmetic" is, I believe, one of the most poignant accounts of a father and son unable to find a common ground on which to meet.

SIMPLE ARITHMETIC

virginia moriconi

geneva, January 15

Dear Father,

Well, I am back in School, as you can see, and the place is just as miserable as ever. My only friend, the one I talked to you about, Ronald Fletcher, is not coming back any more because someone persuaded his mother that she was letting him go to waste, since he was extremely photogenic, so now he is going to become a child actor. I was very surprised to hear this, as the one thing Ronnie liked to do was play basketball. He was very shy.

The flight wasn't too bad. I mean nobody had to be carried off the plane. The only thing was, we were six hours late and they forgot to give us anything to eat, so for fourteen hours we had a chance to get quite hungry but, as you say, for the money you save going tourist class, you should be prepared to make a few little sacrifices.

I did what you told me, and when we got to Idlewild I paid the taxi driver his fare and gave him a fifty-cent tip. He was very dissatisfied. In fact he wouldn't give me my suitcase. In fact I don't know what would have happened if a man hadn't come up just while the argument was going on and when he heard what it was all about he gave the taxi driver a dollar and I took my suit-case and got to the plane on time.

During the trip I thought the whole thing over. I did not come to any conclusion. I know I have been very extravagant and unreasonable about money and you have done the best you can to explain this to me. Still, while I was thinking about it, it seemed to me that there were only three possibilities. I could just have given up and let the taxi driver have the suitcase, but when you realise that if we had to buy everything over again that was in the suitcase we would probably have had to spend at least five hundred dollars, it does not seem very economical. Or I could have gone on arguing with him and missed the plane, but then we would have had to pay something like three hundred dollars for another ticket. Or else I could have given him an extra twenty-five cents which, as you say, is just throwing money around to create a impression. What would you have done?

Anyway I got here, with the suitcase, which was the main thing. They took two week-end privileges away from me because I was late for the opening of School. I tried to explain to M. Frisch that it had nothing to do with me if the weather was so bad that the plane was delayed for six hours, but he said that prudent persons allow for continjensies of this kind and make earlier reservations. I don't care about this because the next two week-ends are skiing week-ends and I have never seen any point in waking up at six o'clock in the morning just to get frozen stiff and endure terrible pain, even if sports are a part of growing up, as you say. Besides, we will save twenty-seven dollars by having me stay in my room.

In closing I want to say that I had a very nice Christmas and I apreciate everything you tried to do for me and I hope I wasn't too much of a bother. (Martha explained to me that you had had to take time off from your honeymoon in order to make Christmas for me and I am very sorry even though I do not think I am to blame if Christmas falls on the twenty-fifth of December, especially since everybody knows that it does. What I mean is, if you had wanted to have a long honeymoon you and Martha could have gotten married earlier, or you could have waited until Christmas was over, or you could just have told me not to come and I would have understood.)

I will try not to spend so much money in the future and I will keep accounts and send them to you. I will also try to remember to do the eye exercises and the exercises for fallen arches that the doctors in New York prescribed.

Love,
Stephen

Dear Stephen,

Thank you very much for the long letter of January fifteenth. I was very glad to know that you had gotten back safely, even though the flight was late. (I do not agree with M. Frisch that prudent persons allow for "continjensies" of this kind, now that air travel is as standard as it is, and the service usually so good, but we must remember that Swiss people are, by and large, the most meticulous in the world and nothing offends them more than other people who are not punctual.)

In the affair of the suitcase, I'm afraid that we were both at fault. I had forgotten that there would be an extra charge for luggage when I suggested that you should tip the driver fifty cents. You, on the other hand, might have inferred from his argument that he was simply asking that the tariff—i.e. the fare, plus the overcharge for the suitcase—should be paid in full, and regulated yourself accordingly. In any event you arrived, and I am only sorry that obviously you had no time to learn the name and address of your benefactor so that we might have paid him back for his kindness.

I will look forward to going over your accounting and I am sure you will find that in keeping a clear record of what you spend you will be able to cut your cloth according to the bolt, and that, in turn, will help you to develop a real regard for yourself.

It is a common failing, as I told you, to spend too much money in order to compensate oneself for a lack of inner security, but you can easily see that a foolish purchase does not insure stability, and if you are chronically insolvent you can hardly hope for peace of mind. Your allowance is more than adequate and when you learn to make both ends meet you will have taken a decisive step ahead. I have great faith in you and I know you will find your anchor to windward in your studies, in your sports, and in your companions.

As to what you say about Christmas, you are not obliged to "apreciate" what we did for you. The important thing was that you should have a good time, and I think we had some wonderful fun together, the three of us, don't you? Until your mother decides where she wants to live and settles down, this is your *home* and you must always think of it that way. Even though I have remarried, I am still your father, first and last, and Martha is very fond of you too, and very understanding about your problems. You may not be aware of it but in fact she is one of the best friends you have. New ideas and new stepmothers take a little getting used to, of course.

Please write to me as regularly as you can, since your letters mean a great deal to me. Please try too, at all times, to keep your marks up to scratch, as college entrance is getting harder and harder in this country, and there are thousands of candidates each year for the good universities. Concentrate particularly on spelling. "Contingency" is difficult, I know, but there is no excuse for only one "p" in "appreciate"! And *do* the exercises.

Love,
Father

Geneva, January 22

Dear Mummy,

Last Sunday I had to write to Father to thank him for my Christmas vacation and to tell him that I got back all right. This Sunday I thought I would write to you even though you are

174

on a cruze so perhaps you will never get my letter. I must say that if they didn't make us write home once a week I don't believe that I would ever write any letters at all. What I mean is that once you get to a point like this, in a place like this, you see that you are supposed to have your life and your parents are supposed to have their lives, and you have lost the connection.

Anyway I have to tell you that Father was wonderful to me and Martha was very nice too. They had thought it all out, what a child of my age might like to do in his vacation, and sometimes it was pretty strenuous, as you can imagine. At the end the School sent the bill for the first term, where they charge you for the extras which they let you have here and it seems that I had gone way over my allowance and besides I had signed for a whole lot of things I did not deserve. So there was a terrible scene and Father was very angry and Martha cried and said that if Father always made such an effort to consider me as a person I should make an effort to consider him as a person too and wake up to the fact that he was not Rockefeller and that even if he was sacrificing himself so that I could go to one of the most expensive schools in the world it did not mean that I should drag everybody down in the mud by my reckless spending. So now I have to turn over a new leaf and keep accounts of every penny and not buy anything which is out of proportion to our scale of living.

Except for that one time they were very affectionate to me and did everything they could for my happiness. Of course it was awful without you. It was the first time we hadn't been together and I couldn't really believe it was Christmas.

I hope you are having a wonderful time and getting the rest you need and please write me when you can.

All my love,
Stephen

175

Geneva, January 29

Dear Father,

Well it is your turn for a letter this week because I wrote to Mummy last Sunday. (I am sure I can say this to you without hurting your feelings because you always said that the one thing you and Mummy wanted was a civilised divorce so we could all be friends.) Anyway Mummy hasn't answered my letter so probably she doesn't aprove of my spelling any more than you do. I am beginning to wonder if maybe it wouldn't be much simpler and much cheaper too if I didn't go to college after all. I really don't know what this education is for in the first place.

There is a terrible scandal here at School which has been very interesting for the rest of us. One of the girls, who is only sixteen, has gotten pregnant and everyone knows that it is all on account of the science instructer, who is a drip. We are waiting to see if he will marry her, but in the meantime she is terrifically upset and she has been expelled from the School. She is going away on Friday.

I always liked her very much and I had a long talk with her last night. I wanted to tell her that maybe it was not the end of the world, that my stepmother was going to have a baby in May, although she never got married until December, and the sky didn't fall in or anything. I thought it might have comforted her to think that grown-ups make the same mistakes that children do (if you can call her a child) but then I was afraid that it might be disloyal to drag you and Martha into the conversation, so I just let it go.

I'm fine and things are just the same.

Love,
Stephen

New York, February 2

Dear Stephen,

It would be a great relief to think that your mother did not "aprove" of your spelling either, but I'm sure that it's not for that reason that you haven't heard from her. She was never any good as a correspondent, and now it is probably more difficult for her than ever. We did indeed try for what you call a "civilised divorce" for all our sakes, but divorce is not an easy thing for any of the persons involved, as you well know, and if you try to put yourself in your mother's place for a moment, you will see that she is in need of time and solitude to work things out for herself. She will certainly write to you as soon as she has found herself again, and meanwhile you must continue to believe in her affection for you and not let impatience get the better of you.

Again, in case you are really in doubt about it, the purpose of your education is to enable you to stand on your own feet when you are a man and make something of yourself. Inaccuracies in spelling will not *simplify* anything.

I can easily see how you might have made a parallel between your friend who has gotten into trouble, and Martha who is expecting the baby in May, but there is only a superficial similarity in the two cases.

Your friend is, or was, still a child, and would have done better to have accepted the limitations of the world of childhood— as you can clearly see for yourself, now that she is in this predicament. Martha, on the other hand, was hardly a child. She was a mature human being, responsible for her own actions and prepared to be responsible for the baby when it came. Moreover I, unlike the science "instructer" am not a drip, I too am responsible for *my* actions, and so Martha and I are married and I will do my best to live up to her and the baby.

Speaking of which, we have just found a new apartment because this one will be too small for us in May. It is right across the street from your old school and we have a kitchen, a dining alcove, a living room, two bedrooms—one for me and Martha, and one for the new baby—and another room which will be for you. Martha felt that it was very important for you to feel that you had a place of your own when you came home to us, and so it is largely thanks to her that we have taken such a big place. The room will double as a study for me when you are not with us, but we will move all my books and papers and paraphernalia whenever you come, and Martha is planning to hang the Japanese silk screen you liked at the foot of the bed. Please keep in touch, and *please* don't forget the exercises.

Love,
Father

Geneva, February 5

178   Dear Father,

There is one thing which I would like to say to you which is that if it hadn't been for you *I* would never have heard of a "civilised divorce", but that is the way you explained it to me. I always thought it was crazy. What I mean is, wouldn't it have been better if you had said, "I don't like your mother any more and I would rather live with Martha," instead of insisting that you and Mummy were always going to be the greatest friends? Because the way things are now Mummy probably thinks that you still like her very much, and it must be hard for Martha to believe that she was chosen, and I'm pretty much confused myself, although it is really none of my business.

You will be sorry to hear that I am not able to do any of the exercises any longer. I cannot do the eye exercises because my room-mate got so fassinated by the stereo gadget that he broke it. (But the School Nurse says she thinks it may be just as well to let the whole thing go since in her opinion there was a good chance that I might have gotten more cross-eyed than ever, fidgeting with the viewer.) And I cannot do the exercises for fallen arches, at least for one foot, because when I was decorating the Assembly Hall for the dance last Saturday, I fell off the stepladder and broke my ankle. So now I am in the Infirmary and the School wants to know whether to send the doctor's bill to you or to Mummy, because they had to call in a specialist from the outside, since the regular School Doctor only knows how to do a very limited number of things. So I have cost a lot of money again and I am very very sorry, but if they were half-way decent in the School they would pay to have proper equipment and not let the students risk their lives on broken stepladders, which is something you could write to the Bookkeeping Department, if you felt like it, because I can't, but you could, and it might do some good in the end.

The girl who got into so much trouble took too many sleeping pills and died. I felt terrible about it, in fact I cried when I heard it. Life is very crewel, isn't it?

I agree with what you said, that she was a child but I think she knew that, from her point of view. I think she did what she did because she thought of the science instructer as a grown-up, so she imagined that she was perfectly safe with him. You may think that she was just bad, because she was a child and should have known better, but I think that it was not entirely her fault since here at School we are all encouraged to take the teachers seriously.

I am very glad you have found a new apartment and I hope you won't move all your books and papers when I come home, because that would only make me feel that I was more of a nuisance than ever.

Love,
Stephen

New York, February 8

Dear Stephen,

This will have to be a very short letter because we are to move into the new apartment tomorrow and Martha needs my help with the packing.

We were exceedingly shocked by the tragic death of

your friend and very sorry that you should have had such a sad experience. Life can be "crewel" indeed to the people who do not learn how to live it.

When I was exactly your age I broke my ankle too—I wasn't on a defective stepladder, I was playing hockey—and it hurt like the devil. I still remember it and you have all my sympathy. (I have written to the School Physician to ask how long you will have to be immobilised, and to urge him to get you back into the athletic program as fast as possible. The specialist's bill should be sent to me.)

I have also ordered another stereo viewer because, in spite of the opinion of the School Nurse, the exercises are most important and you are to do them *religiously*. Please be more careful with this one no matter how much it may "fassinate" your room-mate.

Martha sends love and wants to know what you would like for your birthday. Let us know how the ankle is mending.

Love,
Father

Geneva, February 12

Dear Father,

I was very surprised by your letter. I was surprised that you said you were helping Martha to pack because when you and Mummy were married I do not ever remember you packing or anything like that so I guess Martha is reforming your charactor. I was also surprised by what you said about the girl who died. What I mean is, if anyone had told me a story like that I think I would have let myself get a little worked up about the science instructer because it seems to me that he was a villan too. Of course you are much more riserved than I am.

I am out of the Infirmary and they have given me a pair of crutches, but I'm afraid it will be a long time before I can do sports again.

I hope the new apartment is nice and I do not want anything for my birthday because it will seem very funny having a birthday in School so I would rather not be reminded of it.

> Love,
> Stephen

New York, February 15

Dear Stephen,

This is not an answer to your letter of February twelfth, but an attempt to have a serious discussion with you, as if we were face to face.

You are almost fifteen years old. Shortly you will be up against the stiffest competition of your life when you apply for college entrance. No examiner is going to find himself favourably impressed by "charactor" or "instructer" or "villan" or "riserved" or similar errors. You will have to face the fact that in this world we succeed on our merits, and if we are unsuccessful, on account of sloppy habits of mind, we suffer for it. You are still too young to understand me entirely, but you are not too young to recognise the importance of effort. People who do not make the grade are desperately unhappy all their lives because they have no place in society. If you do not pass the college entrance examinations simply because you are unable to spell, it will be nobody's fault but your own, and you will be gravely handicapped for the rest of your life.

Every time you are in doubt about a word you are to look it up in the dictionary and *memorise* the spelling. This is the least you can do to help yourself.

We are still at sixes and sevens in the new apartment but when Martha accomplishes all she has planned it should be very nice indeed and I think you will like it.

> Love,
> Father

Geneva, February 19

Dear Father,

I guess we do not understand each other at all. If you immagine for one minute that just by making a little effort I could imaggine how to spell immaggine without looking it up and finding that actually it is "imagine," then you are all wrong. In other words, if you get a letter from me and there are only two or three mistakes well you just have to take my word for it that I have had to look up practically every single word in the dictionary and that is one reason I hate having to write you these letters because they take so long and in the end they are not at all spontainious, no, just wait a second, here it is, "spontaneous," and believe me only two or three mistakes in a letter from me is one of the seven wonders of the world. What I'm saying is that I am doing the best I can as you would aggree if you could see my dictionary which is falling apart and when you say I should *memmorise* the spelling I can't because it doesn't make any sence to me and never did.

Love,
Stephen

New York, February 23

Dear Stephen,

It is probably just as well that you have gotten everything off your chest. We all need to blow up once in a while. It clears the air.

Please don't ever forget that I am aware that spelling is difficult for you. I know you are making a great effort and I am very proud of you. I just want to be sure that you *keep trying*.

I am enclosing a small cheque for your birthday because even if you do not want to be reminded of it I wouldn't want to forget it and you must know that we are thinking of you.

Love,
Father

Geneva, February 26

Dear Father,

We are not allowed to cash personal cheques here in the School, but thank you anyway for the money.

I am not able to write any more because we are going to have the exams and I have to study.

Love,
Stephen

New York, March 2

NIGHT LETTER

BEST OF LUCK STOP KEEP ME POSTED EXAM RESULTS

LOVE,
FATHER

Geneva, March 12

Dear Father,

Well, the exams are over. I got a C in English because aparently I do not know how to spell which should not come as too much of a surprise to you. In Science, Mathematics, and Latin I got an A, and in French and History I got a B plus. This makes me first in the class, which doesn't mean very much since none of the children here have any life of the mind, as you would say. I mean they are all jerks, more or less. What am I supposed to do in the Easter vacation? Do you want me to come to New York, or shall I just stay here and get a rest, which I could use?

Love,
Stephen

New York, March 16

Dear Stephen,

I am *immensely* pleased with the examination results. Congratulations. Pull up the spelling and our worries are over.

Just yesterday I had a letter from your mother. She has taken a little house in Majorca, which is an island off the Spanish coast, as you probably know, and she suggests that you should come to her for the Easter holidays. Of course, you are always welcome here—and you could rest as much as you wanted—but Majorca is very beautiful and would certainly appeal to the artistic side of your nature. I have written to your mother, urging her to write to you immediately, and I enclose her address in case you should want to write yourself. Let me know what you would like to do.

Love,
Father

184

Geneva, March 19

Dear Mummy,

Father says that you have invited me to come to you in Majorca for the Easter vacation. Is that true? I would be very very happy if it were. It has been very hard to be away from you for all this time and if you wanted to see me it would mean a great deal to me. I mean if you are feeling well enough. I could do a lot of things for you so you would not get too tired.

I wonder if you will think that I have changed when you see me. As a matter of fact I have changed a lot because I have become quite bitter. I have become bitter on account of this School.

I know that you and Father wanted me to have some expearience of what the world was like outside of America but what you didn't know is that Geneva is not the world at all. I mean, if you were born here, then perhaps you would have a real life, but I do not know anyone who was born here so all the people I see are just like myself, we are just waiting not to be lost any more. I think it would have been better to have left me in some place where I belonged even if Americans are getting very loud and money conscious. Because actually most of the children here are Americans, if you come right down to it, only it seems their parents didn't know what to do with them any longer.

Mummy I have written all this because I'm afraid that I have spent too much money all over again, and M. Frisch says that Father will have a *crise des nerfs* when he sees what I have done, and I thought that maybe you would understand that I only bought these things because there didn't seem to be anything else to do and that you could help me somehow or other. Anyway, according to the School, we will have to pay for all these things.

Concert, Segovia (Worth it)	16.00 (Swiss francs)
School Dance	5.00
English Drama (What do they mean?)	10.00
Controle de l'habitant (?)	9.10
Co-op purchases	65.90
Ballets Russes (Disappointing)	47.00
Librairie Prior	59.30
Concert piano (For practicing)	61.00
Teinturie (They ruined everything)	56.50
Toilet and Medicine	35.00
Escalade Ball	7.00
Pocket Money	160.00
77 Yoghurts (Doctor's advice)	42.40
Book account	295.70
Total	869.90 (Swiss francs)

Now you see the trouble is that Father told me I was to spend about fifty dollars a month, because that was my allowance, and that I was not to spend anything more. Anyway, fifty dollars a month would be about two hundred and ten Swiss francs, and then I had fifteen dollars for Christmas from Granny, and when I got back to School I found four francs in the pocket of my leather jacket and then I had seventy-nine cents left over from New York, but that doesn't help much, and then Father sent me twenty-five dollars for my birthday but I couldn't cash the cheque because they do not allow that here in School, so what shall I do?

It is a serious situation as you can see, and it is going to get a lot more serious when Father sees the bill. But whatever you do I imploar you not to write to Father because the trouble seems to be that I never had a balance foreward, and I am afraid that it is impossible to keep accounts without a balance foreward, and even more afraid that by this time the accounts have gone a little bizerk.

Do you want me to take a plane when I come to Majorca? Who shall I say is going to pay for the ticket?

Please do write me as soon as you can, because the holidays begin on March 30 and if you don't tell me what to do I will be way out on a lim.

> Lots and lots of love,
> Stephen

Geneva, March 26

Dear Father,

I wrote to Mummy a week ago to say that I would like very much to spend my Easter vacation in Majorca. So far she has not answered my letter, but I guess she will pretty soon. I hope she will because the holidays begin on Thursday.

I am afraid you are going to be upset about the bill all over again, but in the Spring term I will start anew and keep you in touch with what is going on.

> Love,
> Stephen

P.S. If Mummy doesn't write what shall I do?

Richard Ford

Over the past century, the vast male culture of the American Midwest has established complex and understated rituals. In a landscape of dusty roads, wayward motels, cutthroat manners, and strict ethics, which advertisments for jeans both mock and consecrate, boys in bashed-up Chevys learn the codes for becoming adults and acquire, almost without knowing it, the necessary skills to take part in the ceremonies of their sex. Richard Ford is this culture's literary anthropologist, and his stark accounts lay bare the reader's accountability. In one of his stories, describing a man looking for a car to steal, Ford asks the reader, "What would you think a man was doing if you saw him in the middle of the night looking in the windows of cars in the parking lot of the Ramada Inn? Would you think he was trying to get his head cleared? Would you think he was trying to get ready for a day when trouble would come down on him? Would you think his girl-friend was leaving him? Would you think he had a daughter? Would you think he was anybody like you?"

Whether fathers or sons, few are happy in Richard Ford's stories. His are cautionary tales; someone always learns something through the quietly brutal events that shape his characters, "anybody like you." The pain is unavoidable, the lesson of the essence. In "Great Falls" (the title is to be taken not only as a geographical place-name but also in its literal meaning), the arch of learning crosses from father to son and back, the son watching his father, the father watching his son during the vital moment of revelation.

GREAT FALLS

richard ford

this is not a happy story. I warn you.

My father was a man named Jack Russell, and when I was a young boy in my early teens, we lived with my mother in a house to the east of Great Falls, Montana, near the small town of Highwood and the Highwood Mountains and the Missouri River. It is a flat, treeless benchland there, all of it used for wheat farming, though my father was never a farmer, but was brought up near Tacoma, Washington, in a family that worked for Boeing.

He—my father—had been an Air Force sergeant and had taken his discharge in Great Falls. And instead of going home to Tacoma, where my mother wanted to go, he had taken a civilian's job with the Air Force, working on planes, which was what he liked to do. And he had rented the house out of town from a farmer who did not want it left standing empty.

The house itself is gone now—I have been to the spot. But the double row of Russian olive trees and two of the outbuildings are still standing in the milkweeds. It was a plain, two-story house with a porch on the front and no place for the cars. At the time, I rode the school bus to Great Falls every morning, and my father drove in while my mother stayed home.

My mother was a tall pretty woman, thin, with black hair and slightly sharp features that made her seem to smile when she wasn't smiling. She had grown up in Wallace, Idaho, and gone to college a year in Spokane, then moved out to the coast, which is where she met Jack Russell. She was two years older than he was, and married him, she said to me, because he was young and wonderful looking, and because she thought they could leave the sticks and see the world together—which I suppose they did for a while. That was the life she wanted, even before she knew much about wanting anything else or about the future.

When my father wasn't working on airplanes, he was going hunting or fishing, two things he could do as well as anyone. He had learned to fish, he said, in Iceland, and to hunt ducks up on the DEW line—stations he had visited in the Air Force. And during the time of this—it was 1960—he began to take me with him on what he called his "expeditions." I thought even then, with as little as I knew, that these were opportunities other boys would dream of having but probably never would. And I don't think that I was wrong in that.

It is a true thing that my father did not know limits. In the spring, when we would go east to the Judith River Basin and camp up on the banks, he would catch a hundred fish in a weekend, and sometimes more than that. It was all he did from morning until night, and it was never hard for him. He used yellow corn kernels stacked onto a #4 snelled hook, and he would rattle this rig-up along the bottom of a deep pool below a split-shot sinker, and catch fish. And most of the time, because he knew the Judith River and knew how to feel his bait down deep, he could catch fish of good size.

It was the same with ducks, the other thing he liked. When the northern birds were down, usually by mid-October, he would take me and we would build a cattail and wheatstraw blind on one of the tule ponds or sloughs he knew about down the Missouri, where the water was shallow enough to wade. We would set out his decoys to the leeward side of our blind, and he would sprinkle corn on a hunger-line from the decoys to where we were. In the evenings when he came home from the base, we would go and sit out in the blind until the roosting flights came and put down among the decoys—there was never calling involved. And after a while, sometimes it would be an hour and full dark, the ducks would find the corn, and the whole raft of them—sixty, sometimes—would swim in to us. At the moment he judged they were close enough, my father would say to me, "Shine, Jackie," and I would stand and shine a seal-beam car light out onto the pond, and he would stand up beside me and shoot all the ducks that were there, on the water if he could, but flying and getting up as well. He owned a Model 11 Remington with a long-tube magazine that would hold ten shells, and with that many, and shooting straight over the surface rather than down onto it, he could kill or wound thirty ducks in twenty seconds' time. I remember distinctly the report of that gun and the flash of it over the water into the dark air, one shot after another, not even so fast, but measured in a way to hit as many as he could.

What my father did with the ducks he killed, and the fish, too, was sell them. It was against the law then to sell wild game, and it is against the law now. And though he kept some for us, most he would take—his fish laid on ice, or his ducks still wet and bagged in the burlap corn sacks—down to the Great Northern Hotel, which was still open then on Second Street in Great Falls, and sell them to the Negro caterer who bought them for his wealthy customers and for the dining car passengers who came through. We would drive in my father's Plymouth to the back of the hotel—always this was after dark—to a concrete loading ramp and lighted door that were close enough to the yards that I could sometimes see passenger trains waiting at the station, their car lights yellow and warm inside, the passengers dressed in suits, all bound for someplace far away from Montana—Milwaukee or Chicago or New York City, unimaginable places to me, a boy fourteen years old, with my father in the cold dark selling illegal game.

The caterer was a tall, stooped-back man in a white jacket, who my father called "Professor Ducks" or "Professor Fish," and the Professor referred to my father as "Sarge." He paid a quarter per pound for trout, a dime for whitefish, a dollar for a mallard duck, two for a speckle or a blue goose, and four dollars for a Canada. I have been with my father when he took away a hundred dollars for fish he'd caught and, in the fall, more than that for ducks and geese. When he had sold game in that way, we would drive out 10th Avenue and stop at a bar called The Mermaid which was by the air base, and he would drink with some friends he knew there, and they would laugh about hunting and fishing while I played pinball and wasted money in the jukebox.

It was on such a night as this that the unhappy things came about. It was late October. I remember the time because Halloween had not been yet, and in the windows of the houses that I passed every day on the bus to Great Falls, people had put pumpkin lanterns, and set scarecrows in their yards in chairs.

My father and I had been shooting ducks in a slough on the Smith River, upstream from where it enters on the Missouri. He had killed thirty ducks, and we'd driven them down to the Great Northern and sold them there, though my father had kept two back in his corn sack. And when we had driven away, he suddenly said, "Jackie, let's us go back home tonight. Who cares about those hard-dicks at The Mermaid. I'll cook these ducks on the grill. We'll do something different tonight." He smiled at me in an odd way. This was not a thing he usually said, or the way he usually talked. He liked The Mermaid, and my mother—as far as I knew—didn't mind it if he went there.

"That sounds good," I said.

"We'll surprise your mother," he said. "We'll make her happy."

We drove out past the air base on Highway 87, past where there were planes taking off into the night. The darkness was dotted by the green and red beacons, and the tower light swept the sky and trapped planes as they disappeared over the flat landscape toward Canada or Alaska and the Pacific.

"Boy-oh-boy," my father said—just out of the dark. I looked at him and his eyes were narrow, and he seemed to be

191

thinking about something. "You know, Jackie," he said, "your mother said something to me once I've never forgotten. She said, 'Nobody dies of a broken heart.' This was somewhat before you were born. We were living down in Texas and we'd had some big blow-up, and that was the idea she had. I don't know why." He shook his head.

He ran his hand under the seat, found a half-pint bottle of whiskey, and held it up to the lights of the car behind us to see what there was left of it. He unscrewed the cap and took a drink, then held the bottle out to me. "Have a drink, son," he said. "Something oughta be good in life." And I felt that something was wrong. Not because of the whiskey, which I had drunk before and he had reason to know about, but because of some sound in his voice, something I didn't recognize and did not know the importance of, though I was certain it was important.

192

I took a drink and gave the bottle back to him, holding the whiskey in my mouth until it stopped burning and I could swallow it a little at a time. When we turned out the road to Highwood, the lights of Great Falls sank below the horizon, and I could see the small white lights of farms, burning at wide distances in the dark.

"What do you worry about, Jackie," my father said. "Do you worry about girls? Do you worry about your future sex life? Is that some of it?" He glanced at me, then back at the road.

"I don't worry about that," I said.

"Well, what then?" my father said. "What else is there?"

"I worry if you're going to die before I do," I said, though I hated saying that, "or if Mother is. That worries me."

"It'd be a miracle if we didn't," my father said, with the half-pint held in the same hand he held the steering wheel. I had seen him drive that way before. "Things pass too fast in your life, Jackie. Don't worry about that. If I were you, I'd worry we might not." He smiled at me, and it was not the worried, nervous smile from before, but a smile that meant he was pleased. And I don't remember him ever smiling at me that way again.

We drove on out behind the town of Highwood and onto the flat field roads toward our house. I could see, out on the prairie, a moving light where the farmer who rented our house to us was disking his field for winter wheat. "He's waited too late with that business," my father said and took a drink, then threw the bottle right out the window. "He'll lose that," he said, "the cold'll kill it." I did not answer him, but what I thought was that my father knew nothing about farming, and if he was right it would be an accident. He knew about planes and hunting game, and that seemed all to me.

"I want to respect your privacy," he said then, for no reason at all that I understood. I am not even certain he said it, only that it is in my memory that way. I don't know what he was thinking of. Just words. But I said to him, I remember well, "It's all right. Thank you."

We did not go straight out the Geraldine Road to our house. Instead my father went down another mile and turned, went a mile and turned back again so that we came home from the other direction. "I want to stop and listen now," he said. "The geese should be in the stubble." We stopped and he cut the lights and engine, and we opened the car windows and listened. It was eight o'clock at night and it was getting colder, though it was dry. But I could hear nothing, just the sound of air moving lightly through the cut field, and not a goose sound. Though I could smell the whiskey on my father's breath and on mine, could hear the motor ticking, could hear him breathe, hear the sound we made sitting side by side on the car seat, our clothes, our feet, almost our hearts beating. And I could see out in the night the yellow lights of our house, shining through the olive trees south of us like a ship on the sea. "I hear them, by God," my father said, his head stuck out the window. "But they're high up. They won't stop here now, Jackie. They're high flyers, those boys. Long gone geese."

There was a car parked off the road, down the line of wind-break trees, beside a steel thresher the farmer had left there to rust. You could see moonlight off the taillight chrome. It was a Pontiac, a two-door hard-top. My father said nothing about it and I didn't either, though I think now for different reasons.

The floodlight was on over the side door of our house and lights were on inside, upstairs and down. My mother had a pumpkin on the front porch, and the wind chime she had hung by the door was tinkling. My dog, Major, came out of the quonset shed and stood in the car lights when we drove up.

"Let's see what's happening here," my father said, opening the door and stepping out quickly. He looked at me inside the car, and his eyes were wide and his mouth drawn tight.

We walked in the side door and up the basement steps into the kitchen, and a man was standing there—a man I had never seen before, a young man with blond hair, who might've been twenty or twenty-five. He was tall and was wearing a short-sleeved shirt and beige slacks with pleats. He was on the other side of the breakfast table, his fingertips just touching the wooden tabletop. His blue eyes were on my father, who was dressed in hunting clothes.

"Hello," my father said.

"Hello," the young man said, and nothing else. And for some reason I looked at his arms, which were long and pale. They looked like a young man's arms, like my arms. His short sleeves had each been neatly rolled up, and I could see the bottom of a small green tattoo edging out from underneath. There was a glass of whiskey on the table, but no bottle.

"What's your name?" my father said, standing in the kitchen under the bright ceiling light. He sounded like he might be going to laugh.

"Woody," the young man said and cleared his throat. He looked at me, then he touched the glass of whiskey, just the rim of the glass. He wasn't nervous, I could tell that. He did not seem to be afraid of anything.

"Woody," my father said and looked at the glass of whiskey. He looked at me, then sighed and shook his head. "Where's Mrs. Russell, Woody? I guess you aren't robbing my house, are you?"

Woody smiled. "No," he said. "Upstairs. I think she went upstairs."

"Good," my father said, "that's a good place." And he walked straight out of the room, but came back and stood in the doorway. "Jackie, you and Woody step outside and wait on me. Just stay there and I'll come out." He looked at Woody then in a way I would not have liked him to look at me, a look that meant he was studying Woody. "I guess that's your car," he said.

"That Pontiac." Woody nodded.

"Okay. Right," my father said. Then he went out again and up the stairs. At that moment the phone started to ring in the living room, and I heard my mother say, "Who's that?" And my father say, "It's me. It's Jack." And I decided I wouldn't go answer the phone. Woody looked at me, and I understood he wasn't sure what to do. Run, maybe. But he didn't have run in him. Though I thought he would probably do what I said if I would say it.

195

"Let's just go outside," I said.

And he said, "All right."

Woody and I walked outside and stood in the light of the floodlamp above the side door. I had on my wool jacket, but Woody was cold and stood with his hands in his pockets, and his arms bare, moving from foot to foot. Inside, the phone was ringing again. Once I looked up and saw my mother come to the window and look down at Woody and me. Woody didn't look up or see her, but I did. I waved at her, and she waved back at me and smiled. She was wearing a powder-blue dress. In another minute the phone stopped ringing.

Woody took a cigarette out of his shirt pocket and lit it. Smoke shot through his nose into the cold air, and he sniffed, looked around the ground and threw his match on the gravel. His blond hair was combed backwards and neat on the sides, and I could smell his aftershave on him, a sweet, lemon smell. And for the first time I noticed his shoes. They were two-tones, black with white tops and black laces. They stuck out below his baggy pants and were long and polished and shiny, as if he had been planning on a big occasion. They looked like shoes some country singer would wear, or a salesman. He was handsome, but only like someone you would see beside you in a dime store and not notice again.

"I like it out here," Woody said, his head down, looking at his shoes. "Nothing to bother you. I bet you'd see Chicago if the world was flat. The Great Plains commence here."

"I don't know," I said.

Woody looked up at me, cupping his smoke with one hand. "Do you play football?"

"No," I said. I thought about asking him something about my mother. But I had no idea what it would be.

"I *have* been drinking," Woody said, "but I'm not drunk now."

The wind rose then, and from behind the house I could hear Major bark once from far away, and I could smell the irrigation ditch, hear it hiss in the field. It ran down from Highwood Creek to the Missouri, twenty miles away. It was nothing Woody knew about, nothing he could hear or smell. He knew nothing about anything that was here. I heard my father say the words, "That's a real joke," from inside the house, then the sound of a drawer being opened and shut, and a door closing. Then nothing else.

Woody turned and looked into the dark toward where the glow of Great Falls rose on the horizon, and we both could see the flashing lights of a plane lowering to land there. "I once passed my brother in the Los Angeles airport and didn't even recognize him," Woody said, staring into the night. "He recognized *me*, though. He said, 'Hey, bro, are you mad at me, or what?' I wasn't mad at him. We both had to laugh."

Woody turned and looked at the house. His hands were still in his pockets, his cigarette clenched between his teeth, his arms taut. They were, I saw, bigger, stronger arms than I had thought. A vein went down the front of each of them. I wondered what Woody knew that I didn't. Not about my mother—I didn't know anything about that and didn't want to—but about a lot of things, about the life out in the dark, about coming out here, about airports, even about me. He and I were not so far apart in age, I

196

knew that. But Woody was one thing, and I was another. And I wondered how I would ever get to be like him, since it didn't necessarily seem so bad a thing to be.

"Did you know your mother was married before?" Woody said.

"Yes," I said. "I knew that."

"It happens to all of them, now," he said. "They can't wait to get divorced."

"I guess so," I said.

Woody dropped his cigarette into the gravel and toed it out with his black-and-white shoe. He looked up at me and smiled the way he had inside the house, a smile that said he knew something he wouldn't tell, a smile to make you feel bad because you weren't Woody and never could be.

It was then that my father came out of the house. He still had on his plaid hunting coat and his wool cap, but his face was as white as snow, as white as I have ever seen a human being's face to be. It was odd. I had the feeling that he might've fallen inside, because he looked roughed up, as though he had hurt himself somehow. My mother came out the door behind him and stood in the floodlight at the top of the steps. She was wearing the powder-blue dress I'd seen through the window, a dress I had never seen her wear before, though she was also wearing a car coat and carrying a suitcase. She looked at me and shook her head in a way that only I was supposed to notice, as if it was not a good idea to talk now.

My father had his hands in his pockets, and he walked right up to Woody. He did not even look at me. "What do you do for a living?" he said, and he was very close to Woody. His coat was close enough to touch Woody's shirt.

"I'm in the Air Force," Woody said. He looked at me and then at my father. He could tell my father was excited.

"Is this your day off, then?" my father said. He moved even closer to Woody, his hands still in his pockets. He pushed Woody with his chest, and Woody seemed willing to let my father push him.

"No," he said, shaking his head.

I looked at my mother. She was just standing, watching. It was as if someone had given her an order, and she was obeying it. She did not smile at me, though I thought she was thinking about me, which made me feel strange.

"What's the matter with you?" my father said into Woody's face, right into his face—his voice tight, as if it had gotten hard for him to talk. "Whatever in the world is the matter with you? Don't you understand something?" My father took a revolver pistol out of his coat and put it up under Woody's chin, into the soft pocket behind the bone, so that Woody's whole face rose, but his arms stayed at his sides, his hands open. "I don't know what to do with you," my father said. "I don't have any idea what to do with you. I just don't." Though I thought that what he wanted to do was hold Woody there just like that until something important took place, or until he could simply forget about all this.

My father pulled the hammer back on the pistol and raised it tighter under Woody's chin, breathing into Woody's face—my mother in the light with her suitcase, watching them, and me watching them. A half a minute must've gone by.

And then my mother said, "Jack, let's stop now. Let's just stop."

My father stared into Woody's face as if he wanted Woody to consider doing something—moving or turning around or anything on his own to stop this—that my father would then put a stop to. My father's eyes grew narrowed, and his teeth were gritted together, his lips snarling up to resemble a smile. "You're crazy, aren't you?" he said. "You're a goddamned crazy man. Are you in love with her, too? Are you, crazy man? Are you? Do you say you love her? Say you love her! Say you love her so I can blow your fucking brains in the sky."

"All right," Woody said. "No. It's all right."

"He doesn't love me, Jack. For God's sake," my mother said. She seemed so calm. She shook her head at me again. I do not think she thought my father would shoot Woody. And I don't

198

think Woody thought so. Nobody did, I think, except my father himself. But I think he did, and was trying to find out how to.

My father turned suddenly and glared at my mother, his eyes shiny and moving, but with the gun still on Woody's skin. I think he was afraid, afraid he was doing this wrong and could mess all of it up and make matters worse without accomplishing anything.

"You're leaving," he yelled at her. "That's why you're packed. Get out. Go on."

"Jackie has to be at school in the morning," my mother said in just her normal voice. And without another word to any one of us, she walked out of the floodlamp light carrying her bag, turned the corner at the front porch steps and disappeared toward the olive trees that ran in rows back into the wheat.

My father looked back at me where I was standing in the gravel, as if he expected to see me go with my mother toward Woody's car. But I hadn't thought about that—though later I would. Later I would think I should have gone with her, and that things between them might've been different. But that isn't how it happened.

"You're sure you're going to get away now, aren't you, mister?" my father said into Woody's face. He was crazy himself, then. Anyone would've been. Everything must have seemed out of hand to him.

"I'd like to," Woody said. "I'd like to get away from here."

"And I'd like to think of some way to hurt you," my father said and blinked his eyes. "I feel helpless about it." We all heard the door to Woody's car close in the dark. "Do you think that I'm a fool?" my father said.

"No," Woody said. "I don't think that."

"Do you think you're important?"

"No," Woody said. "I'm not."

My father blinked again. He seemed to be becoming someone else at that moment, someone I didn't know. "Where are you from?"

199

And Woody closed his eyes. He breathed in, then out, a long sigh. It was as if this was somehow the hardest part, something he hadn't expected to be asked to say.

"Chicago," Woody said. "A suburb of there."

"Are your parents alive?" my father said, all the time with his blue magnum pistol pushed under Woody's chin.

"Yes," Woody said. "Yessir."

"That's too bad," my father said. "Too bad they have to know what you are. I'm sure you stopped meaning anything to them a long time ago. I'm sure they both wish you were dead. You didn't know that. But I know it. I can't help them out, though. Somebody else'll have to kill you. I don't want to have to think about you anymore. I guess that's it."

My father brought the gun down to his side and stood looking at Woody. He did not back away, just stood, waiting for what I don't know to happen. Woody stood a moment, then he cut his eyes at me uncomfortably. And I know that I looked down. That's all I could do. Though I remember wondering if Woody's heart was broken and what any of this meant to him. Not to me, or my mother, or my father. But to him, since he seemed to be the one left out somehow, the one who would be lonely soon, the one who had done something he would someday wish he hadn't and would have no one to tell him that it was all right, that they forgave him, that these things happen in the world.

Woody took a step back, looked at my father and at me again as if he intended to speak, then stepped aside and walked away toward the front of our house, where the wind chime made a noise in the new cold air.

My father looked at me, his big pistol in his hand. "Does this seem stupid to you?" he said. "All this? Yelling and threatening and going nuts? I wouldn't blame you if it did. You shouldn't even see this. I'm sorry. I don't know what to do now."

"It'll be all right," I said. And I walked out to the road. Woody's car started up behind the olive trees. I stood and watched it back out, its red taillights clouded by exhaust. I could see their two heads inside, with the headlights shining behind them. When they got into the road, Woody touched his brakes, and for a moment I could see that they were talking, their heads turned toward each other, nodding. Woody's head and my mother's. They sat that way for a few seconds, then drove slowly off. And I wondered what they had to say to each other, something important enough that they had to stop right at that moment and say it. Did she say, *I love you*? Did she say, *This is not what I expected to happen*? Did she say, *This is what I've wanted all along*? And did he say, *I'm sorry for all this,* or *I'm glad,* or *None of this matters to me*? These are not the kinds of things you can know if you were not there. And I was not there and did not want to be. It did not seem like I should be there. I heard the door slam when my father went inside, and I turned back from the road where I could still see their taillights disappearing, and went back into the house where I was to be alone with my father.

201

Things seldom end in one event. In the morning I went to school on the bus as usual, and my father drove in to the air base in his car. We had not said very much about all that had happened. Harsh words, in a sense, are all alike. You can make them up yourself and be right. I think we both believed that we were in a fog we couldn't see through yet, though in a while, maybe not even a long while, we would see lights and know something.

In my third-period class that day a messenger brought a note for me that said I was excused from school at noon, and I should meet my mother at a motel down 10th Avenue South—a place not so far from my school—and we would eat lunch together.

It was a gray day in Great Falls that day. The leaves were off the trees and the mountains to the east of town were obscured by a low sky. The night before had been cold and clear, but today it seemed as if it would rain. It was the beginning of winter in earnest. In a few days there would be snow everywhere.

The motel where my mother was staying was called the Tropicana, and was beside the city golf course. There was a neon parrot on the sign out front, and the cabins made a U shape behind a little white office building. Only a couple of cars were parked in front of the cabins, and no car was in front of my mother's cabin. I wondered if Woody would be here, or if he was at the air base. I wondered if my father would see him there, and what they would say.

I walked back to cabin 9. The door was open, though a DO NOT DISTURB sign was hung on the knob outside. I looked through the screen and saw my mother sitting on the bed alone. The television was on, but she was looking at me. She was wearing the powder-blue dress she had had on the night before. She was smiling at me, and I liked the way she looked at that moment, through the screen, in shadows. Her features did not seem as sharp as they had before. She looked comfortable where she was, and I felt like we were going to get along, no matter what had happened, and that I wasn't mad at her—that I had never been mad at her.

She sat forward and turned the television off. "Come in, Jackie," she said, and I opened the screen door and came inside. "It's the height of grandeur in here, isn't it?" My mother looked around the room. Her suitcase was open on the floor by the bathroom door, which I could see through and out the window onto the golf course, where three men were playing under the milky sky. "Privacy can be a burden, sometimes," she said, and reached down and put on her high-heeled shoes. "I didn't sleep very well last night, did you?"

"No," I said, though I had slept all right. I wanted to ask her where Woody was, but it occurred to me at that moment that he was gone now and wouldn't be back, that she wasn't thinking in terms of him and didn't care where he was or ever would be.

"I'd like a nice compliment from you," she said. "Do you have one of those to spend?"

"Yes," I said. "I'm glad to see you."

"That's a nice one," she said and nodded. She had both her shoes on now. "Would you like to go have lunch? We can walk across the street to the cafeteria. You can get hot food."

"No," I said. "I'm not really hungry now."

"That's okay," she said and smiled at me again. And, as I said before, I liked the way she looked. She looked pretty in a way I didn't remember seeing her, as if something that had had a hold on her had let her go, and she could be different about things. Even about me.

"Sometimes, you know," she said, "I'll think about something I did. Just anything. Years ago in Idaho, or last week, even. And it's as if I'd read it. Like a story. Isn't that strange?"

"Yes," I said. And it did seem strange to me because I was certain then what the difference was between what had happened and what hadn't, and knew I always would be.

"Sometimes," she said, and she folded her hands in her lap and stared out the little side window of her cabin at the parking lot and the curving row of other cabins. "Sometimes I even have a moment when I completely forget what life's like. Just altogether." She smiled. "That's not so bad, finally. Maybe it's a disease I have. Do you think I'm just sick and I'll get well?"

"No. I don't know," I said. "Maybe. I hope so." I looked out the bathroom window and saw the three men walking down the golf course fairway carrying golf clubs.

"I'm not very good at sharing things right now," my mother said. "I'm sorry." She cleared her throat, and then she didn't say anything for almost a minute while I stood there. "I *will* answer anything you'd like me to answer, though. Just ask me anything, and I'll answer it the truth, whether I want to or not. Okay? I will. You don't even have to trust me. That's not a big issue with us. We're both grown-ups now."

And I said, "Were you ever married before?"

My mother looked at me strangely. Her eyes got small, and for a moment she looked the way I was used to seeing her— sharp-faced, her mouth set and taut. "No," she said. "Who told you that? That isn't true. I never was. Did Jack say that to you? Did your father say that? That's an awful thing to say. I haven't been that bad."

"He didn't say that," I said.

"Oh, of course he did," my mother said. "He doesn't know just to let things go when they're bad enough."

"I wanted to know that," I said. "I just thought about it. It doesn't matter."

"No, it doesn't," my mother said. "I could've been married eight times. I'm just sorry he said that to you. He's not generous sometimes."

"He didn't say that," I said. But I'd said it enough, and I didn't care if she believed me or didn't. It was true that trust was not a big issue between us then. And in any event, I know now that the whole truth of anything is an idea that stops existing finally.

"Is that all you want to know, then?" my mother said. She seemed mad, but not at me, I didn't think. Just at things in general. And I sympathized with her. "Your life's your own business, Jackie," she said. "Sometimes it scares you to death it's so much your own business. You just want to run."

"I guess so," I said.

"I'd like a less domestic life, is all." She looked at me, but I didn't say anything. I didn't see what she meant by that, though I knew there was nothing I could say to change the way her life would be from then on. And I kept quiet.

In a while we walked across 10th Avenue and ate lunch in the cafeteria. When she paid for the meal I saw that she had my father's silver-dollar money clip in her purse and that there was money in it. And I understood that he had been to see her already that day, and no one cared if I knew it. We were all of us on our own in this.

When we walked out onto the street, it was colder and the wind was blowing. Car exhausts were visible and some drivers had their lights on, though it was only two o'clock in the afternoon. My mother had called a taxi, and we stood and waited for it. I didn't know where she was going, but I wasn't going with her.

"Your father won't let me come back," she said, standing on the curb. It was just a fact to her, not that she hoped I would talk to him or stand up for her or take her part. But I did wish then that I had never let her go the night before. Things can be fixed by staying; but to go out into the night and not come back hazards life, and everything can get out of hand.

My mother's taxi came. She kissed me and hugged me very hard, then got inside the cab in her powder-blue dress and high heels and her car coat. I smelled her perfume on my cheeks as I stood watching her. "I used to be afraid of more things than I am now," she said, looking up at me, and smiled. "I've got a knot in my stomach, of all things." And she closed the cab door, waved at me, and rode away.

I walked back toward my school. I thought I could take the bus home if I got there by three. I walked a long way down 10th Avenue to Second Street, beside the Missouri River, then over to town. I walked by the Great Northern Hotel, where my father had sold ducks and geese and fish of all kinds. There were no passenger trains in the yard and the loading dock looked small. Garbage cans were lined along the edge of it, and the door was closed and locked.

As I walked toward school I thought to myself that my life had turned suddenly, and that I might not know exactly how or which way for possibly a long time. Maybe, in fact, I might never know. It was a thing that happened to you—I knew that—and it had happened to me in this way now. And as I walked on up the cold street that afternoon in Great Falls, the questions I asked myself were these: why wouldn't my father let my mother come back? Why would Woody stand in the cold with me outside my house and risk being killed? Why would he say my mother had been married before, if she hadn't been? And my mother herself— why would she do what she did? In five years my father had gone off to Ely, Nevada, to ride out the oil strike there, and been killed by accident. And in the years since then I have seen my mother from time to time—in one place or another, with one man or other—and I can say, at least, that we know each other. But I have never known the answer to these questions, have never asked anyone their answers. Though possibly it—the answer—is simple: it is just low-life, some coldness in us all, some helplessness that causes us to misunderstand life when it is pure and plain, makes our existence seem like a border between two nothings, and makes us no more or less than animals who meet on the road—watchful, unforgiving, without patience or desire.

Rohinton Mistry

      Canada thrives on its diversity. Those who become Canadian citizens adopt the country's generous ethos but, above all, lend the country their own cultural landscape. Through his writing, Rohinton Mistry has given Canada the landscape of his native Bombay and the rich heritage of his Parsi upbringing.

      Reclusive and soft spoken, Mistry began writing after his arrival in Canada in 1975 while working as a clerk in a bank. In 1983 he won a short story competition juried by Mavis Gallant; three years later, he published his first book, *Tales of Firozsha Baag* (in the United States, the book was titled *Swimming Lessons*). He has since won or has been shortlisted for almost every major literary award in the English language. Fathers and sons run through Mistry's universe, from the uneasy son in "Of White Hairs and Cricket" to the heroes of his novels, the much-suffering Gustad Noble and his sons in *Such a Long Journey* to the father-and-son-like couple of luckless tailors in his masterpiece, *A Fine Balance*. Though the association is never explicit, in Mistry's world these relationships stand for continuity of some sort, an emblem of the ongoing and relentless wheel of history. Considering his grandfather's carpentry tools in *Such a Long Journey,* the rebellious Darius reflects, "What did it mean when a hammer like this passed from generation to generation? It meant something satisfying, fulfilling, at the deep centre of one's being. That was all. No need to wrestle further with the meaning of the words."

OF WHITE HAIRS

AND CRICKET

rohinton mistry

the white hair was trapped in the tweezers. I pulled it taut to see if it was gripped tightly, then plucked it.

"Aaah!" grimaced Daddy. "Careful, only one at a time." He continued to read the *Times Of India,* spreading it on the table.

"It *is* only one," I said, holding out the tweezers, but my annoyance did not register. Engrossed in the classifieds, he barely looked my way. The naked bulb overhead glanced off the stainless steel tweezers, making a splotch of light dart across the Murphy Radio calendar. It danced over the cherubic features of the Murphy Baby, in step with the tweezers' progress on Daddy's scalp. He sighed, turned a page, and went on scrutinizing the columns.

Each Sunday, the elimination of white hairs took longer than the last time. I'm sure Daddy noticed it too, but joked bravely that laziness was slowing me down. Percy was always excused from this task. And if I pointed it out, the answer was: your brother's college studies are more important.

Daddy relied on my nimble fourteen-year-old fingers to uproot the signposts of mortality sprouting week after week. It was unappetizing work, combing through his hair greasy with day-old pomade, isolating the white ones, or the ones just beginning to turn—half black and half white, and somehow more repulsive. It was always difficult to decide whether to remove those or let them go till next Sunday, when the whiteness would have spread upward to their tips.

The Sunday edition of the *Times Of India* came with a tabloid of comics: Mandrake the Magician, The Phantom, and Maggie and Jiggs in "Bringing Up Father." The drab yellow tablecloth looked festive with the vivid colours of the comics, as though specially decorated for Sunday. The plastic cloth smelled stale and musty. It was impossible to clean perfectly because of the floral design embossed upon its surface. The swirly grooves were ideal for trapping all kinds of dirt.

Daddy reached up to scratch a spot on his scalp. His aaah surprised me. He had taught me to be tough, always. One morning when we had come home after cricket, he told Mummy and *Mamaiji*, "Today my son did a brave thing, as I would have done. A powerful shot was going to the boundary, like a cannonball, and he blocked it with his bare shin." Those were his exact words. The ball's shiny red fury, and the audible crack—at least, I think it was audible—had sent pain racing through me that nearly made my eyes overflow. Daddy had clapped and said, "Well-fielded, sir, well-fielded." So I waited to rub the agonized bone until attention was no longer upon me. I wish Percy had not lost interest in cricket, and had been there. My best friend, Viraf from A Block, was immensely impressed. But that was all a long time ago, many months ago, now Daddy did not take us for cricket on Sunday mornings.

I paused in my search. Daddy had found something in the classifieds and did not notice. By angling the tweezers I could aim the bulb's light upon various spots on the Murphy Radio calendar: the edges of the picture, worn and turned inward; the threadbare loop of braid sharing the colour of rust with the rusty nail it hung by; a corroded staple clutching twelve thin strips—the perforated residue of months ripped summarily over a decade ago when their days and weeks were played out. The baby's smile, posed with finger to chin, was all that had fully endured the years.

209

Mummy and Daddy called it so innocent and joyous. That baby would now be the same age as me. The ragged perimeter of the patch of crumbled wall it tried to hide strayed outward from behind, forming a kind of dark and jagged halo around the baby. The picture grew less adequate, daily, as the wall kept losing plaster and the edges continued to curl and tatter.

Other calendars in the room performed similar enshroudings: the Cement Corporation skyscraper; the Lifebuoy Soap towel-wrapped woman with long black hair; the Parsi calendar, pictureless but showing the English and Parsi names for the months, and the *roje* in Gujarati beside each date, which Mummy and *Mamaiji* consulted when reciting their prayers. All these hung well past their designated time span in the world of months and years, covering up the broken promises of the Firozsha Baag building management.

210

"Yes, this is it," said Daddy, tapping the paper, "get me the scissors."

Mamaiji came out and settled in her chair on the veranda. Seated, there was no trace of the infirmity that caused her to walk doubled over. Doctors said it was due to a weak spine that could not erect against the now inordinate weight of her stomach. From photographs of Mummy's childhood, I knew *Mamaiji* had been a big handsome woman, with a majestic countenance. She opened her bag of spinning things, although she had been told to rest her eyes after the recent cataract operation. Then she spied me with the tweezers.

"Sunday dawns and he makes the child do that *duleendar* thing again. It will only bring bad luck." She spoke under her breath, arranging her spindle and wool; she was not looking for a direct confrontation. "Plucking out hair as if it was a slaughtered chicken. An ill-omened thing, I'm warning you, Sunday after Sunday. But no one listens. Is this anything to make a child do, he should be out playing or learning how to do *bajaar,* how to bargain with butcher and *bunya.*" She mumbled softly, to allow Daddy to pretend he hadn't heard a thing.

I resented her speaking against Daddy and calling me a child. She twirled the spindle, drawing fibres into thread from the scrap of wool in her left hand as the spindle descended. I watched, expecting—even wishing—the thread to break. Sometimes it did, and then it seemed to me that *Mamaiji* was overcome with disbelief, shocked and pained that it could have happened, and I would feel sorry and rush to pick it up for her. The spindle spun to the floor this time without mishap, hanging by a fine, brand new thread. She hauled it up, winding the thread around the extended thumb and little finger of her left hand by waggling the wrist in little clockwise and counter-clockwise half-turns, while the index and middle fingers clamped tight the source: the shred of wool resembling a lock of her own hair, snow white and slightly tangled.

Mamaiji spun enough thread to keep us all in *kustis*. Since Grandpa's death, she spent more and more time spinning, so that now we each had a spare *kusti* as well. The *kustis* were woven by a professional, who always praised the fine quality of the thread; and even at the fire-temple, where we untied and tied them during prayers, they earned the covetous glances of other Parsis.

I beheld the spindle and *Mamaiji's* co-ordinated feats of dexterity with admiration. All spinning things entranced me. The descending spindle was like the bucket spinning down into the sacred Bhikha Behram Well to draw water for the ones like us who went there to pray on certain holy days after visiting the fire-temple. I imagined myself clinging to the base of the spindle, sinking into the dark well, confident that *Mamaiji* would pull me up with her waggling hand before I drowned, and praying that the thread would not break. I also liked to stare at records spinning on the old 78-rpm gramophone. There was one I was particularly fond of: its round label was the most ethereal blue I ever saw. The lettering was gold. I played this record over and over just to watch its wonderfully soothing blue and gold rotation, and the concentric rings of the shiny black shellac, whose grooves created a spiral effect if the light was right. The gramophone cabinet's warm smell of wood and leather seemed to fly right out of this shellacked

211

spiral, while I sat close, my cheek against it, to feel the hum and vibration of the turntable. It was so cosy and comforting. Like missing school because of a slight cold, staying in bed all day with a book, fussed over by Mummy, eating white rice and soup made specially for me.

Daddy finished cutting out and re-reading the classified advertisement. "Yes, this is a good one. Sounds very promising." He picked up the newspaper again, then remembered what *Mamaiji* had muttered, and said softly to me, "If it is so *duleendar* and will bring bad luck, how is it I found this? These old people—" and gave a sign of mild exasperation. Then briskly: "Don't stop now, this week is very important." He continued, slapping the table merrily at each word: "Every-single-white-hair-out."

There was no real enmity between Daddy and *Mamaiji,* I think they even liked each other. He was just disinclined towards living with his mother-in-law. They often had disagreements over me, and it was always *Mamaiji* versus Mummy and Daddy. *Mamaiji* firmly believed that I was underfed. Housebound as she was, the only food accessible to her was the stuff sold by door-to-door vendors, which I adored but was strictly forbidden; *samosa, bhajia, sevganthia;* or the dinners she cooked for herself, separately, because she said that Mummy's cooking was insipidity itself: "Tasteless as spit, refuses to go down my throat."

So I, her favourite, enjoyed from time to time, on the sly, hot searing curries and things she purchased at the door when Daddy was at work and Mummy in the kitchen. Percy shared, too, if he was around; actually, his iron-clad stomach was much better suited to those flaming snacks. But the clandestine repasts were invariably uncovered, and the price was paid in harsh and unpleasant words. *Mamaiji* was accused of trying to burn to a crisp my stomach and intestines with her fiery, ungodly curries, or of exposing me to dysentery and diphtheria: the cheap door-to-door foodstuff was allegedly cooked in filthy, rancid oil—even machine oil, unfit for human consumption, as was revealed recently by a government investigation. *Mamaiji* retorted that if they did their duty as parents she would not have to resort to secrecy and *chori-chhoopi;* as it was, she had no choice, she could not stand by and see the child starve.

All this bothered me much more than I let anyone know. When the arguments started I would say that all the shouting was giving me a headache, and stalk out to the steps of the compound. My guilty conscience, squirming uncontrollably, could not witness the quarrels. For though I was an eager partner in the conspiracy with *Mamaiji,* and acquiesced to the necessity for secrecy, very often I spilled the beans—quite literally—with diarrhoea and vomiting, which *Mamaiji* upheld as undeniable proof that lack of proper regular nourishment had enfeebled my bowels. In the throes of these bouts of effluence, I promised Mummy and Daddy never again to eat what *Mamaiji* offered, and confessed all my past sins. In *Mamaiji's* eyes I was a traitor, but sometimes it was also fun to listen to her scatalogical reproaches: *"Muà ugheeparoo!* Eating my food, then shitting and tattling all over the place. Next time I'll cork you up with a big *bootch* before feeding you."

213

Mummy came in from the kitchen with a plateful of toast fresh off the Criterion: unevenly browned, and charred in spots by the vagaries of its kerosene wick. She cleared the comics to one side and set the plate down.

"Listen to this," Daddy said to her, "just found it in the paper: 'A Growing Concern Seeks Dynamic Young Account Executive, Self-Motivated. Four-Figure Salary and Provident Fund.' I think it's perfect." He waited for Mummy's reaction. Then: "If I can get it, all our troubles will be over."

Mummy listened to such advertisements week after week: harbingers of hope that ended in disappointment and frustration. But she always allowed the initial wave of optimism to lift her, riding it with Daddy and me, higher and higher, making plans and dreaming, until it crashed and left us stranded, awaiting the next advertisement and the next wave. So her silence was surprising.

Daddy reached for a toast and dipped it in the tea, wrinkling his nose. "Smells of kerosene again. When I get this job, first thing will be a proper toaster. No more making burnt toast on top of the Criterion."

"I cannot smell kerosene," said Mummy.

"Smell this then," he said, thrusting the tea-soaked piece at her nose, "smell it and tell me," irritated by her ready contradiction. "It's these useless wicks. The original Criterion ones from England used to be so good. One trim and you had a fine flame for months." He bit queasily into the toast. "Well, when I get the job, a Bombay Gas Company stove and cylinder can replace it." He laughed. "Why not? The British left seventeen years ago, time for their stove to go as well."

He finished chewing and turned to me. "And one day, you must go, too, to America. No future here." His eyes fixed mine, urgently. "Somehow we'll get the money to send you. I'll find a way."

214

His face filled with love. I felt suddenly like hugging him, but we never did except on birthdays, and to get rid of the feeling I looked away and pretended to myself that he was saying it just to humour me, because he wanted me to finish pulling his white hairs. Fortunately, his jovial optimism returned.

"Maybe even a fridge is possible, then we will never have to go upstairs to that woman. No more obligations, no more favours. You won't have to kill any more rats for her." Daddy waited for us to join in. For his sake I hoped that Mummy would. I did not feel like mustering any enthusiasm.

But she said sharply, "All your *shaik-chullee* thoughts are flying again. Nothing happens when you plan too much. Leave it in the hands of God."

Daddy was taken aback. He said, summoning bitterness to retaliate, "You are thinking I will never get a better job? I'll show all of you." He threw his piece of toast onto the plate and sat back. But he recovered as quickly, and made it into a joke. He picked up the newspaper. "Well, I'll just have to surprise you one day when I throw out the kerosene stoves."

I liked the kerosene stoves and the formidable fifteen-gallon storage drum that replenished them. The Criterion had a little round glass window in one corner of its black base, and I would peer into the murky depths, watching the level rise as kerosene poured through the funnel; it was very dark and cool and mysterious in there, then the kerosene floated up and its surface shone under the light bulb. Looking inside was like lying on Chaupatty beach at night and gazing at the stars, in the hot season, while we stayed out after dinner till the breeze could rise and cool off the walls baking all day in the sun. When the stove was lit and the kitchen dark, the soft orange glow through its little mica door reminded me of the glow in the fire-temple *afargaan*, when there wasn't a blazing fire because hardly any sandalwood offerings had been left in the silver *thaali;* most people came only on the holy days. The Primus stove was fun, too, pumped up hot and roaring, the kerosene emerging under pressure and igniting into sharp blue flames. Daddy was the only one who lit it; every year, many women died in their kitchens because of explosions, and Daddy said that though many of them were not accidents, especially the dowry cases, it was still a dangerous stove if handled improperly.

215

Mummy went back to the kitchen. I did not mind the kerosene smell, and ate some toast, trying to imagine the kitchen without the stoves, with squat red gas cylinders sitting under the table instead. I had seen them in shop windows, and I thought they were ugly. We would get used to them, though, like everything else. At night, I stood on the veranda sometimes to look at the stars. But it was not the same as going to Chaupatty and lying on the sand, quietly, with only the sound of the waves in the dark. On Saturday nights, I would make sure that the stoves were filled, because Mummy made a very early breakfast for Daddy and me next morning. The milk and bread would be arriving in the pre-dawn darkness while the kettle was boiling and we got ready for cricket with the boys of Firozsha Baag.

We always left by seven o'clock. The rest of the building was just starting to wake up: Nariman Hansotia would be aligning, on the parapet of his ground floor veranda, his razor and shaving brush and mirror beside two steaming cups, one of boiling water and the other of tea, and we often wondered if he ever dipped the brush in the wrong cup; and the old spinster Tehmina, still waiting for her cataracts to ripen, would be saying her prayers facing the rising sun, with her duster-coat hoisted up and slung over the left shoulder, her yellowing petticoat revealed, to untie and tie her thick rope-like *kusti* around the waist; and the *kuchrawalli* would be sweeping the compound, making her rounds from door to door with broom and basket, collecting yesterday's garbage. If she happened to cross Tehmina's line of vision, all the boys were sure to have a fine time, because Tehmina, though blurry with cataracts, would recognize the *kuchrawalli* and let loose at her with a stream of curses fouler than any filth in the garbage basket, for committing the unspeakable crime of passing in front of her, thereby polluting her prayers and vitiating their efficacy.

Even Daddy laughed, but he hurried us along as we lingered there to follow the ensuing dialogue. We picked our way through sleeping streets. The pavement dwellers would stretch, and look for a place to relieve themselves. Then they would fold up their cardboard pieces and roll away their plastics before the street sweepers arrived and the traffic got heavy. Sometimes, they would start a small fire if they had something to cook for breakfast, or else try to beg from people who came to the Irani restaurant for their morning *chai* and bun. Occasionally, Mummy would wrap up leftovers from the night before for Daddy and me to distribute to them along the way.

It had been such a long time since we last played cricket. Flying kites had also become a thing of the past. One by one, the things I held dear were leaving my life, I thought gloomily. And Francis. What about poor Francis? Where was he now, I wondered. I wished he was still working in the Baag. That awful thrashing he got in Tar Gully was the fault of Najamai and Tehmina, those stupid old women. And Najamai saying he stole eighty rupees was nonsense, in my opinion; the absent-minded cow must have forgotten where she left the money.

I put down the tweezers and reached for the comics. Daddy looked up. "Don't stop now, it should be perfect this week. There will be an interview or something."

Avoiding his eye, I said stolidly. "I'm going to read the comics," and walked out to the compound steps. When I turned at the doorway Daddy was still looking at me. His face was like *Mamaiji's* when the thread broke and slipped through her fingers and the spindle fell to the floor. But I kept walking, it was a matter of pride. You always did what you said you were going to do.

The comics did not take long. It used to be fun when Daddy and I had a race to the door to grab the *Times*, and pretended to fight over who would read the comics first. I thought of the lines on Daddy's forehead, visible so clearly from my coign of vantage with the tweezers. His thinning hair barely gave off a dull lustre with its day-old pomade, and the Sunday morning stubble on his chin was flecked with grey and white.

Something—remorse, maybe just pity—stirred inside, but I quashed it without finding out. All my friends had fathers whose hair was greying. Surely they did not spend Sunday mornings doing what I did, or they would have said something. They were not like me, there was nothing that was too private and personal for them. They would talk about anything. Especially Pesi. He used to describe for us how his father passed gas, enhancing the narrative with authentic sound effects. Now he was in boarding school. His father was dead.

From our C Block stone steps I could observe the entire length of the compound, up to A Block at the far end. Dr Sidhwa's black Fiat turned in at the gate and trundled laboriously over the roughhewn flagstones of Firozsha Baag. He waved as he went past. He looked so much like Pesi's father. He had the same crow's-feet at the corners of his eyes that Dr Mody used to have, and even their old cars seemed identical, except that Dr Mody healed animals and Dr Sidhwa, humans. Most of us had been treated by him at one time or another. His house and dispensary were within walking distance of Firozsha Baag, even a sick person's walking distance; he was

217

a steadfast Parsi, seen often at fire-temples; and he always drove over for his house calls. What more could we want in a doctor?

The car stopped at the far end of the compound. Dr Sidhwa heaved out, he was a portly man, and reached in for his bag. It must be an emergency in A Block, I decided, for someone to call him on Sunday. He slammed the door, then opened and slammed it again, harder now. The impact rocked the old car a little, but the door shut properly this time. Viraf emerged from the steps of A Block. I waved to him to let him know I was waiting.

Viraf was my best friend. Together we learned bicycling, on a rented contraption of bent spokes and patchwork tyres from Cecil Cycles of Tar Gully: Fifty Paise Per Hour. Daddy used to take us to practise at Chaupatty on the wide pavement by the beach. It was deserted in the early morning—pavement dwellers preferred the narrow side streets—except for pigeons gathering in anticipation of the pigeon-man, who arrived when the streets stirred to life. We took turns, and Daddy ran behind, holding the seat to keep us steady. Daddy also taught the two of us to play cricket. Mummy had been angry when he brought home the bat and ball, asking where the money had come from. His specialty on his own school team had been bowling, and he taught us the leg break and off break, and told us about the legendary Jasu Patel, born with a defective wrist which turned out to be perfect for spin bowling, and how Jasu had mastered the dreaded curl spin which was eventually feared by all the great international batsmen.

Cricket on Sunday mornings became a regular event for the boys in Firozsha Baag. Between us we almost had a complete kit; all that was missing was a pair of bails, and wicket-keeping gloves. Daddy took anyone who wanted to play to the Marine Drive *maidaan,* and organized us into teams, captaining one team himself. We went early, before the sun got too hot and the *maidaan* overcrowded. But then one Sunday, halfway through the game, Daddy said he was going to rest for a while. Sitting on the grass a little distance away, he seemed so much older than he did when he was batting, or bowling leg breaks. He watched us with a faraway expression on his face. Sadly, as if he had just realized something and wished he hadn't.

There was no cricket at the *maidaan* after that day. Since we were not allowed to go alone, our games were now confined to the Firozsha Baag compound. Its flagstoned surface would not accept the points of stumps, and we chalked three white lines on the compound's black stone wall. But the compound was too cramped for cricket. Besides, the uneven ground made the ball bounce and rear erratically. After a few shattered panes of glass and several complaints from neighbours, the games ceased.

I waved again to Viraf and gave our private signal, "OO ooo OO ooo," which was like a yodel. He waved back, then took the doctor's bag and accompanied him into A block. His polite demeanor made me smile. That Viraf. Shrewd fellow, he knew the things to do to make grownups approve of him, and was always welcome at all the homes in Firozsha Baag. He would be back soon.

I waited for at least half an hour. I cracked all my fingers and knuckles, even the thumbs. Then I went to the other end of the compound. After sitting on the steps there for a few minutes, I got impatient and climbed upstairs to find out why Viraf was buttering up the doctor.

But Dr Sidhwa was on his way down, carrying his black bag. I said, "*Sahibji,* doctor," and he smiled at me as I raced up to the third floor. Viraf was standing at the balcony outside his flat. "What's all the *muskaa-paalis* for the doctor?"

He turned away without answering. He looked upset but I did not ask what the matter was. Words to show concern were always beyond me. I spoke again, in that easygoing debonair style which all of us tried to perfect, right arm akimbo and head tilted ever so slightly, "Come on *yaar,* what are your plans for today?"

He shrugged his shoulders, and I persisted, "Half the morning's over, man, don't be such a cry-baby."

"Fish off," he said, but his voice shook. His eyes were red, and he rubbed one as if there was something in it. I stood quietly for a while, looking out over the balcony. His third-floor balcony was my favourite spot, you could see the road beyond Firozsha Baag, and sometimes, on a sunny day, even a corner of Chaupatty beach with the sun gleaming on the waves. From my ground floor veranda the compound's black stone wall was all that was visible.

Hushed voices came from the flat, the door was open. I looked into the dining-room where some A Block neighbours had gathered around Viraf's mother. "How about Ludo or Snakes-and-Ladders?" I tried. If he shrugged again I planned to leave. What else could I do?

"Okay," he said, "but stay quiet. If *Mumma* sees us she'll send us out."

No one saw as we tiptoed inside, they were absorbed in whatever the discussion was about. "*Puppa* is very sick," whispered Viraf, as we passed the sickroom. I stopped and looked inside. It was dark. The smell of sickness and medicines made it stink like the waiting room of Dr Sidhwa's dispensary. Viraf's father was in bed, lying on his back, with a tube through his nose. There was a long needle stuck into his right arm, and it glinted cruelly in a thin shaft of sunlight that had suddenly slunk inside the darkened room. I shivered. The needle was connected by a tube to a large bottle which hung upside down from a dark metal stand towering over the bed.

Viraf's mother was talking softly to the neighbours in the dining-room. ". . . in his chest got worse when he came home last night. So many times I've told him, three floors to climb is not easy at your age with your big body, climb one, take rest for a few minutes, then climb again. But he won't listen, does not want people to think it is too much for him. Now this is the result, and what I will do I don't know. Poor little Viraf, being so brave when the doctor . . ."

Supine, his rotundity had spread into a flatness denying the huge bulk. I remembered calling Viraf a cry-baby, and my face flushed with shame. I swore I would apologize. Daddy was slim and wiry, although there were the beginnings of a small pot, as Mummy called it. He used to run and field with us at cricket. Viraf's father had sat on the grass the one time he took us. The breath came loud and rasping. His mouth was a bit open. It resembled a person snoring, but was uneven, and the sound suggested pain. I noticed the lines on his brow, like Daddy's, only Daddy's were less deep.

Over the rasp of his breath came the voice of Viraf's mother. ". . . to exchange with someone on the ground floor, but that also is no. Says I won't give up my third-floor paradise for all the smell and noise of a ground-floor flat. Which is true, up here even B.E.S.T. bus rattle and rumble does not come. But what use of paradise if you are not alive in good health to enjoy it? Now doctor says intensive care but Parsi General Hospital has no place. Better to stay here than other hospitals, only . . ."

My eyes fixed on the stone-grey face of Viraf's father, I backed out of the sickroom, unseen. The hallway was empty. Viraf was waiting for me in the back room with the boards for Ludo and Snakes-and-Ladders. But I sneaked through the veranda and down the stairs without a word.

The compound was flooded in sunshine as I returned to the other end. On the way I passed the three white stumps we had once chalked on the compound wall's black stone. The lines were very faint, and could barely be seen, lost amongst more recent scribbles and abandoned games of noughts and crosses.

Mummy was in the kitchen, I could hear the roaring of the Primus stove. *Mamaiji,* sinister in her dark glasses, sat by the veranda window, sunlight reflecting off the thick, black lenses with leather blinders at the sides; after her cataract operation the doctor had told her to wear these for a few months.

Daddy was still reading the *Times* at the dining-table. Through the gloom of the light bulb I saw the Murphy Baby's innocent and joyous smile. I wondered what he looked like now. When I was two years old, there was a Murphy Baby Contest, and according to Mummy and Daddy my photograph, which had been entered, should have won. They said that in those days my smile had been just as, if not more, innocent and joyous.

The tweezers were lying on the table. I picked them up. They glinted pitilessly, like that long needle in Viraf's father. I dropped them with a shudder, and they clattered against the table.

Daddy looked up questioningly. His hair was dishevelled as I had left it, and I waited, hoping he would ask me to continue. To offer to do it was beyond me, but I wanted desperately that he should ask me now. I glanced at his face discreetly, from the corner of my eye. The lines on his forehead stood out all too clearly, and the stubble flecked with white, which by this hour should have disappeared down the drain with the shaving water. I swore to myself that never again would I begrudge him my help; I would get all the white hairs, one by one, if he would only ask me; I would concentrate on the tweezers as never before, I would do it as if all our lives were riding on the efficacy of the tweezers, yes, I would continue to do it Sunday after Sunday, no matter how long it took.

Daddy put down the newspaper and removed his glasses. He rubbed his eyes, then went to the bathroom. How tired he looked, and how his shoulders drooped; his gait lacked confidence, and I'd never noticed that before. He did not speak to me even though I was praying hard that he would. Something inside me grew very heavy, and I tried to swallow, to dissolve that heaviness in saliva, but swallowing wasn't easy either, the heaviness was blocking my throat.

I heard the sound of running water. Daddy was preparing to shave. I wanted to go and watch him, talk to him, laugh with him at the funny faces he made to get at all the tricky places with the razor, especially the cleft in his chin.

Instead, I threw myself on the bed. I felt like crying, and buried my face in the pillow. I wanted to cry for the way I had treated Viraf, and for his sick father with the long, cold needle in his arm and his rasping breath; for *Mamaiji* and her tired, darkened eyes spinning thread for our *kustis,* and for Mummy growing old in the dingy kitchen smelling of kerosene, where the Primus roared and her dreams were extinguished; I wanted to weep for myself, for not being able to hug Daddy when I wanted to, and for not ever saying thank you for cricket in the morning and pigeons and bicycles and dreams; and for all the white hairs that I was powerless to stop.

✳

Héctor Murena

To see whether Abraham does indeed fear His wrath, God the All-Knowing orders the old man to sacrifice Isaac, his only son (Genesis 22:1–19). Abraham takes his knife and is about to obey, when an angel stays Abraham's hand and replaces the boy with a sacrificial ram. Many writers have taken up the challenge of this horrific story, which lays bare the darkest side of a father and son relationship. In 1912, Kafka told the story in the form of a parable. Abraham (Kafka conjectures) wanted to perform God's command in the right manner but couldn't believe that he was the one who had been chosen. The world would laugh itself to death, Abraham imagined, to see an unsummoned Abraham come forward with his son. The sacrifice itself didn't horrify him, but the shame! "It is as if," Kafka wrote, "at the end of the year, when the best student was, in all solemnity, about to receive a prize, the worst student rose in the expectant stillness and came forward from his dirty desk in the last row because he had heard his name mistakenly, and the whole class burst out laughing." And Kafka adds this wicked twist: "But perhaps he had made no mistake at all; perhaps his name had really been called out; perhaps it had been the teacher's intention all along to make the reward for the best student simultaneously a punishment for the worst one."

Héctor Murena, a troubled Argentinian novelist and essayist who committed suicide in 1970, explored philosophical variations of classical themes in his half-dozen somewhat ponderous novels. A few of his shorter pieces, however, escape his overwrought style and clearly reveal an original and profound insight. In Argentina, after publishing an influential book of essays, *Original Sin in America* (1954), he became known as the leader of a generation of "parricides," so called by the critic Ezequiel Martínez Estrada because of his critical revisionist readings of the classics of the late nineteenth century. For Murena, neither Abraham nor Isaac are at the center of the tragedy; the conflict between fathers and sons exists almost independently of its victims and executioners.

THE SAW

héctor murena

Translated from the Spanish by Alberto Manguel

i t hangs motionless in the air. Flies circle sluggishly around it, settle on it, obstinately, as if it were something live, an old lion incapable of defending itself, whose oncoming death the flies can sense. But it is not a living being. Even though it is alive. And it will never fail to have a purpose, wherever it might happen to be.

A rudimentary cast-iron arc, almost rectangular, its tensor is a metal blade of tiny teeth, barely separated from one another. A dark wooden handle offers the human fist the possibility of grasping it, an indication of its disposition to serve. If it lacked a handle, its atrocious nature would become immediately obvious; the handle veils the unease, suggests it has been tamed, that a man can use it at his will. And yet, it could be made out of more wood, a complete wooden structure into which the metal teeth might fit, as is the case with other members of its species. It doesn't have one. It is made of cast-iron: iron and steel. Minerals torn from the centre of the earth, subjected to fire, to water, to the hammer; it twisted, resisting the required consistency and shape; it fell once again under the blows, the flames, the water; it shrieked, it whistled, before becoming this blind deep-water fish, still and dauntless. But now its presence alters the order of things;

its weight entails disrupture. It sets forth a new order, a threatening order, not easily repressible.

It dangles from a hook that hangs from a rod parallel to the floor, held up by four vertical poles. Eleven more hooks share the same rod; impaled on them are cuts of meat of various sizes, grayish and scarlet, streaked with seams and marbled layers of fat, offal, plucked fowl pierced through the skin of the neck. Below, on a slab of white marble covered with splinters of bone and crumbs of flesh, squats a huge and iridescent liver; also a skinned young goat whose large pathetic eyes appear to concentrate the pain of a degraded world.

These are the saw's surroundings: violence, mutilation, blood, torture, murder; murder, even though custom has prevented those who practise it to call it by that name. One might be able to tear it away from this place, strip it from the history that has attached itself to it, plunge it suddenly into solitude; it would not be long before it would call unto itself the same blood, it would breed blood, irreductably, and destruction would come and surround it like dreams come to those who sleep. Men know this in the depths of their minds, and try to keep it penned up among its animal victims. Because, if these barriers did not exist, how far, and by what devices, would it penetrate the human realm?

A few metres away, on the wide unpainted wooden shelves propped against one of the lateral walls, a unique collection has been gathered. Green heads of hair with tight and tender locks, others dark and lank and hard; brittle gold-skinned spheres under which can be seen a milky cut of flesh; cones covered in purple blotches, reminiscent of war machines; other, thinner cones, long, reddish reptiles with green and yellow tails; piles of earth-coloured bodies of rough and varied shapes, like pebbles on a beach, strewn by the sea. Stricken in their fibres, lymphatic, in pure circles, brazenly singing their colours, thankful for any shape, the dumb tribe of vegetables loudly reveal that impotence and resignation are the golden secret of all wisdom.

In the humid summer evening, only the flies are stirring, buzzing in a room gradually won over by darkness.

Someone comes in. He comes from the rooms from beyond the shop. Therefore not a stranger, but moving as if he were one: not with the assurance of someone walking through what is his, without questioning the pertinence, even the need of being there, but on tiptoes, creeping, wishing for the weightlessness of a speck of dust that won't disturb the scales. Not a thief: a child. He is five, maybe six years old: he has learned that, according to the rules of the adult world, everyone not standing still or doing what they want, flattering them in fact, is deemed illegal, punishable, for the child's own good, according to them. If one were to judge by his caution, at present the child doesn't have his own good in mind.

The small body, dressed in a grubby shirt and a blue pair of trousers torn at the seat, advances shyly. He decides to turn left and, when he reaches the edge of the counter, he bends down under the marble, sits on his haunches and starts to build a toy mountain out of the sawdust that covers the floor. Is that all? No: after a moment, he lifts his head and looks around him, slowly, uninterested in the task of his hands whose movement suddenly becomes a pretext for discovery. The honey-coloured clump of hair over his forehead accentuates with its shadow the greedy look of the eyes: the lovely beast knows that risk is at the root of all freedom, and even though he sees no one, his sense of smell makes him distrustful, makes him act as if he were preyed upon. But there is no one else there. He keeps on digging in the sawdust. Such patience reveals a surprising obstinacy.

After a while, he stands up; he walks to the other side of the counter; he observes every object; he moves about as if uncertain of what he is looking for. His eyes become fixed on the saw, hanging up high: perhaps he thinks of it as a heraldic weapon, and dreams of holding it one day, of waving it grandly, of conquering vast armies with it. Now it hangs too far away, it is too big; if it were suddenly placed in his hands, he'd cringe away in fright. He has now reached the other end of the counter.

Suddenly his attitude changes.

The fruitless movements and vacant looks disappear, together with the irresolution. In four quick steps he finds himself next to a stool he passed as he entered the room: it has become his prey. Like a thief, he circles around it before pouncing. He grabs it by the legs, drags it up to the counter, climbs on it, stretches his arms towards a wooden drawer sitting on the marble. He turns the key of the drawer and opens it. It is full of gleaming metal disks and rectangles of paper: red, green, brown. Like a thief he has fallen on the money, but not to steal it, to play, though perhaps thieves too imagine they are playing an adventurous game.

He plays, he sinks his fingers in the coins. Maybe there is something evil in this, something vicious, perverse, destructive, damnable. The truth is that the child seems now more beautiful than ever, with that concentrated seriousness of ecstatic moments in which the physical existence is forgotten; his face is tragically lit like that of a poet in a vision. He plays, pulls at the drawer, he wants to examine everything, touch everything. He pulls further. And suddenly the drawer escapes him, falls to the floor; after a thunderous crash, the bills scatter, the coins roll away in all directions. Frowning, the child climbs down quickly. Kneeling, he picks up the money, he tries to repair the mischief.

He hasn't noticed that, for the past couple of minutes, a figure is watching him, standing motionless at the back door.

Then the lights are switched on. Startled, he turns and sees who it is: a tall, massive man, his enormous gut draped in a stained white apron; his arms, tense, are thick and hairy; the brutal face wearing a black moustache whose tips cover the corners of the mouth. As they stare at one another, it becomes obvious that this moment has a long past history; an old wound that has been made raw again.

In silence, the man walks up to the child who jumps to his feet and recoils; in response, the man quickens his step. The victim, always cooperating with his executioner, taunts him by trying to defend itself. The natural contrast between their colours increases: as the child grows pale, until only two pink circles are left around the eyelids, the man's face fills with blood. Anger, as if capable of thought, swells inside him visibly. But anger doesn't think. The man has trapped the child against the counter and fixes him with flaming eyes. But he doesn't see the child. And, if he saw the child, there where the child now stands, he might well shudder. The man's whole aspect—the swollen veins in the neck, the apoplectic face—becomes alarming. Unless he does something, he will explode. What will he do? The child is trembling. If that colossus were to shout, to roar, the knot of tension might dissolve. But he doesn't shout. Only a slight sideways swaying of the body is noticeable. And the hands, the frightening hands? Why doesn't he hit him with them? Why doesn't he raise them and hit the child, make him fall, bleeding, stunned, a lesson taught? It would be better if he did; the child hopes for it. The man appears to consider the possibility. But the appearance is deceiving. He can't hit him. He can't use his hands, they are not his. He is not himself. And the hideous wormlike creature that has taken on his shape, doesn't see, doesn't speak, doesn't hit.

Suddenly, with one hand, the left hand, he grabs hold of the child's forearms, close to the wrists. Under the vise-like grip of those fingers the veins in the small hands turn purple. Imprisoned, one palm against the other, the man forces them sideways against the marble slab. As in a dream, but with the instinctive precision of a task fulfilled for the thousandth time, the hairy right arm does the only thing it can do: it reaches backwards, upwards, until it fastens onto the handle of the saw. Then it descends, holding it vertically, the blade pointing forward.

* * *

The woman who has come in hurriedly through the front door takes no more than three steps and goes no further. Later, she'd be surprised if someone were to ask her why she behaved in that manner; she wouldn't be able to find a reason. And yet, the emotion is so strong her feet seem nailed to the ground.

What does she see?

Nothing out of the ordinary. She sees the butcher holding the forelegs of a kid; she sees her son standing next to the counter, observing the operation. But from that ordinary scene emerges something indescribably atrocious. Nothing more natural than a son observing his father at work; but the child doesn't seem alive; he is like a wax statue, white, cast in horror. Nothing more natural than the butcher at his job. Sawing a bone; however, the job is now no longer human. The man saws, saws without stopping; the machine seems to have gone mad, having cut through the bone ten times, cutting through the flesh now, soon to reach the marble counter and unable to stop even then. The woman doesn't reflect on these details; she merely perceives them. First she thinks of calling out, to indicate her presence; then she realizes she wouldn't succeed; they can't see her, they can't hear her; she doesn't exist for them, they are in another world. This, perhaps, is what causes the strongest impression. Then she turns round and flees.

The man continues at his task, blindly ravaging the forelegs of the kid. At last he stops. As if an alien strength that had animated him until now had suddenly left him, the body relaxes, sags, the pressure of his hands ceases.

The saw falls heavily onto the floor.

The sound of the saw against the tiles wakes the child from the spell into which he seemed to have fallen; his eyes move, he takes in his surroundings; blood comes again to his face. Quickly he scuttles out through the back door.

The man's reaction is more curious; he takes one or two hesitant steps, as if drunk, towards the left; then he sits on the floor, covers his face with both hands and begins to shake convulsively, as if he were crying.

The saw is lying under the counter. It will be picked up later. It will be hung up again on the hook from which it was taken. The order, altered for a moment, will be restored, and it will wait there, motionless, dependent, useful. However, the saw will dream on, up there, in its place. Called into being by men, its presence will always weigh down on the human world with another world, a world in embryo, unimagined, a world that humans have prudently preferred not to imagine. Conceived by a will supposedly free, it will take advantage of every faltering of that will to supplant it with its own dreams. A bolt of lightning harnessed, it will never fail to have a purpose, wherever it might happen to be.

William Faulkner

A writer can have a deep sense of most loving bonds between father and son and yet be a terrible father himself; there is no guaranteed instruction in literary genius. While William Faulkner's "Barn Burning" is a wise, moving story of a son's belief in his father, Faulkner himself held no such hopes for his own children. Throughout his life, he fought halfheartedly against a lack of money and the excess of drink. In an attempt to free himself from both, he accepted a job in Hollywood as a screenwriter for Warner Brothers, where he contracted a nurse to follow him at three paces with a flask of whiskey in a small black bag, "to be produced as needed" in order to make sure the great novelist reached the studio on time. When he left Hollywood, an empty bottle was discovered in his desk, together with a sheet of paper on which he had written five hundred times his ideas for a screenplay: "Boy meets girl." Shortly before his death in 1962, his daughter Jill tried every conceivable ploy to keep him from getting drunk. At last he pushed her away with a grand gesture and asked her, "Who has ever heard of Shakespeare's child?"

The better side of him pronounced the Nobel Prize acceptance speech of 1950. "Man will not merely endure: he will prevail because he has a soul, a spirit capable of compassion and sacrifice and endurance." And he added, "The writer's duty is to write about these things."

BARN BURNING

william faulkner

the store in which the Justice of the Peace's court was sitting smelled of cheese. The boy, crouched on his nail keg at the back of the crowded room, knew he smelled cheese, and more: from where he sat he could see the ranked shelves close-packed with the solid, squat, dynamic shapes of tin cans whose labels his stomach read, not from the lettering which meant nothing to his mind but from the scarlet devils and the silver curve of fish—this, the cheese which he knew he smelled and the hermetic meat which his intestines believed he smelled coming in intermittent gusts momentary and brief between the other constant one, the smell and sense just a little of fear but mostly of despair and grief, the old fierce pull of blood. He could not see the table where the Justice sat and before which his father and his father's enemy (*our enemy* he thought in that despair; *ourn! mine and hisn both! He's my father!*) stood, but he could hear them, the two of them that is, because his father had said no word yet:

"But what proof have you, Mr. Harris?"

"I told you. The hog got into my corn. I caught it up and sent it back to him. He had no fence that would hold it. I told him so, warned him. The next time I put the hog in my pen. When he came to get it I gave him enough wire to patch up his pen. The

next time I put the hog up and kept it. I rode down to his house
and saw the wire I gave him still rolled on to the spool in his yard.
I told him he could have the hog when he paid me a dollar pound
fee. That evening a nigger came with the dollar and got the hog.
He was a strange nigger. He said, 'He say to tell you wood and hay
kin burn.' I said, 'What?' 'That whut he say to tell you,' the nigger
said. 'Wood and hay kin burn.' That night my barn burned. I got
the stock out but I lost the barn."

"Where is the nigger? Have you got him?"

"He was a strange nigger, I tell you. I don't know what
became of him."

"But that's not proof. Don't you see that's not proof?"

"Get that boy up here. He knows." For a moment the
boy thought too that the man meant his older brother until Harris
said, "Not him. The little one. The boy," and crouching, small for
his age, small and wiry like his father, in patched and faded jeans
even too small for him, with straight, uncombed, brown hair and
eyes gray and wild as storm scud, he saw the men between himself and the table part and become a lane of grim faces, at the end
of which he saw the Justice, a shabby, collarless, graying man in
spectacles, beckoning him. He felt no floor under his bare feet; he
seemed to walk beneath the palpable weight of the grim turning
faces. His father, stiff in his black Sunday coat donned not for the
trial but for the moving, did not even look at him. *He aims for me
to lie,* he thought, again with that frantic grief and despair. *And I
will have to do hit.*

"What's your name, boy?" the Justice said.

"Colonel Sartoris Snopes," the boy whispered.

"Hey?" the Justice said. "Talk louder. Colonel Sartoris?
I reckon anybody named for Colonel Sartoris in this country can't
help but tell the truth, can they?" The boy said nothing. *Enemy!
Enemy!* he thought; for a moment he could not even see, could
not see that the Justice's face was kindly nor discern that his voice
was troubled when he spoke to the man named Harris: "Do you
want me to question this boy?" But he could hear, and during

those subsequent long seconds while there was absolutely no sound in the crowded little room save that of quiet and intent breathing it was as if he had swung outward at the end of a grape vine, over a ravine, and at the top of the swing had been caught in a prolonged instant of mesmerized gravity, weightless in time.

"No!" Harris said violently, explosively. "Damnation! Send him out of here!" Now time, the fluid world, rushed beneath him again, the voices coming to him again through the smell of cheese and sealed meat, the fear and despair and the old grief of blood:

"This case is closed. I can't find against you, Snopes, but I can give you advice. Leave this country and don't come back to it."

His father spoke for the first time, his voice cold and harsh, level, without emphasis: "I aim to. I don't figure to stay in a country among people who . . ." he said something unprintable and vile, addressed to no one.

"That'll do," the Justice said. "Take your wagon and get out of this country before dark. Case dismissed."

His father turned, and he followed the stiff black coat, the wiry figure walking a little stiffly from where a Confederate provost's man's musket ball had taken him in the heel on a stolen horse thirty years ago, followed the two backs now, since his older brother had appeared from somewhere in the crowd, no taller than the father but thicker, chewing tobacco steadily, between the two lines of grim-faced men and out of the store and across the worn gallery and down the sagging steps and among the dogs and half-grown boys in the mild May dust, where as he passed a voice hissed:

"Barn burner!"

Again he could not see, whirling; there was a face in a red haze, moonlike, bigger than the full moon, the owner of it half again his size, he leaping in the red haze toward the face, feeling no blow, feeling no shock when his head struck the earth, scrabbling up and leaping again, feeling no blow this time either and tasting no blood, scrabbling up to see the other boy in full flight and himself already leaping into pursuit as his father's hand jerked him back, the harsh, cold voice speaking above him: "Go get in the wagon."

It stood in a grove of locusts and mulberries across the road. His two hulking sisters in their Sunday dresses and his mother and her sister in calico and sunbonnets were already in it, sitting on and among the sorry residue of the dozen and more movings which even the boy could remember—the battered stove, the broken beds and chairs, the clock inlaid with mother-of-pearl, which would not run, stopped at some fourteen minutes past two o'clock of a dead and forgotten day and time, which had been his mother's dowry. She was crying, though when she saw him she drew her sleeve across her face and began to descend from the wagon. "Get back," the father said.

"He's hurt. I got to get some water and wash his . . ."

"Get back in the wagon," his father said. He got in too, over the tail-gate. His father mounted to the seat where the older brother already sat and struck the gaunt mules two savage blows with the peeled willow, but without heat. It was not even sadistic; it was exactly that same quality which in later years would cause his descendants to over-run the engine before putting a motor car into motion, striking and reining back in the same movement. The wagon went on, the store with its quiet crowd of grimly watching men dropped behind; a curve in the road hid it. *Forever* he thought. *Maybe he's done satisfied now, now that he has . . .* stopping himself, not to say it aloud even to himself. His mother's hand touched his shoulder.

"Does hit hurt?" she said.

"Naw," he said. "Hit don't hurt. Lemme be."

"Can't you wipe some of the blood off before hit dries?"

"I'll wash to-night," he said. "Lemme be, I tell you."

The wagon went on. He did not know where they were going. None of them ever did or ever asked, because it was always somewhere, always a house of sorts waiting for them a day or two days or even three days away. Likely his father had already arranged to make a crop on another farm before he . . . Again he had to stop himself. He (the father) always did. There was something about his wolflike independence and even courage when the advantage was at least neutral which impressed strangers, as if they got from his latent ravening ferocity not so much a sense of dependability as a feeling that his ferocious conviction in the rightness of his own actions would be of advantage to all whose interest lay with his.

That night they camped, in a grove of oaks and beeches where a spring ran. The nights were still cool and they had a fire against it, of a rail lifted from a nearby fence and cut into lengths—a small fire, neat, niggard almost, a shrewd fire; such fires were his father's habit and custom always, even in freezing weather. Older, the boy might have remarked this and wondered why not a big one; why should not a man who had not only seen the waste and extravagance of war, but who had in his blood an inherent voracious prodigality with material not his own, have burned everything in sight? Then he might have gone a step farther and thought that that was the reason: that niggard blaze was the living fruit of nights passed during those four years in the woods hiding from all men, blue or gray, with his strings of horses (captured horses, he called them). And older still, he might have divined the true reason: that the element of fire spoke to some deep mainspring of his father's being, as the element of steel or of powder spoke to other men, as the one weapon for the preservation of integrity, else breath were not worth the breathing, and hence to be regarded with respect and used with discretion.

But he did not think this now and he had seen those same niggard blazes all his life. He merely ate his supper beside it and was already half asleep over his iron plate when his father called him, and once more he followed the stiff back, the stiff and ruthless limp, up the slope and on to the starlit road where, turning, he could see his father against the stars but without face or depth—a shape black, flat, and bloodless as though cut from tin in the iron folds of the frockcoat which had not been made for him, the voice harsh like tin and without heat like tin:

"You were fixing to tell them. You would have told him."
He didn't answer. His father struck him with the flat of his hand
on the side of the head, hard but without heat, exactly as he had
struck the two mules at the store, exactly as he would strike either
of them with any stick in order to kill a horse fly, his voice still
without heat or anger: "You're getting to be a man. You got to
learn. You got to learn to stick to your own blood or you ain't going
to have any blood to stick to you. Do you think either of them, any
man there this morning, would? Don't you know all they wanted
was a chance to get at me because they knew I had them beat?
Eh?" Later, twenty years later, he was to tell himself, "If I had said
they wanted only truth, justice, he would have hit me again." But
now he said nothing. He was not crying. He just stood there.
"Answer me," his father said.

"Yes," he whispered. His father turned.

"Get on to bed. We'll be there to-morrow."

To-morrow they were there. In the early afternoon the
wagon stopped before a paintless two-room house identical almost
with the dozen others it had stopped before even in the boy's ten
years, and again, as on the other dozen occasions, his mother and
aunt got down and began to unload the wagon, although his two
sisters and his father and brother had not moved.

"Likely hit ain't fitten for hawgs," one of the sisters said.

"Nevertheless, fit it will and you'll hog it and like it," his
father said. "Get out of them chairs and help your Ma unload."

The two sisters got down, big, bovine, in a flutter of
cheap ribbons; one of them drew from the jumbled wagon bed a
battered lantern, the other a worn broom. His father handed the
reins to the older son and began to climb stiffly over the wheel.
"When they get unloaded, take the team to the barn and feed
them." Then he said, and at first the boy thought he was still
speaking to his brother: "Come with me."

"Me?" he said.

"Yes," his father said. "You."

"Abner," his mother said. His father paused and looked

237

back—the harsh level stare beneath the shaggy, graying, irascible brows.

"I reckon I'll have a word with the man that aims to begin to-morrow owning me body and soul for the next eight months."

They went back up the road. A week ago—or before last night, that is—he would have asked where they were going, but not now. His father had struck him before last night but never before had he paused afterward to explain why; it was as if the blow and the following calm, outrageous voice still rang, repercussed, divulging nothing to him save the terrible handicap of being young, the light weight of his few years, just heavy enough to prevent his soaring free of the world as it seemed to be ordered but not heavy enough to keep him footed solid in it, to resist it and try to change the course of its events.

Presently he could see the grove of oaks and cedars and the other flowering trees and shrubs where the house would be, though not a house yet. They walked beside a fence massed with honeysuckle and Cherokee roses and came to a gate swinging open between two brick pillars, and now, beyond a sweep of drive, he saw the house for the first time and at that instant he forgot his father and the terror and despair both, and even when he remembered his father again (who had not stopped) the terror and despair did not return. Because, for all the twelve movings, they had sojourned until now in a poor country, a land of small farms and fields and houses, and he had never seen a house like this before. *Hit's big as a courthouse* he thought quietly, with a surge of peace and joy whose reason he could not have thought into words, being too young for that: *They are safe from him. People whose lives are a part of this peace and dignity are beyond his touch, he no more to them than a buzzing wasp: capable of stinging for a little moment but that's all; the spell of this peace and dignity rendering even the barns and stable and cribs which belong to it impervious to the puny flames he might contrive . . .* this, the peace and joy, ebbing for an instant as he looked again at the stiff black back, the stiff and implacable limp of the figure which was not dwarfed by the house, for the reason that it had never looked big anywhere and which now, against the serene columned backdrop, had more than ever that impervious quality of something cut ruthlessly from tin, depthless, as though, side-wise in the sun, it would cast no shadow. Watching him, the boy remarked the absolutely undeviating course which his father held and saw the stiff foot come squarely down in a pile of fresh drop-pings where a horse had stood in the drive and which his father could have avoided by a simple change of stride. But it ebbed only for a moment, though he could not have thought this into words either, walking on in the spell of the house, which he could even want but without envy, without sorrow, certainly never with that ravening and jealous rage which unknown to him walked in the ironlike black coat before him: *Maybe he will feel it too. Maybe it will even change him now from what maybe he couldn't help but be.*

      They crossed the portico. Now he could hear his father's stiff foot as it came down on the boards with clocklike finality, a sound out of all proportion to the displacement of the body it bore and which was not dwarfed either by the white door before it, as though it had attained to a sort of vicious and ravening minimum not to be dwarfed by anything—the flat, wide, black hat, the for-mal coat of broadcloth which had once been black but which had now that friction-glazed greenish cast of the bodies of old house flies, the lifted sleeve which was too large, the lifted hand like a curled claw. The door opened so promptly that the boy knew the Negro must have been watching them all the time, an old man with neat grizzled hair, in a linen jacket, who stood barring the door with his body, saying, "Wipe yo foots, white man, fo you come in here. Major ain't home nohow."

      "Get out of my way, nigger," his father said, without heat too, flinging the door back and the Negro also and entering, his hat still on his head. And now the boy saw the prints of the stiff foot on the doorjamb and saw them appear on the pale rug behind the machinelike deliberation of the foot which seemed to bear (or transmit) twice the weight which the body compassed. The Negro was shouting "Miss Lula! Miss Lula!" somewhere behind them, then the boy, deluged as though by a warm wave by a suave turn of carpeted stair and a pendant glitter of chandeliers and a mute gleam of gold frames, heard the swift feet and saw her too, a lady—perhaps he had never seen her like before either—in a gray, smooth gown with lace at the throat and an apron tied at the waist and the sleeves turned back, wiping cake or biscuit dough from her hands with a towel as she came up the hall, looking not at his father at all but at the tracks on the blond rug with an expression of incredulous amazement.

"I tried," the Negro cried. "I tole him to . . ."

"Will you please go away?" she said in a shaking voice. "Major de Spain is not at home. Will you please go away?"

His father had not spoken again. He did not speak again. He did not even look at her. He just stood stiff in the center of the rug, in his hat, the shaggy iron-gray brows twitching slightly above the pebble-colored eyes as he appeared to examine the house with brief deliberation. Then with the same deliberation he turned; the boy watched him pivot on the good leg and saw the stiff foot drag round the arc of the turning, leaving a final long and fading smear. His father never looked at it, he never once looked down at the rug. The Negro held the door. It closed behind them, upon the hysteric and indistinguishable woman-wail. His father stopped at the top of the steps and scraped his boot clean on the edge of it. At the gate he stopped again. He stood for a moment, planted stiffly on the stiff foot, looking back at the house. "Pretty and white, ain't it?" he said. "That's sweat. Nigger sweat. Maybe it ain't white enough yet to suit him. Maybe he wants to mix some white sweat with it."

Two hours later the boy was chopping wood behind the house within which his mother and aunt and the two sisters (the mother and aunt, not the two girls, he knew that; even at this distance and muffled by walls the flat loud voices of the two girls emanated an incorrigible idle inertia) were setting up the stove to prepare a meal, when he heard the hooves and saw the linen-clad

man on a fine sorrel mare, whom he recognized even before he
saw the rolled rug in front of the Negro youth following on a fat
bay carriage horse—a suffused, angry face vanishing, still at full
gallop, beyond the corner of the house where his father and
brother were sitting in the two tilted chairs; and a moment later,
almost before he could have put the axe down, he heard the
hooves again and watched the sorrel mare go back out of the yard,
already galloping again. Then his father began to shout one of the
sisters' names, who presently emerged backward from the kitchen
door dragging the rolled rug along the ground by one end while
the other sister walked behind it.

"If you ain't going to tote, go on and set up the wash
pot," the first said.

"You, Sarty!" the second shouted. "Set up the wash pot!"
His father appeared at the door, framed against that shabbiness,
as he had been against that other bland perfection, impervious to
either, the mother's anxious face at his shoulder.

"Go on," the father said. "Pick it up." The two sisters
stooped, broad, lethargic; stooping, they presented an incredible
expanse of pale cloth and a flutter of tawdry ribbons.

"If I thought enough of a rug to have to get hit all the
way from France I wouldn't keep hit where folks coming in would
have to tromp on hit," the first said. They raised the rug.

"Abner," the mother said. "Let me do it."

"You go back and git dinner," his father said. "I'll tend
to this."

From the woodpile through the rest of the afternoon the
boy watched them, the rug spread flat in the dust beside the bub-
bling wash-pot, the two sisters stooping over it with that profound
and lethargic reluctance, while the father stood over them in turn,
implacable and grim, driving them though never raising his voice
again. He could smell the harsh homemade lye they were using;
he saw his mother come to the door once and look toward them
with an expression not anxious now but very like despair; he saw his
father turn, and he fell to with the axe and saw from the corner of

his eye his father raise from the ground a flattish fragment of field stone and examine it and return to the pot, and this time his mother actually spoke: "Abner. Abner. Please don't. Please, Abner."

Then he was done too. It was dusk; the whippoorwills had already begun. He could smell coffee from the room where they would presently eat the cold food remaining from the mid-afternoon meal, though when he entered the house he realized they were having coffee again probably because there was a fire on the hearth, before which the rug now lay spread over the backs of the two chairs. The tracks of his father's foot were gone. Where they had been were now long, water-cloudy scoriations resembling the sporadic course of a lilliputian mowing machine.

It still hung there while they ate the cold food and then went to bed, scattered without order to claim up and down the two rooms, his mother in one bed, where his father would later lie, the older brother in the other, himself, the aunt, and the two sisters on pallets on the floor. But his father was not in bed yet. The last thing the boy remembered was the depthless, harsh silhouette of the hat and coat bending over the rug and it seemed to him that he had not even closed his eyes when the silhouette was standing over him, the fire almost dead behind it, the stiff foot prodding him awake. "Catch up the mule," his father said.

When he returned with the mule his father was standing in the black door, the rolled rug over his shoulder. "Ain't you going to ride?" he said.

"No. Give me your foot."

He bent his knee into his father's hand, the wiry, surprising power flowed smoothly, rising, he rising with it, on to the mule's bare back (they had owned a saddle once; the boy could remember it though not when or where) and with the same effortlessness his father swung the rug up in front of him. Now in the starlight they retraced the afternoon's path, up the dusty road rife with honeysuckle, through the gate and up the black tunnel of the drive to the lightless house, where he sat on the mule and felt the rough warp of the rug drag across his thighs and vanish.

"Don't you want me to help?" he whispered. His father did not answer and now he heard again that stiff foot striking the hollow portico with that wooden and clocklike deliberation, that outrageous overstatement of the weight it carried. The rug, hunched, not flung (the boy could tell that even in the darkness) from his father's shoulder struck the angle of wall and floor with a sound unbelievably loud, thunderous, then the foot again, unhurried and enormous; a light came on in the house and the boy sat, tense, breathing steadily and quietly and just a little fast, though the foot itself did not increase its beat at all, descending the steps now; now the boy could see him.

"Don't you want to ride now?" he whispered. "We kin both ride now," the light within the house altering now, flaring up and sinking. *He's coming down the stairs now,* he thought. He had already ridden the mule up beside the horse block; presently his father was up behind him and he doubled the reins over and slashed the mule across the neck, but before the animal could begin to trot the hard, thin arm came round him, the hard, knotted hand jerking the mule back to a walk.

In the first red rays of the sun they were in the lot, putting plow gear on the mules. This time the sorrel mare was in the lot before he heard it at all, the rider collarless and even bareheaded, trembling, speaking in a shaking voice as the woman in the house had done, his father merely looking up once before stooping again to the hame he was buckling, so that the man on the mare spoke to his stooping back.

"You must realize you have ruined that rug. Wasn't there anybody here, any of your women . . ." he ceased, shaking, the boy watching him, the older brother leaning now in the stable door, chewing, blinking slowly and steadily at nothing apparently. "It cost a hundred dollars. But you never had a hundred dollars. You never will. So I'm going to charge you twenty bushels of corn against your crop. I'll add it in your contract and when you come to the commissary you can sign it. That won't keep Mrs. de Spain quiet but maybe it will teach you to wipe your feet off before you enter her house again."

Then he was gone. The boy looked at his father, who still had not spoken or even looked up again, who was now adjusting the logger-head in the hame.

"Pap," he said. His father looked at him—the inscrutable face, the shaggy brows beneath which the gray eyes glinted coldly. Suddenly the boy went toward him, fast, stopping as suddenly. "You done the best you could!" he cried. "If he wanted hit done different why didn't he wait and tell you how? He won't get no twenty bushels! He won't git none! We'll gether hit and hide hit! I kin watch . . ."

"Did you put the cutter back in that straight stock like I told you?"

"No, sir," he said.

"Then go do it."

That was Wednesday. During the rest of that week he worked steadily, at what was within his scope and some which was beyond it, with an industry that did not need to be driven nor even commanded twice; he had this from his mother, with the difference that some at least of what he did he liked to do, such as splitting wood with the half-size axe which his mother and aunt had earned, or saved money somehow, to present him with at Christmas. In company with the two older women (and on one afternoon, even one of the sisters), he built pens for the shoat and the cow which were a part of his father's contract with the landlord, and one afternoon, his father being absent, gone somewhere on one of the mules, he went to the field.

They were running a middle buster now, his brother holding the plow straight while he handled the reins, and walking beside the straining mule, the rich black soil shearing cool and damp against his bare ankles, he thought *Maybe this is the end of it. Maybe even that twenty bushels that seems hard to have to pay for just a rug will be a cheap price for him to stop forever and always from being what he used to be;* thinking, dreaming now, so that his brother had to speak sharply to him to mind the mule: *Maybe he even won't collect the twenty bushels. Maybe it will all add up and balance and vanish—corn, rug, fire; the terror and grief, the being pulled two ways like between two teams of horses—gone, done with for ever and ever.*

Then it was Saturday; he looked up from beneath the mule he was harnessing and saw his father in the black coat and hat. "Not that," his father said. "The wagon gear." And then, two hours later, sitting in the wagon bed behind his father and brother on the seat, the wagon accomplished a final curve, and he saw the weathered paintless store with its tattered tobacco- and patent-medicine posters and the tethered wagons and saddle animals below the gallery. He mounted the gnawed steps behind his father and brother, and there again was the lane of quiet, watching faces for the three of them to walk through. He saw the man in spectacles sitting at the plank table and he did not need to be told this was a Justice of the Peace; he sent one glare of fierce, exultant, partisan defiance at the man in collar and cravat now, whom he had seen but twice before in his life, and that on a galloping horse, who now wore on his face an expression not of rage but of amazed unbelief which the boy could not have known was at the incredible circumstance of being sued by one of his own tenants, and came and stood against his father and cried at the Justice: "He ain't done it! He ain't burnt . . . "

"Go back to the wagon," his father said.

"Burnt?" the Justice said. "Do I understand this rug was burned too?"

"Does anybody here claim it was?" his father said. "Go back to the wagon." But he did not, he merely retreated to the rear of the room, crowded as that other had been, but not to sit down this time, instead, to stand pressing among the motionless bodies, listening to the voices:

"And you claim twenty bushels of corn is too high for the damage you did to the rug?"

"He brought the rug to me and said he wanted the tracks washed out of it. I washed the tracks out and took the rug back to him."

245

"But you didn't carry the rug back to him in the same condition it was in before you made the tracks on it."

His father did not answer, and now for perhaps half a minute there was no sound at all save that of breathing, the faint, steady suspiration of complete and intent listening.

"You decline to answer that, Mr. Snopes?" Again his father did not answer. "I'm going to find against you, Mr. Snopes. I'm going to find that you were responsible for the injury to Major de Spain's rug and hold you liable for it. But twenty bushels of corn seems a little high for a man in your circumstances to have to pay. Major de Spain claims it cost a hundred dollars. October corn will be worth about fifty cents. I figure that if Major de Spain can stand a ninety-five dollar loss on something he paid cash for, you can stand a five dollar loss you haven't earned yet. I hold you in damages to Major de Spain to the amount of ten bushels of corn over and above your contract with him, to be paid to him out of your crop at gathering time. Court adjourned."

It had taken no time hardly, the morning was but half begun. He thought they would return home and perhaps back to the field, since they were late, far behind all other farmers. But instead his father paced on behind the wagon, merely indicating with his hand for the older brother to follow with it, and crossed the road toward the blacksmith shop opposite, pressing on after his father, overtaking him, speaking, whispering up at the harsh, calm face beneath the weathered hat: "He won't git no ten bushels neither. He won't git one. We'll . . ." until his father glanced for an instant down at him, the face absolutely calm, the grizzled eyebrows tangled above the cold eyes, the voice almost pleasant, almost gentle:

"You think so? Well, we'll wait till October anyway."

The matter of the wagon—the setting of a spoke or two and the tightening of the tires—did not take long either, the business of the tires accomplished by driving the wagon into the spring branch behind the shop and letting it stand there, the mules nuzzling into the water from time to time, and the boy on the seat with the idle reins looking up the slope and through the sooty tunnel of the shed where the slow hammer rang and where his father sat on an upended cypress bolt, easily, either talking or listening, still sitting there when the boy brought the dripping wagon up out of the branch and halted it before the door.

"Take them on to the shade and hitch," his father said. He did so and returned. His father and the smith and a third man squatting on his heels inside the door were talking, about crops and animals; the boy squatting too in the ammoniac dust and hoof-pairings and scales of rust, heard his father tell a long and unhurried story out of the time before the birth of the older brother even when he had been a professional horsetrader. And then his father came up beside him where he stood before a tattered last year's circus poster on the other side of the store, gazing rapt and quiet at the scarlet horses, the incredible poisings and convolutions of tulle and tights and the painted leers of comedians, and said, "It's time to eat."

But not at home. Squatting beside his brother against the front wall, he watched his father emerge from the store and produce from a paper sack a segment of cheese and divide it carefully and deliberately into three with his pocket knife and produce crackers from the same sack. They all three squatted on the gallery and ate, slowly, without talking; then in the store again, they drank from a tin dipper tepid water smelling of the cedar bucket and of living beech trees. And still they did not go home. It was a horse lot this time, a tall rail fence upon and along which men stood and sat and out of which one by one horses were led, to be walked and trotted and then cantered back and forth along the road while the slow swapping and buying went on and the sun began to slant westward, they—the three of them—watching and listening, the older brother with his muddy eyes and his steady, inevitable tobacco, the father commenting now and then on certain of the animals, to no one in particular.

It was after sundown when they reached home. They ate supper by lamplight, then, sitting on the doorstep, the boy watched the night fully accomplish, listening to the whippoorwills and the frogs, when he heard his mother's voice: "Abner! No! No! Oh, God. Oh, God. Abner!" and he rose, whirled, and saw the altered light through the door where a candle stub now burned in a bottle neck on the table and his father, still in the hat and coat, at once formal and burlesque as though dressed carefully for some shabby and ceremonial violence, emptying the reservoir of the lamp back into the five-gallon kerosene can from which it had been filled, while the mother tugged at his arm until he shifted the lamp to the other hand and flung her back, not savagely or viciously, just hard, into the wall, her hands flung out against the wall for balance, her mouth open and in her face the same quality of hopeless despair as had been in her voice. Then his father saw him standing in the door.

"Go to the barn and get that can of oil we were oiling the wagon with," he said. The boy did not move. Then he could speak.

"What . . ." he cried. "What are you . . ."

"Go get that oil," his father said. "Go."

Then he was moving, running, outside the house, toward the stable: this the old habit, the old blood which he had not been permitted to choose for himself, which had been bequeathed him willy nilly and which had run for so long (and who knew where, battening on what of outrage and savagery and lust) before it came to him. *I could keep on,* he thought. *I could run on and on and never look back, never need to see his face again. Only I can't. I can't,* the rusted can in his hand now, the liquid sploshing in it as he ran back to the house and into it, into the sound of his mother's weeping in the next room, and handed the can to his father.

"Ain't you going to even send a nigger?" he cried. "At least you sent a nigger before!"

This time his father didn't strike him. The hand came even faster than the blow had, the same hand which had set the can on the table with almost excruciating care flashing from the can toward him too quick for him to follow it, gripping him by the back of his shirt and on to tiptoe before he had seen it quit the can, the face stooping at him in breathless and frozen ferocity, the cold, dead voice speaking over him to the older brother who leaned against the table, chewing with that steady, curious, sidewise motion of cows:

"Empty the can into the big one and go on. I'll catch up with you."

"Better tie him up to the bedpost," the brother said.

"Do like I told you," the father said. Then the boy was moving, his bunched shirt and the hard, bony hand between his shoulder-blades, his toes just touching the floor, across the room and into the other one, past the sisters sitting with spread heavy thighs in the two chairs over the cold hearth, and to where his mother and aunt sat side by side on the bed, the aunt's arms about his mother's shoulders.

"Hold him," the father said. The aunt made a startled movement. "Not you," the father said. "Lennie. Take hold of him. I want to see you do it." His mother took him by the wrist. "You'll hold him better than that. If he gets loose don't you know what he is going to do? He will go up yonder." He jerked his head toward the road. "Maybe I'd better tie him."

"I'll hold him," his mother whispered.

"See you do then." Then his father was gone, the stiff foot heavy and measured upon the boards, ceasing at last.

Then he began to struggle. His mother caught him in both arms, he jerking and wrenching at them. He would be stronger in the end, he knew that. But he had no time to wait for it. "Lemme go!" he cried. "I don't want to have to hit you!"

"Let him go!" the aunt said. "If he don't go, before God, I am going up there myself!"

"Don't you see I can't?" his mother cried. "Sarty! Sarty! No! No! Help me, Lizzie!"

Then he was free. His aunt grasped at him but it was too late. He whirled, running, his mother stumbled forward on to her knees behind him, crying to the nearer sister: "Catch him, Net! Catch him!" But that was too late too, the sister (the sisters were twins, born at the same time, yet either of them now gave

249

the impression of being, encompassing as much living meat and volume and weight as any other two of the family) not yet having begun to rise from the chair, her head, face, alone merely turned, presenting to him in the flying instant an astonishing expanse of young female features untroubled by any surprise even, wearing only an expression of bovine interest. Then he was out of the room, out of the house, in the mild dust of the starlit road and the heavy rifeness of honeysuckle, the pale ribbon unspooling with terrific slowness under his running feet, reaching the gate at last and turning in, running, his heart and lungs drumming, on up the drive toward the lighted house, the lighted door. He did not knock, he burst in, sobbing for breath, incapable for the moment of speech; he saw the astonished face of the Negro in the linen jacket without knowing when the Negro had appeared.

"De Spain!" he cried, panted. "Where's . . ." then he saw the white man too emerging from a white door down the hall. "Barn!" he cried. "Barn!"

"What?" the white man said. "Barn?"

"Yes!" the boy cried. "Barn!"

"Catch him!" the white man shouted.

But it was too late this time too. The Negro grasped his shirt, but the entire sleeve, rotten with washing, carried away, and he was out that door too and in the drive again, and had actually never ceased to run even while he was screaming into the white man's face.

Behind him the white man was shouting, "My horse! Fetch my horse!" and he thought for an instant of cutting across the park and climbing the fence into the road, but he did not know the park nor how high the vine-massed fence might be and he dared not risk it. So he ran on down the drive, blood and breath roaring; presently he was in the road again though he could not see it. He could not hear either: the galloping mare was almost upon him before he heard her, and even then he held his course, as if the very urgency of his wild grief and need must in a moment more find him wings, waiting until the ultimate instant to hurl himself aside and into the weed-choked roadside ditch as the horse thundered past and on, for an instant in furious silhouette against the stars, the tranquil early summer night sky which, even before the shape of the horse and rider vanished, stained abruptly and violently upward: a long, swirling roar incredible and soundless, blacking the stars, and he springing up and into the road again, running again, knowing it was too late yet still running even after he heard the shot and, an instant later, two shots, passing now without knowing he had ceased to run, crying "Pap! Pap!", running again before he knew he had begun to run, stumbling, tripping over something and scrabbling up again without ceasing to run, looking backward over his shoulder at the glare as he got up, running on among the invisible trees, panting, sobbing, "Father! Father!"

At midnight he was sitting on the crest of a hill. He did not know it was midnight and he did not know how far he had come. But there was the glare behind him now and he sat now, his back toward what he had called home for four days anyhow, his face toward the dark woods which he would enter when breath was strong again, small, shaking steadily in the chill darkness, hugging himself into the remainder of his thin, rotten shirt, the grief and despair now no longer terror and fear but just grief and despair. *Father. My father,* he thought. "He was brave!" he cried suddenly, aloud but not loud, no more than a whisper. "He was! He was in the war! He was in Colonel Sartoris' cav'ry!" not knowing that his father had gone to that war a private in the fine old European sense, wearing no uniform, admitting the authority of and giving fidelity to no man or army or flag, going to war as Malbrouck himself did: for booty—it meant nothing and less than nothing to him if it were enemy booty or his own.

The slow constellations wheeled on. It would be dawn and then sun-up after a while and he would be hungry. But that would be to-morrow and now he was only cold, and walking would cure that. His breathing was easier now and he decided to get up and go on, and then he found that he had been asleep because he knew it was almost dawn, the night almost over. He could tell that from the whippoorwills. They were everywhere now among the dark trees below him, constant and inflectioned and ceaseless, so that, as the instant for giving over to the day birds drew nearer and nearer, there was no interval at all between them. He got up. He was a little stiff, but walking would cure that too as it would the cold, and soon there would be the sun. He went on down the hill, toward the dark woods within which the liquid silver voices of the birds called unceasing—the rapid and urgent beating of the urgent and quiring heart of the late spring night. He did not look back.

Dan Jacobson

Dan Jacobson was born in South Africa, spent some time in a kibbutz in Israel, and finally settled in England in 1958. His stories, which he began publishing in 1953, have always sprung, he has said, from the memory of a particular person or an incident that will "suddenly turn in its sleep and show how much life there was still in it." Then comes a time for "curiosity, speculation, invention, the righting or the aggravation of old wrongs, a playful or malicious juxtaposition of quite different people and incidents upon those recollected, a readiness at all stages to subject the results to rough handling, to sudden reversals and abridgements." In the end, Jacobson maintains, the story must surprise him, so that it won't collapse the moment he turns his back on it.

Life itself sometimes provided the afterword, offering sequels more melodramatic or pathetic than anything Jacobson might have dared to invent. In the case of "The Zulu and the Zeide," Jacobson discovered that the man on whom he had based the character of Harry Grossman eventually became senile and very difficult to cope with. Jacobson explains, "So his children hired an African male servant to look after him, as I write of him doing for his father. But because times had changed and the family had prospered, these two did not wander about on foot, as my characters do, but instead drove about in a car, with the African at the wheel. One of their favorite drives was to 'Israel,' which the old man had developed an inordinate desire to visit before his life ended. They would drive to a spot in the empty countryside around Johannesburg; the driver would point at the veld ahead of them and say, 'There's Israel,' and his employer would sit Moses-like in the seat of his car, looking out upon the promised land."

THE ZULU AND THE ZEIDE

dan jacobson

old man Grossman was worse than a nuisance. He was a source of constant anxiety and irritation; he was a menace to himself and to the passing motorists into whose path he would step, to the children in the streets whose games he would break up, sending them flying, to the householders who at night would approach him with clubs in their hands, fearing him a burglar; he was a butt and a jest to the African servants who would tease him on street corners.

It was impossible to keep him in the house. He would take any opportunity to slip out—a door left open meant that he was on the streets, a window unlatched was a challenge to his agility, a walk in the park was as much a game of hide-and-seek as a walk. The old man's health was good, physically; he was quite spry, and he could walk far, and he could jump and duck if he had to. And all his physical activity was put to only one purpose: to running away. It was a passion for freedom that the old man might have been said to have, could anyone have seen what joy there could have been for him in wandering aimlessly about the streets, in sitting footsore on pavements, in entering other people's homes, in stumbling behind advertisement hoardings across undeveloped building plots, in toiling up the stairs of fifteen-storey blocks of flats in which he had no business, in being brought home by large young policemen who winked at Harry Grossman, the old man's son, as they gently hauled his father out of their flying-squad cars.

'He's always been like this,' Harry would say, when people asked him about his father. And when they smiled and said: 'Always?' Harry would say, 'Always. I know what I'm talking about. He's my father, and I know what he's like. He gave my mother enough grey hairs before her time. All he knew was to run away.'

Harry's reward would come when the visitors would say: 'Well, at least you're being as dutiful to him as anyone can be.'

It was a reward that Harry always refused. 'Dutiful? What can you do? There's nothing else you can do.' Harry Grossman knew that there was nothing else he could do. Dutifulness had been his habit of life: it had had to be, having the sort of father he had, and the strain of duty had made him abrupt and begrudging: he even carried his thick, powerful shoulders curved inwards, to keep what he had to himself. He was a thick-set, bunch-faced man, with large bones, and short, jabbing gestures; he was in the prime of life, and he would point at the father from whom he had inherited his strength, and on whom the largeness of bone showed now only as so much extra leanness that the clothing had to cover, and say: 'You see him? Do you know what he once did? My poor mother saved enough money to send him from the old country to South Africa; she bought clothes for him, and a ticket, and she sent him to her brother, who was already here. He was going to make enough money to bring me out, and my mother and my brother, all of us. But on the boat from Bremen to London he met some other Jews who were going to South America, and they said to him: "Why are you going to South Africa? It's a wild country, the savages will eat you. Come to South America and you'll make a fortune." So in London he exchanged his ticket. And we don't hear from him for six months. Six months later he gets a friend to write to my mother asking her please to send him enough money to pay for his ticket back to the old country—he's dying in Argentina, the Spaniards are killing him, he says, and he must come home. So my mother borrows from her brother to bring him back again. Instead of a fortune he brought her a new debt, and that was all.'

But Harry was dutiful, how dutiful his friends had reason to see again when they would urge him to try sending the old man to a home for the aged. 'No,' Harry would reply, his features moving heavily and reluctantly to a frown, a pout, as he showed how little the suggestion appealed to him. 'I don't like the idea. Maybe one day when he needs medical attention all the time I'll feel differently about it, but not now, not now. He wouldn't like it, he'd be unhappy. We'll look after him as long as we can. It's a job. It's something you've got to do.'

More eagerly Harry would go back to a recital of the old man's past. 'He couldn't even pay for his own passage out. I had to pay the loan back. We came out together—my mother wouldn't let him go by himself again, and I had to pay off her brother who advanced the money for us. I was a boy—what was I?—sixteen, seventeen, but I paid for his passage, and my own, and my mother's and then my brother's. It took me a long time, let me tell you. And then my troubles with him weren't over.' Harry even reproached his father for his myopia; he could clearly enough remember his chagrin when shortly after their arrival in South Africa, after it had become clear that Harry would be able to make his way in the world and be a support to the whole family, the old man—who at that time had not really been so old—had suddenly, almost dramatically, grown so short-sighted that he had been almost blind without the glasses that Harry had had to buy for him. And Harry could remember too how he had then made a practice of losing the glasses or breaking them with the greatest frequency, until it had been made clear to him that he was no longer expected to do any work. 'He doesn't do that any more. When he wants to run away now he sees to it that he's wearing his glasses. That's how he's always been. Sometimes he recognizes me, at other times, when he doesn't want to, he just doesn't know who I am.'

What Harry said about his father sometimes failing to recognize him was true. Sometimes the old man would call out to his son, when he would see him at the end of a passage, 'Who are you?' Or he would come upon Harry in a room and demand of him, 'What do you want in my house?'

'Your house?' Harry would say, when he felt like teasing the old man. 'Your house?'

'Out of my house!' the old man would shout back.

'Your house? Do you call this your house?' Harry would reply, smiling at the old man's fury.

Harry was the only one in the house who talked to the old man, and then he didn't so much talk to him, as talk of him to others. Harry's wife was a dim and silent woman, crowded out by her husband and the large-boned sons like himself that she had borne him, and she would gladly have seen the old man in an old-age home. But her husband had said no, so she put up with the old man, though for herself she could see no possible better end for him than a period of residence in a home for aged Jews which she had once visited, and which had impressed her most favourably with its glass and yellow brick, the noiseless rubber tiles in its corridors, its secluded grassed grounds, and the uniforms worn by the attendants to the establishment. But she put up with the old man; she did not talk to him. The grandchildren had nothing to do with their grandfather—they were busy at school, playing rugby and cricket, they could hardly speak Yiddish, and they were embarrassed by him in front of their friends; and when the grandfather did take any notice of them it was only to call them Boers and *goyim* and *shkotzim* in sudden quavering rages which did not disturb them at all.

The house itself—a big single-storeyed place of brick, with a corrugated iron roof above and a wide stoep all round— Harry Grossman had bought years before, and in the continual rebuilding the suburb was undergoing it was beginning to look old-fashioned. But it was solid and prosperous, and withindoors curiously masculine in appearance, like the house of a widower.

The furniture was of the heaviest African woods, dark, and built to last, the passages were lined with bare linoleum, and the few pictures on the walls, big brown and grey mezzotints in heavy frames, had not been looked at for years. The servants were both men, large ignored Zulus who did their work and kept up the brown gleam of the furniture.

It was from this house that old man Grossman tried to escape. He fled through the doors and the windows and out into the wide sunlit streets of the town in Africa, where the blocks of flats were encroaching upon the single-storeyed houses behind their gardens. And in these streets he wandered.

It was Johannes, one of the Zulu servants, who suggested a way of dealing with old man Grossman. He brought to the house one afternoon Paulus, whom he described as his 'brother'. Harry Grossman knew enough to know that 'brother' in this context could mean anything from the son of one's mother to a friend from a neighbouring *kraal*, but by the speech that Johannes made on Paulus's behalf he might indeed have been the latter's brother. Johannes had to speak for Paulus, for Paulus knew no English. Paulus was a 'raw boy', as raw as a boy could possibly come. He was a muscular, moustached and bearded African, with pendulous ear-lobes showing the slits in which the tribal plugs had once hung; and on his feet he wore sandals the soles of which were cut from old motor-car tyres, the thongs from red inner tubing. He wore neither hat nor socks, but he did have a pair of khaki shorts which were too small for him, and a shirt without any buttons: buttons would in any case have been of no use for the shirt could never have closed over his chest. He swelled magnificently out of his clothing, and above there was a head carried well back, so that his beard, which had been trained to grow in two sharp points from his chin, bristled ferociously forward under his melancholy and almost mandarin-like moustache. When he smiled, as he did once or twice during Johannes's speech, he showed his white, even teeth, but for the most part he stood looking rather shyly to the side of Harry Grossman's head, with his hands behind his back and his bare knees bent a little forward, as if to show how little he was asserting himself, no matter what his 'brother' might have been saying about him.

His expression did not change when Harry said that it seemed hopeless, that Paulus was too raw, and Johannes explained what the baas had just said. He nodded agreement when Johannes explained to him that the baas said that it was a pity that he knew no English. But whenever Harry looked at him, he smiled, not ingratiatingly, but simply smiling above his beard, as though saying: 'Try me.' Then he looked grave again as Johannes expatiated on his virtues. Johannes pleaded for his 'brother'. He said that the baas knew that he, Johannes, was a good boy. Would he, then, recommend to the baas a boy who was not a good boy too? The baas could see for himself, Johannes said, that Paulus was not one of these town boys, these street loafers: he was a good boy, come straight from the *kraal*. He was not a thief or a drinker. He was strong, he was a hard worker, he was clean, and he could be as gentle as a woman. If he, Johannes, were not telling the truth about all these things, then he deserved to be chased away. If Paulus failed in any single respect, then he, Johannes, would voluntarily leave the service of the baas, because he had said untrue things to the baas. But if the baas believed him, and gave Paulus his chance, then he, Johannes, would teach Paulus all the things of the house and the garden, so that Paulus would be useful to the baas in ways other than the particular task for which he was asking the baas to hire him. And, rather daringly, Johannes said that it did not matter so much if Paulus knew no English, because the old baas, the *oubaas,* knew no English either.

It was as something in the nature of a joke—almost a joke against his father—that Harry Grossman gave Paulus his chance. For Paulus was given his chance. He was given a room in the servants' quarters in the back yard, into which he brought a tin trunk painted red and black, a roll of blankets, and a guitar with a picture of a cowboy on the back. He was given a houseboy's outfit of blue denim blouse and shorts, with red piping round the edges, into which he fitted, with his beard and physique, like a king in exile in some pantomime. He was given his food three times a day, after the white people had eaten, a bar of soap every week, cast-off clothing at odd intervals, and the sum of one pound five shillings per week, five shillings of which he took, the rest being left at his request, with the baas, as savings. He had a free after-noon once a week, and he was allowed to entertain not more than two friends at any one time in his room. And in all the particulars that Johannes had enumerated, Johannes was proved reliable. Paulus was not one of these town boys, these street loafers. He did not steal or drink, he was clean and he was honest and hard-working. And he could be gentle as a woman.

260

It took Paulus some time to settle down to his job; he had to conquer not only his own shyness and strangeness in the new house filled with strange people—let alone the city, which, since taking occupation of his room, he had hardly dared to enter—but also the hostility of old man Grossman, who took immediate fright at Paulus and redoubled his efforts to get away from the house upon Paulus's entry into it. As it happened, the first result of this persistence on the part of the old man was that Paulus was able to get the measure of the job, for he came to it with a willingness of spirit that the old man could not vanquish, but could only teach. Paulus had been given no instructions, he had merely been told to see that the old man did not get himself into trouble, and after a few days of bewilderment Paulus found his way. He simply went along with the old man.

At first he did so cautiously, following the old man at a distance, for he knew the other had no trust in him. But later he was able to follow the old man openly; still later he was able to walk side by side with him, and the old man did not try to escape from him. When old man Grossman went out, Paulus went too, and there was no longer any need for the doors and windows to be watched, or the police to be telephoned. The young bearded Zulu and the old bearded Jew from Lithuania walked together in the

streets of the town that was strange to them both; together they
looked over fences of the large gardens and into the shining foyers
of the blocks of flats; together they stood on the pavements of the
main arterial roads and watched the cars and trucks rush between
the tall buildings; together they walked in the small, sandy parks,
and when the old man was tired Paulus saw to it that he sat on a
bench and rested. They could not sit on the bench together, for
only whites were allowed to sit on the benches, but Paulus would
squat on the ground at the old man's feet and wait until he judged
the old man had rested long enough, before moving on again.
Together they stared into the windows of the suburban shops, and
though neither of them could read the signs outside the shops,
the advertisements on billboards, the traffic signs at the side of
the road, Paulus learned to wait for the traffic lights to change
from red to green before crossing a street, and together they
stared at the Coca-cola girls and the advertisements for beer and
the cinema posters. On a piece of cardboard which Paulus carried
in the pocket of his blouse Harry had had one of his sons print the
old man's name and address, and whenever Paulus was uncertain
of the way home, he would approach an African or a friendly-
looking white man and show him the card, and try his best to
follow the instructions, or at least the gesticulations which were
all of the answers of the white men that meant anything to him.
But there were enough Africans to be found, usually, who were
more sophisticated than himself, and though they teased him for
his 'rawness' and for holding the sort of job he had, they helped
him too. And neither Paulus nor old man Grossman were aware
that when they crossed a street hand-in-hand, as they sometimes
did when the traffic was particularly heavy, there were white men
who averted their eyes from the sight of this degradation, which
could come upon a white man when he was old and senile and
dependent.

     Paulus knew only Zulu, the old man knew only Yiddish,
so there was no language in which they could talk to one another.
But they talked all the same: they both explained, commented and

complained to each other of the things they saw around them, and often they agreed with one another, smiling and nodding their heads and explaining again with their hands what each happened to be talking about. They both seemed to believe that they were talking about the same things, and often they undoubtedly were, when they lifted their heads sharply to see an aeroplane cross the blue sky between two buildings, or when they reached the top of a steep road and turned to look back the way they had come, and saw below them the clean impervious towers of the city thrust nakedly against the sky in brand-new piles of concrete and glass and face-brick. Then down they would go again, among the houses and the gardens where the beneficent climate encouraged both palms and oak trees to grow indiscriminately among each other—as they did in the garden of the house to which, in the evenings, Paulus and old man Grossman would eventually return.

In and about the house Paulus soon became as indispensable to the old man as he was on their expeditions out of it. Paulus dressed him and bathed him and trimmed his beard, and when the old man woke distressed in the middle of the night it would be for Paulus that he would call—'Der schwarzer,' he would shout (for he never learned Paulus's name), 'vo's der schwarzer'— and Paulus would change his sheets and pyjamas and put him back to bed again. 'Baas Ziede', Paulus called the old man, picking up the Yiddish word for grandfather from the children of the house.

And that was something that Harry Grossman told everyone of. For Harry persisted in regarding the arrangement as a kind of joke, and the more the arrangement succeeded the more determinedly did he try to spread the joke, so that it should be a joke not only against his father but a joke against Paulus too. It had been a joke that his father should be looked after by a raw Zulu: it was going to be a joke that the Zulu was successful at it. 'Baas Zeide! That's what der schwarzer calls him—have you ever heard the like of it? And you should see the two of them, walking about in the streets hand-in-hand like two schoolgirls. Two clever ones, der schwarzer and my father going for a promenade, and between them I tell you you wouldn't be able to find out what day of the week or what time of day it is.'

And when people said, 'Still that Paulus seems a very good boy,' Harry would reply:

'Why shouldn't he be? With all his knowledge, are there so many better jobs that he'd be able to find? He keeps the old man happy—very good, very nice, but don't forget that that's what he's paid to do. What does he know any better to do, a simple kaffir from the *kraal*? He knows he's got a good job, and he'd be a fool if he threw it away. Do you think,' Harry would say, and this too would insistently be part of the joke, 'if I had nothing else to do with my time I wouldn't be able to make the old man happy?' Harry would look about his sitting-room, where the floorboards bore the weight of his furniture, or when they sat on the stoep he would measure with his glance the spacious garden aloof from the street beyond the hedge. 'I've got other things to do. And I had other things to do, plenty of them, all my life, and not only for myself.' What these things were that he had had to do all his life would send him back to his joke. 'No, I think the old man has just found his level in *der schwarzer*—and I don't think *der schwarzer* could cope with anything else.'

Harry teased the old man to his face too, about his 'black friend', and he would ask his father what he would do if Paulus went away; once he jokingly threatened to send the Zulu away. But the old man didn't believe the threat, for Paulus was in the house when the threat was made, and the old man simply left his son and went straight to Paulus's room, and sat there with Paulus for security. Harry did not follow him: he would never have gone into any of his servants' rooms least of all that of Paulus. For though he made a joke of him to others, to Paulus himself Harry always spoke gruffly, unjokingly, with no patience. On that day he had merely shouted after the old man, 'Another time he won't be there.'

Yet it was strange to see how Harry Grossman would always be drawn to the room in which he knew his father and

Paulus to be. Night after night he came into the old man's bed-room when Paulus was dressing or undressing the old man; almost as often Harry stood in the steamy, untidy bathroom when the old man was being bathed. At these times he hardly spoke, he offered no explanation of his presence: he stood dourly and silently in the room, in his customary powerful and begrudging stance, with one hand clasping the wrist of the other and both supporting his waist, and he watched Paulus at work. The backs of Paulus's hands were smooth and black and hairless, they were paler on the palms and at the finger nails, and they worked deftly about the body of the old man, who was submissive under the ministrations of the other. At first Paulus had sometimes smiled at Harry while he worked, with his straightforward, even smile in which there was no invita-tion to a complicity in patronage, but rather an encouragement to Harry to draw forward. But after the first few evenings of this work that Harry had watched, Paulus no longer smiled at his mas-ter. And while he worked Paulus could not restrain himself, even under Harry's stare, from talking in a soft, continuous flow of Zulu, to encourage the old man and to exhort him to be helpful and to express his pleasure in how well the work was going. When Paulus would at last wipe the gleaming soap-flakes from his dark hands he would sometimes, when the old man was tired, stoop low and with a laugh pick up the old man and carry him easily down the passage to his bedroom. Harry would follow; he would stand in the passage and watch the burdened, barefooted Zulu until the door of his father's room closed behind them both.

Only once did Harry wait on such an evening for Paulus to reappear from his father's room. Paulus had already come out, had passed him in the narrow passage, and had already subduedly said: 'Good night, baas,' before Harry called suddenly:

'Hey! Wait!'

'Baas,' Paulus said, turning his head. Then he came quickly to Harry. 'Baas,' he said again, puzzled and anxious to know why his baas, who so rarely spoke to him, should suddenly have called him like this, at the end of the day, when his work was over.

Harry waited again before speaking, waiting long enough for Paulus to say: 'Baas?' once more, and to move a little closer, and to lift his head for a moment before letting it drop respectfully down.

'The *oubaas* was tired tonight,' Harry said. 'Where did you take him? What did you do with him?'

'Baas?' Paulus said quickly. Harry's tone was so brusque that the smile Paulus gave asked for no more than a moment's remission of the other's anger.

But Harry went on loudly: 'You heard what I said. What did you do with him that he looked so tired?'

'Baas—I—' Paulus was flustered, and his hands beat in the air for a moment, but with care, so that he would not touch his baas. 'Please baas.' He brought both hands to his mouth, closing it forcibly. He flung his hands away. 'Johannes,' he said with relief, and he had already taken the first step down the passage to call his interpreter.

'No!' Harry called. 'You mean you don't understand what I say? I know you don't,' Harry shouted, though in fact he had forgotten until Paulus had reminded him. The sight of Paulus's startled, puzzled, and guilty face before him filled him with a lust to see this man, this nurse with the face and the figure of a warrior, look more startled, puzzled, and guilty yet; and Harry knew that it could so easily be done, it could be done simply by talking to him in the language he could not understand. 'You're a fool,' Harry said. 'You're like a child. You understand nothing, and it's just as well for you that you need nothing. You'll always be where you are, running to do what the white baas tells you to do. Look how you stand! Do you think I understood English when I came here?' Harry said, and then with contempt, using one of the few Zulu words he knew: '*Hamba!* Go! Do you think I want to see you?'

'*Au* baas!' Paulus exclaimed in distress. He could not remonstrate; he could only open his hands in a gesture to show that he knew neither the words Harry used, nor in what he had been remiss that Harry should have spoken in such angry tones to him. But Harry gestured him away, and had the satisfaction of seeing Paulus shuffle off like a schoolboy.

Harry was the only person who knew that he and his father had quarrelled shortly before the accident that ended the old man's life took place; this was something that Harry was to keep secret for the rest of his life.

Late in the afternoon they quarrelled, after Harry had come back from the shop out of which he made his living. Harry came back to find his father wandering about the house, shouting for *der schwarzer,* and his wife complaining that she had already told the old man at least five times that *der schwarzer* was not in the house: it was Paulus's afternoon off.

Harry went to his father, and when his father came eagerly to him, he too told the old man, 'Der *schwarzer's* not here.' So the old man, with Harry following, turned away and continued going from room to room, peering in through the doors. 'Der *schwarzer's* not here,' Harry said. 'What do you want him for?'

Still the old man ignored him. He went down the passage towards the bedrooms. 'What do you want him for?' Harry called after him.

The old man went into every bedroom, still shouting for *der schwarzer.* Only when he was in his own bare bedroom did he look at Harry. 'Where's *der schwarzer?*' he asked.

'I've told you ten times I don't know where he is. What do you want him for?'

'I want *der schwarzer.*'

'I know you want him. But he isn't here.'

'I want *der schwarzer.*'

'Do you think I haven't heard you? He isn't here.'

'Bring him to me,' the old man said.

'I can't bring him to you. I don't know where he is.' Then Harry steadied himself against his own anger. He said quietly: 'Tell me what you want. I'll do it for you. I'm here, I can do what *der schwarzer* can do for you.'

'Where's *der schwarzer?*'

'I've told you he isn't here,' Harry shouted, the angrier for his previous moment's patience. 'Why don't you tell me what you want? What's the matter with me—can't you tell me what you want?'

'I want *der schwarzer.*'

'Please,' Harry said. He threw out his arms towards his father, but the gesture was abrupt, almost as though he were thrusting his father away from him. 'Why can't you ask it of me? You can ask me—haven't I done enough for you already? Do you want to go for a walk?—I'll take you for a walk. What do you want? Do you want—do you want—?' Harry could not think what his father might want. 'I'll do it,' he said. 'You don't need *der schwarzer.*'

Then Harry saw that his father was weeping. The old man was standing up and weeping, with his eyes hidden behind the thick glasses that he had to wear: his glasses and his beard made his face a mask of age, as though time had left him nothing but the frame of his body on which the clothing could hang, and this mask of his face above. But Harry knew when the old man was weeping—he had seen him crying too often before, when they had found him at the end of a street after he had wandered away, or even, years earlier, when he had lost another of the miserable jobs that seemed to be the only ones he could find in a country in which his son had, later, been able to run a good business, drive a large car, own a big house.

'Father,' Harry asked, 'what have I done? Do you think I've sent *der schwarzer* away?' Harry saw his father turn away, between the narrow bed and the narrow wardrobe. 'He's coming—' Harry said, but he could not look at his father's back, he could not look at his father's hollowed neck, on which the hairs that Paulus had clipped glistened above the pale brown discolorations of age—Harry could not look at the neck turned stiffly away from him while he had to try to promise the return of the Zulu. Harry dropped his hands and walked out of the room.

No one knew how the old man managed to get out of the house and through the front gate without having been seen.

But he did manage it, and in the road he was struck down. Only a man on a bicycle struck him down, but it was enough, and he died a few days later in the hospital.

Harry's wife wept, even the grandsons wept; Paulus wept. Harry himself was stony, and his bunched, protuberant features were immovable; they seemed locked upon the bones of his face. A few days after the funeral he called Paulus and Johannes into the kitchen and said to Johannes: 'Tell him he must go. His work is finished.'

Johannes translated for Paulus, and then, after Paulus had spoken, he turned to Harry. 'He says, yes baas.' Paulus kept his eyes on the ground; he did not look up even when Harry looked directly at him, and Harry knew that this was not out of fear or shyness, but out of courtesy for his master's grief—which was what they could not but be talking of, when they talked of his work.

'Here's his pay.' Harry thrust a few notes towards Paulus, who took them in his cupped hands, and retreated.

Harry waited for them to go, but Paulus stayed in the room, and consulted with Johannes in a low voice. Johannes turned to his master. 'He says, baas, that the baas still has his savings.'

Harry had forgotten about Paulus's savings. He told Johannes that he had forgotten, and that he did not have enough money at the moment, but would bring the money the next day. Johannes translated and Paulus nodded gratefully. Both he and Johannes were subdued by the death there had been in the house.

And Harry's dealings with Paulus were over. He took what was to have been his last look at Paulus, but this look stirred him again against the Zulu. As harshly as he told Paulus that he had to go, so now, implacably, seeing Paulus in the mockery and simplicity of his houseboy's clothing, to feed his anger to the very end Harry said: 'Ask him what he's been saving for. What's he going to do with the fortune he's made?'

Johannes spoke to Paulus and came back with a reply. 'He says, baas, that he is saving to bring his wife and children

268

from Zululand to Johannesburg. He is saving, baas,' Johannes said, for Harry had not seemed to understand, 'to bring his family to this town also.'

The two Zulus were bewildered to know why it should have been at that moment that Harry Grossman's clenched, fist-like features should suddenly seem to have fallen from one another, nor why he should have stared with such guilt and despair at Paulus, while he cried, 'What else could I have done? I did my best,' before the first tears came.

Ethan Canin

A Jewish legend, recorded in the Babylonian Talmud, tells that on his deathbed a certain man bequeathed "the barrel of earth to one son, the barrel of bones to the second, the barrel of hackled wool to the third." The sons did not know what their father had meant, so they went to the rabbi, who asked them: "Do you have land?" They replied, "Yes." "Do you have cattle?" "Yes." "Do you have felt cloaks?" "Yes." "If so," said the rabbi, "This is what your father had in mind."

Every father must, by needs, teach something to his son. Whether the teaching is intended or whether the lesson is acknowledged, what was meant to be taught and what was thought to be learned, are questions not easily answered. A passing remark, a gesture, a swing in a game of golf can hold everything we need to impart and everything we are capable of receiving. "The Year of Getting to Know Us" deliberately points to the plural, to the mutual commerce between a father and his son. Of Canin's stories, the poet Robert Coles has written that they "linger in the mind, provoke laughter and sadness, provide wisdom of the best kind—life's small ironies that touch and inform the heart."

THE YEAR OF
GETTING TO KNOW US

ethan canin

i told my father not to worry, that love is what matters,
and that in the end, when he is loosed from his body, he can look
back and say without blinking that he did all right by me, his son,
and that I loved him.

And he said, "Don't talk about things you know nothing
about."

We were in San Francisco, in a hospital room. IV tubes
were plugged into my father's arms; little round Band-Aids
were on his chest. Next to his bed was a table with a vase of
yellow roses and a card that my wife, Anne, had brought him. On
the front of the card was a photograph of a golf green. On the
wall above my father's head an electric monitor traced his
heartbeat. He was watching the news on a TV that stood in the
corner next to his girlfriend, Lorraine. Lorraine was reading a
magazine.

I was watching his heartbeat. It seemed all right to me:
the blips made steady peaks and drops, moved across the screen,
went out at one end, and then came back at the other. It seemed
that this was all a heart could do. I'm an English teacher, though,
and I don't know much about it.

"It looks strong," I'd say to my mother that afternoon over the phone. She was in Pasadena. "It's going right across, pretty steady. Big bumps. Solid."

"Is he eating all right?"

"I think so."

"Is *she* there?"

"Is Lorraine here, you mean?"

She paused. "Yes, Lorraine."

"No," I said. "She's not."

"Your poor father," she whispered.

I'm an only child, and I grew up in a big wood-frame house on Huron Avenue in Pasadena, California. The house had three empty bedrooms and in the back yard a section of grass that had been stripped and leveled, then seeded and mowed like a putting green. Twice a week a Mexican gardener came to trim it, wearing special moccasins my father had bought him. They had soft hide soles that left no imprints.

My father was in love with golf. He played seven times every week and talked about the game as if it were a science that he was about to figure out. "Cut through the outer rim for a high iron," he used to say at dinner, looking out the window into the yard while my mother passed him the carved-wood salad bowl, or "In hot weather hit a high-compression ball." When conversations paused, he made little putting motions with his hands. He was a top amateur and in another situation might have been a pro. When I was sixteen, the year I was arrested, he let me caddie for the first time. Before that all I knew about golf was his clubs—the Spalding made-to-measure woods and irons, Dynamiter sand wedge, St. Andrews putter—which he kept in an Abercrombie & Fitch bag in the trunk of his Lincoln, and the white leather shoes with long tongues and screw-in spikes, which he stored upside down in the hall closet. When he wasn't playing, he covered the club heads with socks that had little yellow dingo balls on the ends.

272

He never taught me to play. I was a decent athlete—could run, catch, throw a perfect spiral—but he never took me to the golf course. In the summer he played every day. Sometimes my mother asked if he would take me along with him. "Why should I?" he answered. "Neither of us would like it."

Every afternoon after work he played nine holes; he played eighteen on Saturday, and nine again on Sunday morning. On Sunday afternoon, at four o'clock, he went for a drive by himself in his white Lincoln Continental. Nobody was allowed to come with him on the drives. He was usually gone for a couple of hours. "Today I drove in the country," he would say at dinner, as he put out his cigarette, or "This afternoon I looked at the ocean," and we were to take from this that he had driven north on the coastal highway. He almost never said more, and across our blue-and-white tablecloth, when I looked at him, my silent father, I imagined in his eyes a pure gaze with which he read the waves and currents of the sea. He had made a fortune in business and owed it to being able to see the truth in any situation. For this reason, he said, he liked to drive with all the windows down. When he returned from his trips his face was red from the wind and his thinning hair lay fitfully on his head. My mother baked on Sunday afternoons while he was gone, walnut pies or macaroons that she prepared on the kitchen counter, which looked out over his putting green.

I teach English in a high school now, and my wife, Anne, is a journalist. I've played golf a half-dozen times in ten years and don't like it any more than most beginners, though the two or three times I've hit a drive that sails, that takes flight with its own power, I've felt something that I think must be unique to the game. These were the drives my father used to hit. Explosions off the tee, bird flights. But golf isn't my game, and it never has been, and I wouldn't think about it at all if not for my father.

Anne and I were visiting in California, first my mother, in Los Angeles, and then my father and Lorraine, north in Sausalito, and Anne suggested that I ask him to play nine holes one morning. She'd been wanting me to talk to him. It's part of the project we've started, part of her theory of what's wrong—although I don't think that much is. She had told me that twenty-five years changes things, and since we had the time, why not go out to California.

She said, "It's not too late to talk to him."

My best friend in high school was named Nickie Apple. Nickie had a thick chest and a voice that had been damaged somehow, made a little hoarse, and sometimes people thought he was twenty years old. He lived in a four-story house that had a separate floor for the kids. It was the top story, and his father, who was divorced and a lawyer, had agreed never to come up there. That was where we sat around after school. Because of the agreement, no parents were there, only kids. Nine or ten of us, usually. Some of them had slept the night on the big pillows that were scattered against the walls: friends of his older brothers', in Stetson hats and flannel shirts; girls I had never seen before.

Nickie and I went to Shrier Academy, where all the students carried around blue-and-gray notebooks embossed with the school's heraldic seal. SUMUS PRIMI the seal said. Our gray wool sweaters said it; our green exam books said it; the rear window decal my mother brought home said it. My father wouldn't put the sticker on the Lincoln, so she pressed it onto the window above her kitchen sink instead. IMIRP SUMUS I read whenever I washed my hands. At Shrier we learned Latin in the eighth grade and art history in the ninth, and in the tenth I started getting into some trouble. Little things: cigarettes, graffiti. Mr. Goldman, the student counselor, called my mother in for a premonition visit. "I have a premonition about Leonard," he told her in the counseling office one afternoon in the warm October when I was sixteen. The office was full of plants and had five floor-to-ceiling windows that let in sun like a greenhouse. They looked over grassy, bushless knolls. "I just have a feeling about him."

That October he started talking to me about it. He called me in and asked me why I was friends with Nickie Apple, a boy going nowhere. I was looking out the big windows, opening and closing my fists beneath the desk top. He said, "Lenny, you're a bright kid—what are you trying to tell us?" And I said, "Nothing. I'm not trying to tell you anything."

Then we started stealing, Nickie and I. He did it first, and took things I didn't expect: steaks, expensive cuts that we cooked on a grill by the window in the top story of his house; garden machinery; luggage. We didn't sell it and we didn't use it, but every afternoon we went someplace new. In November he distracted a store clerk and I took a necklace that we thought was diamonds. In December we went for a ride in someone else's car, and over Christmas vacation, when only gardeners were on the school grounds, we threw ten rocks, one by one, as if we'd paid for them at a carnival stand, through the five windows in Mr. Goldman's office.

"You look like a train station," I said to my father as he lay in the hospital bed. "All those lines coming and going everywhere."

He looked at me. I put some things down, tried to make a little bustle. I could see Anne standing in the hall just beyond the door.

"Are you comfortable, Dad?"

"What do you mean, 'comfortable'? My heart's full of holes, leaking all over the place. Am I comfortable? No, I'm dying."

"You're not dying," I said, and I sat down next to him. "You'll be swinging the five iron in two weeks."

I touched one of the tubes in his arm. Where it entered the vein the needle disappeared under a piece of tape. I hated the sight of this. I moved the bedsheets a little bit, tucked them in. Anne had wanted me to be alone with him. She was in the hall, waiting to head off Lorraine.

"What's the matter with her?" he asked, pointing at Anne.

"She thought we might want to talk."

"What's so urgent?"

Anne and I had discussed it the night before. "Tell him what you feel," she said. "Tell him you love him." We were eating dinner in a fish restaurant. "Or, if you don't love him, tell him you don't."

"Look, Pop," I said now.

"What?"

I was forty-two years old. We were in a hospital and he had tubes in his arms. All kinds of everything: needles, air, tape. I said it again.

"Look, Pop."

276

Anne and I have seen a counselor, who told me that I had to learn to accept kindness from people. He saw Anne and me together, then Anne alone, then me. Children's toys were scattered on the floor of his office. "You sound as if you don't want to let people near you," he said. "Right?"

"I'm a reasonably happy man," I answered.

I hadn't wanted to see the counselor. Anne and I have been married seven years, and sometimes I think the history of marriage can be written like this: People Want Too Much. Anne and I have suffered no plague; we sleep late two mornings a week; we laugh at most of the same things; we have a decent house in a suburb of Boston, where, after the commuter traffic has eased, a quiet descends and the world is at peace. She writes for a newspaper, and I teach the children of lawyers and insurance men. At times I'm alone, and need to be alone; at times she does too. But I can always count on a moment, sometimes once in a day, sometimes more, when I see her patting down the sheets on the bed, or watering the front window violets, and I am struck by the good fortune of my life.

Still, Anne says I don't feel things.

It comes up at dinner, outside in the yard, in airports as we wait for planes. You don't let yourself feel, she tells me; and I tell her that I think it's a crazy thing, all this talk about feeling. What do the African Bushmen say? They say, Will we eat tomorrow? Will there be rain?

When I was sixteen, sitting in the back seat of a squad car, the policeman stopped in front of our house on Huron Avenue, turned around against the headrest, and asked me if I was sure this was where I lived.

"Yes, sir," I said.

He spoke through a metal grate. "Your daddy owns this house?"

"Yes, sir."

"But for some reason you don't like windows."

He got out and opened my door, and we walked up the porch steps. The swirling lights on the squad car were making crazy patterns in the French panes of the living room bays. He knocked. "What's your daddy do?"

I heard lights snapping on, my mother moving through the house. "He's in business," I said. "But he won't be home now." The policeman wrote something on his notepad. I saw my mother's eye through the glass in the door, and then the locks were being unlatched, one by one, from the top.

* * *

When Anne and I came to California to visit, we stayed at my mother's for three days. On her refrigerator door was a calendar with men's names marked on it—dinner dates, theater— and I knew this was done for our benefit. My mother has been alone for fifteen years. She's still thin, and her eyes still water, and I noticed that books were lying open all through the house. Thick paperbacks—*Doctor Zhivago, The Thorn Birds*—in the bathroom and the studio and the bedroom. We never mentioned my father, but at the end of our stay, when we had packed the car for our drive north along the coast, after she'd hugged us both and we'd backed out of the driveway, she came down off the lawn into the street, her arms crossed over her chest, leaned into the window, and said, "You might say hello to your father for me."

We made the drive north on Highway 1. We passed mission towns, fields of butter lettuce, long stretches of pumpkin farms south of San Francisco. It was the first time we were going to see my father with Lorraine. She was a hairdresser. He'd met her a few years after coming north, and one of the first things they'd done together was take a trip around the world. We got postcards from the Nile delta and Bangkok. When I was young, my father had never taken us out of California.

His house in Sausalito was on a cliff above a finger of San Francisco Bay. A new Lincoln stood in the carport. In his bedroom was a teak-framed king-size waterbed, and on the walls were bits of African artwork—opium pipes, metal figurines. Lorraine looked the same age as Anne. One wall of the living room was glass, and after the first night's dinner, while we sat on the leather sofa watching tankers and yachts move under the Golden Gate Bridge, my father put down his Scotch and water, touched his jaw, and said, "Lenny, call Dr. Farmer."

It was his second one. The first had been two years earlier on the golf course in Monterey, where he'd had to kneel, then sit, then lie down on the fairway.

At dinner the night after I was arrested, my mother introduced her idea. "We're going to try something," she said. She had brought out a chicken casserole, and it was steaming in front of her. "That's what we're going to do. Max, are you listening? This next year, starting tonight, is going to be the year of getting to know us better." She stopped speaking and dished my father some chicken.

"What do you mean?" I asked.

"I mean it will be to a small extent a theme year. Nothing that's going to change every day of our lives, but in this next year I thought we'd all make an attempt to get to know each other better. Especially you, Leonard. Dad and I are going to make a better effort to know you."

"I'm not sure what you mean," said my father.

"All kinds of things, Max. We'll go to movies together, and Lenny can throw a party here at the house. And I personally would like to take a trip, all of us together, to the American Southwest."

"Sounds all right to me," I said.

"And Max," she said, "you can take Lenny with you to play golf. For example." She looked at my father.

"Neither of us would like it," he said.

"Lenny never sees you."

I looked out the window. The trees were turning, dropping their leaves onto the putting green. I didn't care what he said, one way or the other. My mother spooned a chicken thigh onto my plate and covered it with sauce. "All right," my father said. "He can caddie."

"And as preparation for our trip," my mother said, "can you take him on your Sunday rides?"

My father took off his glasses. "The Southwest," he said, wiping the lenses with a napkin, "is exactly like any other part of the country."

Anne had an affair once with a man she met on an assignment. He was young, much younger than either of us—in his late twenties, I would say from the one time I saw him. I saw them because one day on the road home I passed Anne's car in the lot of a Denny's restaurant. I parked around the block and went in to surprise her. I took a table at the back, but from my seat in the corner I didn't realize for several minutes that the youngish-looking woman leaning forward and whispering to the man with a beard was my wife.

I didn't get up and pull the man out with me into the parking lot, or even join them at the table, as I have since thought might have been a good idea. Instead I sat and watched them. I could see that under the table they were holding hands. His back was to me, and I noticed that it was broad, as mine is not. I remember thinking that she probably liked this broadness. Other than that, though, I didn't feel very much. I ordered another cup of coffee just to hear myself talk, but my voice wasn't quavering or fearful. When the waitress left, I took out a napkin and wrote on it, "You are a forty-year-old man with no children and your wife is having an affair." Then I put some money on the table and left the restaurant.

"I think we should see somebody," Anne said to me a few weeks later. It was a Sunday morning, and we were eating breakfast on the porch.

"About what?" I asked.

On a Sunday afternoon when I was sixteen I went out to the garage with a plan my mother had given me. That morning my father had washed the Lincoln. He had detergent-scrubbed the finish and then sun-dried it on Huron Avenue, so that in the workshop light of the garage its highlights shone. The windshield molding, the grille, the chrome side markers, had been cloth-dried to erase water spots. The keys hung from their magnetic sling near the door to the kitchen. I took them out and opened the trunk. Then I hung them up again and sat on the rear quarter panel to consider what to do. It was almost four o'clock. The trunk of my father's car was large enough for a half-dozen suitcases and had been upholstered in a gray medium-pile carpet that was cut to hug the wheel wells and the spare-tire berth. In one corner, fastened down by straps, was his toolbox, and along the back lay the golf bag. In the shadows the yellow dingos of the club socks looked like baby chicks. He was going to come out in a few minutes. I reached in, took off four of the club socks, and made a pillow for my head. Then I stepped into the trunk. The shocks bounced once and stopped. I lay down with my head propped on the quarter panel and my feet resting in the taillight berth, and then I reached up, slammed down the trunk, and was in the dark.

This didn't frighten me. When I was very young, I liked to sleep with the shades drawn and the door closed so that no light entered my room. I used to hold my hand in front of my eyes and see if I could imagine its presence. It was too dark to see anything. I was blind then, lying in my bed, listening for every sound. I used to move my hand back and forth, close to my eyes, until I had the sensation that it was there but had in some way been amputated. I had heard of soldiers who had lost limbs but still felt them attached. Now I held my open hand before my eyes. It was dense black inside the trunk, colorless, without light.

When my father started the car, all the sounds were huge, magnified as if they were inside my own skull. The metal scratched, creaked, slammed when he got in; the bolt of the starter shook all the way through to the trunk; the idle rose and leveled; then the gears changed and the car lurched. I heard the garage door glide up. Then it curled into its housing, bumped once, began descending again. The seams of the trunk lid lightened in the sun. We were in the street now, heading downhill. I lay back and felt the road, listened to the gravel pocking in the wheel wells.

I followed our route in my mind. Left off Huron onto Telscher, where the car bottomed in the rain gulley as we turned, then up the hill to Santa Ana. As we waited for the light, the idle made its change, shifting down, so that below my head I heard the individual piston blasts in the exhaust pipe. Left on Santa Ana, counting the flat stretches where I felt my father tap the brakes, numbering the intersections as we headed west toward the ocean. I heard cars pull up next to us, accelerate, slow down, make turns. Bits of gravel echoed inside the quarter panels. I pulled off more club socks and enlarged my pillow. We slowed down, stopped, and then we accelerated, the soft piston explosions becoming a hiss as we turned onto the Pasadena freeway.

"Dad's rides," my mother had said to me the night before, as I lay in bed, "would be a good way for him to get to know you." It was the first week of the year of getting to know us better. She was sitting at my desk.

"But he won't let me go," I said.

"You're right." She moved some things around on a shelf. The room wasn't quite dark, and I could see the outline of her white blouse. "I talked to Mr. Goldman," she said.

"Mr. Goldman doesn't know me."

"He says you're angry." My mother stood up, and I watched her white blouse move to the window. She pulled back the shade until a triangle of light from the streetlamp fell on my sheets. "Are you angry?"

"I don't know," I said. "I don't think so."

"I don't think so either." She replaced the shade, came over and kissed me on the forehead, and then went out into the hall. In the dark I looked for my hand.

A few minutes later the door opened again. She put her head in. "If he won't let you come," she said, "sneak along."

On the freeway the thermal seams whizzed and popped in my ears. The ride had smoothed out now, as the shocks settled into the high speed, hardly dipping on curves, muffling everything as if we were under water. As far as I could tell, we were still driving west, toward the ocean. I sat halfway up and rested my back against the golf bag. I could see shapes now inside the trunk. When we slowed down and the blinker went on, I attempted bearings, but the sun was the same in all directions and the trunk lid was without shadow. We braked hard. I felt the car leave the freeway. We made turns. We went straight. Then more turns, and as we slowed down and I was stretching out, uncurling my body along the diagonal, we made a sharp right onto gravel and pulled over and stopped.

My father opened the door. The car dipped and rocked, shuddered. The engine clicked. Then the passenger door opened. I waited.

If I heard her voice today, twenty-six years later, I would recognize it.

"Angel," she said.

I heard the weight of their bodies sliding across the back seat, first hers, then his. They weren't three feet away. I curled up, crouched into the low space between the golf bag and the back of the passenger compartment. There were two firm points in the cushion where it was displaced. As I lay there, I went over the voice again in my head: it was nobody I knew. I heard a laugh from her, and then something low from him. I felt the shift of the trunk's false rear, and then, as I lay behind them, I heard the contact: the crinkle of clothing, arms wrapping, and the half-delicate, muscular sounds. It was like hearing a television in the next room. His voice once more, and then the rising of their breath, slow; a minute of this, maybe another, then shifting again, the friction of cloth on leather seat and the car's soft rocking. "Dad," I whispered. Then rocking again; my father's sudden panting, harder and harder, his half-words. The car shook violently. "Dad," I whispered. I shouted, "Dad!"

The door opened.

His steps kicked up gravel. I heard jingling metal, the sound of the key in the trunk lock. He was standing over me in an explosion of light.

He said, "Put back the club socks."

I did and got out of the car to stand next to him. He rubbed his hands down the front of his shirt.

"What the hell," he said.

"I was in the trunk."

"I know," he said. "What the goddamn."

The year I graduated from college, I found a job teaching junior high school in Boston. The school was a cement building with small windows well up from the street, and dark classrooms in which I spent a lot of time maintaining discipline. In the middle of an afternoon that first winter a boy knocked on my door to tell me I had a phone call. I knew who it was going to be.

"Dad's gone," my mother said.

He'd taken his things in the Lincoln, she told me, and driven away that morning before dawn. On the kitchen table he'd left a note and some cash. "A lot of cash," my mother added, lowering her voice. "Twenty thousand dollars."

I imagined the sheaf of bills on our breakfast table, held down by the ceramic butter dish, the bank notes ruffling in the breeze from the louvered windows that opened onto his green. In the note he said he had gone north and would call her when he'd

settled. It was December. I told my mother that I would visit in a
week, when school was out for Christmas. I told her to go to her
sister's and stay there, and then I said that I was working and had
to get back to my class. She didn't say anything on the other end
of the line, and in the silence I imagined my father crisscrossing
the state of California, driving north, stopping in Palm Springs
and Carmel, the Lincoln riding low with the weight.

"Leonard," my mother said, "did you know anything like
this was happening?"

During the spring of the year of getting to know us
better I caddied for him a few times. On Saturdays he played early
in the morning, when the course was mostly empty and the grass
was still wet from the night. I learned to fetch the higher irons as
the sun rose over the back nine and the ball, on drying ground,
rolled farther. He hit skybound approach shots with backspin,
chips that bit into the green and stopped. He played in a foursome
with three other men, and in the locker room, as they changed
their shoes, they told jokes and poked one another in the belly.
The lockers were shiny green metal, the floor clean white tiles
that clicked under the shoe spikes. Beneath the mirrors were jars
of combs in green disinfectant. When I combed my hair with
them it stayed in place and smelled like limes.

We were on the course at dawn. At the first fairway the
other men dug in their spikes, shifted their weight from leg to leg,
dummy-swung at an empty tee while my father lit a cigarette and
looked out over the hole. "The big gun," he said to me, or, if it was
par three, "The lady." He stepped on his cigarette. I wiped the
head with the club sock before I handed it to him. When he took
the club, he felt its balance point, rested it on one finger, and
then, in slow motion, he gripped the shaft. Left hand first, then
right, the fingers wrapping pinkie to index. Then he leaned down
over the ball. On a perfect drive the tee flew straight up in the air
and landed in front of his feet.

Over the weekend his heart lost its rhythm for a few seconds. It happened Saturday night, when Anne and I were at the house in Sausalito, and we didn't hear about it until Sunday. "Ventricular fibrillation," the intern said. "Circus movements." The condition was always a danger after a heart attack. He had been given a shock and his heartbeat had returned to normal.

"But I'll be honest with you," the intern said. We were in the hall. He looked down, touched his stethoscope. "It isn't a good sign."

The heart gets bigger as it dies, he told me. Soon it spreads across the x-ray. He brought me with him to a room and showed me strips of paper with the electric tracings: certain formations. The muscle was dying in patches, he said. He said things might get better, they might not.

My mother called that afternoon. "Should I come up?"

"He was a bastard to you," I said.

When Lorraine and Anne were eating dinner, I found the intern again. "I want to know," I said. "Tell me the truth." The intern was tall and thin, sick-looking himself. So were the other doctors I had seen around the place. Everything in that hospital was pale—the walls, the coats, the skin.

He said, "What truth?"

I told him that I'd been reading about heart disease. I'd read about EKGs, knew about the medicines—lidocaine, propranolol. I knew that the lungs filled up with water, that heart failure was death by drowning. I said, "The truth about my father."

The afternoon I had hidden in the trunk, we came home while my mother was cooking dinner. I walked up the path from the garage behind my father, watching the pearls of sweat on his neck. He was whistling a tune. At the door he kissed my mother's cheek. He touched the small of her back. She was cooking vegetables, and the steam had fogged up the kitchen windows and dampened her hair. My father sat down in the chair by the window and opened the newspaper. I thought of the way the trunk

285

rear had shifted when he and the woman had moved into the back
of the Lincoln. My mother was smiling.

"Well?" she said.

"What's for dinner?" I asked.

"Well?" she said again.

"It's chicken," I said. "Isn't it?"

"Max, aren't you going to tell me if anything unusual
happened today?"

My father didn't look up from the newspaper. "Did anything unusual happen today?" he said. He turned the page, folded
it back smartly. "Why don't you ask Lenny?"

She smiled at me.

"I surprised him," I said. Then I turned and looked out
the window.

286

"I have something to tell you," Anne said to me one
Sunday morning in the fifth year of our marriage. We were lying in
bed. I knew what was coming.

"I already know," I said.

"What do you already know?"

"I know about your lover."

She didn't say anything.

"It's all right," I said.

It was winter. The sky was gray, and although the sun
had risen only a few hours earlier, it seemed like late afternoon. I
waited for Anne to say something more. We were silent for several
minutes. Then she said, "I wanted to hurt you." She got out of bed
and began straightening out the bureau. She pulled my sweaters
from the drawer and refolded them. She returned all our shoes to
the closet. Then she came back to the bed, sat down, and began
to cry. Her back was toward me. It shook with her gasps, and I put
my hand out and touched her. "It's all right," I said.

"We only saw each other a few times," she answered.
"I'd take it back if I could. I'd make it never happen."

"I know you would."

"For some reason I thought I couldn't really hurt you."

She had stopped crying. I looked out the window at the tree branches hung low with snow. It didn't seem I had to say anything.

"I don't know why I thought I couldn't hurt you," she said. "Of course I can hurt you."

"I forgive you."

Her back was still toward me. Outside, a few snowflakes drifted up in the air.

"*Did* I hurt you?"

"Yes, you did. I saw you two in a restaurant."

"Where?"

"At Denny's."

"No," she said. "I mean, where did I hurt you?"

The night he died, Anne stayed awake with me in bed.
"Tell me about him," she said.

"What about?"

"Stories. Tell me what it was like growing up, things you did together."

"We didn't do that much," I said. "I caddied for him. He taught me things about golf."

That night I never went to sleep. Lorraine was at a friend's apartment and we were alone in my father's empty house, but we pulled out the sheets anyway, and the two wool blankets, and we lay on the fold-out sofa in the den. I told stories about my father until I couldn't think of any more, and then I talked about my mother until Anne fell asleep.

In the middle of the night I got up and went into the living room. Through the glass I could see lights across the water, the bridges, Belvedere and San Francisco, ships. It was clear outside, and when I walked out to the cement carport the sky was lit with stars. The breeze moved inside my nightclothes. Next to the garage the Lincoln stood half-lit in the porch floodlight. I opened the door and got in. The seats were red leather and smelled of limes and cigarettes. I rolled down the window and took the key from the glove compartment. I thought of writing a note for Anne, but didn't. Instead I coasted down the driveway in neutral and didn't close the door or turn on the lights until the bottom of the hill, or start the engine until I had swung around the corner, so that the house was out of sight and the brine smell of the marina was coming through the open windows of the car. The pistons were almost silent.

I felt urgent, though I had no route in mind. I ran one stop sign, then one red light, and when I reached the ramp onto Highway 101, I squeezed the accelerator and felt the surge of the fuel-injected, computer-sparked V-8. The dash lights glowed. I drove south and crossed over the Golden Gate Bridge at seventy miles an hour, its suspension cables swaying in the wind and the span rocking slowly, ocean to bay. The lanes were narrow. Reflectors zinged when the wheels strayed. If Anne woke, she might come out to the living room and then check for me outside. A light rain began to fall. Drops wet my knees, splattered my cheek. I kept the window open and turned on the radio; the car filled up with wind and music. Brass sounds. Trumpets. Sounds that filled my heart.

The Lincoln drove like a dream. South of San Francisco the road opened up, and in the gully of a shallow hill I took it up over a hundred. The arrow nosed rightward in the dash. Shapes flattened out. "Dad," I said. The wind sounds changed pitch. I said, "The year of getting to know us." Signposts and power poles were flying by. Only a few cars were on the road, and most moved over before I arrived. In the mirror I could see the faces as I passed. I went through San Mateo, Pacifica, Redwood City, until, underneath a concrete overpass, the radio began pulling in static and I realized that I might die at this speed. I slowed down. At seventy drizzle wandered in the windows again. At fifty-five the scenery stopped moving. In Menlo Park I got off the freeway.

It was dark still, and off the interstate I found myself on a road without streetlights. It entered the center of town and then left again, curving up into shallow hills. The houses were large on

288

either side. They were spaced far apart, three and four stories tall, with white shutters or ornament work that shone in the perimeter of the Lincoln's headlamps. The yards were large, dotted with eucalyptus and laurel. Here and there a light was on. Sometimes I saw faces: someone on an upstairs balcony; a man inside the breakfast room, awake at this hour, peering through the glass to see what car could be passing. I drove slowly, and when I came to a high school with its low buildings and long athletic field I pulled over and stopped.

The drizzle had become mist. I left the headlights on and got out and stood on the grass. I thought, This is the night your father has passed. I looked up at the lightening sky. I said it, "This is the night your father has passed," but I didn't feel what I thought I would. Just the wind on my throat, the chill of the morning. A pickup drove by and flashed its lights at me on the lawn. Then I went to the trunk of the Lincoln, because this was what my father would have done, and I got out the golf bag. It was heavier than I remembered, and the leather was stiff in the cool air. On the damp sod I set up: dimpled white ball, yellow tee. My father would have swung, would have hit drives the length of the football field, high irons that disappeared into the gray sky, but as I stood there I didn't even take the clubs out of the bag. Instead I imagined his stance. I pictured the even weight, the deliberate grip, and after I had stood there for a few moments, I picked up the ball and tee, replaced them in the bag, and drove home to my wife.

The year I was sixteen we never made it to the American Southwest. My mother bought maps anyway, and planned our trip, talking to me about it at night in the dark, taking us in her mind across the Colorado River at the California border, where the water was opal green, into Arizona and along the stretch of desert highway to New Mexico. There, she said, the canyons were a mile deep. The road was lined with sagebrush and a type of cactus, jumping cholla, that launched its spines. Above the desert, where a man could die of dehydration in an afternoon and a morning, the peaks of the Rocky Mountains turned blue with sun and ice.

We didn't ever go. Every weekend my father played golf, and at last, in August, my parents agreed to a compromise. One Sunday morning, before I started the eleventh grade, we drove north in the Lincoln to a state park along the ocean. Above the shore the cliffs were planted with ice plant to resist erosion. Pelicans soared in the thermal currents. My mother had made chicken sandwiches, which we ate on the beach, and after lunch, while I looked at the crabs and swaying fronds in the tide pools, my parents walked to the base of the cliffs. I watched their progress on the shallow dunes. Once when I looked, my father was holding her in his arms and they were kissing.

She bent backward in his hands. I looked into the tide pool where, on the surface, the blue sky, the clouds, the reddish cliffs, were shining. Below them rock crabs scurried between submerged stones. The afternoon my father found me in the trunk, he introduced me to the woman in the back seat. Her name was Christine. She smelled of perfume. The gravel drive where we had parked was behind a warehouse, and after we shook hands through the open window of the car, she got out and went inside. It was low and long, and the metal door slammed behind her. On the drive home, wind blowing all around us in the car, my father and I didn't say much. I watched his hands on the steering wheel. They were big and red-knuckled, the hands of a butcher or a carpenter, and I tried to imagine them on the bend of Christine's back.

Later that afternoon on the beach, while my mother walked along the shore, my father and I climbed a steep trail up the cliffs. From above, where we stood in the carpet of ice plant, we could see the hue of the Pacific change to a more translucent blue—the drop-off and the outline of the shoal where the breakers rose. I tried to see what my father was seeing as he gazed out over the water. He picked up a rock and tossed it over the cliff. "You know," he said without looking at me, "you could be all right on the course." We approached the edge of the palisade, where the ice plant thinned into eroded cuts of sand. "Listen," he said. "We're here on this trip so we can get to know each other a little bit." A hundred yards below us waves broke on the rocks. He lowered his voice. "But I'm not sure about that. Anyway, you don't *have* to get to know me. You know why?"

"Why?" I asked.

"You don't have to get to know me," he said, "because one day you're going to grow up and then you're going to *be* me." He looked at me and then out over the water. "So what I'm going to do is teach you how to hit." He picked up a long stick and put it in my hand. Then he showed me the backswing. "You've got to know one thing to drive a golf ball," he told me, "and that's that the club is part of you." He stood behind me and showed me how to keep the left arm still. "The club is your hand," he said. "It's your bone. It's your whole arm and your skeleton and your heart." Below us on the beach I could see my mother walking the water-line. We took cut after cut, and he taught me to visualize the impact, to sense it. He told me to whittle down the point of energy so that the ball would fly. When I swung he held my head in position. "Don't just watch," he said. "See." I looked. The ice plant was watery-looking and fat, and at the edge of my vision I could see the tips of my father's shoes. I was sixteen years old and waiting for the next thing he would tell me.

ACKNOWLEDGEMENTS

Canin, Ethan, "The Year of Getting to Know Us," from *Emperor of the Air*. Copyright © 1988 by Ethan Canin. Reprinted by permission of Houghton Mifflin Company. All rights reserved.

Desai, Anita, "A Devoted Son," from *Games at Twilight*. Copyright © 1978 by Anita Desai. Reproduced by permission of the author, c/o Rogers, Coleridge & White Ltd., 20 Powis Mews, London W11 1JN.

Ford, Richard, "Great Falls," from *Rock Springs*, published by Alfred A. Knopf. Copyright © 1987 by Richard Ford. Reprinted by permission of the author.

Jacobson, Dan, "The Zulu and the Zeide," from *A Long Way to London*. Copyright © 1958 by Dan Jacobson.

Mistry, Rohinton, "Of White Hairs and Cricket," from *Tales from Firozsha Baag*. Copyright © 1987 by Rohinton Mistry. Reprinted by permission of Westwood Creative Artists Ltd. (U.S. only) and McClelland & Stewart Inc. (Canada only).

Moriconi, Virginia, "Simple Arithmetic." Copyright © 1964, renewed 1992 by the Estate of Virginia Moriconi. Reprinted by permission of the Literary Executor.

Murena, Héctor, "The Saw," from *El Coronel de Caballería y Otros Cuentos*, translated by Alberto Manguel. Copyright © 1956 by Héctor Murena. Translation copyright © 1997 by Alberto Manguel.

Ōe, Kenzaburō, "Aghwee the Sky Monster," from *Teach Us to Outgrow Our Madness*, translated by John Nathan. Translation copyright © 1977 by John Nathan; used by permission of Grove/Atlantic, Inc.

Acknowledgements

O'Faolain, Sean, "Innocence," from *Teresa and Other Stories*. Copyright © 1947 by Sean O'Faolain. Reproduced by permission of the Estate of Sean O'Faolain, c/o Rogers, Coleridge & White Ltd., 20 Powis Mews, London W11 1JN.

Okri, Ben, "In the Shadow of War," from *Stars of the New Curfew*. Copyright © 1988 by Ben Okri. Used by permission of Viking Penguin, a division of Penguin Books USA Inc.

Ramírez, Sergio, "The Perfect Game," translated by Nick Caistor. Originally published in English in his collection of short stories, *Stories* (London Readers International, 1986). Translation copyright © 1988 by Nick Caistor.

Schulz, Bruno, "Father's Last Escape," from *Sanatorium under the Hourglass*. Copyright © 1978 by Jacob Schulz. Reprinted by permission of Walker & Co.

Tremain, Rose, "Over," from *Evangelista's Fan*. Copyright © 1996 by Rose Tremain. Reprinted by permission of Richard Scott Simon Limited.

Wideman, John Edgar, "Casa Grande," from *The Stories of John Edgar Wideman*. Copyright © 1992 by John Edgar Wideman. Reprinted by permission of Pantheon Books, a division of Random House, Inc.

AUTHOR BIOGRAPHIES

Ambrose Bierce (USA, 1842–c.1914) Bierce's fame rests on two short story collections: *Tales of Soldiers and Civilians* (1891, republished as *In the Midst of Life*); and *Can Such Things Be?* (1893). He is also the author of the caustic *Devil's Dictionary* (1906).

Ethan Canin (USA, b. 1960) Ethan Canin is the author of two collections of short stories, *Emperor of the Air* (1988) and *The Palace Thief* (1994), and the novel *Blue River* (1992).

Stephen Crane (USA, 1871–1900) A novelist and short-story writer, Crane is best known for his novel *The Red Badge of Courage* (1895). His other books include *Maggie: A Girl of the Streets* (1893), *The Little Regiment* (1896), *George's Mother* (1896), *The Third Violet* (1897), *The Open Boat and Other Stories* (1898), and *The Monster* (1898). He also wrote poetry and autobiographical sketches.

Anita Desai (India, b. 1937) Desai has written several novels, including *Cry, the Peacock* (1963), *Voices in the City* (1965), *Bye-Bye Blackbird* (1971), *Fire on the Mountain* (1977), *Clear Light of Day* (1980), *In Custody* (1984), and *Journey to Ithaca* (1995).

William Faulkner (USA, 1897–1962) Most of Faulkner's novels are set in the fictional Mississippi county of Yoknapatawpha: *Sartoris* (1929), *The Sound and the Fury* (1929), *As I Lay Dying* (1930), *Sanctuary* (1931), *Light in August* (1932), *Absalom, Absalom* (1936), *Intruder in the Dust* (1948). He won the Nobel Prize in 1950.

F. Scott Fitzgerald (USA, 1896–1940) After publishing his first story in 1919, Fitzgerald wrote his first novel, *This Side of Paradise,* a year later. This was followed by *The Beautiful and the Damned* (1922), *Tales of the Jazz Age* (1922), *The Great Gatsby* (1925), and *Tender Is the Night* (1934). His essays and notes were collected posthumously in *The Crack-Up* (1945).

Richard Ford (USA, b. 1944) Winner of the 1996 Pulitzer Prize for *Independence Day* (1995), Richard Ford is the author of *A Piece of My Heart* (1976), *The Sportswriter* (1986), *Wildlife* (1990), and the short story collections *Rock Springs* (1987) and *Women with Men* (1997).

Dan Jacobson (South Africa, b. 1929) Jacobson is the author of *The Trap* (1955), *A Dance in the Sun* (1956), *The Price of Diamonds* (1957), *Evidence of Love* (1960), *The Rape of Tamar* (1970) and *The Confessions of Joseph Baisz* (1977). His autobiography is *Time and Time Again* (1985).

Franz Kafka (Czechoslovakia, 1883–1924) Kafka's work, a keystone of modern literature, includes the posthumous novels *The Trial* (1925), *The Castle* (1926), and *Amerika* (1927), as well as many brilliant short stories, such as "Metamorphosis" (1912).

Rohinton Mistry (India/Canada, b. 1952) One book of Mistry's short stories, *Tales of Firozsha Baag* (published under the title *Swimming Lessons and Other Stories from Firozsha Baag* in 1987 in the United States) and two novels, *Such a Long Journey* (1991) and *A Fine Balance* (1995), have placed Mistry among the best writers of his generation.

Virginia Moriconi (USA, 1924–1987) Moriconi is the author of one book of extraordinary short stories, *The Mark of St. Crispin* (1978) and four novels—*The Distant Trojans* (1948), *Black Annis* (1982), *The Princes of Kew* (1984), and *Arrows of Longing* (1985).

Héctor Murena (Argentina, 1923–1975) Murena's novels include the trilogy *La fatalidad de los cuerpos* (1955), *Las leyes de la noche* (1958) and *Los herederos de la promesa* (1965). His stories were collected in *El centro del infierno* (1956).

Kenzaburō Ōe (Japan, b. 1935) Several of this novelist and short-story writer's books are available in English: *A Personal Matter* (1964), *The Silent Cry* (1967), and *Teach Us to Outgrow Our Madness* (1977). Ōe has won many of Japan's major literary awards, including the Akutagawa and the Tanizaki prizes. He won the Nobel Prize in 1994.

Sean O'Faolain (Ireland, 1900–1991) O'Faolain was editor of *The Bell* and director of the Arts Council of Ireland. He was the author of short stories, first collected in *Midsummer Night Madness* (1932), and several novels: *A Nest of Simple Folk* (1933), *Bird Alone* (1936), and *Come Back to Erin* (1940). He also wrote four volumes of Irish biography.

Ben Okri (Nigeria, b. 1954) Now living in England, Okri published his first novel, *Flowers and Shadows* (1980) when he was twenty-six years old. His other books include *The Landscapes Within* (1981), *Incidents at the Shrine* (1986), *The Famished Road* (1990), and *Astonishing the Gods* (1995).

Sergio Ramírez (Nicaragua, b. 1942) Ramírez served as vice-president of Nicaragua in 1985. His novel *To Bury Our Fathers* and his short-fiction collection *Stories* were published in English translation in 1984 and 1986 respectively.

Bruno Schulz (Poland, 1892–1942) Only two of Schulz's books survive: *The Street of the Crocodiles* (1934) and *Sanatorium under the Sign of the Hourglass* (1937). At the time of his death, he was working on a novel, *The Messiah,* of which nothing remains.

Rose Tremain (England, b. 1943) Tremain's novels include *Sadler's Birthday* (1976), *Letter to Sister Benedicta* (1978), *The Swimming Pool Season* (1985), *Restoration* (1989), *Sacred Country* (1992), and *The Way I Found Her* (1997). She has also published a volume of short stories, *The Colonel's Daughter* (1984), and a biography of Stalin.

José García Villa (Philippines, b. 1914) The author of two novels and a book of short stories, *Footnote to Youth* (1933), all written in English, Villa's poetry and fiction has been collected in three volumes: *Essential Villa* (1965), *Portable Villa* (1962) and *Selected Stories* (1962).

John Edgar Wideman (USA, b. 1941) Wideman's many books include *A Glance Away* (1967), *The Lynchers* (1973), *Hurry Home* (1979), *Damballah* (1981), *Hiding Place* (1981), *Sent for You Yesterday* (1983), *Reuben* (1987), *Fever* (1989), and two memoirs, *Brothers and Keepers* (1984) and *Fatheralong* (1994). His stories were collected in *All Stories Are True* (1992).